FILTHY
RICH
VAMPIRES

Three Queens

FILTHY RICH VAMPIRES

Three Queens

GENEVA LEE

NEW YORK TIMES & INTERNATIONALLY BESTSELLING AUTHOR

Entangled Publishing, LLC
644 Shrewsbury Commons Ave., STE 181
Shrewsbury, PA 17361
rights@entangledpublishing.com

Amara is an imprint of Entangled Publishing, LLC.

Visit our website at www.entangledpublishing.com.

Edited by Yezanira Venecia
Cover art and design by Geneva Lee
Stock art by Gluiki/Adobestock, lavendertime/Adobestock, rodjulian/
Adobestock, Csaba Peterdi/Adobestock, NilsZ/Adobestock, helenagl/
Adobestock, and wooster/Adobestock
Interior design by Britt Marczak

ISBN 978-1-64937-645-9

Manufactured in the United States of America

First Edition April 2024

10 9 8 7 6 5 4 3 2 1

ALSO BY GENEVA LEE

For you

At Entangled, we want our readers to be well-informed. If you would like to know if this book contains any elements that might be of concern for you, please check the back of the book for details.

CHAPTER ONE

Julian

"Lord Julian Rousseaux and his fiancée, Thea Melbourne." The attendant stepped away after his announcement, making room for us to begin our descent down the stairs.

The whispers started immediately. I spared a single glance to the ballroom below. The royalty of the vampire world mingled with familiars young and old under enchanted glass chandeliers hanging in midair. The effect was no less stunning now than it had been centuries ago. The room's arched windows were draped with snow-laden garlands, each laced with frosted ivy. In the very center of the space, a large evergreen sparkled with lights that winked in and out like stars in the night sky.

The room was filled with lingering remnants of magic, bits of enchantments that had survived the curse. But despite the wintery theme, everyone here was dressed in gowns that revealed tempting amounts of flesh, or tuxedos without jackets. It was the Solstice in name only. A chance for immortals to show off their wealth and witches to show off their dwindling skills. But I didn't care about any of that.

I was only interested in confirming the rumors circling the room—that Julian Rousseaux was off the market.

Heads bowed and eyes darted as the news of my engagement rippled over the crowd. Only one pair of eyes remained fixed on me. My mother's pupils were inky black as she glowered at us, and next to me, my mate stumbled. It was only enough for me to notice.

But I noticed.

Still, it was nothing compared to the anger rolling off the woman at my side.

I met Thea's furious glare with the most charming smile I could muster, but her eyes only narrowed. She righted herself carefully, regaining her composure and balance.

"Sorry," I whispered.

Thea muttered something about cliffs and warnings, but she squared her shoulders and turned a blinding smile on me. I knew better than to trust that smile. I was in trouble. Again.

"Yes, you are," she murmured, maintaining her composure masterfully, "but I'm not about to let your mother see us fighting."

"I'll make it up to you later," I promised, placing my hand over hers as we started down the stairs. There was a collective gasp from the crowd, and the murmurs turned into scandalized whispers.

"You forgot your gloves," Thea said at about the moment I realized the same thing.

"Thanks for reminding me," I said drily.

"No problem." Her grin widened and finally reached her eyes. She was enjoying this. "I might have remembered sooner, but I was recovering from a near-death experience."

"Now you're just being dramatic."

"Should we go back to the car?" she suggested, guessing correctly that I didn't have any with me. I'd been so focused on her—on the ring she now wore—that I hadn't thought to grab them from the glove compartment.

But I was already guiding her to the next step, and the bare hands sent a message all on their own. "Let's not worry about it."

"Rebel." She arched an eyebrow as she stepped delicately down to the plush ivory runner that lined the stairs. I kept my eyes on her, ignoring the curious eyes stalking us below. Let them talk.

I was not convinced Thea's choice of footwear was safe, especially on these ancient stairs, regardless of the carpet. They did, however, have many other enticing qualities, like making her tall enough to easily kiss while also turning her legs into temptation itself. Later, I planned to lift her off her feet and fuck her against a wall with those heels digging into my back.

Thea's breath caught as she read my thoughts, her cheeks flushing into a tantalizing shade. Then the scent of sweet melon bloomed around me. "Promise?"

"Absolutely," I muttered as I lifted her hand to my mouth and kissed it.

She blushed more deeply, and my nostrils flared as I drank in the arousal drenching her. I hadn't intended to cause that reaction, even if I appreciated it, but the kiss had given me a chance to show off the ring she now wore over her satin gloves. If we were forced to attend these archaic rituals, I'd put our presence to good use. The announcement, the kiss, even my forgotten gloves—only spread the news faster.

I was truly off the market.

Permanently.

"What are you up to?" Thea said under her breath.

"Gossip travels fast, my love."

The crowd parted before us as we made our way toward my family. It was customary to greet the matriarch upon arrival.

This was the real test. If Sabine decided to raise hell, it would start an entirely new rumor. I probably should have warned Thea about that, too.

But Thea glided next to me, offering gracious smiles to the strangers gawking at her. When we reached my parents, she greeted them warmly.

Dominic Rousseaux smirked, giving me a subtle nod, indicating he appreciated our tactics. It was something he wouldn't dare say in front of his wife, but it spoke volumes. My mate was beginning to win him over. My brothers, even Benedict, would side with me if it came down to it. That only left one holdout regarding my family's position on my choice of partner.

My mother's upper lip curled as we approached, revealing the fangs she seemed to have ready whenever Thea was around. I bristled, drawing my shoulders up in a show of strength. There was a time when she might have been able to take me. She was thousands of years older, with more battle experience. But I had something she didn't have.

A mate. One I would die to protect.

"Mother," I said softly. "Happy Solstice."

She blinked, her eyes shifting between us before landing on our joined hands.

"You forgot gloves," she said with a sniff of disapproval. "I'll see a servant brings some *immediately*."

"That's not necessary. I will be quite safe. I have no desire to touch anyone but *my mate* this evening." I raised my voice enough that the eavesdroppers around us caught the last bit. If anyone had doubts about my betrothal, learning we were mated might answer their questions.

"Nonsense." She snapped her fingers, and an attendant appeared beside her. "My son forgot his gloves. Fetch him a pair."

"Please," Thea added in a whisper.

Sabine's dark gaze swiveled to her. My mother wore a wine-colored gown that snaked across her shoulder and draped elegantly down her back. Her black hair was twisted into twin braids that wrapped around her head like a crown. She was the angel of death incarnate, complete with stained red lips that suggested she might have recently dined on someone's heart. Next to her, Thea glowed in her gold-feathered gown. Even flustered, there was a joy that radiated from her like the warmth of a perfect spring morning. They were polar opposites—my mother was midnight and Thea the promise of a new day.

"At least your fiancée has some sense," my mother continued. "Perhaps she'll be able to convince you to respect our traditions."

"Indeed," I said coolly, fighting the urge to smile. It wasn't exactly a blessing, but referring to Thea as my fiancée was an acknowledgment of our relationship—a public acknowledgment.

"You look lovely," my father interjected, stepping closer to take Thea's hand. "And congratulations to you both."

Next to him, Sabine pressed her lips into a thin line. Apparently, that was taking things a bit too far. But it was done.

Our engagement had been publicly recognized by the family matriarch and her consort.

Thea took a deep breath, undoubtedly clued in to what I was thinking. "Happy Solstice to you both. I am honored to join your family."

The moment couldn't have been more deliberate if it had been staged. We were all taking our cues and playing our parts for our audience. When the attendant returned with my gloves, I took them. Sabine cleared her throat once I'd pulled them on, clearly relieved that I was going to maintain *some* decorum.

"We should make the rounds." She waved at her spouse. "Come along."

My father rolled his eyes slightly as he offered his arm, but he took his place at her side without complaint.

"Before you go," I said, stopping her, "I've arranged to take a private villa on the west side of the island."

"Oh?" Quiet rage seethed from her, but she shrugged. "I suppose you need more space for whatever it is you do."

"Rather, more romance," I said with a smirk. "We have been given clear expectations by the Council."

Thea spluttered next to me, tilting slightly as if my words had nearly knocked her over.

But my mother remained composed, even as her eyes shadowed ominously. "Of course. There is *that*."

"There is," I agreed.

"I suppose we won't be seeing much of you after this evening?"

"Not until the new year," I said firmly.

"They'll expect you on New Year's Eve," she said.

"Send us the details. I'll see what I can do."

Sabine smiled, revealing that deadly beauty I'd learned to fear as a child. "It's not optional."

I simply tilted my head. Message received. I'd played my hand and won, but this game wouldn't end tonight. We were expected to follow this macabre tour wherever their whims took us next. And we had more Rites to face.

My parents slipped into the crowd, accepting well-wishes from everyone.

"That went better than expected," I said, tugging at my bow tie, but when I looked over at my mate, she was practically boiling.

"Dark corner, *now*," she ordered, jerking her head away from the party, toward the shadowed corridors leading away from the ballroom.

Something told me she didn't want a moment alone to get her hands on me.

CHAPTER TWO

Thea

I wasn't angry with Julian. I was furious. I'd spent the whole day wondering and worrying about what he was up to while I'd coped with learning what I truly was. Meanwhile, he'd been plotting all of this. Even the proposal...

I pushed away the pain of that to focus on my outrage and anger.

It took longer than it should have to get away from the ball, since everyone wanted to congratulate us. I'd seen a few of the people here at other events, but they were all strangers. Julian's brothers were nowhere to be found, and Jacqueline was late. By the time Julian darted out an open patio door, my face ached from my forced smile. I let it fall as we made our way across a covered stone courtyard. Strings of lights hung across the vaulted wood ceiling, adding a warm glow.

"I see plenty of dark corners," I muttered as he kept going.

"I assume you want some privacy." His words were flat and cautious. He knew why I wanted to be alone with him.

Maybe that's why he guided me down stone steps into a lush garden below. Julian paused as we arrived at the bottom and turned to me.

I protested as he stooped and reached for my leg. "What do

you think you're doing?"

"Don't worry. I'm not trying to have my way with your ankle," he said drily as his fingers wrapped around it, and he gestured for me to lift my foot.

"Good." I crossed my arms to show that I was in no mood. Julian slipped my heel off, then reached for the other. I groaned with relief as I wiggled my toes. The gold heels were very beautiful but very tall, and an hour wearing them on the hard marble floor inside had made my feet throb.

"Better?" He straightened, his fingers hooked under my heels. I nodded but refused to smile. "I'm still mad at you."

"I know." His teeth raked over his lower lip, like he was biting back a smirk. At least he had some survival instinct. "I didn't want to make you anxious about tonight."

"So, instead, you humiliated me?" I demanded. I didn't wait for him to answer before I continued into the garden. My bare feet sank into the plush blanket of grass, which was surprisingly cool given the temperature. I wrapped my arms around my shoulders and looked up at the night sky. There were so many people nearby, but I felt alone. Here amongst vampires and witches, I only had one person to talk to about how I was feeling.

How was I supposed to talk to him when he was the reason I was upset?

"Are you cold?" Julian asked as he joined me.

I shook my head. "You shouldn't have done that."

"I know." He took a deep breath and maintained a slight distance. "I'm sorry. I didn't think it would humiliate you."

Genuine frustration coated his words, and I felt the tug of our mating bond. He meant it. He was hurting. He needed me. Right now, he probably felt the same urge. But I resisted its call.

"Is the announcement why you proposed tonight?" I asked him.

"I proposed last night," he reminded me.

"You know what I mean."

A volley of curses spouted from his thoughts, and I raised my brows.

"Was that because you were called out, or because you just realized that you're a dumbass?"

"Maybe both," he said grimly. "I didn't think."

"That's clear."

"I didn't plan to propose last night, but once it was settled, I wanted to tell the world as soon as possible. So, I did decide to give you the ring before." He paused and turned to me, his face shadowed under the moonlight. "I never considered how that might feel to you. I just…"

I already knew how that thought ended. I didn't need to read his mind. He'd said once that he wanted to shout it from the rooftops that we had mated. Which was an entirely different matter.

"So, most of the vampire world knows we're engaged, but can they tell that we're mated?" I asked him.

"Anyone who got close enough to say hello, maybe. There are a lot of creatures in there, though."

There were a lot of scents, in other words.

"I should have asked your permission," he added.

I resisted the urge to roll my eyes because I was pretty sure they would go so far they'd get stuck. "You don't need my permission. I just want to know what you're planning. I nearly fell down the stairs when the attendant made that announcement."

"I wouldn't have let you," he said huskily, but I held up a warning finger.

"That isn't the point. We're a team. No secrets. No lies. We promised each other."

He considered this for a second, pushing a strand of dark hair off his forehead. "I thought it would make you anxious."

"But?" I prompted, knowing there was more.

"The Solstice is treasured by vampires. I knew if there was any chance my mother would publicly give her blessing, it would be here."

"Because she's in the Christmas spirit?" I muttered. That didn't sound like Sabine.

"Because she cares more about what the strangers in there

think than about her family's feelings," he said bitterly. "She would never lose face in front of that many important vampires."

"I see. But is this really getting her approval?" I thought of how Jacqueline had told me she needed her mother's blessing to marry. Julian *acted* like he could—and would—do whatever he wanted... "Can we get married without her approval?"

"Yes," he said firmly.

"Legally?"

"In the mortal world," he said softly.

I shut my eyes. For all their talk of evolution, sometimes vampires were terribly, insultingly old-fashioned. "Why didn't you just tell me that to begin with?"

Julian closed the space between us and took my chin in his bare hands. He'd slipped off the gloves he'd been asked to wear, and I'd been too preoccupied to notice. "Because I didn't want you to have one more second of doubt about us. I didn't want you to worry about what the Vampire Council might say—or my parents. We're getting married."

"And if we did it without their blessing?"

"There would be consequences," he admitted in a gruff tone. His eyes grew as dark as the night sky above.

"You would be disowned," I guessed.

He searched my face for a moment, then laughed quietly. "So Jacqueline told you about the stunt with the werewolf in Rome."

I nodded. "Julian, I don't want you to lose your family."

"Even my mother?" He smirked.

I managed to hold my tongue.

"No one will come between us. That is the vow I made to you when we mated. You are the most important person in my life, and if all we have is each other, that is enough for me." His thumb brushed over my lips. "That is a sacrifice you already made for me."

"But if I could find my mom and talk to her," I confessed, "I would fight like hell to keep her, too." Even after everything she had done—after the lies and secrets—I missed her like hell.

"We will find her, my love," he promised, "and I won't spring any more surprise announcements on you."

"And you'll tell me when you're going to drive off a cliff?" I asked drily.

"I swear. Stake through the heart." He hooked an arm around my waist and drew me closer.

Without my shoes on, I barely came to his chest. It made it harder to kiss him but easier to listen to his heartbeat.

"No stakes are getting anywhere near this heart," I informed him.

"Not with my terrifying mate around." He grinned down at me. Moonlight glinted in his dark hair, and I grabbed hold of his lapels and tugged him lower so I could run my hands through it.

"I believe you promised me dark corners," I whispered. "But we seem to be standing out in the open."

An irresistible smirk twisted his mouth. "We could put on a show."

"I'm done with scandals for the evening." But even as I spoke, my body ached for him. Since The Second Rite, we'd found every opportunity we could manage to be alone. Someone had even taken to leaving a tray of food at our door when we inevitably missed a meal, but today had been different. Julian had stayed away, planning his romantic cliffside proposal, and we had barely seen each other.

"What's going on in that wicked mind of yours?" he asked, leaning to lick my lower lip.

I moaned, pleasure rocketing to my core. "Find a dark corner, and I'll show you."

Julian took my hand, his eyes devouring me for a moment before he began toward the garden. I'd expected him to lead us back toward the ball and one of the many shadowy corridors I'd spotted during our exit. Right now, I would settle for a tall bush as privacy. We were a few steps around a hedge when I realized he'd taken me into a labyrinth.

"I hope you know your way around this," I said, gripping his hand tightly.

"Afraid to be left alone with me for too long?" he teased.

"Just wondering if a hedge can withstand us."

He laughed, pausing to twirl me into his arms. "Should we find out?" He leaned to kiss me, and I melted into him. He could have me—all of me—wherever he wanted, and he knew it.

His hand slipped under my gown's strap and slid it from my shoulder. I gasped, breaking the kiss slightly as he slid the other one free.

"Here?" I asked innocently, nibbling on my lower lip.

A hungry growl ripped through him, his dark eyes trained on that lower lip with predatory intensity. I swallowed as my body responded to the beast before me. Tugging away from him, I reached for my zipper and pulled it down.

"This will make it easier," I whispered, letting the gown fall and puddle at my feet.

The provocative nature of the dress didn't leave many undergarment options, so I'd skipped them altogether. And with my shoes in Julian's hands, there wasn't a stitch on me.

Almost.

Julian seemed to expand, his breath growing labored while I slipped my engagement ring free and took off my final clothing items: my gloves. I slid the ring back on and casually dropped the gloves. He raked midnight eyes down me, rubbing his chin with his free hand as if considering what to do about the situation he was in. It was obvious he wanted me, and not in a gentle, tender way. No, tonight amongst rival bloodlines and strange vampires, that primal monster inside him—the one I felt rousing inside me now—was restless. He was on edge. He needed a way to dull the protective compulsion he felt now.

Without thinking, I slipped my hand between my legs and touched myself. The shadows in his eyes darkened until there was no hint of white. He was more animal than male now, and I was what he needed. Bringing my drenched fingers to his mouth, I brushed one over his lip.

My shoes fell to the ground as his hand shot up and grabbed my wrist before I could pull away. His black eyes never left my face as he lifted my fingers once more to his mouth and sucked them clean—one at a time.

I stumbled a little on my feet, my flesh singing with want, but I righted myself and looked him in the eye. "Is that what you want?"

His growl trembled through me.

"You can have it," I promised him sweetly. "If you can catch me."

Wrenching my hand free, I sprinted away. Before he realized what I was doing, I darted around a turn in the maze and then again at the next one I saw. I didn't stand a chance against his vampire senses, but the labyrinth might give his predator a moment to prowl.

And when he caught me, it would be worth the wait.

CHAPTER THREE

Julian

"You can have it—if you can catch me."

And then Thea dashed into the night, vanishing like a mischievous nymph. Darkness swallowed me. She wanted to play a game. She would learn exactly how dangerous that prospect was with me—and I would enjoy delivering the lesson.

Sucking in a deep breath, I closed my eyes and let the beast inside me take over. When I opened them, the world had shifted. It was no longer cast in the shadows of night. My supernatural eyesight painted it in brilliant jeweled tones. Emerald hedges. Sapphire sky. Flowers of garnet and amethyst. Billowing blooms of night-scented stock spilled their sweet aroma, mixing with the sensual notes of jasmine on the evening air.

But she rose above it all. I caught sight of movement—a ruby aura darting through the leafy maze. Sweet melon spiked with cloves floated toward me on the breeze, and my control snapped like an overextended chain.

I launched into the labyrinth. I couldn't resist it if I tried. She pulled me toward her like an anchoring point. I followed her scent. It lingered so thickly I tasted it on my tongue, my thoughts turning to her other flavors—the sweetness between her legs, the richness of her blood. I needed her.

Now.

I caught up with her in less than a minute. Thea yelped as I rounded a corner in a blur and swept her into my arms. Her arms coiled around my neck tightly as I flashed forward without slowing.

I didn't stop to savor my victory and the reward she'd promised me. Not until I reached the center of the maze, where a marble gazebo awaited. When I finally halted, she stared breathlessly up at me.

"You caught me," she murmured, her voice drowned by the blood rushing through my veins. "Now, what will you do with me?"

I growled in response.

Her answering tremble lifted the corner of my mouth, flashing her a fang. Carrying her toward the gazebo, I studied every line of her face. She was made for me. I'd never done anything to deserve such perfection, but I would claim it.

My cock swelled in my pants as I considered what I wanted to do with her.

Thea stroked a finger down my cheek.

"How do you want me?"

My eyes narrowed, but the bloodlust didn't ebb. I was too far gone. I could only think in terms of flesh and teeth.

I placed her gently onto a stone bench. Thea's eyes shadowed as she spread her legs. My hunger vibrated inside me as I drank in the sight of her splayed before me in invitation. Her nipples beaded in the night air, and a slick sheen between her legs betrayed her arousal. My gaze traveled upward, reaching her sinful mouth, and lingered. Her tongue swept over her lips, and its movement became the center of my universe. When it retreated into her mouth, her teeth sank into her bottom lip with artless sensuality.

I unfastened my belt with one quick movement and undid my trousers. My fingers closed over my shaft, stroking it as I freed my cock. Thea tracked the movement, hunger shining in her eyes. I was already moving closer when her index finger curled to beckon me forward.

"Show me who this belongs to," I ordered her.

Thea lowered onto the soft grass and stared up at me in total supplication. Her hand reached up and took hold of me before she leaned and took me in her mouth. I hissed with satisfaction as her lips closed around me. Her cheeks hollowed as she worshipped with adoring eyes, moving up and down with hunger that threatened to push me over the edge.

"I love seeing you on your knees for me," I muttered, "but I need to fuck you."

Her eyes rounded, but she pulled back with deliberate, teasing slowness, her lips popping as she released me. Still, her hand stayed wrapped around my shaft, and I watched as she leaned forward and licked a slow circle around its tip.

That did it.

Lifting her, I laid her across the bench. She writhed as I kicked off my shoes one at a time before shucking off my pants. Straddling the stone bench, I grabbed hold of her hips and lifted them up until her swollen sex swept across the crown of my cock.

"Fuck," I groaned as I felt her wetness. "You're *drenched*."

Thea whimpered, her eyes shining in the moonlight, as she bucked her hips, trying to get closer.

"Do you want this?" I dragged my cock down her seam, coating myself in her. She managed a small nod. "You ran from me. Why should I give it to you?"

Thea hesitated for only a minute before a wicked smile carved across her face. Maybe she heard the answer I wanted in my mind. Maybe she *just knew.*

"It's mine," she said with a calculated slowness, pressing herself against my tip.

"Oh?" I pushed in a little.

"Mine," she repeated. "You're mine, Julian, and I want you."

Fuck, that was the right answer. I thrust hard, burying myself in her completely. Her body arced up, a throaty cry escaping her lips. I held her ass off the bench and began pistoning with long, deep strokes. She met every movement with her hips, moving in perfect unison as we fought our way to climax.

Lowering my head, I caught her nipple in my mouth and flicked its tip with my tongue. Thea moaned, and I moved to the two perfect scars on her creamy flesh. Pressing a kiss to them, I reared my head and let her catch sight of my fangs before I sank them into the scars so near to her heart.

Her blood was sweetest here. I drank deeply, my fangs and cock drawing her blood and her orgasm. She tightened around me, her arm hooking around my neck to hold me there as she gasped and panted, and when she gushed around my cock, I released her breast and came with a roar, her blood still coating my lips.

Thea sagged across the bench, and I lifted her, wrapping my arms around her.

"That..." She trailed away, her eyes glinting.

"I want to do that to you forever," I confessed in a harsh whisper.

"You can," she said softly.

But there was only one thought in my mind as I held her there, her body still pulsating over me. I didn't want her for any lifetime. I wanted her for all of mine.

"Thea," I murmured, reaching to brush a loose strand of hair from her flushed cheek, "I want this forever. I want *you* forever." Her head tilted, confusion blinking in her eyes, and then, slowly, understanding. I knew what I wanted. She'd promised to marry me, but I wanted more. I needed more. "Let me make you a vampire."

CHAPTER FOUR

Thea

The summery air felt heavier against my damp, fevered skin. I stared at Julian, watching as his eyes contracted in the moonlight. He blinked, and they returned to the brilliant blue that always stole my breath away. Not tonight, though. His words had knocked the wind and all thoughts out of my head. I clung to him, trying to process what he was saying.

Let me make you a vampire.

The last time this subject had come up, Julian had slipped into beast mode. I studied his face, trying to figure out what had changed. I mean, apart from pretty much everything. We were mated, engaged, and seriously testing the boundaries of my magic.

He remained silent, his hand pressed to my cheek. After a minute, he raised his eyebrows, and I realized he was waiting for an answer.

"No!" I blurted out, surprising myself.

Julian flinched, his body tightening beneath me. Rejection shot through me, but it wasn't my own. It was his. It twisted in my gut before settling heavily inside me like lead. Its weight pulled at me, making every inch of my body throb with agony. The last time I'd felt this way was when he'd broken my heart in Paris. One word had hurt him that badly.

One word had broken his heart.

Julian gently unsheathed himself and guided me onto the bench. I immediately missed his skin against mine, but he turned away before I could explain myself. Getting to his feet, he reached for his pants.

"I'll find your dress," he said distantly as he yanked them on. He didn't bother with his shoes as he started back toward the hedge maze with bare feet.

"Wait!" I called, scrambling to stand. My head swam from the sudden movement after such recent physical exertion, and I swayed. I caught myself on the bench as Julian turned. In an instant, he was by my side.

"Are you okay?" he asked through gritted teeth. Even with his hands on my waist to keep me upright, he kept his eyes trained over my shoulder.

"Just dizzy." I smiled, but he continued to stare past me. "Let me explain."

"That's not necessary." His tone remained clipped. "It's your decision to make."

"Don't do this," I whispered. Reaching out, I tugged on the lapel of his tuxedo jacket, trying to urge him to look at me. He wrapped a hand around my wrist and pried himself free. "Julian!"

"Don't worry. I'll get over it." He forced himself to meet my eyes, his mouth tipping at the corners in an attempted smile.

I shook my head, trying to think clearly as his pain pummeled me. "I need to think about it." I forced the words out. "I was just surprised."

"It's not something you should have to think about," he said carefully, then nodded toward the maze. "Let me find your dress."

"Julian, we can talk about this." I clutched his hand in my own, refusing to let him go. "I love you."

"I love you, too," he echoed, but it sounded hollow, like I'd wrung the words from him. He pulled his hand free and waited for me to explain myself.

But how was I supposed to explain that despite my surprise, my answer had been an instinct that even I didn't understand? "It's just…immortality is a big decision."

"I wasn't going to turn you on the spot." He paused, and when I still didn't respond, he turned. Julian disappeared into the labyrinth without so much as a glance in my direction. I hesitated, wondering if it was better to wait for him to cool down. But the intensity of his emotions only ratcheted up with each step he took. This wasn't the type of pain he could walk off.

I ran after him. I was not going to let my mate walk around feeling like he'd just been gutted and left to die. He caught me around the waist at the second turn, my dress and gloves already over his arm, my shoes hooked on his fingers.

"Where are you going?" he asked.

"After you," I said, panting heavily. I'd run as fast as I could, and I was paying for it now. On the other hand, Julian had managed to race through the maze and back with his supernatural speed without a hair out of place.

He passed my gown to me, pivoting away as I slipped it over my head.

"Oh, top that!" I snapped as I smoothed it into place and grabbed my shoes. I didn't bother to put them on. I doubted the Vampire Council wanted me to aerate the lawn with my stilettos. "What did you expect me to say?"

"You've agreed to marry me," he pointed out, turning to me with black eyes. "We've mated. You asked me to turn you before. What changed?"

There was too much misery in his words. It stung, but beneath it, fear lingered.

That didn't mean I was going to agree to this before thinking it through, though. I crossed my arms, my shoes dangling from my right hand. "As you just said, in the last month, I've gotten engaged, bound my soul to yours, found out I'm probably a siren, and agreed to have your vampire babies! I just need a damn minute to process some shit before I have to make one more life-altering decision!"

His mouth twitched. "So you are going to have my babies, huh?"

"Dammit, Julian!" I screamed with frustration. Tears burned my eyes, and I reached to wipe them away. "We don't even know if I can, but I won't be able to if I'm a turned vampire, right?"

He nodded hesitantly.

"Can you see why I need to think about this?" I asked, softening a bit.

"But you didn't say you needed to think—"

"I did," I interjected, but he ignored me.

"You said *no*," he finished.

I opened my mouth to respond, but suddenly, Julian pushed me behind him.

"What—"

"Someone's coming," he hissed. His whole body expanded as he took on a defensive posture, looming large in front of me as if ready to attack an oncoming threat. I started to reach for him but stopped myself. I had no idea how he would react, given how taut his tether appeared to be and considering that I'd placed him on the very edge with my rejection.

Footsteps rustled around the corner, but just as my heart began to race, Julian relaxed. A second later, Jacqueline appeared. She strode out of the night, her fair skin and hair glowing under the stars. Her deep purple dress blended with the exotic blossoms lacing the hedge maze. Its skirt rippled as she sauntered toward us with a smirk on her red lips.

"There you are," she said, an almost musical hint of a French accent in her voice. "People are looking for you, but I see you've been *occupied*."

I could only imagine how we looked. Jacqueline's nostrils flared, and I realized that wasn't the only thing that gave us away. Undoubtedly, her vampire senses were picking up exactly what we'd been up to in the garden. And if she could...

I guessed coming back covered in each other's scents would help the gossip travel faster. That was what Julian wanted.

"We're on our way. We went out for air," Julian said stiffly.

"Is that what you kids are calling it these days?" she teased him but remained tense. She shot me a curious look but didn't press him for more information. Instead, her hand lashed out and grabbed mine. A deep growl rumbled through Julian, which Jacqueline shushed. "I want to see the ring."

Julian rolled his eyes as Jacqueline did an appropriate amount of *ooh*ing and *aah*ing.

"I always loved this ring," she told me. "It fits you perfectly."

I fumbled for something to say. "He had it sized." My throat constricted, emotions starting to choke me.

"It fits *you*," she clarified.

"Oh." I managed to bob my head.

Jacqueline glanced between us, her eyes narrowing, her smile slipping to a frown. "Okay." She dropped my hand. "Spill. What's going on with you two?"

"Nothing," we both said.

"Sure," she said flatly. Releasing a resigned sigh, she hooked her arm through mine. "Can you two stop fighting for a second?"

"We're not fighting," I said quickly, but Julian only shrugged a shoulder.

Jacqueline ignored me. "It's my family," she told us. "They're here. I knew they would be. At least, I suspected it, but..."

"And that's bad because of the werewolf thing?" I guessed.

Her throat slid as she nodded.

"It's bad because they haven't spoken to me in over a century," she said gloomily. "I was hoping you two might distract them so they don't get any ideas about setting me up with someone."

"Would they?" I asked, thinking of what she'd told me earlier. According to Jacqueline, she was an outcast.

"I don't know," she admitted, "but if you two were with me, there would be plenty of people wanting to talk to you instead."

"So, we're interference?"

"Yes." She looked at Julian. "Maybe if they see you two together, they'll realize that I was right to stop the engagement when I did."

It was a desperate hope, but I knew that sometimes the only thing keeping hope alive was sheer determination. I looped my arm through hers.

"We've got you."

"I'm not entirely certain your parents will want to see me," Julian said mysteriously. The two vampires shared a look.

Reaching out with my mind, I listened, hoping he had more he needed to say to me privately. It was clear there was more to this story than what I'd been told. But either he didn't want me to hear it or his mind was entirely blank, because all I discovered was cool, black silence.

"Can I borrow your fiancée?" she asked.

"That's up to her."

Julian and I needed to talk. I knew that, and so did he. But maybe we needed a moment to collect our thoughts first. I swallowed hard and nodded. "Sure. I'd be honored to be your sidekick."

"Thank you." She threw her delicate arms around me and squeezed. When she finally released me, Julian was nowhere to be seen. Frustration burned through me, but I managed a smile. Jacqueline, however, wrinkled her nose. "Let's find the powder room first. You smell…"

"That bad, huh?" I asked flatly.

"No one will doubt that you're mated," she teased. "Come on."

We walked, arm in arm, through the maze and back to the party.

"You seemed surprised your parents are here," I said quietly.

She sighed and glanced over at me. "They tend to stay away from the season since…"

Since she had humiliated them by bringing a werewolf to a gala and introducing him as her boyfriend, all to get out of marrying her best friend—my mate.

"But they came tonight?" I asked as the sprawling estate came into view. Lights and laughter drifted toward us on the balmy air. "Why now?"

Jacqueline's mouth tightened, her eyes glued to the party ahead like a prisoner walking toward her own execution. "There's only one reason they would come."

I waited as she stopped and collected herself.

Finally, she turned to me with sad eyes. "I'm a firstborn pureblood. They're here because I have to get married."

CHAPTER FIVE

Julian

I stalked back to the party with a mussed tuxedo and wounded pride. More vampires and witches had arrived in our absence, and the ballroom was packed. Under the sparkling glass chandeliers, the beautiful, elite members of our society mingled and flirted. Everywhere I looked, I spotted flirtations meant to secure alliances. I made it two steps inside the door before I was accosted by a pair of vampires. The female looked about my mother's age—if that meant anything—but something in the way she carried herself told me she was even older. Or maybe it was the high neckline and modest cut of her dress. She angled herself close to me. Her bored, much younger trophy husband waited silently at her side.

"Julian," she said, her tone gushing with syrupy feminine coyness, "I am thrilled to see you've made a match."

I kept a careful distance and managed a forced smile. "I believe I'm the lucky one."

Lucky? I'd fallen in love with a mortal. Her average life expectancy meant I'd be lucky to have fifty years with Thea—and fifty years wasn't long enough.

"...as I was telling Randolph." The female placed a gloved hand on my arm, and I realized she'd been talking the whole time. Not that it was likely to be important. Still, she continued. "It's reassuring to see so many purebloods upholding traditional values."

"Oh?" I raised an eyebrow despite myself.

"With the threats to our way of life, we need to maintain the bloodlines by any means necessary," she said in a conspiratorial whisper. "Tell me. From what bloodline does your fiancée hail?"

"It's an ancient line," I told her, hoping it would be enough to sate her.

"But she's magical?"

I hesitated before nodding. We wouldn't be able to keep Thea's nature a secret forever, and now that the Council knew, word of her powers was likely to spread. For now, we would keep the details to ourselves. Until we knew more about her siren blood, it was safer to keep it quiet.

And then there was the matter of her father.

I pushed the thought away. My eyes skimmed the room for my betrothed or my best friend, who had yet to return from wherever they'd gone.

"Good. I trust you won't waste time." The female's sugary demeanor slipped, and her face darkened.

"I plan to marry Thea as soon as possible," I promised. If it was up to me, we would already be married.

But it wasn't up to me. I had my family and the Council to contend with, though they weren't the ones who worried me.

Thea was.

Because the thought of losing her, the thought of her remaining mortal, the thought of her dying...

"Good, but I'm talking about children. We need to strengthen our numbers," the strange woman said, drawing my attention to her guarded face.

"Am I meant to uphold traditions or personally breed an army?" I asked her carefully.

She laughed, but her eyes watched me warily. "Why can't it be both?" She sniffed me and smiled, revealing her fangs. "It seems you've already taken up the task."

I trained my face into a blank stare, unwilling to give away that I knew precisely what she was talking about. I glanced away from her and caught Lysander and Sebastian watching me with amusement. One glare and they straightened up before heading my way to help their brother out.

"Excuse me," Sebastian interrupted whatever grossly inappropriate comment the older female planned to make next. "My brother is needed…"

"Elsewhere," Lysander finished for him.

I groaned internally. They were about as helpful as two left shoes, but the female blinked flirtatiously at them.

"I suppose one of you will be next," she said in that cloying voice.

Sebastian winked at her, his eyes darting to her husband. "Unfortunately, it seems you're off the market."

"Oh!" She giggled, buying his false flattery. "I'm old enough to be your mother."

"You don't look a day over three hundred," he said seriously.

"You're a charmer. I'm sure you will break plenty of hearts next year."

"I'm sure he will." I grabbed my brother's shoulder and steered him in the opposite direction. "Excuse us."

My brothers fell into step beside me, providing a much-needed buffer between me and the rest of the guests.

"Where is the lovely Thea?" Lysander asked.

"Or should we listen for her song?" Sebastian added.

I glared at Lysander, who made a point of looking confused. He lifted his hands defensively. "I didn't know it was a secret."

"Who else have you told?" I whispered, hoping no one had caught Sebastian's stupid joke.

"Just us," he dodged.

"And by us…"

"The family," he admitted.

I muttered a curse under my breath.

"I didn't know I was supposed to keep it from—"

"It's fine," I cut him off. "Fuck, I need a drink."

I could still taste Thea on my tongue. Despite our disagreement, I found myself torn between taking a minute to calm down and immediately finding her. I knew what would happen if I found her—and it wouldn't solve anything.

"Follow me," Sebastian said, a wicked glint in his eyes.

We bypassed the waiters serving blood-and-champagne cocktails and continued down an empty hall. "Where are you taking me?"

"Don't worry. We'll keep you safe," Sebastian teased. His grin faltered when I didn't even smile. "There's a bar on the lower level, and it's full of the expensive shit."

Trust my wayward brothers to know where they kept the good stuff. I looked over my shoulder, thinking of Thea and Jacqueline.

"Unless you need to stay," Lysander said, an edge to his voice.

I considered for a moment. Thea was with Jacqueline, and regardless of what my best friend said, I was not the right person to run interference where her parents were concerned. They'd never given up on Jacqueline and me marrying, even long after my tenacious mother had. Despite the werewolf incident, I suspected they would have forced Jacqueline if I hadn't publicly refused the match, knowing she wanted an out. That was the part that my old friend had left out of her story to Thea. Mostly because it was me and not her family that was responsible for Jacqueline being exiled from polite society in the first place. Bringing her as a guest of the Rousseaux family was the first step in officially restoring her reputation. But if her parents were here, they were up to something.

"He probably needs to find his fiancée," Sebastian said. "Tether a little tight tonight?"

"Don't be an asshole," I muttered, speeding up. But each step I took was harder, as if he was right. I felt a restless stir of magic in my veins. Was it Thea's magic calling out to mine? Or was my magic growing anxious about leaving her behind? I wasn't waiting around to find out.

They caught up with me quickly.

"Someone is in a good mood," Lysander noted. There was no derision in his words. "Need to talk?"

"Careful," Sebastian warned him. "You'll have to take a blood-vow."

"Remind me not to invite you to the wedding."

"No way! I love weddings, and who else is going to be your best man?" he demanded.

"Me," Lysander said.

I rolled my eyes as we reached a winding staircase that descended to the floor below. "Maybe we'll elope."

"Good luck with that."

"Yeah, no way Sabine will let you off that lightly," Lysander agreed with him.

I took the stairs two at a time, both of my brothers following at my heels. At the bottom, we found ourselves in a large lounge. As promised, a fully stocked bar comprised the far corner. The rest of the room was decorated in deep browns and greens that smacked of earthy masculinity. Oversize chairs sat throughout the rest of the space, each complemented by a polished oak side table.

"I think this is where they banish the husbands when the females need to talk," Lysander told me.

I thought of the young vampire husband I'd just met. Lysander might be right. Males like my father, who had seen plenty of action on the battlefield and was well-respected among the Council, might be invited to important meetings, but plenty of trophy husbands needed a place to wait quietly for their wives to see to important matters.

Sebastian flashed to the bar and found a bottle of Scotch. He lifted it triumphantly over his head.

"Stop showboating and start drinking," I ordered him. My fangs ached from keeping them retracted.

"For someone who just gleefully pissed our mother off by surprising everyone with news of your engagement, you seem awfully depressed," Lysander pointed out as Sebastian sauntered over, cradling three glasses and the bottle.

"Not to mention that you reek of sexy siren, and I saw you disappear toward the garden." Sebastian waggled his blond eyebrows, and I swiped a glass from him.

"Pour," I ordered. I needed to wash the taste of Thea out of my mouth so I could think clearly.

Sebastian bowed dutifully and did as he was told. I took a long sip of my drink, savoring its pleasant burn.

"Need something stronger?" he asked. "The Council arranged

for a *cortège* to be available tonight. I could send for one."

It wasn't surprising to hear a *cortège* was present. With this many vampires and familiars in one place, it was a smart precaution. Not every vampire's control grew with age. It was best to have a supply of fresh blood at the ready, and there were always humans willing to serve our appetites in exchange for help or the promise of being turned into one of us.

I shook my head. "I already fed."

"On Thea?" Lysander guessed.

Sebastian remained silent as he dropped into a chair and downed his Scotch before pouring another.

"I only feed on Thea." My admission was met with barely suppressed shock. I cleared my throat to explain. "It's part of our arrangement. We don't share each other."

"Are you certain that's wise?" Lysander asked carefully.

"Yeah, how are you going to feel in a couple of decades?"

I ignored Sebastian. I should have known that he wouldn't understand, but Lysander was different. In so many ways, the two were alike, but Lysander had been in love once. Deeply in love, and it had ended poorly. Sometimes I wondered if the cockiness was an act designed to cover up an irreparably broken heart.

"I would never share Thea," I said gruffly. "I can't ask her to do the same."

"You're comparing apples to oranges," Lysander said with a sigh, "but I understand."

"I don't," Sebastian said.

"Is that why you're upset?"

I shook my head. "No, it's not." I looked into Lysander's eyes and dared to finally admit the burden weighing on my soul. The truth I'd refused to acknowledge because even thinking it killed me. "I don't think I should marry Thea."

CHAPTER SIX

Thea

"It's a little late for that."

Jacqueline didn't bother to hide her amusement as I inspected the fresh bite marks on the swell of my breast while trying to adjust my gown to cover them. I looked around the bathroom for something that might help. A row of mahogany stalls sat empty behind us. I was grateful no one else was using the restroom, especially given the condition I was in. Turning back to the sinks, my gaze slid down the granite counter to a basket of folded towels and expensive hand lotion. I grabbed one of the hand towels and turned back to the mirror. Jacqueline eyed me in the reflection as she checked her lipstick. It was perfect, naturally.

I, on the other hand, was a freaking mess.

"He usually does some vampire thing to make them heal faster," I grumbled as I dabbed at the damp hair curling around my forehead and neck. Julian had managed to loosen my carefully pinned curls, but it was the bite marks that stood out, and there was nothing I could do about them. They weren't bleeding anymore, but they refused to seal back to their normal pearly scar tissue.

He must have been too distracted in the garden to remember to heal them. No. He'd been too upset.

Because I had said no.

"Let me." She didn't wait for permission and stepped in front of me. There was a blur of motion, and then she dabbed the spots gently before stepping away. "Good as new."

"Was that a good idea?" I asked her.

Something primal had overtaken Julian in the garden. I'd sensed it simmering below the surface of the gentleman vampire he'd presented upon our arrival. When it had stirred inside me, his magic responding to his agitation, I'd acted. But whatever relief I'd given him had been short-lived. "He might freak if he smells another vampire on me."

Her crimson lips twitched. "I can handle Jules," she promised. "He's acting like a real alphahole, huh?"

"Yeah." I frowned as I returned to fix the rest of myself. Jacqueline stepped behind me, shooing my hands away, and began redoing my hair. "I thought vampires were matriarchal."

Laughter bubbled from her. "We are. Our males are driven to protect their women, but since you two mated..."

"All that primitive, beastly compulsion is directed at me?" I guessed.

"You did pick a fight with his mother," she pointed out.

"Why does that matter?" I knew what everyone thought about my impending duel with Sabine, including my mate. Maybe that was why he was acting jumpier than usual.

"Do you think you can win?" Jacqueline asked me seriously.

"Yes." I had a plan, but it would only work if Sabine didn't know about it.

Jacqueline didn't press for more information. She just shot me an impressed smile. "Normally, Julian's protective instincts would be split between his mother and you. Right now, he views his mother as a threat, so..."

"I get all the alphahole energy." I sighed. It made sense—in a twisted vampire way.

"But that doesn't explain why he looked like you just kicked his puppy." Jacqueline tucked a pin between her teeth and waited for an explanation as she twisted a strand of my hair into place.

"He asked to make me a vampire," I confessed in a whisper.

Jacqueline's hands froze, her eyes flickering to mine. "And you said...?"

"No." My shoulders slumped. I'd said no. He had me there. Even if I'd meant that I needed to think about it, I'd still rejected him.

To my surprise, she rolled her eyes. "What did he expect? To turn you on the spot? That's a huge decision."

"Thank you!" I threw my hands in the air. "I just wasn't expecting it. Not with everything going on, and the Council wants me knocked up, like, yesterday. How can he even think about it?"

"So, that's what you two were up to in the garden." She snorted, shaking her head. "The problem is that he's not thinking. He's *feeling*. He's afraid."

It was hard to think of my mate as being afraid of anything, but I'd seen his eyes wild with terror. He'd been afraid the night Camila had attacked me, and he'd looked the same following The Second Rite.

"If you were a vampire, you'd be less breakable," she explained.

"He didn't want to turn me before. What changed?" There was something else driving him. I'd sensed an almost imperceptible shift in him since before we'd left San Francisco. He couldn't lie to me.

"Try reading his mind?" She shrugged.

I shook my head, causing a curl to tumble loose. She tutted and returned to fixing me. "He isn't thinking about it. I mean, he can shield some thoughts from me."

"And you don't want to pry?"

"I reached out, and he maintained radio silence." I swallowed. "I want him to talk to me. Do you think it's because I'm a siren?"

"I don't know," she said softly. "I'll speak with him."

"Thank you." My words were thick on my tongue. Maybe my mate could share whatever haunted him more easily with a friend. I wished it wasn't the case, but the only thing that mattered was that he worked through it.

I studied Jacqueline in the mirror, noticing that her fingers trembled slightly.

"Do you want to talk about your parents?" I asked her softly.

"Not really," she admitted. "I need to just get it over with. It's worse not knowing."

"I get that." I laughed humorlessly. "If there's anything I can do, please tell me."

"Stick with me?" She bit her lower lip. I'd never seen her so out of sorts. "And don't let me rip off their heads?"

I hoped she was joking about the second request, but I couldn't be sure. I nodded either way. "Done. What are you going to do if they want you to get married?"

"I don't think they give a shit, but the Council's stipulations are for every pureblood to marry, so how do I get off the hook?"

I wished I had an answer for her.

"The worst part is that it's all a ploy to boost the population," she said miserably. "They want babies."

"I know." I gulped, and she gave me a sympathetic grin.

"I'm not the maternal type," she admitted.

"Maybe you'll meet someone who inspires you," I said weakly.

Her face blanched, pain glistening in her eyes. Jacqueline didn't speak. She didn't have to, because I knew what a broken heart looked like.

"You already did," I murmured. Turning toward her, I took her hands.

"Some things aren't meant to be," she said quickly. She pulled away and dabbed the corners of her eyes, staining the fingertips of her gloves with mascara.

"If you ever want to talk," I offered.

She bobbed her head. "Thank you, but—"

Jacqueline fell silent as the restroom door swung open and someone entered. The vampire—a statuesque blonde—stopped two steps inside.

"We're just finishing up," I said, trying to act normally.

But she ignored me, her gaze pinned on my friend. Looking over to Jacqueline, I cringed to find her glaring at the stranger.

"Jacqueline." The stranger sneered at her. "I had no idea you would be here."

"You didn't?" Jacqueline's eyebrow arched. "I find that surprising. I was told the DuBois family had a prospect to present."

Something clicked into place. The same thing that must have occurred to Jacqueline when she found out her parents would also be in attendance. Had they known she was coming? Did they plan to trap her? Maybe it was the uneasy tension crackling between the two of them that warned me to remain silent. Regardless, I didn't say a word.

"The Council's new policies apply to *everyone*. No exceptions."

"I am not marrying someone because of an edict. If you think for a second that you can force me to—" Jacqueline began.

"I wouldn't dream of forcing you to do anything," she cut her off. "I wouldn't even ask. You made your feelings clear on the matter. Have you changed your mind?"

Jacqueline's jaw tightened as she shook her head. "Have you, Mother?"

The confirmation only told me what I'd already guessed from looking at them. They had the same willowy body, the same honey-blond hair and full lips, and they shared the same murderous expression. But it was the way her mother carried herself—with the poise of someone powerful—that gave away her position in the DuBois family.

"No, I haven't." A hateful smile carved over her face. She moved toward the sinks, brushing past Jacqueline like she was nothing.

"What's your plan?" Jacqueline demanded, planting her hands on her hips.

Her mother placed a clutch on the counter and took out a gold-plated tube of lipstick. She uncapped it and twisted the bottom. "Why does it matter to you?"

"Why does it..." Jacqueline didn't trail away; she spluttered.

Her fair skin reddened, and I realized she was on the verge of exploding. I took a step forward and placed a hand on her arm.

"Who is your friend?" her mother asked, watching us in the reflection.

I didn't miss the distaste in her voice.

"Don't pretend," Jacqueline said angrily. "You know exactly who she is."

Her mother recapped her lipstick, sighing as she dropped it into her bag, and turned to me. "Daphné DuBois." She didn't offer her hand. "And you are?"

"Thea Melbourne," I said softly.

"And how do you know my prodigal daughter?" Daphné asked. "Or has she finally moved on from werewolves?"

I had half a mind to grab Jacqueline's hand and pretend to be her girlfriend just to piss this bitch off, but that might have made things worse, so I hesitated.

"She's Julian's fiancée," Jacqueline said with a raised chin.

"Oh. I heard about that." Daphné looked away from me like she'd just been informed I was an insect. I supposed gossip might travel quickly, but it usually wasn't the good news that traveled fastest.

"So, if you were hoping to rekindle your plan, you're shit out of luck." Jacqueline grinned at her.

"So vulgar." Her mother tugged at her elbow-length glove. "Believe me. I have no intention of going back on my promise to you. You are no longer my daughter in the eyes of the family."

Jacqueline swayed ever so slightly, and I gripped her arm tightly in case she started to fall over.

"But you will marry me off," she accused.

"I wouldn't dream of it." Her mother rolled her eyes. "We're here to present your sister."

All the defiance rolling off Jacqueline vanished in an instant. Her mouth fell open in numb horror. "You can't. You wouldn't."

"Jessica is pureblood and, as far as we're concerned, our eldest child."

"But she's a child," Jacqueline whispered. "She's not ready."

"Age, it seems, doesn't matter, does it?" Shadows fell over her mother's face, a brittle smile playing on her lips as she beheld her daughter. "We don't have a choice. The Council demanded it."

"Jessica is only three hundred years old!" Jacqueline lunged for her, but Daphné stepped to the side. "You can't do this!"

"It's done. Your sister understands what is required of her. She is making the rounds with your father now." The satisfaction in her voice told me everything I needed to know about why Jacqueline had chosen exile over duty.

I remembered what Julian had said—that vampires didn't marry until they were at least five hundred years old. If that was true, then I understood why Jacqueline was panicking.

Daphné started toward the door with a smug grin. When she reached it, Jacqueline yelled the last thing I would have expected.

"Stop! I'll do it," she cried.

"Jacqueline," I said quickly. "Think about this."

But I was too late. Again.

"Not quite good enough. Everyone's getting married these days." Daphné's hand paused on the door as Jacqueline sobbed her final offer.

"I'll marry whoever you want."

CHAPTER SEVEN

Julian

"I wasn't expecting that." Sebastian poured me another drink. I forced a smile, and he nodded slightly in return. He could be a jackass, but he knew when matters were serious.

"Me neither," Lysander muttered as he held up his glass for a refill with one hand and raked the other through his hair. "I don't get it. You're crazy about her."

"Certifiably insane," Sebastian added.

I took a deep breath, my eyes finding the ground as I explained. "I am. I know it. But maybe that's the problem. I can't think straight with her around, and I need to think straight. When I don't, things get out of hand."

"Like *challenging Mom to a duel* out of hand?" Lysander said flatly.

"Exactly." I nodded and took a long draw from my glass. "I still haven't figured out how to get her out of that."

"Mother is just trying to scare you," Sebastian pointed out. "You know it's not about Thea slapping her. It's about... everything."

He was right, but that didn't make the situation any easier to swallow. "Thea doesn't even understand the expectations—and if we have children…"

Lysander wrinkled his nose. "Judging by the way you smell, that will be any minute."

"She's too young—for any of it. She deserves a life." Wasn't that the whole problem? Was that the fear she kept to herself? She'd given up her whole world to be with me, and in return, she was being forced to meet the Council's demands—not a fair exchange for the life filled with music she'd given up for us.

"Where is this really coming from?" Lysander asked me quietly.

I swallowed another gulp of Scotch, letting it burn away my hesitance. "It's the tether. I can't trust it. I'm never sure if I'm doing the right thing for her or if I'm just acting on some lingering caveman genes."

Sebastian piped up. "Have you asked her?"

I glared over at him.

Lysander tipped his head and grinned. "He has a point. Have you?"

"Yes," I said with a groan. "I mean, I think I have."

"Sounds like you haven't to me." Sebastian smirked over the rim of his glass. "If you're worried that you're being an asshole, just ask her."

It could not be that easy. Could it?

"Look," Lysander said, sinking against the couch cushion, "do you want to marry Thea?"

"Yes."

He stabbed a finger in the air. "You didn't even hesitate. Why are you having second thoughts? You two just need to talk more and breed less."

"Charming." I shot him a thin smile.

"Don't shoot the messenger."

"There's something else." I swished the remaining liquid in my cup, wondering if I should just keep the rest to myself. Since the concern preoccupying me would affect them, I plunged forward. "I asked Thea to become a vampire."

"Wow." Sebastian blinked and sat up straighter in his chair.

"Mother is going to flip the fuck out."

I ignored him and turned to Lysander. He didn't say anything. He didn't move. After a moment of utter silence, he cleared his throat. "Sebastian is right. You know that."

"It's my decision," I reminded him.

"When?"

"Earlier tonight," I said.

"I meant when do you plan to turn her?" he clarified, still visibly shaken by my confession.

"I don't know. It was an impulse. The last time the subject came up, we weren't mated." Then, I'd been able to think more clearly, even with the constant urge to consummate our relationship. Why was it harder to keep a clear head now? "I thought it was a bad idea then."

"And that's changed," Lysander said. It wasn't a question.

"My life is tied to hers. Our magic is bound. We live or die together," I said softly. At least as far as I was concerned. If Thea remained mortal, my life would end with hers. I would see to it.

"Does she know that?" he asked me.

It had never come up, but somehow I knew she did. I nodded.

"So, screw what Mom thinks and do it." Passion burned in his words. This was a predicament he understood from experience. "Don't make the mistake I made. You'll spend eternity regretting it if a peaceful death is denied to you."

There would be no eternity. Somehow I knew that my magic was linked to Thea's, and if hers were extinguished...

"Sabine isn't the problem," I said grimly. "Thea said no."

"*Fuck.*" Sebastian managed to draw the single syllable into five.

"Did she give you a reason?" Lysander stood to retrieve a new bottle of Scotch.

"Several. She's young. We don't know much about her powers. I think she's worried the Council will refuse our marriage if she can't produce an heir."

"Wait," Sebastian interrupted. "Can she even carry a vampire baby?"

"Maybe." Lysander gave me a look that told me he might have shared the possibility of Thea being a siren with the family, but he'd kept the rest under wraps. We hadn't filled the rest of the family in on the theory that Thea's father might have been a vampire. We couldn't be certain until we knew more. But it would change everything—and it would prove that a siren could carry and give birth to a vampire's baby.

But there was one obvious problem with that solution.

Thea was a siren. Not a vampire. If I got her pregnant, she might not give birth to a vampire at all. It was another reason I hadn't given up my search for Kelly Melbourne.

"We need to find her parents," Lysander said, echoing my thoughts.

"We know nothing about her father," I reminded him.

"Then we find her mother."

I rolled my eyes at his casual plan. "What do you think I've been trying to do all this time?"

"Do you really want me to answer that?" he said with a smirk.

"No," I admitted. "I've been looking, okay?"

"You could ask for help."

"I have several detectives on the case."

Lysander released a long-suffering sigh. "How many times do I need to remind you that I'm the family expert? Finding things is what I do for a living."

"You're just looking for all the old shit you've lost over the centuries," Sebastian teased.

Lysander ignored him because it was somewhat true. No one knew exactly what my brother had misplaced, but he'd been driven to near madness trying to find whatever it was. He'd taken up archeology to cope with his obsession.

"I can find her if you give me what they've found so far."

"It's pretty thin," I warned him.

"Family expert," he repeated, tapping his chest for emphasis.

"I'll have T-shirts made," I promised. I finished my drink and placed the glass on the table. Standing, I looked toward the door.

"We should get back."

"Before we leave, promise me one thing." Lysander got up and looked me dead in the eye. "Promise you won't call off your engagement. Love is too rare to surrender so easily."

I stared at him as his words sank in. I'd spent nine hundred years alone. I'd cared for a few females and bedded even more, but I had never loved until Thea, which meant I hadn't lived a day of those nine hundred years. "I promise."

"Then we better go find your fiancée."

"And I need to make the rounds," Sebastian said with a wink. "Someone has to be as bored as I am."

"Jacqueline is here," I told him, "and so are her parents. You could save her."

"Excellent." He rubbed his hands together. "She's always up for an adventure."

By "adventure," I assumed my brother meant that she was always ready to stir shit up. Considering the raw wound her parents had inflicted upon her, she might be more than eager to make a scene.

Sebastian continued ahead of us, but I stopped Lysander at the door.

"The Council enacted The Rites permanently," I warned him. "If they have their way, we'll be suffering through these events for years instead of months."

"I know." His throat slid as his dark eyes flickered away, looking to some distant memory. "Hopefully, they get it out of their system quickly."

Although my parents had turned my brothers, they'd done it together in an ancient ceremony. By vampire laws, that meant each of my siblings was considered pureblood. That meant none of them were getting out of making a match until the Council reversed the policy.

"Maybe I'll find myself a siren," he said with a practiced smile. It looked worn and comfortable on his face, but I could see how brittle it was at the edges. I couldn't imagine how he managed it—managed to live without the female he loved. I didn't think I could last a day, and there was no way I would consider taking another lover, let alone a wife.

Lysander's eyes studied me for a second as if he knew what I was thinking. "A Rousseaux answers when duty calls."

Not so long ago, I'd said the same to Sebastian. I'd even believed it until I met Thea. Now she was the only one I served. It was all the more reason to give her the family name. But did Lysander actually believe that? Could he believe that after everything he'd endured in the name of this family?

I wasn't so sure.

I was only certain of one thing. I clapped a hand on his shoulder. "Come on. Let's get back to it before we're missed."

When we reached the party, the guests had spread into the wings to make room for dancing in the entry hall. By the patio doors, a small orchestra played Mozart as couples waltzed around the Solstice tree. I searched the crowd for Thea but couldn't spot her. Given that most creatures towered over her, this wasn't a huge surprise. But I sensed her nearby. Closing my eyes, I turned my search inward and called to her magic.

Where are you? I sent the thought out, wondering if she was close enough to hear it.

"Excuse me," I told my brother. "I need to find my mate."

Moving across the dance floor, I found an open door and stepped into the night.

I went outside. Find me.

It took considerable restraint to not prowl amongst the guests sniffing her out like a wild animal. I shoved my hands in my pockets and looked up to count the stars while I waited. My gaze snagged on Orion, and I smiled to see the winter constellation burning in the darkness. Even with all the enchantments around the Veiled Quarter, the night refused to bend to magic's will.

"There you are," a soft voice interrupted my thoughts.

I turned to Thea slowly, allowing myself to drink in every inch of her. Every minute she grew more beautiful, and at night she outshone every star.

She bit her lip, shifting anxiously on her feet, and I snapped out of my daze.

"What's wrong?" I asked her.

"I don't even know where to begin," she admitted, "but I need your help." She chewed harder on her lip, as if she wasn't sure I would offer it.

I held out my hand. "Always," I promised and meant it. With her by my side, all my doubts and worries faded. Maybe I was wrong. Maybe I only thought clearly with her near me. "What happened?"

"It's Jacqueline," she said seriously, grabbing my hand and tugging me back toward the dancing. "She had a run-in with her mother."

"That will happen." I nodded for her to continue as our fingers twined together.

But before she could tell me anything else, the music stopped abruptly. The dancers whirled to a halt, and everyone looked around with confusion until an attendant appeared at the top of the stairs to announce a late arrival.

All around us, vampires and familiars craned for a peek of the latecomer, and as they moved forward, I caught a glimpse.

"Oh shit," I muttered, earning a concerned glance from my mate, who was too short to see the storm no longer on the horizon—but crashing upon our shores.

"Who is it?" she asked, clutching my arm with her other hand.

Before I could answer, the attendant bellowed his announcement, and I knew that my engagement wouldn't be the juiciest gossip of the night.

"Announcing Madame Camila Drake."

CHAPTER EIGHT

Thea

Camila looked good in black. I stared as she smiled down at her confused audience. All around me, vampires and familiars began to talk about her. They didn't show the prodigal vampire heiress the courtesy of lowering their voices, but I couldn't focus on what they were saying. Not with Julian's sister this close to us. Camila reached for the railing, her fingers ghosting over it while she sauntered down the stairs with the slick ease of a panther.

Julian's fingers closed over mine. "Don't leave my sight."

We might have left matters unresolved the last time we'd seen his sister, but I didn't miss the worried tone in his voice.

Camila showing her face here felt like a threat. Mostly because everyone here believed she was dead. Even Sabine had seemed to doubt us when we'd told her the truth.

Camila's gloves came up well past her elbows and accounted for covering the most skin of anything she wore. I didn't have to look around the ballroom to know that every male's gaze was glued to her. Not with the black lace gown that hung off her shoulders by a thin strap. It draped artfully between her breasts. The gown's waist narrowed to a diamond brooch pinned right below her navel. Lace gathered there before flowing into a daring skirt. The fabric's folds were the only thing covering her nude body.

"What is she doing here?" I asked, even though my mate knew as little as I did.

"We should find my brothers."

Translation: the evening was about to get ugly.

I didn't know what would happen when Sabine came face-to-face with her daughter. Bloodshed seemed likely.

The crowd parted as Camila swept onto the dance floor. A few vampires murmured hellos, but nearly everyone kept their distance. No one seemed angry or afraid. They all seemed confused. If they knew the truth—that Camila was a member of the Mordicum, the group that had attacked the opera in Paris—they might behave differently.

I strained checking for the red slash tattooed on her neck, but it had been covered or removed. She was playing it safe, it seemed.

"I see Lysander," I whispered to Julian.

Julian led us quietly through the crowd, weaving in and out of groups. I knew he didn't want to attract attention. My heart slowed inside my chest but beat with such force that it almost hurt. There was a determination to it that must be coming from Julian. Turning worried eyes on my mate, I searched for signs of how he felt.

We were only a few feet from Lysander when everyone began speaking at once. I looked over my shoulder to see what was going on and stopped in my tracks, forcing Julian to halt with me.

"Julian." I said his name carefully. He turned and followed my eyes. A string of curses fell from his lips, and his strong hand gripped mine more tightly. He only hesitated for a moment as he saw his mother moving through the room to intercept his sister. Then he began pushing through the crowd.

"Don't let go," he ordered me as we made our way out through the onlookers. "And don't start a fight."

"Me? What about you?" I frowned. On the list of those present who were most likely to start a fight, I had to be a lot lower than him.

"You challenged my mother to a duel," he reminded me with a lowered voice.

"That was different," I muttered as I pinned a smile to my face. Nearly everyone present was focused on the impending collision between presumed-dead daughter and infuriated vampire mother. But a few watched us curiously as we made our way toward them.

"What about her husband?"

"I thought she was dead."

"Where are her children?"

My stomach churned as I caught snatches of what those around us were saying. Maybe Julian was right; I needed to let him take the lead. I knew as much about the night Camila supposedly died as I'd been able to discover through his thoughts. I suspected there was more to the story than even he knew.

"Sabine doesn't look surprised," a simpering voice said nearby.

"She probably orchestrated the whole thing. I wonder where she's been hiding her," another added.

I turned to stare daggers at them. Neither Sabine nor Camila topped my list of favorite people, but they were my family. The females fell quickly silent under my stare.

You're truly terrifying when you're angry, my love.

Julian's voice sounded amused in my head, but I caught the note of grim uncertainty in it.

"Thanks," I said, pressing closer to him.

Camila and Sabine stopped a few feet from each other, surveying the other with an unsettling calm. Seeing them both together, I was struck by how much they looked alike. It wasn't just their features. They both stood like queens. I couldn't imagine what Camila had gone through that gave her the courage to face her mother now. Not after hearing about how innocent she'd once been.

"Daughter," Sabine said, her voice carrying over the crowd, which hushed as soon as she spoke, "you've returned to us."

There was a pause, and I caught Camila's lips curling slightly. "I was uncertain if I would be welcome."

Sabine remained composed, her face revealing nothing. "I have suffered many a Solstice without you. The gods have seen fit that I endure no more."

"Indeed." A current of hostility rippled through that single word, but no one seemed to catch it. "Then I submit to you for forgiveness for my absence."

"No forgiveness is necessary."

"What the fuck?" Julian grumbled, speeding up his pace.

I didn't know what to make of the oddly formal greeting. It felt rehearsed, as if they'd been preparing for this moment, but I knew that couldn't be true. Sabine had been genuinely surprised to learn her daughter was alive.

At least, I thought she had been.

Sabine moved forward and embraced Camila, a single bloody tear sliding down her cheek. Was I dreaming?

Maybe we had died. Maybe Julian had really driven over a cliff and we weren't at the Solstice Ball at all. I was in purgatory or a very confusing version of hell.

Sabine's gaze fell on us, and I saw the truth. Her eyes remained sharp, almost predatory, as if she expected to be attacked at any moment.

Just go along with it.

I turned surprised eyes on my mate when I heard his thoughts, but he was looking straight ahead at his family. Shifting in my heels, I did my best to look mildly curious or surprised or any emotion other than stabby. Things were complicated enough. How much worse would it get trying to navigate a fake family alliance?

Sabine pulled back and carefully dabbed her eye. The movement was graceful and precise, and it sent a message. The ice queen Sabine Rousseaux had feelings—but she was completely in control of them, even during a miraculous homecoming.

"Your brother," she said to Camila, taking her shoulders and turning her to face us. "It seems we have cause for two celebrations tonight."

Now I knew for a fact that shit was about to go down, but before I could brace myself, Camila flew forward—right at Julian.

CHAPTER NINE

Julian

I shoved Thea behind me before Camila attacked, earning an exasperated cry from my mate. I'd hear about this later, but for now, my instinct to protect her took hold. Camila reached me a split second later and threw her arms around my neck. The hug caught me by surprise, nearly toppling me to the ground.

"We need to talk," Camila whispered in my ear before wrenching back and staring at me. Tears sparkled in her eyes, but I had no doubt that they were as contrived as her performance. She gripped my forearms and loudly said, "I've missed you."

"Me too," I said through gritted teeth. Barely managing a smile, I played along with her act. "I have so many questions."

"Indeed," my mother agreed, sweeping up beside her daughter. "Perhaps we should head home."

Thea cleared her throat behind me as if to remind us she was still there. It was silly, considering that I was currently monitoring her breathing and knew that she was precisely thirteen inches behind me. I gently tugged free of my sister and stepped away, allowing Thea to move to my side. Placing a possessive hand on the small of her back, I shot my family a sharp smile. "Thea and I have other arrangements."

"They can wait." If my smile was sharp, Sabine's cut like a razor's edge.

"Julian," Thea murmured. "It's fine."

I wasn't so certain. I doubted anyone believed that Camila had just stumbled into the Solstice Ball after more than a two-hundred-year absence. There would be talk, and I doubted anyone would consider her resurrection a miracle. Which meant there would also be questions.

More disturbing was the fact that she had chosen now to make her move.

"Nonsense." Something dark simmered in my sister's eyes. "I came to dance—if someone will ask me."

I glanced at Thea, who bobbed her head once, her eyes darting between the two of us like a caged animal. She didn't trust Camila. Neither did I, but...

"Go." Thea nudged me.

"Yes," Sabine added, "I'll keep an eye on your fiancée."

"That's very reassuring," I said flatly.

Thea rolled her eyes a little, but she remained resolute. No music played, but we were all dancing around the truth. I sighed and offered Camila my arm. My twin looped hers through it.

"Play!" Sabine yelled at the confused orchestra, who immediately scrambled to pick up where they had left off.

I led Camila toward the center of the crowded room as Tchaikovsky drifted through the air. Taking her waist, I whirled her into the first steps of a waltz.

"What the fuck are you doing here?" I guided our movements so that I could keep an eye on Thea, which was no small feat.

Camila's gaze traveled to mine's destination, and she let out a breathy giggle. "Afraid someone will steal her, or afraid our mother will kill her?"

"Does it matter?" I asked with a tight voice.

"It should, since you've been allowing your mate to sleep under our mother's roof."

"With me at her side," I reminded her.

"Ahh." She smiled as if she'd just been handed a prize. "And now I've taken you from her."

I managed a quick nod, my eyes pinned to where Thea waited with Sabine. They didn't speak, but I felt the tension from across the room. I dared to look around for a moment and found all eyes on Camila and me, even as couples began to trickle onto the dance floor to join us.

They were probably hoping to eavesdrop, but thanks to the orchestra and the crowded space, that would be almost impossible. Was that why Camila had chosen tonight to approach me?

"I'll keep this brief," my sister murmured, as if she was aware of the ears around us. "I apologize for the dramatic entrance, but I didn't have a choice."

"Every vampire here thinks you died forty years ago," I hissed at her.

"And every vampire here believes this is a happy reunion." She grinned. "Act like it."

Maybe I should just strangle her and get it over with, but I was too intrigued—and I wasn't the only one. I forced a smile as a curious pair dared to drift across the dance floor toward us. "Fuck."

"What?" Camila asked, her eyes flickering around the space.

"You showed up to tell me a secret in a room of nosy vampires." I had no choice but to turn us in the opposite direction to evade the couple. My spine locked as I lost sight of Thea, my heart beginning to race at a distinctly human rate.

"She's fine," Camila told me. "I can see her. Mother is with her still."

"And I should trust you?"

"Do you have a choice?" Camila gripped my hand and spun herself out, allowing me to move to where I could see my mate.

I saw Thea's eyebrow raise across the room, a smile tugging on her red lips.

Everything okay?

I couldn't hear her sigh, but I felt it in my bones. Thea tilted her head once—the barest of nods—to remind me that she was completely in control.

"That's a neat trick," Camila said.

"I don't know what you're talking about," I said swiftly.

She huffed a laugh. "Really? Because it seems like you're having a conversation with your mate from across the room."

"Why are you here?" I demanded again. "If it's so dire, tell me already."

"To warn you," she said softly.

Every muscle in my body contracted, and my fangs protracted, anticipating danger. "Of what?"

"I had no choice but to make an appearance. I had to reach you immediately."

"Heard of a phone?"

"I don't trust anyone else," she whispered. For a moment, the composed facade lifted, and I saw under her veil. Her eyes scanned the room anxiously, as if anticipating danger around every corner.

"You trust me?" I found that hard to believe after our last conversation. If it could even be called that. Camila had murdered my driver and forced her way into my car, demanding answers my blood-vow wouldn't allow me to give her.

Or my conscience.

Something was different about my sister. Maybe the cruelty she'd suffered at the hands of her abusive vampire husband had taken a toll on her. But if she had died, as she claimed, and been brought back, I couldn't help wondering if all of her had come back. There was no depth in her eyes. Their once bright blue color had dimmed to a flat silver. Something vital was missing or tainted. Something I couldn't bring myself to name.

"Like I said, I don't have a choice. I had to trust someone."

"And you picked me?" I slowed our pace as the music shifted into a new piece. "I'm flattered."

"I'm not here to endure your sarcasm," she snapped.

"And I'm not here to be a pawn in whatever you and the Mordicum are planning," I growled.

"I'm not here because of the Mordicum. I'm here for you—as a favor."

"A favor like the time you nearly killed my mate?" Anger seethed inside me. Camila had confounded me since I'd discovered she was alive. One minute, she was saving my life. The next, she was burning down my house. Any minute now, she might rip out my throat. I didn't know what to expect, but it seemed better to keep her where I could see her—and far away from Thea.

"You should be thanking me." My twin blinked, the veil now fully back in place as a coy smile sat on her lips. "I motivated you to claim her."

"I'll send you a fruit basket."

"Have it delivered to *Paradeisos*," she said with a slight shrug.

"Do you really think our family is going to welcome you back?"

"With open arms. Mother's guilt is cloying. She reeks of it. And Father? He'll do whatever she tells him to."

"And then what?" I demanded. "You'll hand us all to this cult of yours."

"I haven't decided," she admitted with startling honesty. "I'm not here on behalf of the Mordicum, but that doesn't mean I've abandoned their cause." Her voice dropped to a whisper. "Can you honestly tell me this is what you want? Ballrooms and rituals and babies? Vampires are meant for more than this."

"Like what? Acting as animals? Attacking unarmed creatures? Excuse me if I don't buy it." I allowed myself to look her in the eyes, ignoring the panic expanding in my chest as I looked away from Thea.

"Anything is better than sitting around toothless and pretending nothing has changed." Her lips pressed into a thin line.

So, she was disgusted, but that didn't mean she was right. "You still haven't answered my question. Why are you here? Why now? Just to make a scene, so Mommy will be forced to let you crash on the couch?"

"I was told your room would be available." Her smirk chilled the blood in my veins. "Or did you change your mind about the house outside Sidari?"

I stopped abruptly, and a pair of dancers nearly crashed into us. They picked up their pace and moved swiftly away, the rest of those on the floor following suit. I checked on Thea one more time.

But she wasn't watching me. She was speaking to my mother, and even from here, I knew they were arguing.

"Why the fuck are you here?" I asked Camila, not bothering to make my demand quietly. Vampires and familiars waltzed around us, carefully avoiding where we stood. With any luck, they only caught snatches of our conversation as they passed.

Camila's eyes never left mine. If she cared that others might hear, she showed no signs of it. "To save your mate's life."

CHAPTER TEN

Thea

Anxiety tightened my chest as I watched Julian dance with his twin. Maybe the feeling was mine. Maybe it was his. I suspected we both felt stressed. Next to me, Sabine hissed instructions under her breath. I was only half paying attention until she hit me with:

"You are not to leave the sight of a Rousseaux from now on."

"What?" I whipped my head around, abandoning my vigil over Julian and Camila to stare at her. She had to be joking.

"As head of this family, I am in charge of your welfare," she murmured, a false smile still pinned to her face. It hadn't faltered for one moment since she'd welcomed her daughter back into the fold.

"You've made it clear that I'm not a member of this family," I seethed in a low voice. "I can take care of myself."

"That is debatable." Her electric-blue eyes flashed toward me with a look that was clearly meant to be withering. When I didn't shrink, she continued. "Julian's public announcement put me in a tenuous position. I could have disavowed you both right then and there, but I am a loving mother."

Loving? Perhaps by ancient vampiric standards. Not by

modern expectations, though.

I straightened to my full height, which wasn't very impressive, but that wasn't the point. I was not about to back down from Sabine Rousseaux. Julian said that vampires were a matriarchal culture. Maybe Sabine's sons and husband didn't challenge her enough. That changed now. "I don't need you to be my mother. I have one. Thanks."

"And where is yours?" The tips of Sabine's fangs were visible just below her painted upper lip. She waited for a response, but I clamped my mouth shut. "Oh yes. She has vanished."

"What do you want from me, Sabine?" I pivoted to face her. This wasn't about my mother or Julian or saving face in front of a room full of her peers. She was up to something.

"What do I want?" she echoed. "Some respect would be a nice start."

"Respect is earned, and you've done nothing to win mine." I crossed my arms and waited for her next volley.

Her nostrils flared slightly as my words hit her. I didn't look away from her even as her pupils dilated and began to swallow the whites of her eyes. I was about to back away when she grabbed my arm and marched me out of the ballroom. Only a few people around us seemed to notice. One of them was Sebastian.

He stepped into our path, and I smelled Scotch on him. His bow tie hung loosely from his unbuttoned collar. He'd clearly had more to drink than my mate, but he didn't flinch when Sabine growled at him. "Going somewhere?"

"We need a breath of fresh air," she snapped at him.

"I'll join you." He moved to my side, casting a concerned look at me, and crooked his arm.

I slipped mine through it with a grateful smile and was rewarded by Sabine releasing her hold on me. Julian's family escorted me back to the patio, but we only went a few steps past the doors before Sabine turned on me.

"Listen up, you little bitch," she snarled. "We're stuck with each other. You made sure of that when you tethered my son, so unless you want me to rip your head off and end his misery, you will do as I command."

"Misery?" I repeated her delightful phrasing with disbelief. Did she really believe that? I yanked my arm from Sebastian's. He scrambled to grab hold of me, but I was already advancing the short distance to her. "Does it make you feel better to tell yourself these lies because your children are miserable? So miserable that one of them *pretended to be dead* for nearly forty years? I'm not the one he needs free of."

"Is that so?" She narrowed her eyes as the barb struck, but she didn't back down. "And who will lead this family? You?"

"Or that psychopath of a daughter you have in there." I shrugged. "Or maybe you could just leave them all be."

"Thea," Sebastian said my name in a low voice, but I ignored him.

"Let them live their lives," I pressed on. "Or does that scare you?"

Her smile sent an icy shot racing down my spine. "You talk of fear like you have none, and still you've yet to name the time and date for our duel."

I rolled my eyes, but Sebastian stiffened.

"Mom," he said. "Now is not the time."

"It could be—if she were female enough to stand by her actions."

"Fine!" I threw my hands up. "Next week—unless you want to throw down right here."

Sabine inhaled deeply and nodded. "Next week will do. I look forward to ending this once and for all."

Before I could get off another retort, she sashayed back to the party. As soon as she was out of sight, I sighed and let my head fall back. One of the greatest nights of my life was quickly turning into what Julian would call a shit show. Was it so much to ask for one moment of peace?

Swiveling to where Sebastian stood, I found him staring at me with horror. It contorted his usually charming face. I'd never seen him look so out of sorts.

"What is it now?" I braced myself for him to tell me that the sky was falling.

"You can't really fight her," he said in a hoarse whisper.

"You heard her." I hitched a thumb in the direction Sabine had walked. "She isn't going to let this go."

"Yes, because she thinks she has to fight you." He grabbed my arm, his eyes going wild.

I tried to shake free of him. "It's a duel."

"What do you think that means?" he demanded. "You have to find a way to make this right with her. I just got my brother back. I can't lose him again."

"Why would you lose him?" Maybe Sebastian needed to lay off the booze.

"Because the last time someone he loved died, he went to sleep for over thirty fucking years. This time he won't bother with that." Sebastian shook me as he yelled. "He'll just pick another fight to lose and finish what he started in Paris."

"Paris? What happened in Paris?" I asked slowly.

"Your mate"—he spat the word at me like it was a betrayal— "tried to get his heart ripped out by a bunch of vampires in a bar."

"But why…"

But I knew why. I hadn't gone to such extreme measures in San Francisco to cope with my broken heart. I'd simply shut out the world. But shutting out the world for a vampire was almost impossible.

I swallowed, trying to calm the sickening feeling in my stomach. "Is that why she wants someone to watch me all the time?"

"What?" he said, looking confused. "I don't know anything about that, but I do know that if you duel Sabine and she kills you—"

"Kills?" I interrupted. "We're dueling, not fighting to the death!"

"What the fuck do you think a vampire duel is?" he exploded, shoving his hands through his hair. He turned in a circle, as if it might clear his head, but when he came back round to me, he looked more frustrated than before.

I closed my eyes, trying to process what he was telling me. "You're saying that your mother thinks I want to fight her to the death?"

"Pretty much."

"And no one bothered to explain this technicality to me?" I was going to have a word or two with Julian when he stopped prancing around in circles with his murderous twin.

"I assumed my brother would have talked you out of it," he said with gritted teeth.

I peeked at him and shook my head. "Nope. Maybe he has more faith in me than you do."

"That's not what this is about. You won't get a single swing at her before she ends you."

"She hates me that much," I mused, scratching an itch on my neck, wondering if I was signing myself up for the worst mother-in-law in history.

"No. It's just how vampires work. What do you think happened to our grandmother when Sabine married our father? There can only be one matriarch in a family, and if the lucky bride has no family, she takes her husband's with force."

"Wait." I shook my head. He was not telling me that I had to overthrow Sabine, was he? No wonder she took everything I said the wrong way. "What—"

"There you are," Julian interrupted us, looking relieved. "I've been looking for you everywhere."

"We've been right here," I muttered.

My mate cast a concerned glance between the two of us. "Should I be worried?"

"Nope," Sebastian lied cheerfully. "We just needed some air."

But I wasn't going to pretend everything was okay, because it wasn't. I'd had enough drama for one evening. Now I wanted the truth.

"What happened to your grandmother?" I asked Julian.

He shot a poisoned look at his brother. "There's no need to tell her about that."

"No need?" Sebastian scoffed. "You're wrong, brother. She needed to know before you decided to put a ring on it. In fact, she needed to know about it when you were stupid enough to fall in love with her."

"Hey!" I cried.

"No offense," Sebastian said, not bothering to look at me.

"It won't happen. Times have changed," Julian said tersely.

But my heart pounded in my chest. Not because of my frayed nerves. No, this time it was because of Julian—or rather, something he was feeling.

I stamped one foot. "If someone doesn't tell me what's going on right now, I will move this stupid duel to tomorrow! What happened to your grandmother?"

Julian's eyes darkened at my threat, and I braced myself as if he might throw me over his shoulder and run off with me. Before he could, Sebastian cleared his throat and answered my question.

"Sabine killed her. Our mother killed our grandmother—and now it's your turn to kill her."

CHAPTER ELEVEN

Thea

I was not in the holiday spirit. Maybe it was the breezy summer air drifting over my bare shoulders thanks to the Veiled Quarter's enchantments, but I suspected it had more to do with what I'd learned last night.

I was supposed to kill Sabine—or she was going to kill me.

Just another fun vampire tradition.

At least it had distracted me from Julian's offer to turn me. Something he hadn't brought up again.

He gripped my hand tightly as we wove through the busy streets. Everyone around us looked like tourists on vacation, with their floppy-brimmed hats, sandals, and sun-kissed skin, except for one thing. Each person we passed was laden down with packages. Far too many to be the average souvenir haul. Then there was the electricity in the air, fueled by the panic that hovered around shopping malls during the Christmas season. But unlike the average tourist trap, the quarter held both familiar and supernatural delights. A potion-making shop sat next to a store touting designer names like Chanel and Louis Vuitton. Next to them was a jewelry store and an absinthe bar. There appeared to be something for everyone here.

"Who do we need to buy presents for?" I asked, trying to muster a little enthusiasm to tackle the chore. Usually, I loved shopping for presents. Until now, I'd spent the holidays with my mother and friends—people I knew what to gift. How was I supposed to buy gifts for my new vampire family?

Particularly given that they all expected me to kill their matriarch any day.

"Need?" he repeated, maneuvering me past a cluster of people waiting outside a bakery, its windows filled with cakes decorated to resemble yule logs. Judging from the rich chocolate frosting covering them and the sweet scent drifting out the shop door, I couldn't blame them.

My mouth watered, but I tamped down on my craving. We had a job to do. "Yes. Do you all exchange gifts?"

He shook his head as we darted into an alley that led away from the crowded main avenue. I couldn't help noticing my mate's gaze darted around the cobbled street and plaster walls as we passed through the shadowed corridor as if he expected someone to attack. He'd been on edge since last night. We both had. I doubted it was for the same reason.

"We draw names," he told me. "My family did it the night before we arrived, but don't worry. I made it clear to my mother we'd be spending Christmas alone."

"Oh." That made things easier, and I'd much rather send gifts and stay home with Julian. "Who did you get?"

I prayed it wasn't Sabine. The only gift I imagined might delight her was a deadly weapon—and arming her was the last thing I needed to do at the moment.

"I got Benedict," he said grimly, "and you got Thoren."

"Me?" I couldn't help being surprised. Last night was the first indication that I was considered a Rousseaux.

"Jacqueline insisted," he explained, "and Sebastian and Benedict backed her up."

I came to a sudden stop, forcing him to do the same. "They did?"

He nodded. "But that doesn't mean I've forgiven Benedict. Maybe I'll get him a pet rat."

"We'll get him a tie," I mumbled, still processing this information. I wasn't sure how Benedict felt about me, especially since he was so politically motivated and I was a thorn in the family's side. But if he'd stood up for me, maybe he didn't resent me after all.

"Good idea," Julian agreed. "If he steps out of line again, I can strangle him with it."

"That would be festive." I couldn't help laughing, even though my heart remained burdened. How had I wound up entangled with an entire family of murderous vampires?

Julian shifted toward me. His large body loomed over me, haloed by the afternoon light. I drank in the sight of him: the sharp, chiseled lines of his face, the unearthly blue of his eyes, and the sinful, full lips that I would never get enough of.

"Wondering why you put up with me?" he asked as if he was the one who could read minds.

His effect was so dizzying that when I tried to shake my head, I swore I saw stars. "I know why I put up with you," I murmured, "but your family..."

His answering chuckle slid over me, making me tingle *everywhere*. As our eyes locked, his pupils dilated until only a thin ring of electric blue remained. I wasn't the only one affected, it seemed, but it looked like he was doing a better job of fighting it.

"Exactly why we should make a new family." A gloved finger traced my collarbone, sending emissaries of pleasure down my body. My nipples peaked, my breasts growing heavy and swollen. Last night, we'd left the ball and gone straight to our new residence: a cozy—by vampire standards—villa on the far end of the island. But rather than taking me to bed, Julian had shown me to our room, then disappeared to make a few phone calls. I'd fallen asleep waiting for him. Now I realized why I'd been so on edge: I craved him.

Maybe it was the mating bond's vise-grip on us still. Or perhaps it was some primitive drive to procreate that The Second Rite had instilled in us both. All I knew was that every inch of me longed for him. Not only my body but my soul. I felt incomplete when we were apart, and with our minds so caught up in the drama with his family, it was like I was torn in two.

Julian edged me back until I bumped into the plaster wall of the building behind me. In the distance, street noise echoed, but it felt a million miles away. There was only him—only his hard body pressing me against the wall, and then his mouth exploring the sensitive spot behind my ear. I was dimly aware that anyone could turn down the alley at any moment, but I didn't care. All I wanted was *more*. A low growl rumbled in Julian's chest as he dragged his lips down my neck. Our bodies were in control, and it seemed they thought we'd gone too long without contact, too.

"Is this a good idea?" It took every bit of self-restraint I had to get the question out.

"Vampires feed in back alleys all the time," he said darkly, continuing past my neck to the hollow at the base of my throat. He paused. "Do you want me to stop, my love?"

That was the last thing I wanted, but I was torn between wanting him then and there and knowing how exposed we were.

In the end, my need for distraction won out.

"No," I moaned, giving in to the instinct taking hold of me. I braced a hand against the wall and moved the other to the bulge in his pants. Slipping my hand down the front of them, I gripped him in my hand.

"Fuck," he bit out as I stroked his velvet hardness. Encouraged, I reached with my other hand to undo his belt, then his fly. He drew a ragged breath when I freed his cock. "I need to be inside you."

"What's stopping you?" I breathed.

His mouth crashed into mine, a fang stinging my lower lip. I gasped at the jolt of pleasure-laced pain, and he nipped it harder. A coppery tang flowered on my tongue as he pushed his own inside my mouth and captured it. Julian's hand closed over my wrist, moving it away from his cock. The kiss smothered my protest, becoming more demanding. More possessive. I gave in to it and melted against him.

Julian shoved my skirt to my waist and lifted me off my feet. I wrapped my legs around his waist, and he groaned as he nudged against the lace barrier of my panties.

I drew back and looked him square in his obsidian eyes. "Don't rip them off. We aren't done shopping."

His eyes narrowed dangerously as he glowered down at me. "Fine." A hand reached between us and shoved the obstruction to the side. "I can work with that." He brushed his thick tip along me until I was panting. "Do you know what I want for Christmas?"

I managed a sound between a yes and a moan, and he chuckled.

"I want to spend the entire day making you come." His mouth brushed over mine, igniting another ember of need inside me. "Consider it my standing wish list."

I'd be more than happy to give him just that if I didn't die from want in this alley.

"Is that so?" he asked, and I realized I must have spoken aloud. "We can't have that."

A low sob of pleasure spilled from me as he slid home, burying himself with one smooth thrust. My thighs tightened possessively around his waist, earning another smug laugh followed by a dark shudder as he withdrew slightly and bucked against me again.

I'm yours. His offer echoed in my head, and I began to pant. *Tell me.*

"You're mine," I whispered fiercely. "You belong to me."

"Fuck yeah, I do," he growled, pistoning harder and faster.

My shoulders scraped against the ancient plaster wall, making my skin sing as he drove inside me.

"Mine," I repeated like an incantation. "Mine."

The arm bracing me tightened as he sped up, his breath ragged and uneven. His hand pressed between us again, a finger finding the center of my hunger. I unraveled around him, the same word spilling from my lips as I unspooled over him. I cried out, and he emptied inside me. When he finally stilled, I dissolved into his embrace, boneless and spent.

We stayed like that for a few minutes, soaking up the stolen moment. Finally, Julian drew back and studied me with a self-satisfied grin.

"What are you smirking about?" I muttered as we began to untangle ourselves.

"I can't help it," he said, giving me a kiss. "I always feel smug when I claim my mate."

"Oh yeah?" I lifted an eyebrow.

He tilted his head, his eyes full of sudden challenge. "Do you need me to show you again?"

Before I could answer, someone cleared their throat behind us. Julian instantly went rigid, his entire being on alert, as an amused voice said, "I'd rather you didn't."

CHAPTER TWELVE

Julian

I placed Thea gently on her feet, smoothing her skirt down to cover her. Shoving my dick into my pants, I sucked in a calming breath—which did nothing to actually calm me—and turned toward my sister's voice. Camila's flat smile told me that she'd seen more than she cared to, and so had her companion. Next to her, Jacqueline covered her mouth, her entire body shaking with silent laughter.

"It's not wise to sneak up on a vampire," I ground out as I finished buckling my belt.

Jacqueline snorted. "It's not wise to screw your mate in an alley on Corfu."

Thea moved behind me, taking my hand and squeezing it slightly. It was a reminder that the females weren't our enemies. Could she sense the blood rage that clawed inside me, waiting to be unleashed?

I'd placed my mate in a dangerous situation and left us both defenseless. Looking over my shoulder, I swallowed against the knot in my throat. "I'm sorry."

"For what?" Thea lifted her eyebrows, looking confused.

"Because we might have been big, bad monsters out to get

you," Camila explained before I could, the amusement gone from her voice, "and he had his guard down."

"'Might have been'?" Thea repeated. She remained unconvinced that my sister wasn't a threat, and she had good reason. Camila had attacked her in San Francisco.

"It's obvious," she said, shrugging off Thea's comment. "I would know."

Of all of us, she was the only one who understood how tethering fucked with the mind. She understood, but it was clear that she didn't empathize.

Her husband had taken her against her will, tethering her during The Rites nearly two centuries ago. How had he managed to control the impulse to protect her? Choosing to hurt her instead? I couldn't imagine doing that to Thea.

"Is that why you're grouchy?" Thea asked me, stepping to my side.

She belonged there. I would never treat her as Willem had Camila. Thea was my equal.

"I'm not grouchy," I said gruffly.

"Sure." She patted my arm before turning her attention to the others. "Out doing some holiday shopping?"

"Hardly." Camila brushed a loose strand of hair out of her eyes. "But if Mother asks, that's what we were doing."

"What *are* you doing?" I asked pointedly.

"We came to look for you." Jacqueline shot me a warning look. "Your mother thought it was best if someone went with your sister, so I got stuck babysitting."

Once Camila and Jacqueline had been best friends—closer than I was with either of them. That, like so many things, had changed when Camila married Willem Drake. Her absence had allowed Jacqueline and me to get closer, but now that Camila was back, I'd half expected them to resume their friendship. Clearly, I was wrong. Maybe they had both changed too much, or maybe Camila wanted to keep us all at arm's length. It was probably part of whatever she was planning. Jacqueline must have guessed it, too.

"I could have come alone," Camila said.

Jacqueline smiled wolfishly at her. "Sabine didn't think so."

Time to change the subject.

"I'm sure Mother wanted to make you feel welcome. I assume she's too busy to go with you herself." While we rarely celebrated Christmas Day with one another, gifts were expected—and Sabine loved to send flashy presents. One year I'd woken to find a Ferrari parked in my driveway. But considering The Rites were happening, I suspected she was busy overseeing plans for New Year's Eve.

"You found us," Thea piped up. "We were trying to find presents."

"You should reconsider your methods," Camila said drily.

A flood of hot rage burst through me, and I glanced with surprise at my mate. She showed no outward signs of being angry, but I knew the feeling had come from her.

"Maybe we should walk," Jacqueline suggested, striding forward.

Thea bit her lip and looked at me before releasing my hand and joining my best friend. We both knew that Camila wanted to talk to me alone. She'd made that clear last night with her ominous warning.

I watched as Thea hurried to Jacqueline and looped arms with her.

"You can help me," she said to her. "I need to find a present for Thoren."

Jacqueline's groan suggested she understood the difficulty of the task.

I followed them, Camila falling into step beside me. We walked slowly even as the others sped up.

"I'm surprised you let her out of your sight," my sister said as they disappeared around the mouth of the alley.

"I don't own Thea. She can do as she pleases." But even as I spoke, my tether tugged inside me, urging me to move faster—to stay close to her.

"Even if that means putting her in danger?" she asked.

I fell silent. My sister's sandals slapped against her heels as we made our way down the dark passage.

"Why did you really come back?" I finally asked.

"I told you. I—"

"The real reason," I cut her off. I didn't buy that she was concerned for my mate. Camila hadn't suddenly decided to return to vampire society to deliver a vague warning.

"What I told you was true," she said carefully, "but I left some things out."

"Such as?"

"I told you there were factions within the Council with their own agendas," she started.

"Factions your dead husband is behind." Maybe my sister had actually been driven insane by what happened. I forced myself to consider that possibility as we stepped onto the bustling street. Searing-hot afternoon light greeted us, and I reached for the sunglasses I kept in my pocket.

"What if I'm right?" she asked. "Are you willing to risk Thea's life to find out?"

I was going about this the wrong way. I'd been asking the wrong question. "Why do you care if someone goes after Thea? And don't lie and give me some 'because I'm your sister' bullshit."

She laughed. The sound, like breaking glass, caused several people around us to stop. "Fine. I don't care because of Thea," she admitted. "I care because of who is after her."

CHAPTER THIRTEEN

Jacqueline

The shop was a collection of centuries and places. Its mismatched items were crammed into every available nook and cranny like a closet for forgotten objects and times. Antique tobacco pipes sat next to carved chess sets. An entire wall featured battle-tested shields. I wondered what had happened to the vampires who had carried them. No one I'd known through the years would abandon a shield that carried them safely through a fight. The entire place seemed to be devoted to a particular type of creature—one who found himself on the battlefield and felt less comfortable when he left it. No wonder Thea had chosen to come inside to find her present for the gift exchange.

I lingered a few feet behind her, watching as each step she took kicked up a small cloud of dust from the Persian rug under her feet. The dust matched the cobwebs hanging from the old wooden beams overhead and the store's musty aroma of old steel and pipe smoke. The shop was so full that each step took careful maneuvering to avoid knocking something from a shelf.

Normally, I enjoyed shopping. No. I *loved* shopping. It wasn't just that this wasn't my cup of tea. Today was different. Maybe it was that I'd been roped into chaperoning Camila, the last person

I wanted to be with, or perhaps it was the idea of being stuck in Greece with half the vampire population for the holidays. Deep down, though, I knew it all came down to a stupid slip of the tongue.

I had agreed to enter The Rites, the very thing I'd been avoiding for the last couple of centuries.

"What do you think of this?" Thea asked, holding up what appeared to be a polished drinking horn.

I managed a tight smile and shook my head. "Your guess is as good as mine."

"Ugh. How did I get stuck with Thoren?" she grumbled as we left the small shop and headed toward the next. "Do you think someone sells clothes for ancient Vikings?"

"Ancient?" I couldn't help laughing at that.

Thea's mouth fell open in that adorable way that reminded me why my best friend had fallen in love with her. "I'm so sorry!"

"Don't be. I look good for my age."

Thea giggled and continued shopping. She rifled through a stack of books on a table, not bothering to look up as she asked, "Do you want to talk about it?"

Her words dashed any hope I had that I was acting normally.

I sighed and moved next to her, absently picking up a heavy green tome. "You were there. What am I supposed to do?"

After all these years, it never occurred to me that my mother might make a power move, but she had, and I'd been unprepared. Now I had to face the possibility of marriage—something I'd never considered. An arranged marriage made the prospect even worse, but could I really let Jessica suffer because of my choices?

"Did anything happen after we left? Did you talk to her or your sister?" Thea glanced over, her lips drawn with sympathy. They fell farther when I shook my head.

"After Camila's grand entrance, I lost track of them. I think they left early," I said bitterly. Somehow, despite my conversation with my mother, Camila's arrival had been the low point of the evening. I didn't dare look around to see if Julian and his renegade sister were tailing us still. I was too angry at Camila at the moment. For a lot of reasons, but mostly for showing up here when I was already stressed.

"What are you going to do?" Thea asked, bringing my attention back to the matter at hand.

"I thought I asked you that," I reminded her. I dropped the book onto the table, sending a cloud of antique dust into the air.

"You can't get married just to protect your sister." Thea gave up on her search and nodded for us to leave. "I mean, what does she want?"

"She's too young to know what she wants," I snapped and instantly regretted it. Thea showed no sign of annoyance at my outburst, so I went on. "Besides, if it's true and the Council is pushing for her to marry, it wasn't her choice to begin with. Though I doubt my parents fought them on it. Why are families so complicated?"

Thea's soft smile told me she understood, and I knew she did. She'd sat by her mother's side at the hospital, and from what I knew of her past, she'd nearly killed herself making sure they'd been able to make ends meet while she was in school. In truth, she understood better than I did. For the last couple of centuries, I'd been enjoying the exile life while my sister dealt with my parents' expectations.

I'd taken the coward's way out to avoid being forced to marry Julian—or any other vampire, for that matter. Then, I'd believed in marrying for love, but centuries had proven very few of my species felt the same.

"I owe her," I said. "Marriage for vampires isn't like what you and Julian have. It's just a contractual obligation. Nothing more."

Both of us fell silent as we strolled along the crowded street. I looked over my shoulder to see my best friend and his twin leaving the shop behind us. Frustration bubbled inside me as I watched the two of them argue.

I didn't even have that with Jessica anymore, thanks to being disowned. I could do this arranged marriage for my sister. I'd given up on love a long time ago, having learned my lesson the hard way.

"Is that what it should be?" Thea asked thoughtfully. "Is that what you want?"

I rolled my eyes, not trusting myself to answer. I'd given up on something like what Julian and Thea had years ago.

Looking up, I found her studying me with her unnervingly green eyes. They'd gotten brighter since the first time we met. It was proof of the magic stirring inside her.

"Was there someone?" she asked as we stopped outside a weapons dealer. The question was delicate, which meant she already knew my answer.

"No one that matters anymore." I squeezed the words through my aching throat. I wouldn't cry about this. Not in public. Not in front of her or Julian, and especially not in front of Camila.

My eyes locked with Thea's, and I knew she saw the pain there. I knew she saw the lie behind my words. But she sucked in a breath and said cheerfully, "We'll just have to find you a superhot familiar, then."

"Exactly," I said with relief, eager to move on from the topic. I needed to distract myself. Nothing could change the past, and if my future involved marriage, she was probably right. "It's the least I deserve."

"You deserve a lot more," she murmured before quickly looking at the window display. Her eyes lingered on a longsword. "Let's skip this shop. I think Julian's family has enough weapons."

I snorted in agreement. "At least you didn't get Sabine."

"True." Thea groaned. "Or Camila. I can't believe she just showed up like nothing happened. She tried to kill me, and now we're spending the holidays together."

"Welcome to being a vampire," I said tightly. "If you think mortal holidays are tense, wait until you spend one with *them*."

"Were you and Camila close?"

Her words sent a lump forming in my throat. I swallowed and nodded. "We were. A long time ago. I was closer to her than Julian once."

Admitting that hurt worse than I'd expected. The confession stirred the ache inside me as I remembered how it used to be.

"I know everyone says she was different, before..." Thea trailed off. "But it's hard to imagine."

"She was different," I said softly. "She might as well be a stranger now."

"A homicidal one at that," Thea added. "Do you think you two could be friends again?"

"No," I said so quickly that Thea's eyebrows raised. "Not after how she hurt everyone."

She sighed and glanced over her shoulder. "I'm not sure Julian can forgive her, either."

The next shop featured an assortment of couture gowns aimed at the wealthy vampire tourists who spent their winters here throwing balls and orgies. Thea started to walk past it, but I grabbed her hand and dragged her inside.

"I don't need any more dresses," she informed me, twisting her new engagement ring around her finger.

"We're not looking for you. We're looking for me." I'd finally thought of the perfect distraction.

"I don't think you need more, either," she said.

"I need a maid of honor dress." I planted a hand on my hip and leveled a meaningful stare at her. "Don't I?"

"Oh!" Her eyes widened, shock turning to delight. "Yes, yes, you do."

"Good. You weren't planning to ask someone else, right?" It was a good distraction from my own broken heart.

Thea's answering smile was wistful, and I wondered if she was thinking of the human friends she'd lost by choosing Julian.

"Come on." I looped my arm through hers. "Have you thought about where you want to get married?"

"Do I have a say in it?" She shook her head with a laugh. "I would marry Julian in a parking lot. All that matters is that I'm marrying him."

"A parking lot?" I scrunched up my nose. "I think you better let me plan the wedding."

"With Sabine?" A smile danced on her lips, and we both broke into a fit of giggles as we stepped inside.

We each found separate racks and began to look when the sales associate approached us. She was dressed in an elegant ivory sheath that displayed her flawless vampire skin, her blond hair twisted up and pinned at the back of her neck. She sniffed the air, frowning when she caught Thea's mixed scent. She might not know who Thea was, but two things were clear: she smelled like a vampire, and she was mortal. Most of the time, that meant some vampire playboy had brought one of his *cortège* with him on vacation.

The saleswoman walked by Thea and headed straight to me. "May I help you, mademoiselle?"

"Yes." I smiled sweetly. "I came to look for a gown for my friend's wedding. I'm the maid of honor." I gestured to Thea pointedly.

"Oh, and will this be a formal event?" she said in a brittle voice, still ignoring Thea.

Clearly, I needed to teach her a thing or two about manners. My fingers paused on a lilac gown with a delicately beaded bodice.

"I assume." I looked over her shoulder at where Thea stood, watching us. "Sabine will insist, don't you think?"

"Sabine?" the saleswoman echoed. She blinked rapidly as her brain processed the name.

"Sabine Rousseaux." I pointed at Thea. "That's her future daughter-in-law."

That did the trick.

The female's eyes bugged from her head, but she collected herself quickly and whipped around. "It's an honor to meet you," she gushed at Thea. "Are you looking for a wedding gown?"

"No," I said when I saw my friend's flustered face. "We'll probably go to Paris for that."

"Of course!" She waved a hand around. "Have you picked any colors yet?"

The saleswoman's attitude had changed instantly. Not only because she wouldn't dare insult a future Rousseaux, but also because she was probably seeing dollar signs. A Rousseaux wedding would rival human royalty. Everyone would be there, and no expense would be spared.

Thea glared at me, and I resisted the urge to laugh. "Um, blue, maybe?"

"Let me see what I can find." The saleswoman disappeared into the back of the store to find more dresses and probably have a panic attack.

Thea marched over to me. "Are you amused?"

"Very." I nodded with a grin. "I always enjoy deflating a smug vampire."

"You have plenty around here," she whispered as the sales associate returned with an armful of dresses.

Thea took a seat near the dressing rooms, refusing a dozen offers of champagne, and waited for me to try the gowns on. I started with a dreamy cornflower blue gown that flowed to my feet, swirling as I walked.

"Ohh! Pretty!" Thea clapped her hands when I came out wearing it.

"But do you like it?"

"It's gorgeous, but I care more about whether *you* like it," she said.

"You don't have an opinion?" I studied myself in the mirror, tugging at the waistline.

"I want you to be happy," she said firmly.

I glanced at her reflection in the mirror and shook my head. "You realize that if you don't have an opinion, Sabine actually *will* plan your whole wedding."

She probably would regardless.

A shadow passed over Thea's face, passing as quickly as it had appeared. "I meant what I said earlier. I only care about marrying Julian."

She meant it. I knew that. But that wouldn't save her from

some overblown vampire wedding. Not if Sabine was involved.

Movement caught my eye, and a moment later, Julian and Camila joined us. Suddenly, I felt self-conscious as Camila gave both of us a withering look. The frustration I'd felt over getting stuck with her for the day was dangerously close to boiling over. Why had she bothered to come back if she was going to act like we were all beneath her every chance she got? But before I could snap at her, she moved to look at dresses. My best friend strode over, hands shoved in his pockets.

"I thought we were shopping for Christmas," he said.

"We needed a break," I told him. "We have no clue what to get Thoren, and we have a wedding to plan."

Julian smirked, tossing a possessive look at his future bride. "Yes, you do."

"Go ahead and plan it," Thea said, feigning annoyance. "I need to use the restroom."

He started to join her, but she held up a hand. "It's not that kind of bathroom break, babe. I'll be right back."

I bit back a laugh at her rejection. Next to me, Julian tilted his head, looking peeved, his eyes growing darker as he watched her leave.

"You're going to suffocate her," I informed him.

"Really?" He ran a hand through his hair, glaring over at his sister. "I was being told I'm not protective enough."

"By her?" I hitched a thumb at Camila. "She's batshit crazy."

"But I'm not deaf," Camila called, continuing to peruse the rack.

Camila and I glared at each other from across the shop. It was hard to believe that we'd once been inseparable. Now Camila seemed hell-bent on causing as much trouble for her family as she could. What I told Thea earlier was true—it was like she was a total stranger.

"I trust Thea, but maybe she's right," he said in a lowered voice.

"That would be a first." I couldn't bear to look at Camila—not after what she'd done. I still couldn't believe she'd had the audacity to show up last night.

Camila abandoned her pursuit and joined us, flashing a look of frustration in my direction. "I'll just join you if you're going to talk about me."

"We aren't talking about you," I lied.

I expected her to fight me on this, but she didn't respond. Instead, her nostrils flared, and she whirled toward Julian. "Where is Thea?"

"Bathroom. Why?"

But Camila was already rushing through the store. Julian and I looked at each other and dashed after her, stopping just in time to see a male whisper something in Thea's ear. He turned, keeping his face angled away from us. I barely caught a glimpse before my eyes settled on Thea's horrified expression.

CHAPTER FOURTEEN

Thea

It wasn't that big of a deal. At least that's what I kept telling myself. Julian had insisted we leave immediately, along with Jacqueline and his sister. None of them said a word on the drive back to the villa we'd taken on the northern point of the island. It had made for a long ride.

I tossed my purse on a teak table in the entryway and made my way toward the kitchen. Other than the bedroom, it was my favorite room in the house—and not just because it was where we kept the food. Two massive islands with stone counters sat opposite each other, a sink in one and the stove in the other. Behind them, a large white pantry and oversize refrigerator waited. The unusual arrangement of the kitchen also offered unbroken floor-to-ceiling windows, looking out over the sea, around the kitchen. The view wasn't only spectacular. It was calming.

Instantly, some of the tension in my shoulders melted away as I stared at the waters stretching around me. But peace was fleeting.

"I want to know everything he said," Julian commanded as he entered the space.

I refused to look at him as I yanked open the refrigerator door. "First, I want to know who he was!"

It was the only question I'd asked after my encounter with the stranger at the bridal shop. When the man whispered in my ear, I'd been rattled, but it was the look on the others' faces—like they'd seen a ghost—that shook me to my core. None of them had answered me.

"Don't be a brat," Camila said, joining us.

I peeked around the door and glared daggers at her. "You sound like your mother."

Her nostrils flared, and I knew I'd hit my mark.

Jacqueline went straight to a barstool and sat. "Look, Thea, we just need to know what he said to you. It's important."

Her words were musical—soothing, almost—and I wondered if she was letting a little of her compulsion slip through.

I grabbed a bottle of orange juice, uncapped it, and took a swig. I had a choice to make. I could keep torturing them for acting so oddly, or I could take a chance that answering them would get me what I wanted. I screwed the lid back on the bottle and slid it into the fridge. Closing the door, I slumped against it and gave in. "He told me that he knew what I was and that he had answers." I waited for one of them to respond, but no one did. "He was probably lying."

"Maybe," Jacqueline said cautiously.

Camila shook her head and jabbed a finger in Julian's direction. "This is what I warned you about!"

"Wait, warned him about what?" I asked. "He said you made some vague threat."

Julian pinched the bridge of his nose, and I realized there was a lot more to this story. "There has to be an explanat—"

"You know what the explanation is!" Camila exploded. "Don't be an idiot!"

"I'm trying to think," he said, beginning to pace the length of the room.

Well, my plan hadn't worked, which meant it was time for plan B. "Tell me what's going on right now. Who was he?"

I expected to activate Julian's tether—something I decided I would feel guilty about later—but it was Jacqueline who answered. "I didn't get the best look at him, but I'm sure it was Willem Drake."

"It was," Camila confirmed.

Instantly, I felt numb. My relationship with Julian's twin might be strained—at best—but I couldn't believe how close I'd been to the vampire who had tethered and tortured her for years.

"How would he know about me? About what I am?" I asked.

Julian, apparently, had other concerns. He advanced on his sister. "I find it strange that you both showed up in Corfu."

"You think we came together?" Camila's mouth puckered on the question.

"I don't know what to think, but I find it suspicious."

"I told you he was behind this. I warned you." Her voice rose, but under its angry timbre, I heard something else. Pain.

"Tell me everything," I cut in. "Everything you told him"—I pointed to my mate—"and whatever you've left out."

I waited for her to refuse or offer some coy riddle. Instead, she surprised me and began to talk. We listened without comment to Camila's story about why she was here. When she finally trailed away, I looked to Julian.

"I don't understand why Willem is interested in Thea." He dropped onto a barstool, his gaze snagging on something out the window. It lingered there, but when I followed it, I saw nothing but endless blue. I wondered what he saw.

"For her magic—whatever it is. Have you figured it out yet?"

Don't trust her. Julian's voice echoed in my head.

"We don't even know if it is magic," he lied smoothly.

Camila cocked her head, staring at him for a moment. Did they have that weird twin superpower where they could sense each other's thoughts? Did she know it was a lie?

"Whatever it is," she said after a moment, "he's not the only one who knows about it. The Mordicum does as well."

"I don't know why so many people are interested in a magical nobody," I grumbled.

Camila shook her head. "Because it's old magic. The witch you saw in San Francisco smelled it on you."

"What witch?" Jacqueline asked.

"Your new bestie went to see a fortune teller. She had her palm read," Camila revealed to everyone.

"You what?" Julian turned on me, his face slack. Jacqueline only dropped her head and sighed. "How could you do that, knowing about magic?"

"I didn't," I snapped. Why was I the one being interrogated? "Olivia dragged me inside. I thought it was just some act. Fortune telling isn't real."

"Haven't you seen enough to know that there is so much more to this world than you thought? Letting her see your palm..." He shook his head, and I didn't know what was worse: seeing his disappointment or feeling it. It hollowed out my stomach and left me feeling sick.

But I had questions of my own. "How did you know about that?"

"The Mordicum was searching for you," she said with a shrug, as if announcing her friends stalking me was no big deal.

"The vampire on the corner," I said, recalling the creature I'd spotted that day. "You were having me followed!"

Camila clicked her tongue. "No. We were trying to find you."

"Why?" Julian demanded.

"We have our reasons," she said cryptically.

A second later, Julian had her by the throat. Her sandaled feet kicked a few inches above the floor as she struggled for air. "Not good enough," he roared. "You can't have it both ways. Them or us."

"Julian!" I grabbed the back of his shirt. "Don't! Julian!"

For one harrowing moment, I wasn't sure if he would release or kill her until she fell in a pile at his feet, gasping.

"Me," she said, rubbing her neck. "I choose *me*."

"I'm not sure where that leaves us," he said through gritted teeth. "But I won't allow you to risk the people I love while you play spy."

"Fine." Ice chilled her words. "Take your chances. I only came to help."

"You came to help yourself," he accused.

"Killing her"—she pointed at me—"serves no purpose of mine. You can either take the help I can give you or take your chances."

"Get out," he snarled, stalking out of the kitchen.

"No!" I yelled before he made it farther than that. "If she's right and Willem is after me, we're going to need help."

I don't trust her.

I shot him a warning look that said neither did I, but we needed allies. More importantly than that, we needed to know why her husband was interested in me. Julian took a deep breath and moved to the doorframe. I stole a glance at Jacqueline to see where she stood. Our eyes met, and she nodded slightly.

Jacqueline cleared her throat and asked, "So, Willem is interested in Thea and her magic, but what is he really after? Why has he stayed hidden for all of these years? What's his agenda?"

"I don't know why he stayed hidden," Camila said.

"Why did you?" Jacqueline asked pointedly. It was impossible to imagine them as best friends. There was an edge to their dislike of each other that I couldn't quite comprehend.

I didn't expect Camila to answer. I doubted any of us did.

"Because the Mordicum was building an army," she said, shocking us. "And if Willem pretended to be dead, I know he had a reason. Perhaps he's after the same thing."

"And what is that?" I smothered a groan of frustration.

Malevolence gleamed in her eyes. "I was wrong. I thought Willem was pulling the Vampire Council's strings. But he's not. He's unraveling them and their lies—once and for all."

CHAPTER FIFTEEN

Julian

The moon hung high above the Ionian Sea by the time I closed the door—*and locked it*—behind our guests. I slumped against it, drawing my gloves off one at a time. Stretching my liberated fingers, I considered what we'd learned.

Not a whole fucking lot.

It was conjecture—a guessing game that could prove as dangerous as remaining ignorant of the situation. Had it really only been a few weeks ago that my biggest worry was keeping my dick in my pants and Thea's virginity intact? Now that she was my mate, things should be simpler. We'd faced the Council, and I had no doubt we'd get through the rest of The Rites. The hard part was supposed to be over, but now we had a duel, a wedding, and a war looming on the horizon. Maybe things would never be easy again.

My phone vibrated in my pocket, and I let it go to voicemail. Only a few people had this number. I didn't want to talk to any of them. The only person I cared to speak to was still in the kitchen. I made it two steps down the hall before it started ringing again.

I yanked it out, frowning when I saw my mother's name flash on the screen. I rejected the call.

I only made it one more step before it rang a third time. For a moment, I considered hurling it into the lapping waves below the house, but I knew better. She'd just send someone over—or worse, come herself.

"What?" I answered.

"Oh good, you're there," she said casually. "We need to discuss the holidays."

I swallowed a groan. "We already did. We'll see you on New Year's."

"That was before your sister came home."

I heard the soft click of her nails on wood. I could almost see her sitting at her desk, calendar spread before her as she devised new ways to torture us over the holidays.

"So?"

"So," she said in a seething voice that cut across the line, "we need to present a united front while I figure out what's going on."

"I don't see what that has to do with the holidays," I grumbled.

"How would it look to have our family spend Christmas apart?"

"Normal?" I continued down the hall, stopping short of the kitchen.

"You and your siren will come over for Christmas morning," she ordered, adding, "and bring the presents."

She hung up before I could respond.

"Fuck!" I yelled, debating if I should call her back.

Thea popped her head out of the kitchen, a tired smile on her face. "Something wrong?"

Instead of answering, I threw my phone on the floor so hard its screen shattered and a few pieces went skidding along the hardwood floor.

"I hope you had insurance on that," she said quietly.

"My mother wants us to play happy family for Christmas." I'd expected more quality time with my family when I was summoned to attend The Rites. I'd told myself that a year of that would pass quickly. To a vampire, it was practically a blip.

What I hadn't anticipated was finding someone who made me

want to spend all day making love in bed.

"Maybe it won't be that bad." Her grin slipped like she was trying to drum up some enthusiasm for the idea. She held out a hand, and I felt the irresistible tug to go toward her. Maybe it was the tether. Maybe it was love. I didn't care.

Reaching for her hand, I twined our fingers together and felt a weight lift off my shoulders.

Thea sighed happily, as if she was experiencing the same relief. "That's better."

I studied her in the moonlight shining through the expansive windows. The day had faded so quickly that no one had gotten around to turning on any lights. In the dark, quiet space, I could hear her heart beating; I could savor the gentle draw of her breath, the slight rise and fall of her throat.

"I'll get us out of it," I promised her.

She stared up at me, her eyes full of stars. "It's not like we had other plans."

"I did." I angled my face over hers. "I planned to spend the entire time cataloging every single sound you make."

"That sounds boring," she said with a snort.

My tongue lashed over my lower lip. "It won't be."

"Oh, so it's not for scientific purposes?" she asked breathlessly.

"Do you want me to show you?" I asked.

Thea grabbed my shirt with her free hand, her eyes fluttering over me. "I do," she said, adding, "later."

"Later?" I repeated, arching an eyebrow.

"We should probably talk."

"That is the last thing we need to do." We'd been talking all afternoon. It hadn't gotten us anywhere.

"Be serious."

"I am," I said somberly. "We need to take a break from worrying about vague threats for a damn minute and just be together."

"It's just…" She trailed off, her teeth nibbling at her lower lip.

"Yes, my love?"

She didn't speak, but sadness surged through me in a sudden, uncontrollable wave. Cupping her jaw, I lifted her face to mine and found tears swimming in her eyes.

"Sorry," she said, blinking furiously. "I don't know what's wrong with me."

Instantly, the world fell away. I forgot about the desire straining my pants and family drama and everything but her. Gathering her in my arms, I held her.

"Do you want to tell me?" I asked her after a few minutes.

"It's stupid," she croaked.

"I doubt that." I brushed my palm over her hair and kissed her forehead.

"It's...Christmas."

I blinked. "And my family? Believe me, the idea of spending Christmas with them makes me want to cry, too."

"Not that." She laughed a little. "I've never spent Christmas on my own."

"I'm here," I said stiffly.

"I meant without my family," she said quickly.

I heard what she didn't say: *without my mom.*

"It was never a big deal in our house." She continued: "We couldn't afford for it to be, but we had traditions, you know?"

I'd been so wrapped up in vampire politics that it hadn't occurred to me the holiday might be important to her.

"Like what?"

She pulled away, shrugging like she was already coaching herself to let this go.

I wouldn't let her.

"The usual stuff."

"Like?" I prompted.

"What every family does," she said. "Probably the same stuff your family does. Decorate a tree. Bake cookies. Watch cheesy movies."

I didn't respond.

Her eyes widened. "You do that stuff, right?"

"Watch cheesy movies and hang ornaments? No."

"But the other stuff..." She trailed away weakly.

"My parents are from the ancient world," I reminded her. "We used to celebrate Saturnalia, but we haven't done that for years."

Now she was looking at me like I'd grown a second head.

"But cookies..."

"Sabine isn't the kind of mom who bakes cookies."

"I guess I assumed you participated more because of the gift exchange..." She shook her head a little, as if waking from a daze. "What are we going to do on Christmas then?"

"It'll be a quiet family Christmas. Open presents." I was fairly certain vampires and humans shared that pastime. "Try not to kill one another."

"You do that every day." She frowned. "I can't believe you don't have any traditions."

There was an ache in her voice—pain from remembering the life she'd given up. But it was more than that. Thea thought she was without family this year.

I would prove she was not.

"Tell you what," I said, coming up with a plan. "Tomorrow, let's make our own traditions."

She rolled her eyes, but I caught her hand and brought it to my lips.

"Not like that," I said before reconsidering. "Okay, maybe a little like that, but seriously, tomorrow we'll have our own Christmas."

She stayed silent for a minute before nodding. "If you're sure..."

"I am," I promised. I was going to make her forget all of this for one day. It might be the most important gift I could give to her.

"Okay," she said, a wicked smirk playing at her mouth. "And maybe tonight—"

She was over my shoulder before she could finish, laughing as I hauled her toward the bedroom.

CHAPTER SIXTEEN

Thea

Of all the moments Julian had surprised me since I'd met him, this had to be the strangest yet. I'd woken to an empty bed and finally found him in the kitchen—wearing an apron and a red Santa hat. In front of him, the kitchen counter was strewn with bags of flour and sugar, jars of sprinkles, and an impressive collection of cookie cutters. I stopped and stared.

"What..." I blinked a few times and realized I was about to ask the wrong question. "How did you do all of this?"

"I made a few calls." He shrugged as if he hadn't managed to dredge up a Christmas miracle in a matter of hours. "Will this be enough?"

I snorted as I stepped closer and inspected everything. "Are we making cookies for everyone in Greece?"

"Too much, then?" he asked flatly.

"No." I spun to him. "It's perfect." I reached up and flicked the white pom-pom on the end of his hat. "This is a nice touch."

"I thought I could play Santa." His face smoothed into a serious expression. "You do Santa, right?"

I grinned at him. I knew what he meant, but I couldn't help thinking dirty thoughts. "I haven't done him before, but I'm reconsidering."

"We have cookies to bake," he said, but the corners of his lips tugged up.

"And we have all day," I reminded him.

"But we have traditions to create. Speaking of…" He flashed out of the room before I could tell him that I wouldn't mind coming up with some clothing-optional traditions of our own. A split second later, he reappeared and plopped a hat on me.

"What's this?" I asked, laughing, as I reached up and felt the velvet.

"You're my elf," he teased.

"What? I should be your Mrs. Claus." I tried to swipe the hat from my head, but he swatted my hand away.

"You aren't my wife," he reminded me, leaning closer to add, "*yet.*"

"So I get upgraded when you make an honest woman of me?" I raised an eyebrow.

"Exactly." He swiped a kiss across my lips that left me wanting more. "By next Christmas."

"Next…Christmas…" I repeated breathlessly as he began digging into cabinets.

He stopped, his hand clenching a knob so tightly that his knuckles went white. "Were you hoping for a longer engagement?"

Frustration bloomed in my chest, and I knew instantly that it wasn't mine but his. Despite his agitation, his mind remained blank. No, not blank. He was shutting me out.

"Would you be mad if I said yes?" I asked genuinely.

He paused. "Not mad, exactly."

"But frustrated," I guessed based on how he felt.

"The sooner I make you my wife, the better," he muttered before returning to his search.

What the hell was this about? The Council? Or the cryptic threats Camila spoke of? Or the stupid Rites?

"Is that what you want?" I demanded.

"Of course it is."

He couldn't lie to me, but he was holding back.

I grabbed one of the cookbooks stacked at the end of the kitchen island. "Because if that's true, we don't have to wait to get married."

"Elope?" His voice peaked on the word.

I nodded, paging absently through the book even as my heart began to race.

"You want to elope?"

I shrugged and murmured as I pretended to be engrossed in a recipe, "Sure, why not?"

Was it his heart pounding or mine? I rubbed my chest with my free hand. I wanted to be his wife. No part of me doubted that I belonged to him. He was mine forever. I wanted to marry him. How could it be any other way? He was my mate.

"Thea." Julian dropped a hand over mine to keep me from turning another page. "Why are you lying to me?"

"I'm... What? Why would you think that?" I stammered. Was it my heart? Was that how he knew the truth?

I wasn't ready to get married. Not yet. Not while my world felt like it had been turned inside out.

"Because you've been studying a Greek cookbook for the last couple of minutes." He tilted his head toward it.

My eyes flew to the page and found he was right. I closed my eyes and inhaled deeply before turning to face him. "I *do* want to marry you."

"But?"

I shook my head. He needed to understand. I had to make him understand. "There's no but. I want to marry you. I want to be your wife. It's just that...I want my mom to be there."

Julian sighed. "Is that what's been bothering you?"

"Mostly," I admitted. "I know it's impossible."

He blinked rapidly. "Why would that be impossible?"

Where should I start? There was the fact that we didn't know where she was or if she was hiding from us. That might make it harder, but it wasn't what made it impossible. "She told me to choose," I reminded him. "Even if we found her…"

You don't think she would come.

Somehow it was easier to have him think it than it was for me to admit it.

"Well, we have plenty of time," he said as he wrapped his arms around me.

I swallowed, hoping I wasn't about to start an argument. "But you want me to be Mrs. Claus by next Christmas."

"Well, it is phase two of my tradition planning," he admitted, nuzzling against my neck. He inhaled deeply, and a new emotion flowered inside me: desire.

Part of me wanted him to sink his fangs into my neck, lift me onto the counter, and make me forget the ache growing inside me. But I knew it wouldn't be that easy to distract myself from how I was feeling.

"We don't know how long it will take to find her," I finally said. "It's silly anyway. She made it clear she wants nothing to do with me."

And why should I care either way? She'd lied to me for years. She had kept the truth from me. And when I'd finally discovered the truth about the real world—about the world I secretly belonged to—she had refused to open up.

Julian took a step back and planted his hands on my shoulders. "It's not silly to want your mom around."

"You never want your mom around," I reminded him drily.

"My mother is homicidal, and no matter what you think, your mom loves you. I knew that the moment I met her."

"When she demanded I kick your ass to the curb?" I asked him.

"She wants to protect you. I would never blame her for that." He hooked his index finger under my chin and tilted my face to his. "In fact, I owe her for it. She kept you safe for me. I owe her everything."

The electric blue of his irises blazed, and my mouth went dry. He meant it. Every word.

"I don't want to wait to get married," I said softly, admitting the other half of my shame. "I should wait until we find her. I should refuse to marry you until she's back. But I don't want to."

Julian's shoulders slumped, relief washing over his face. "Thank the gods."

It was easier this way. We both knew that. "So we elope?"

"Elope?" He chuckled. "Do you think my mother will allow us to elope?"

Crap on a cracker. "So, we aren't just getting married. We're having a wedding."

"A big one," he said apologetically. "But for now, we have a bigger problem."

My eyes rounded. What could be wrong now? I could only imagine after all the craziness of yesterday. "What?"

But Julian held up the cookbook with a laugh. "I can't find a single recipe for Christmas cookies."

CHAPTER SEVENTEEN

Thea

The kitchen was surprisingly well stocked, considering it belonged to a vampire. Outside, the winter sky was clear, and buttery sunlight seeped into the room. Julian's cell phone was plugged in and playing Christmas music softly in the background. I cracked an egg into the stainless steel mixing bowl. This was how I would spend holidays for the rest of my life. If Julian had his way and I became a vampire, that would be a very long time. The idea sent a smile to my lips.

"Can you find me a whisk?" I asked Julian, then thought better of it. "That's the one that has metal—"

"I know what a whisk is," he cut me off as he grabbed one from a nearby drawer.

"Sorry. You said you've never made Christmas cookies before."

"I have been in a kitchen once or twice." He looped an arm around me, drawing me closer as I beat the eggs. I'd already shown him how to cream the sugar and butter together. A fang nipped at my shoulder, and I nearly sent my whisk flying. A bit of beaten egg hit the counter as he murmured, "I feel like you're doing all the work."

"Is that why you're trying to distract me?" I asked as I wiped up my mess.

"This?" Another nip sent my toes curling against the tile floor. "You find this distracting?"

I swatted behind me. "Seriously? Do you want to make cookies or…"

"Or?" he prompted. "Are you getting other ideas?"

"Just measure the flour," I said with a sigh.

Julian moved a few feet away, holding up his hands in surrender. I knew better than to trust him to keep those hands to himself. Not that I wanted him to, exactly.

He picked up his phone to check the recipe we'd found online for basic sugar cookies. "I can't believe there were no cookie recipes in the books."

I glanced at the stack he'd had delivered and laughed. "I can't believe you bought a bunch of cookbooks written in Greek."

"Why's that a problem?" he asked as he measured two cups out of the bag.

I suppressed a groan as I slowly added the eggs into the creamed sugar mixture. "You can read Greek."

"Fluently."

"What languages don't you speak fluently?" It had to be a shorter list than the ones he knew.

"Do you really want me to answer that?" A cocky grin slid onto his face, and I found myself lost in him for a second. "Um, I'm no expert, but I think the eggs go into the bowl, my love."

"What?" I blinked and turned my attention back to the mixer—and the puddle of carefully beaten eggs I'd poured onto the counter next to it. "Oh shit." I flipped the mixer off. Some of the eggs had made it in, but it looked like about half hadn't. "Stop distracting me!"

"What did I do?" His eyes narrowed. "I was measuring flour like you asked me to do."

"You were being charming," I muttered.

His mouth twitched, and I braced for another disarming smile. "And that's a problem?"

"Definitely." I reached for the carton of eggs, but my hand came up empty.

Looking up, I found Julian had moved around the island with a bowl and whisk. Not that he was any less tempting with some granite between us. He grinned at me as if he knew what I was thinking. A moment later, he slid the bowl to me. "Here you go."

"Thank you." I took the eggs, flipped the mixer back on, and focused on adding it to the bowl.

"Now what?" he asked when I switched the mixer back off.

"We sift the dry ingredients and add them to this," I said. "Then the dough needs to chill for an hour before we can bake."

"A whole hour? What should we do?" I didn't miss the wicked current running through his words. My core tightened as various ways we could pass that hour came to mind.

But I kept my face blank and shrugged. "Clean up?"

Julian pressed his palms to the counter and leaned in my direction. "You forget that I can feel your emotions, my love. I had no idea cleaning up got you so hot and bothered."

"Maybe I like a shining sink." I arched an eyebrow.

He barked a laugh. "It's okay. We have other traditions to see to."

"Other traditions?" I liked the sound of that. Our lovemaking had been desperate last night, each of us wanting—no, needing—more than normal. It made sense. We hadn't had a moment to breathe, let alone think, since we'd arrived in Corfu.

"You'll see," he said cryptically.

"I can read your thoughts, remember?" I turned the dough out onto the counter and mounded it into a ball.

"You'll ruin all the fun," he warned me.

Rolling my eyes, I wrapped the dough up and turned to put it in the fridge. "Fine. Be all charming and mysterious."

"As you wish," he whispered in my ear, and I whirled around to find myself in his arms. Julian pressed a kiss to the curve of my neck. "Ready for our next tradition?"

I hooked an arm around his shoulder, offering my lips to him, but instead, he grabbed my hand and dragged me toward the living room. "Close your eyes."

"Fine." My exasperation was all for show. In truth, my heart beat wildly in my chest as I wondered what my mate planned to do to me.

"Okay, you can open them," he whispered.

I peeked through my lashes and gasped. A giant pine tree had been erected in the corner of the room. Under it, baskets full of decorations waited along with a few random branches and a small model boat.

"You found a tree," I murmured, my voice breaking a little as my throat swelled.

"I wish I could pretend it was some grand act, but it's tradition here, too," he admitted as he led me closer. "In Greece, they decorate boats as well. You'll see many of them on the water, but lots of homes have small ones."

I bent down and picked up a branch. "Olive tree?"

He nodded. "In ancient times, they decorated olive branches. I thought..." He paused and cleared his throat. Glancing up, I realized he was nervous. "I thought we could add some of the Greek traditions, so we remember our first Christmas together."

Our first Christmas. I'd been so caught up in grieving for what I'd lost that I hadn't spent enough time considering what I'd been given. Moving to face him, I reached to brush the stubble peppering his jawline.

"Sorry. I didn't shave," he muttered.

Because he'd been doing all of this for us, but mostly for me—to give me the holidays I missed.

"I love you," I whispered.

"So, I'm not fucking this all up?" He brushed his palm down my shoulder. "I want to give you everything."

I shook my head, a light laugh escaping my lips. "Don't you see? You've already given me everything. More than I ever dreamed of."

"Including an extended family made up of crazy vampires? And death threats? And—"

I pressed my index fingers to his perfectly carved lips. "Everything," I cut him off. "I want to spend every Christmas with you."

"You will," he promised in a thick voice.

"For eternity," I whispered.

Julian stilled, not even a breath moving his broad chest. Finally, he opened his mouth and spoke slowly. "Thea, are you saying what I think you are saying?"

I swallowed, allowing the fear hammering inside me to slide down my throat. "I want you to turn me."

He stared at me, still not breathing.

"I'm sure," I told him. "I think I've wanted it since the moment I found out what you were. I was just scared to admit it to you, and when you asked me at the ball, I wasn't expecting it. You'd seemed so against it before, and I panicked."

"What changed?" he asked, his voice hoarse.

"I remembered that I always feel less scared when I talk to you."

"There's a lot you don't know about becoming a vampire." He drew in a shuddering breath. "You should know how it works before you agree."

"Fine." I shrugged, a bright smile finding my face. "But it won't change my mind. I know what I want. There's just one thing."

Julian waited for me to find the right words. But even though I meant everything I said, I needed to make one thing clear.

"I want to wait until after we're married." I cleared my throat before adding, "And I think we have to consider the Vampire Council's demand."

"An heir," he said flatly. "There's something you should know. With Camila back..."

"She's technically the eldest Rousseaux." I'd already figured this part out.

"The Council may argue that she's a Drake now, as well as her children. Willem forced her to take his name. They weren't happy about that, so they might throw a fit. But it doesn't change that she is back. We can use this to our advantage. At least for a while."

He gripped my arms and looked me dead in the eye. "If The Rites go well, the Council may drop their demands for us to produce an heir entirely."

The tension in my chest grew instead of diminishing at his words.

"I thought it was expected of males to…reproduce."

"Yes, but I won't let them expect it of you." He searched my face. "I'm saying you don't have to have a baby."

"Oh. That's good."

"Is it?" he asked softly.

My eyes found the floor. I studied my chipped toenail polish. Had Sabine noticed? Of course she had. No wonder she didn't believe I could take her place. She must be thrilled at Camila's return—if only because I could never measure up to being the matriarch of her family. "You never wanted babies, and I'm young." I forced a smile onto my face before looking up to him. "We can make a family when we're ready."

"If that's what you want." I couldn't read the darkness swirling in his eyes any more than I could understand the tight cord wrapped around my heart.

"What I want is you," I reminded him. "I want to spend forever with you."

"And you will," he vowed, then glanced over at the tree. "Should we move on to this tradition?"

I shook my head, my fingers hooking into his waistband. "I have a better idea."

I flashed him a grin before I dropped before him, one knee at a time. The wool area rug scraped at my bare skin, but I ignored it as I unfastened his trousers. Julian's eyes hooded when I wrapped my hands around his shaft. Leaning forward, I kept my eyes pinned to his as I swirled my tongue over the crest of his cock.

"Christ, Thea," he grunted as I lowered my mouth fully over him. "You are the hottest thing I've ever seen."

I moaned in response, earning me another grunt of pleasure from my mate. I bobbed my mouth over him, pulling off enough to lick around his tip.

Fisting my hand around him, I dragged it roughly from the hilt up. A primal rumble tore from his chest, and in an instant, he'd lifted me to my feet. Our mouths collided as he carried me toward the couch.

"I need to be inside you," he growled against my mouth.

I wrapped my hand around the back of his neck, wetting my lips with my tongue. Between the talk of turning me and everything else, his magic rattled inside me. It wanted to be let out. It wanted to possess me. "Don't be gentle. I want it hard."

A curse fell from his lips as he lowered me. "Turn around."

A dark thrill shot through me as I did as he instructed.

"Bend over."

I folded over the sofa's arm obediently. His hands were rough as he yanked off my pants. Julian's powerful body bent over me, dropping to kiss the small of my back. I whimpered as his fingers kneaded my rear.

"I want to make this a tradition," he whispered before sinking his fangs into my tender skin.

A sob of pleasure tore through me as he fed. Was my body learning what to expect from his bite, or had I started to long for the pain as much as his touch?

"What do you think?" He stood and positioned himself behind me.

"Yes," I panted.

Julian cursed as he slid inside me slowly, allowing me time to adjust to him. Strong hands gripped my hips as he pulled out slightly. I wriggled, trying to push against him. His low chuckle rasped down my neck. "Impatient, are we?"

He pushed in a little, and I bit down on a moan.

"I take it back," he said gruffly. "This is the hottest thing I've ever seen. You have the most perfect ass. It's a work of art."

"Stop looking and start—" A thrust strangled my complaint. But it wasn't enough. "I want you," I gasped out, realizing that I was going to have to unleash him myself. "I need you to fuck me hard."

I felt his control snap, even though he stilled. "You're playing a dangerous game, pet."

A dark shiver raced down me when he used my old nickname.

"Teach me a lesson," I purred.

Julian reached forward and gathered my ponytail in his hand, wrapping it around his wrist, then gently tugged my head back. "Ask nicely."

His magic spread its wings inside me, waiting for me to speak.

"Please," I said softly.

"You want it hard? You want a lesson?"

"Please!" I tried to nod, but I couldn't move my head.

Julian bent, bringing his lips to the shell of my ear. His stubble scratched the sensitive skin, and I nearly came. "I live to serve you."

And then he relinquished the last of his self-control. Julian drove into me, yanking me by the hair so that my neck was stretched. He tugged my head to the side, kissing along my throat as he battered into me.

Darkness wrapped around me, binding my pleasure to his. I reached to the hand on my hip, trying to drive him faster and deeper. Julian shoved it away before delivering a stinging smack to my butt. I arched, wanting more pain, and I knew how to get it now. I pushed, and he punished. We clawed and tore until finally his fangs plunged into the scars on my neck.

Release rocketed through me, clenching around him and setting him free. We soared higher and then crashed together.

When he finally withdrew, I felt his heat spilling between my legs. I reached for it, some hidden piece of me wanting to feel the proof of our union. I closed my eyes and sucked in a deep breath as I felt the slick remnants. I was so sensitive that I shuddered as an aftershock rocked me.

I felt Julian watching me, and then he delivered an order I was powerless to resist.

"Don't stop."

CHAPTER EIGHTEEN

Julian

The world went black as I watched Thea touch herself. She glanced over her shoulder, biting down on her lower lip. It was all I could do not to take her again on the spot.

"I love how it feels after," she confessed, her cheeks turning pink. "I love this, and I love how I can still feel your bite."

Something rumbled inside my chest, and she grinned.

"Do you enjoy torturing me?" I asked her, edging closer. Placing my hand between her legs, I coaxed her fingers in circles.

"A little." She gasped, her whole body flinching from tiny jolts of pleasure.

"Maybe I should torture you." I seized her hand and held it still. She squirmed against the pressure, seeking release, and I chuckled. I brought my lips to her ear and whispered, "It sucks to want something you can't have."

Thea grumbled something under her breath. She ground herself against our hands. She wouldn't take no for an answer, and I loved her for it.

"So, it seems you want two orgasms as a holiday tradition?" I began moving my hand again and earned a pleased moan.

"Only two?" she asked between panting breaths.

She could never have enough. This was a predicament I understood a little too well. If it was up to me, we would never leave our bedroom unless it was to screw in a different room. But life kept getting in the way of that. If I made her a vampire, though...

I pushed the thought away and did my best to ignore the dark pang I felt at the possibility. She might change her mind when she learned what she would endure being turned—and what she would have to give up.

The truth was that I'd never had a choice. The moment we mated, I knew I would give in to my selfish need to keep her if she asked me to turn her, regardless of the reasons I shouldn't. I couldn't live without her. I couldn't live without my soul.

"Julian." My name lingered on her lips, calling me back to her. "I want to see you."

I cursed in a low voice. There was no way I could resist her appeal. I grabbed her hips and spun her around. "Spread your legs, my love." I cupped her chin with one hand, the other taking over the unfinished business between her thighs.

Her eyes rolled back as I pressed the palm of my hand to her swollen flesh. The flush of her cheeks spread down her neck, across her collarbone, and then the scent of cloves and night-blooming jasmine seeped into the air. My fangs ached, still extended from feeding a few minutes ago. It was all I could do to resist going in for seconds.

But it was her eyes that captivated me. She locked her gaze on mine as her breath became shallow and labored. "Tell me you love me."

Pain edged her request, and then I felt it inside me: uncertainty.

My tether tightened around me. How could she doubt how I felt about her? How could I show her?

"I love you," I murmured, never breaking eye contact. She moaned, and her hips began to match the rhythm of my hand. "When I say I love you, I mean that I was born for you. I exist for you. You are the air I breathe. You are the blood in my veins. You are part of me, my love."

She cracked open as I finished speaking, and I claimed her mouth, tasting her release in the kiss. Her body trembled, and she swayed, but I held her chin firmly as I delivered every lingering ounce of pleasure I could coax from her.

When I finally broke the kiss, she collapsed into my arms, and I held her, repeating the words I'd spoken like a talisman to ward off any further doubt. After a few minutes, I helped her dress before pointing to the tree.

"Tree or cookies?" I asked.

"Definitely cookies. I need sugar after that." Her lopsided grin sent a possessive thrill racing through me.

I shoved my hands in my pockets before I lost control again and we spent the whole day half naked. "Okay. You have to show me what to do next."

We wandered back into the kitchen. Thea went to the sink and washed her hands, and I laughed. "What?" she said indignantly. "I don't want them to taste like sex."

"I think if you could make cookies taste like sex, you'd be on to something." But I followed suit as she preheated the oven and got the dough out of the fridge. Reaching for a towel, I dried my hands and watched as she sprinkled flour on the countertops.

"We don't want them to stick," she explained.

"No sticking. Got it." I didn't bother to tell her I'd figured that much out, mostly because she was so adorable as she showed me how to do everything.

"This is the hard part." She unwrapped the dough and let it fall to the counter with a smack. "You have to get it rolled out just right."

"Let me." I took the French rolling pin and bumped her out of the way.

Thea's lips pursed as I began rolling out the dough, like she was holding back some commentary. But after a minute, she sighed. "You've done this before."

"I have rolled out dough in my time on this planet," I admitted.

"You told me—"

"That I'd never made Christmas cookies," I cut in. "That part is true, but I have cooked before."

"You know how to cook?"

"I've picked up a few things." I shrugged, wondering if now was the time to mention the flirtation I'd had with Le Cordon Bleu at the turn of the twentieth century.

"You went to Le Cordon Bleu," she said with shock, and I realized I'd let my mental shields slip. "You might have mentioned that."

"Only for a few weeks. I needed something to do."

"You needed something to do?" she repeated, still staring at me.

"Believe it or not, living for hundreds of years can get a bit tedious. Sometimes, I dabble."

"What else do you dabble in?" she asked suspiciously.

Before I could stop myself, several of my past hobbies came to mind.

"Wait, you play how many instruments?" She'd caught the fleeting thoughts. "And medical school? Really?"

"There are times when that comes in handy," I explained.

She planted a hand on her hip, shaking her head. "Like when? Are there lots of occasions for casual doctoring?"

"I studied medicine before the Plague. Vampires don't get sick. It was useful."

"You... The Plague." Her arms fell limply to her sides as she processed this.

"I'll tell you some other time," I promised her. It was a long, depressing story. Not the kind of thing I wanted to relive during the holidays. I placed the rolling pin on the counter next to the evenly rolled-out dough. "How did I do?"

Her eyes narrowed as she examined my work. "Okay, I guess."

"Okay?" I scoffed.

"Well, I expected more from the Julia Child of vampires," she said with a shrug.

I ignored her and grabbed a cookie cutter from the basket. I put it dead center and pressed down. "Like this?"

"Stop," she ordered me. "You have to plan it out." She shooed me away and seized the basket. Frowning as she studied the cut I'd left in the middle of the dough, she went to work placing cookies all around like a crazy puzzle. She chewed on her lip as she concentrated, and I forgot entirely about the cookies. I was mesmerized by her.

She wasn't human. We knew that now. But I'd never been with someone who felt so mortal—so alive. I could see why this meant something to her. I felt it—the connection each movement made with her past. My own past was twisted and hazy. I'd forgotten half of what I'd experienced in my life so far.

She was so young, and now, she wanted me to turn her. After that...

"Now we put them on a tray," she announced, interrupting my shielded thoughts.

"What do we do with this?" I pointed to the remaining dough on the counter.

"Roll it back out and make more cookies." She flashed me a mischievous smile as she plucked a small piece from it. "But we eat some of it."

I grimaced. "Raw cookie dough?"

"Seriously?" She gawked at me. "Don't tell me... You know what, never mind."

She pulled off another piece and held it to my mouth.

"Do I have to?" I asked with a frown.

"You'll rip people's heads off and drink blood, but you're getting freaked out by some raw eggs?"

I groaned and opened my mouth obediently. Thea popped the dough into it and waited.

Chewing slowly, I was surprised to find that I didn't hate it. "Not bad."

"Wait until you try chocolate chip cookie dough. It will change your life," she promised me. "I think it's my favorite."

"I already have a favorite snack," I said darkly.

Thea backed away, wagging a finger. "We will never finish these cookies if you start getting ideas."

I held my hands up in surrender. Today was about making memories. I'd have to behave.

When we were done with both batches, we set to work decorating, which was a lot messier but more fun. It turned out Thea had a soft spot for frosting, too.

"All done," I announced.

"You're too fast," she grumbled. Turning, she smacked my nose with the end of her frosting knife.

I glowered at her, a bit of red frosting in my direct line of sight. She burst into laughter, and I seized my chance. Lifting her onto the counter, I bracketed my arms around her. Thea's legs circled my waist, and she wiped the bit of frosting off my nose with a giggle.

"Sorry. Don't be grumpy."

"I'm not grumpy," I muttered.

Her eyebrow arched up, but my phone began to ring before we could discuss the matter further. I pulled it out to check the screen and froze.

"I need to take this," I explained as I accepted the call. "What's up?"

The caller rattled off the information I'd been anticipating and dreading for weeks. When I hung up, Thea watched me with anxious eyes. She twisted her fingers together and swallowed. "Who was that?"

But it wasn't who that mattered. It was the message.

"A friend," I told her, taking a deep breath. "Thea, we found your mother."

CHAPTER NINETEEN

Thea

I now understood there was a difference between a human and a vampire's idea of how to celebrate Christmas. *Paradeisos* had been transformed into a winter wonderland since we'd packed up and left the family home a few days ago.

"'A quiet family Christmas'?" I repeated Julian's words back to him as I took in the decorations. Garlands draped the door and window frames. Two large evergreens flanked the entrance, covered in a frosting of glittering white ornaments and large white poinsettias. I felt like I'd wandered into a very fancy—and very snooty—hotel lobby.

"It seems my mother is pulling out all the stops." Tension wound through Julian's words as he surveyed the scene. He'd been quiet on the drive from our end of the island, and he still seemed preoccupied. He lifted the boxes we'd brought. "I'll put these under the tree."

He continued around the corner into the living room, but I lingered. The truth was that I needed a minute. I'd thought I would be fine by the time we arrived, but now I realized that was wishful thinking. Too much had happened over the last week, and now I was supposed to do what? Drink eggnog and sing vampire carols by the tree?

"Hey." A friendly voice interrupted my thoughts, and I turned to find Jacqueline moving toward me. She looked softer than usual, opting for gloss over crimson lipstick and an ivory sweater that draped nearly to her knees. Her hair was pulled up in a loose bun, soft curls tumbling from it.

I forced a smile, feeling a little overdressed in my champagne-colored silk pantsuit. I'd been too nervous to ask Julian how formal things were going to be. "I should have worn jeans."

"Nonsense. You look gorgeous." Jacqueline wrapped her arms around me, and I caught a whiff of sun-soaked peaches and freesia. I had no idea if it was really expensive perfume or her supernatural scent, but I instantly relaxed. She took a step back and studied me. "How are you?"

I knew from her lowered voice that Julian had told her my mother had been found. For all I knew, she was the one who'd called with the news. Of course, "found" was a slight stretch. She'd been located. We knew where she was. What happened next was less certain.

"I'm good," I said, mustering up as much sugar as I could to coat the lie.

"Uh-huh." Jacqueline clucked her tongue. "Look, if you don't want to talk to me about it, no big deal. But if you do, I'm here."

"I know." I took a deep breath and managed a much smaller but more genuine smile. "I'm not really sure what I need."

"Are you going to make contact? Or send someone to her? Or...?" She trailed off, but I could guess the last question on her mind.

Was I going to go to my mom?

I knew because it was the question I'd been asking myself since we'd received the news.

"Julian's leaving it up to me," I explained.

Her eyebrows shot up. "And how do you feel about that?"

"Part of me loves that he's letting me make the choice," I said before hesitating.

"But?" she prompted.

"I don't know what to do," I burst out, my words bouncing off the polished tiled floors more loudly than I'd anticipated. I seized control of myself before I wrecked my eye makeup with tears. "She didn't want me."

Jacqueline sighed sympathetically as she draped an arm around my shoulder and pulled me close to her. "That is not true. She doesn't want *Julian*," she whispered. "She's your mother. Of course she wants *you*."

My eyes darted to her. "Because mothers are so unconditionally accepting when it comes to their children, huh?"

"Touché," she said with a hollow laugh. "But, really, your relationship with your mom is different."

"Speaking of, have you talked to yours?"

"Well, I wasn't invited for Christmas, and she hasn't returned my calls, so... At least you don't have a vampire mom," she said, sounding miserable.

But was my mom any better? I wasn't sure. Yes, I'd grown up with a loving mother. She'd supported me through years of lessons. She'd cheered me on at every recital and performance, even when she was undergoing treatments.

But she'd also lied to me my whole life—about the real world and my true place in it.

Had she ever wanted me to have the career I'd dreamed of while practicing for hours? How could she, knowing it might expose me to the world? I thought of Diana, the witch who'd been on the panel for my senior final; she had leveraged her magic into a spectacular career. But how many creatures from our world recognized what she was? I couldn't help but think my mother must have known she would have to tell me, so why hadn't she?

Why hadn't she told me about the real world—warned me about the dangers waiting for me? She loved me, but was her love poison—to both of us?

"I need answers," I finally said.

Jacqueline nodded. "I understand." She paused for a moment

as if considering her words. "If you want me to go with you, I will. She might be less hostile to me."

"You're still a vampire," I pointed out. I was grateful for the offer, and I might take her up on it—if I found the courage to go.

"Yes, but I'm not sleeping with you." She winked. "And I'm much more charming than Julian."

"Charming?" Julian's deep voice was as dry as kindling. "Who are you trying to seduce this time?"

"No one," she lied for me. "Stop eavesdropping. This is girl talk."

He rolled his eyes, hitching a thumb in the direction of the living room. "According to Sabine, she isn't waiting a minute more for stragglers."

"Stragglers, huh? That's a kinder word than I expected her to use," I said.

"I might have censored what she really said," he admitted. Julian extended his hand. Like at the ball, it was bare—a decision we'd both made together. From now on in public, gloves were mandatory for both of us. But in private—even amongst his family—we wanted to send a message. We were not merely a couple. We were mates, and nothing would separate us.

"Let's go before she gets violent," Jacqueline suggested, smiling at our joined hands.

"She's always violent," I grumbled, earning a laugh from them.

"It makes her easy to shop for," Jacqueline said nonchalantly.

"So, I guess you got the short stick," I said. I'd been wondering who had gotten Sabine in the holiday gift exchange.

Julian sighed and turned pleading eyes on his best friend. "Tell me you didn't buy her a weapon."

"I can't believe you even asked that. Of course not. I got her something to go with her weapons. A girl needs accessories."

"Does Chanel make scabbards now?" Julian smirked, but our amusement collectively evaporated when we entered the living room.

"Finally!" Sabine wore a white velvet dressing gown, and her dark hair fell in lush waves over her shoulder. Her stunning face was free of makeup, but everything about her was still polished and sophisticated.

"Let me guess—she woke up like this?" I murmured to Julian.

"It is Christmas morning," she shot back. I should know better than to whisper around vampires. Sabine checked the delicate gold watch on her wrist. "For a few minutes, at least. You could have arrived before noon."

"No one told me we were expected at dawn." Julian bypassed her complaints and led me to a loveseat as far from her as possible.

"Like you were sleeping in," Lysander teased.

I blushed as I recalled the lazy morning we'd spent in bed, but managed to keep my face studiously blank.

"It's Christmas. There's no reason to rush," Julian said smoothly. His arm dropped possessively around my shoulder, and I snuggled into his clove-and-woodsmoke scent.

"You haven't been waiting to open presents," Sebastian said, dropping to the rug next to the tree.

"What are you, five? Some things never change." Julian shook his head at his younger brother.

The ribbing continued despite their mother's sighs. At least listening to them go at it about Christmas felt normal. I couldn't say the same for the rest of the scene before me. The tree itself was easily ten feet tall and decorated with golden feathers and fruit, but the most impressive part was the mountain of presents under it—each wrapped with a compulsive level of detail. I bit my lip as I spotted our gifts to Benedict and Thoren, wondering if we should have put more effort into them. Then I realized there were far too many presents for a simple gift exchange.

"I thought it was just an exchange," I said without thinking.

"It's been a long time since I had all my children under the same roof. I might have gone a bit over the top," Sabine said in a lofty voice. She took an armchair by the unlit fireplace, looking more like a queen on her throne than a mother on Christmas morning. Dominic moved to stand behind her, looking the part of a protective knight. "And, Julian, your package arrived yesterday. I assumed it's a gift of some sort, so I put it under the tree."

"I wondered," he said tightly. "Celia wasn't sure she could get it here in time. It's for Thea."

"Me?"

"It's our first Christmas together. I got you a present." He shrugged like he didn't see the big deal.

"I didn't... I mean, I haven't had a chance to get you anything," I stumbled, looking for the right words.

"When would you have time with finals and traveling? *And* my sister trying to kill you? *And* Council ordinances?" He glared at Camila, who didn't look remotely remorseful.

"You can hardly blame Camila for that reaction," Sabine said. Of course she could justify her daughter's homicidal tendencies. It was probably genetic.

"Let's focus on being together," Dominic suggested. He held up a crystal glass that was clearly full of liquor. "Maybe everyone should have a drink."

I turned to Julian, but he was already standing to do as his father suggested.

From her throne, Sabine glowered at yet another delay, so I scrounged up the least controversial topic I could come up with. "What do you serve for Christmas dinner? Maybe I could help you in the kitchen later."

My olive branch was met with a sharp smile that made my stomach clench. "You have to ask what delicacy vampires enjoy during the holidays? Although, now that you mention it, I suppose we have to feed the human."

"Mortal," Julian corrected her. "Thea isn't human."

"We aren't eating later?" Lysander looked like he might riot. He'd clearly misread Sabine's far-from-subtle threat.

"There was a time when vampires lived on blood alone," Sabine said with a sniff. She reached up to swipe her husband's glass and took a sip.

"Like, a million years ago." Lysander rolled his eyes.

"The Mordicum believes—" Camila started, but Benedict cut her off swiftly.

"No politics today," he suggested gently.

"What will you do with your time?" Jacqueline asked in a sugary sweet tone laced with venom.

"Don't start," Sabine warned everyone. "We're going to have a lovely, peaceful family Christmas."

Everyone turned to stare at her.

I didn't know peaceful was in her vocabulary.

I bit back a laugh at Julian's thought, but when I looked up, Camila's eyes gleamed with mischief.

"You're right," she said. "Why argue when we have something exciting to discuss?"

"Camila." Julian said her name softly, but she ignored him.

"I just thought that since we were all here, it's a good time to talk about the future." She blinked innocently, but the wicked glint remained. "So, will you be getting married before or after your mate duels our mother to the death?"

CHAPTER TWENTY

Julian

So much for my mother's peaceful family Christmas. I thrust the Scotch I'd poured for Thea into her hands and angled myself carefully between where she sat and the rest of my family. This earned me an annoyed groan from my mate. I ignored her. If things went to blows, it wouldn't be the first holiday ruined by family squabbles. But Thea wasn't a vampire, and I wouldn't allow her to be injured while everyone played insult roulette with one another.

"It's quite the predicament," Camila continued. "If they duel now, there will either be no one to plan the wedding or no bride to walk down the aisle. But waiting would put a damper on the celebration, wouldn't it?"

Sebastian loosed a heavy sigh. "When did you become such a bitch?"

"At least I'm not the family whore," she said with a shrug.

"Enough!" My father's voice boomed across the room, and everyone fell silent. "Your mother has been putting this celebration together for days, so if you cannot behave like civilized creatures for the next two hours, you can leave." His gaze took turns landing on each of us.

No one spoke, and I finally sat down next to Thea, who was biting back a grin.

You like him, don't you?

She nodded a little as she sipped her drink.

"I guess you haven't knocked her up yet if she's drinking," Lysander said casually, and everyone groaned. I tossed a pillow at his head. "What? I was just curious."

"About the status of my uterus?"

He rubbed his head where the pillow had hit him. "Well, when you put it like that."

Before another fight began, Sebastian interrupted loudly, "Can we open presents now?"

"That seems like a good idea," our father said tightly. "Shall I?"

Sabine's nod was stiff, but it was enough. He moved to the tree and picked up a small package. "To Jacqueline," he read the tag, "from Benedict."

I swallowed a laugh as he handed the gift to my queasy-looking friend. Thea elbowed me in the ribs. I guess she had noticed the tension between those two.

"Yep," she said quietly to her glass.

Benedict had a massive crush on Jacqueline when we were kids. I think he wanted to marry her.

Thea's eyebrows shot up, but she said nothing as we watched Jacqueline unwrap the gift nervously.

I don't think he's ever realized that Jacqueline much prefers females.

My attention was drawn back by Jacqueline's gasp. The torn paper fell from her fingers, revealing a Tiffany Blue Box.

"Holy shit," Thea muttered.

Apparently, he still doesn't realize, I added.

"Benedict, you shouldn't have..." Jacqueline shook her head dizzily as she stared at the unopened box.

"It was my assistant." He shrugged, but the thickness of his words betrayed the lie. Still, he forged on. "I don't even know what it is."

She didn't speak as she lifted the lid. A moment later, she held up a delicate silver necklace with a single petite diamond. Her eyes lifted to his, color finding her cheeks. "Thank you. It's lovely."

He nodded as Sebastian complained loudly, "I hope no one

bought me fancy shit."

It turned out Thoren had gotten Sebastian. He tore into his present and unearthed a Metallica T-shirt. "Is this vintage?" he asked giddily as he held it up.

"Got it in '83," Thoren replied tersely. It was hard to imagine him attending anything as loud as a concert.

The gift-giving continued. Sebastian had bought Lysander a very old, very expensive bottle of Scotch that he immediately cracked open. I had no doubt the bottle would be gone before dinner. Lysander's gift to our father was more sentimental. He'd found a few pieces of pottery on one of his excavations outside Rome.

"Should those be in a museum?" Thea asked under her breath as Dominic turned them over with a far-off look.

They probably belonged to him a couple thousand years ago.

She giggled, earning a reproachful look from Sabine, not realizing I was serious. My mother's anger was short-lived when she opened her present from Jacqueline.

"It's stunning," she gushed, showing off the sleek, artfully designed scabbard.

Jacqueline shrugged at us. "A vampire makes them in Venice. He has a secret studio behind one of the tourist mask traps."

At least she hadn't included a blade to go with it.

Dominic picked up a small package, not bothering to look at the tag, and carried it to Camila with a small smile. "It's not much."

There was no mistaking the emotion in his voice, and he turned away quickly as she ripped off the paper. When she lifted the lid, she only stared into the box. No one spoke for a moment.

"I'm sorry," Dominic finally said. "It was a bad idea. I just thought—"

"You kept her," Camila cut him off, lifting a clay doll from it.

"Of course," he said softly.

I remembered the day he'd brought the doll home from a trip to Germany when we were only a few hundred years old. I'd laughed and called it childish, but Camila had loved it. Over the following centuries, dolls became more realistic, and while I'd gone off to fight through my adolescent years, she'd stayed home to collect them. But this doll had always been special to her. It had remained in her quarters until the day she'd married Willem and left home.

"Thank you." She cradled it to her.

An ache burst across my chest, and it took me a moment to realize it wasn't my pain I was feeling. Glancing down, I found Thea's eyes full of tears, and I knew what she was thinking: When were we going to let Camila see her children again?

I wished I had an answer. More than that, I wished I believed it was a good idea to let her anywhere near them.

After a moment, Camila carefully placed the doll back in the box and looked up. "There's a box for Julian there."

Dominic picked up the gift she'd pointed to and passed it to me.

"I'm afraid it's less thoughtful," she said as I removed my arm from Thea's shoulders to open it.

Inside the package, I found a pair of gold cufflinks engraved with a looping *J* and *T*.

"I thought you could wear them for the wedding." There was no derision in her voice—no scheming or wicked intentions.

I nodded my thanks. "I will." I cleared my throat and gestured to the simple white boxes Thea and I had brought. "Those are for Benedict and Thoren."

Next to me, Thea squirmed, and I knew she was thinking about how small our gifts must seem compared to the grand gestures everyone else had made.

My dad passed one to each of them. They shared a look as he undid the simple twine we'd tied them with. Benedict got his open first, and he blinked with surprise. Thoren looked more delighted.

"Cookies?" Benedict asked, looking over at us.

"You already have everything," I said flatly, earning another elbow in the rib from my mate.

"We made them," she said, a slight tremble in her voice.

"Both of you?" Benedict looked even more shocked.

"I didn't poison them," I reassured him, adding, "Thea wouldn't let me."

Thoren seemed to have no such concern, because he was already polishing off the first one. "These are great. I don't think I've ever had homemade cookies. Thanks."

"Ever?" Thea squeaked, shrinking a little at the look my mother shot in her direction.

Benedict took a bite more tentatively but grinned as he tasted it. "Not bad."

Thea relaxed, and I leaned to kiss her forehead.

"Told you they would love them," I whispered.

"Well, now that we're done with the exchange," Sabine began as she stood and moved toward the tree, "I have some presents for my children."

"Wait." I stopped her, looking at my mate's empty hands. "Thea still needs her present."

"Yeah," Sebastian piped up. "Who had her?"

It took me all of five seconds to look around and calculate the only person who had yet to give anyone a present.

"Mother?" I said, my voice soft with poison.

"I've been very busy," she snapped, cupping one of her curls to check that her hair was still in place. "I must have forgotten."

There was a collective murmur of disapproval from the group. A second later, a wadded T-shirt landed on Thea's lap.

"You can have mine," Sebastian said. "You're a musician, right? You can appreciate it. Hope you don't mind, Thoren."

Our brother shrugged, sugar cookie crumbs dusting his lips. "It's cool, but she can't have my cookies."

"Thank you," Thea said to them. "I can always make more cookies."

"Let me know when you do."

I'd never seen Thoren so enthusiastic about...*anything*.

"Now that we've settled that." My mother started to reach for a package under the tree, but I stood swiftly and nudged her away.

"Our other gifts can wait. Thea deserves a proper present," I told her. My brothers might have saved the day, but I wasn't going to let this slide. There was no doubt in my mind that she had snubbed Thea purposefully. My mate might have reacted with grace, but she deserved a reminder of how important she was, not only to me but this entire family.

It was easy to spot the box, even though it was tucked behind the tree. It was still wrapped in the brown paper from the courier. I lifted it carefully, afraid to damage it—hoping it hadn't been damaged in transit. I'd probably have to kill someone if it was.

Thea's eyes widened into full moons when I turned to hand it to her.

CHAPTER TWENTY-ONE

Thea

Every head in the room turned to watch as Julian placed the enormous box in front of me. Judging by its size, it was not another priceless piece of jewelry. That was a relief. I still hadn't adjusted to the expensive engagement ring I now wore—and I hadn't dared to ask how much it was worth. I was pretty sure I didn't want to know. I shot my mate a questioning look as I reached to carefully tug the paper. He held it upright for me with a rakish grin that made my heart skip a beat.

"Oh, just rip it," Sebastian said impatiently. He really was like a little kid, but he seemed to enjoy watching everyone else open presents as much as opening them himself.

I stuck my tongue out at him and carefully plucked away the paper. Just because it wasn't the right size for jewelry didn't make it less valuable. Knowing Julian, there was probably some ancient Ming dynasty vase in there or something equally ridiculous.

But as I peeled the paper away, I found a simple shipping crate. I had expected a box. I looked up at Julian, who winked at me. "Allow me."

He shooed Sebastian from where he sat near our feet. His brother grumbled as he moved so that Julian could place it carefully on the ground.

"Do we need something to pry it open—" I hadn't finished the question before Julian pried off the lid with his bare fingers. I guess vampires didn't need silly things like tools.

Inside the crate was a mountain of packing peanuts. It took me a moment to fish them off, but I froze when I caught the first glimpse of the present hiding beneath. "Is it...?"

I didn't wait for him to tell me before I started throwing the peanuts out of the crate.

"My floor!" Sabine whined, but no one paid attention. Everyone was waiting to see what I was about to unearth.

I felt my heart pounding in my throat as I stared at the ancient wooden case.

"How old is this?" My voice cracked on the question.

"The case?" Julian asked. "Or what's inside?"

Oh my...

My fingers trembled as I lifted it from the crate, spilling even more of the packing materials on the pristine floor. Sebastian, who had lost interest in the present, began tossing them at Lysander like snow. I barely noticed as I saw the name stamped into the wood.

"It's not really," I said breathlessly.

Julian knelt next to me, the rakish grin turning to a boyish smile. "Open it."

It took me a moment to figure out the antique clasp. I held my breath as I raised the lid. For a second, I thought I was hallucinating. Tucked carefully inside was the most beautiful cello I'd ever seen. Never in my life had I expected to be sitting so close to an instrument like this, let alone given it.

"Pick it up," Julian urged.

"Touch it? Are you insane? It's a *Stradivarius*." I shrank away from it, afraid to even breathe on it wrong.

"It's *your* Stradivarius," he corrected me.

"I think I'm going to pass out," I murmured. The truth was that I'd avoided playing since we left San Francisco. At first I'd told myself it was because I'd needed a break after practicing so tirelessly to pass my final performance, but it had been almost two weeks since then—

the longest I'd ever gone since I started playing, because...

Because I couldn't stop thinking about what Diana had told me—that my talent wasn't the result of all the practice, all the love I felt for the instrument. She'd said it was magic. Now I knew it was the product of my siren blood. Knowing that had changed something inside me, something that was still hurt over my mother's betrayal. I was only beginning to make peace with being a siren, only starting to understand what that meant.

And despite the beauty and rarity of the cello sitting in front of me, calling to me, begging to be played, I wondered if that wounded part of me—the part of me that roared at the lies I'd been fed—would ever be healed. If playing would ever feel peaceful again.

I was still staring at it, still not reaching for it, when Sabine swept toward us with a huff. "Really? You gave her the Stradivarius? It was worth over ten million a decade ago."

Someone whistled—Lysander, maybe—and Julian shook his head. "It's meant to be played."

"Oh, so that's why you bought it two hundred years ago and never touched it?" Sabine asked drily.

"I rarely play," he said, hitting me with my second shock of the afternoon.

"You...what...?" I sputtered. I almost smacked him, but I didn't dare risk the cello, even if...even if I wasn't certain where it fit into my life anymore.

"He never told you that he plays as well?" Camila asked, mirroring their mother's dry disapproval.

"Played," he corrected her. "It's been decades... Longer. A century."

I couldn't process any of this. Too many emotions swirled inside me.

"I can't accept this," I said finally. It belonged in a museum or at least in the hands of someone who deserved to play it—someone whose talent wasn't the result of a magic trick.

To my surprise, he shrugged. "Fine."

"What?" Jacqueline demanded from across the room.

"She doesn't have to accept it. It was already hers. She is my mate."

Dammit, what other insane, priceless objects did I now incidentally own because of that fact?

He leaned closer, bringing his mouth to my ear. "It was always meant for you. I've just been keeping it safe."

Despite the confusion I felt, love swelled in my chest, his and mine mixing together until I thought I might burst. I felt a brush of dark magic sweep through me—a silent reminder that he wasn't simply saying these things. When he said what was his was now mine, he meant it. There was no other possibility. We were two halves of one soul.

Knowing that made the loss of my past—my world—easy to bear, and maybe someday I might pick up the cello to play, to feel the power of that music thrumming through me. Maybe someday I would learn to love the music and the magic.

I closed my eyes, allowing myself to feel the peace that came with that realization. Warmth spread through me like a burning light, and when I opened them again, that fire blazed in Julian's eyes.

"Will you play it for us, Thea?" Benedict broke in.

"I probably need to tune it first." It was a good excuse. Although it was in excellent condition, if it had traveled from God knows where, it likely needed a little attention. But there was one matter the cello would solve.

"Later, then," Sabine said impatiently, causing my own patience to snap.

"Yes, later." I smiled at her, allowing my lips to curl a little too much, to show a little more teeth than usual. "And now we can get this messy business of a duel behind us."

The room fell silent. Even Sabine went so still that she looked like a terrifying statue of an avenging goddess.

"Excuse me?" Only her lips moved.

"The duel," I repeated. "I know you were eager to get it over with."

"I don't think you understand," she seethed, edging close enough that Julian let out a low growl.

"You told me to pick anything I could hold in my—what did you call them—'fragile fingers'?" I repeated the words she'd used the morning after we'd survived The Second Rite.

"I meant a weapon." I could see her fangs now. Julian shifted his body slightly between us but didn't rise.

"You didn't say that, did you?" I met her shocked stare without blinking. "I mean, the pen is mightier than the sword, so I suppose the bow is deadlier than the knife." I only prayed Sabine hadn't dabbled like her son, but something told me that music wasn't violent enough to be one of her hobbies.

She blinked. "I've had a few lessons. I'm certain that—"

"Oh, give it up, darling," Dominic interjected as he moved to her side. "She has you on this one."

"You don't think I can play the cello?"

"As brilliantly as Thea does?" Julian asked, and I resisted the urge to shy away from the compliment. He didn't know, didn't realize that it was a source of pain. "I guess you two can duel each other in a couple of decades."

"Or," Dominic said gently, "you can be more careful with your words next time."

His eyes smiled at me from across the room. It was clear he approved of my tactic, even if he wasn't inclined to rub his wife's nose in it.

Sabine took another threatening step toward me, forcing Julian to rise to his feet entirely, but she didn't come closer. "Next time, I will be more careful."

"Next time?" I snorted, even as relief washed through me like a cleansing wave. "I'm not an idiot. There's not going to be a next time. And to be clear, I have no intention of challenging you for the role of family matriarch—that's all yours."

Muffled laughter surrounded us, but Julian and Sabine remained toe to toe. Finally, Dominic took her by the shoulders and steered her back to the tree. "Let's open those presents now."

• • •

The rest of the afternoon was less tense. By the time Lysander passed out Christmas crackers to everyone, half of the family was drunk. I was too busy staring at the crate to even pop mine, too busy battling the desire to give in and pick it up. Just once. To see how it felt.

"Do you need to be alone with it?" Julian asked as he placed a paper crown on my head.

I looked up, startled, to discover everyone else was wearing one, too.

"Sorry," I murmured. "I can't believe someone is letting me touch a Stradivarius." Had I earned that? Would I ever?

"Touch? I thought you were going to duel," he whispered in my ear, kissing its shell. A ripple of pleasure danced through me. "Well played, by the way. But next time?"

"Mm-hmm," I hummed, lost to the stolen kisses he planted on my neck while everyone else caroused.

"Let me in on your plan so I'm not losing my mind. I've been having nightmares about you and swords for a week."

"Sorry!" In truth, I'd been enjoying Sabine's annoyance over the whole thing. Instead of looking forward to killing me, I'd left her wondering why I was so foolishly confident.

"It was a masterstroke," Jacqueline agreed, pushing into a nonexistent space on the loveseat. I moved closer to Julian to give her room. She sighed as she surveyed the room. "You survived your first vampire Christmas."

"I did," I said with a nod. Outside, the sky had faded to twilight, painting the water's surface in pastel hues. It was getting late. My stomach growled as if to prove the point. I glanced at Julian. "So, really, will there be dinner, or do you all crack open some O negative for the holidays?"

"There will be dinner," he promised, "but let's find you something to eat." He stood and pulled me to my feet.

"I'll save your spot," Jacqueline called after us, throwing her legs across the cushions like she owned the place.

"Keep an eye on my cello," I called back, and she gave me a thumbs-up. I wouldn't put it past Sabine to spirit it away, to deem it too precious for my mortal fingers, to prove my greatest fear: that

I didn't deserve it.

The kitchen was a welcome reprieve from the loud scene in the living room, even if it was bigger than my apartment in San Francisco.

"Let's see what we've got." Julian strode to a double-doored Sub-Zero refrigerator and opened it.

"Is that O negative?" I called out, spotting the blood bags filling the door's compartments.

"We're more A- positive types." He grinned over his shoulder before continuing his search. "There's some *foie gras* and fancy jam and a lot of stuff I assume is for dinner."

"Fancy jam," I said, moving to rummage through the pantry. I found a loaf of bread and a jar of peanut butter.

"Very sophisticated." Julian handed the jam to me.

"Well, I am a Stradivarius owner now. It goes with the territory." I spread a thick layer of peanut butter on one slice. Julian smirked over me, and I rolled my eyes. "I'm hungry and it's fast, okay?"

"It's not that." He stepped behind me and wrapped his arms around my waist. Nuzzling into my neck, he murmured, "That's twice now that you said it was your cello."

"Oh." I swallowed as I joined the slices together. I hadn't realized that. I wasn't sure what it meant that I both coveted it and feared it. "I meant *our* cello."

He laughed, and the sound bolted through me to pool in my core. "It's *yours*, my love. It's all yours."

I abandoned my sandwich and spun around. Coiling my arms around his neck, I stared up at him. "All of it?"

"Every last possession. Every last cent."

He meant it. Not that it mattered. I'd never had enough of anything, especially money, for that kind of thing to matter to me.

"And you?" I asked quietly.

"Every last breath."

His face angled over mine, hesitating for one delicious moment before he brought his lips to mine. Whisky lingered on his breath, sharpening the taste of his mouth. My tongue swept across his, wanting to taste more of him. Julian groaned, pressing my body closer to his, as he invaded. We lingered, exploring and claiming each other, as our magic wrapped and wound together in strands of light and dark that I felt even with my eyes closed. When he finally broke away, we were both panting and his eyes were black.

"Maybe we should skip dinner," I suggested with a raised brow. My stomach, apparently not liking the sound of that, growled again.

"Eat your sandwich," he ordered through gritted teeth.

My tether yanked me away, and I found myself whipping around to grab it. His low chuckle slid over me as I took a huge bite and wriggled happily.

"That's what I thought."

"I always want to eat," I said with a full mouth.

He laughed again and brought his lips to my ear. "Finish that up, and we'll head home."

If we make it that far. A vision of us pulled over to the side of the road so I could climb onto his lap flashed through my mind, and I nearly choked.

"Slow down," he warned.

I only ate faster. I washed the sandwich down with a glass of milk—the only thing other than blood or booze that they had to drink—and turned to him.

"You ready?" he asked.

I nodded, but before he could take a step, I grabbed his hand. "Wait."

Julian paused, concern etching his features.

"I've been thinking." I took a deep breath and plunged ahead. "I want to see my mother."

He didn't say anything, but I saw the muscle working in his jaw.

"We don't have to leave right now," I said quickly, even if part of me was ready to go. "But I need to make things right with her."

"I'll arrange for us to leave right away." His face and thoughts betrayed nothing.

Which was probably going to make the next bit worse.

"I was thinking maybe Jacqueline should go with me."

"Because your mother hates me," he said flatly.

"No… Okay, yes," I admitted.

"You aren't going to see your mother without me."

"She's my mom; I should make the decision. Is there something you're not telling me?"

"It's too dangerous."

I felt confused. "You said she was in Venice."

Why she was in Venice was beyond me. As far as I knew, she'd never even left America. Then again, it turned out I didn't know as much about her as I thought.

"Venice?" a voice so sharp it stung interrupted. Camila stepped to the counter and relaxed against it. "What about Venice?"

"It's none of your business," Julian said through clenched teeth.

My mate might not be able to lie to me, but he was definitely leaving something out. I turned to Camila. "My mom is in Venice. I want to see her. She's not…well."

Camila's gaze met her brother's.

"Don't," Julian said.

She ignored him and looked to me. "If she's in Venice, they have her."

"Who?" I asked even as dread filled me.

"The Mordicum."

I froze, staring blankly at him until this information processed. When it did, tears pricked my eyes. "How could you?"

I didn't wait for him to answer before I stomped out of the room.

CHAPTER TWENTY-TWO

Jacqueline

I stared at the text I'd received from my mother a few minutes ago, reading it for the hundredth time.

Come over tomorrow.

That was all it said. Not Happy Christmas or hello. Nope, just a blatant demand. That couldn't be good. I should be pleased she was reaching out to me. It was what I wanted, wasn't it?

Wasn't it?

I looked at the Tiffany box sitting on the side table next to the loveseat. There was an easy solution to this problem. If she wanted me to get married—if that's what it would take to save my sister from marrying far too young—Benedict would marry me. I knew that.

I'd always known that.

Just like I knew he'd been in love with me for centuries. Just like I knew the reason he acted like he hated me was because he'd never gotten over my almost-engagement to Julian. If Benedict only knew the truth, how would he feel then?

The real question, though, was could I do it? Benedict was incredibly handsome in a politician sort of way. I mean, so what if his hair was too perfectly combed, his skin too dewy, and his smile always camera-ready? He was usually a nice guy, notwithstanding his role in putting my best friends through The Second Rite without warning.

None of those were the real reasons I couldn't bear to consider it. I knew exactly why it turned my stomach to think about taking a husband, particularly Benedict. But it had been over two centuries since I'd lost that reason. Why not just get it over with?

I swallowed and swung my legs over the side of the couch. Should I do it now or wait until after I talked with my mother? She couldn't object to him. Even if he wasn't technically born a vampire, he'd been turned by pureblood parents and given the proper ceremonial rites. That made him as big a catch as Julian.

Almost.

My toes swayed across the floor as I contemplated. She might not be thrilled with the match, but maybe it was better not to let her have a say. Who knew what vampires she had her eye on? What if she demanded I marry some random pureblood?

Better not give her a choice.

I took a deep breath and pushed to my feet. I made it a single step before Thea appeared in the doorway, tears streaming down her cheeks. She gestured toward the front door. So much for my plan. At least Benedict wasn't going anywhere.

I snuck out of the room. Sabine was too busy admiring something sparkly that Dominic had given her, and the boys were all drunk. No one even noticed as I slipped away.

I found Thea in the foyer, hugging her arms across her chest. All my worries about Benedict and my family and marriage vanished when I got a good look at her. I rushed to her side. "What's wrong?"

"My mom," she said in a creaky voice. "The Mordicum has her."

"What?" I shook my head. It was clear this was news to her, too. "How did you find out?"

"Camila," she whispered.

My stomach hollowed out. There had been a time when

Camila was the kindest person I knew. Gentle. Sweet, even though she'd had a streak of Rousseaux passion. Now? She was a fox in the chicken coop.

"You can't trust her," I said flatly. I still hadn't figured out why she'd been welcomed back so easily by her family. Surely Julian and I weren't the only ones who mostly saw a stranger instead of his sister. "She lies."

"I wasn't lying about that," Camila announced as she joined us.

I ignored her and took Thea by the shoulders. "What do you want?"

"I want to get out of here before I go crazy," she said in a small voice.

"And Julian?"

She cringed, and I knew I didn't need to press for more information there. If he'd known, why hadn't he told her? Why hadn't he told me?

"Trouble in *Paradeisos*," Camila said in a singsong voice.

Something snapped inside me, and I whirled on her. "Shut the fuck up."

Camila's smile faltered as she backed away from me. "Jacqueline, I—"

"I don't really give a shit," I told her. "I don't know why you're back here. I don't know why you're playing games with your family."

"If you had any idea what they did to me," she hissed.

"I have a pretty good idea about everything, and none of it makes how you're acting okay." She looked like I'd slapped her, but I took no pleasure in it. I relished calling Sabine on her shit or telling Julian like it was, but when it came to Camila, the only emotion I could drum up was exhaustion.

I wrapped an arm around Thea's slight shoulders and steered her toward the door.

We'd nearly reached it when Camila called out, "He didn't know. He only suspected."

I resisted the urge to look back at her, even though I caught the slight tremor in her voice. Opening the door, I nudged Thea through it. Julian was going to be pissed, but I would deal with him later.

"Maybe I should go with you," Camila added.

"You've done enough."

She stepped toward me, biting her lower lip. For a split second, she looked like the Camila I used to know. "Please, Jacqueline. I didn't mean to... I should come. The Mordicum knows me."

"There isn't room for you." I let the door slam closed between us, wishing it felt better to walk away.

My Porsche was parked in the side drive next to Julian's sedan and a row of motorcycles belonging to three of his brothers. My car, with its canary yellow exterior, was the flashiest of the lot. The Rousseaux coven tended to go for more sophisticated automobiles or bikes. Thea didn't speak as she climbed inside.

"Should I be worried Julian will fly out the door and leap onto my hood?" I asked as I hit the ignition button. The stereo blared some dreadful pop song, and I turned it down quickly. "Because aluminum dents easily."

"I don't think he'll come after us," she said grimly.

"He fucked up that bad, huh?"

"Maybe I'm overreacting." She watched the house as I pulled out of the drive with absolutely no idea where I was going. "But if he suspected, he should have told me."

"Yes." I nodded in agreement as we raced along the coastal highway leading along the edge of Corfu. "But—and hear me out—perhaps he did not want to worry you during the holidays."

I heard her eyes roll even though I was focused on the winding road. "He should have told me."

I agreed with her. "Sometimes our lovers think they're protecting us when they're really hurting us."

"That sounds like experience talking," she said softly.

"I wish that wasn't true." I'd wished for so long that I'd nearly tricked myself into actually forgetting about the past. But the past was exactly that. I couldn't change it. All I could do was concentrate on the future, even if the future meant finally letting go altogether. "So, should we head to Venice?"

"Julian was going to make the arrangements," she said, looking over her shoulder into the night behind us. Was she hoping to see him following us? Or, like me, was she as eager to leave her problems back there?

"If we go to the house, I can get my wallet and book airfare," she mused. "There has to be something available."

I snorted before I could stop myself.

"You're right," she said with a heavy sigh that spoke of the weight she was carrying on her shoulders. "It's Christmas. We're never going to catch a flight."

"Don't worry about it." I couldn't help smiling as I delivered one piece of good news. "I might not be a Rousseaux, but I still have a private jet."

CHAPTER TWENTY-THREE

Julian

Camila was beginning to make an art out of dropping bombshells. I glared at her when she returned to the kitchen and Thea didn't. I wondered if it was considered a *faux pas* to spill blood on Christmas.

"Was that necessary?" I growled.

She didn't so much as flinch. Instead, she met my glare with one of her own. It was still strange to meet her eyes after all this time apart. Sebastian hadn't been wrong earlier when he'd called her a bitch. She was far from the Camila we had all doted on. Part of me wondered if, under different circumstances, I might like this version of her more. But right now, she was a colossal pain in my ass.

"I thought mates couldn't keep secrets from each other," she said, grabbing the open jar of peanut butter and sniffing it. Her nose wrinkled before she set it down. "Why do we even have that? Why pretend we need anything other than blood?"

I didn't bother to tell her it was for Sebastian. Our kid brother loved the shit. She didn't really care. It was just another one of her political statements. "Call your people and get them to release her mother."

Her eyebrow arched into a question mark. "Why would they

listen to me?"

"I thought you were their leader."

"Don't be stupid," she said with a laugh that raked down my frayed nerves. "The Mordicum and I share common interests, but I'm not their leader. In fact, I've been on my own for a while."

"Is that why you spout their beliefs every chance you get?" I demanded.

"I happen to agree with them about the vampire's place on the food chain." She shrugged. "But they're using me as much as I'm using them."

"For what?" I was in real danger of losing my temper now. Growing up, Camila had never picked fights, but wherever she'd been in the last few decades, she'd learned how to handle herself. That was precisely why I was worried about losing control. Our mother would be pissed if one of us wound up thrown through a window.

She leaned forward, beckoning with her finger, and I moved closer.

"Wouldn't you like to know?" she whispered. Camila laughed at my expression and dashed out of the room just as my fist cracked the marble counter.

Things had gotten out of hand. It couldn't be a coincidence that Camila was here. She was sowing seeds of discord. Was that her plan? To destroy us from the inside out? And if so, was that on the Mordicum's missive? Or was she driven by pure spite?

I stared after her, questioning why she was really here—and what I was going to do about it.

We couldn't avoid dealing with it for much longer, but right now, I needed to find Thea. Stalking into the living room, I found it empty.

I wound my way through the main level before descending into the lower level. A search of our former bedroom came up empty. I found my brothers in the billiards room with an open bottle of Scotch and boxes of Christmas cookies.

"Want one?" Sebastian asked, holding up a glass.

I shook my head. "Have you seen Thea?"

"Lost her already?" Lysander's head popped up from the couch.

I ignored him and surveyed the room, realizing someone else was missing. "What about Jacqueline?"

"She was on the phone," Thoren said. "She looked upset."

Of course he would notice. He was the most thoughtful of my brothers.

"Maybe she's with Camila," Sebastian offered.

Jacqueline was more likely to be having a tea party with our mother than she was to be willingly hanging out with Camila. I wondered if they would ever reconcile or if their friendship was over forever.

"They're around somewhere." Benedict shrugged before aiming his pool cue and taking a shot.

I didn't bother to stick around for more help from them. It didn't bode well that my best friend and my mate were missing, especially if Jacqueline was worked up. Racing upstairs, I threw open the door and discovered Jacqueline's car was gone.

"Fuck."

I had royally screwed up this time. Thea was safe, but if she'd left without a word, she was also pissed.

I'd started to walk out the door when I remembered our presents. If I couldn't soothe Thea, maybe the Stradivarius could. Maybe I'd play for her. Although given how long it had been, that might not win me any points. I turned and headed into the living room just as my mother wandered in from the hall. Her frown deepened when she saw everyone had left.

"What is going on?" Sabine demanded as I collected presents. She hovered next to me. "Where is everyone?"

"I think your peaceful family Christmas is over. At least if Camila has anything to say about it," I said without looking at her. After the stunt she'd pulled, I was out of fucks to give about what she wanted.

"Your brothers?"

"Drinking their way through the liquor cabinet. I have no idea where Dad is, and I don't care." I needed to find Thea. Now. "I need to go."

"We haven't even had supper," she continued to complain.

Now she was talking about food? Of course she was. The only thing my mother disliked more than being shown up was when others changed her plans. "So, you aren't planning to eat my fiancée?"

Sabine's response could best be summed up as withering. She stood by as I picked up the cufflinks that Camila had given me. There were a handful of other gifts, but I left them.

"Aren't you going to take those? I went shopping," my mother said with a sniff.

"What a hardship." Given that my mate had taken off with my best friend without a word, I wasn't in the mood to deal with my mother's emotional state. I was, however, ready for a fight. I stood and turned a glare on her. "As long as you persist in treating Thea like she is below you—below our family—I don't want *anything* to do with you."

Her throat slid, but she didn't blink. "Anything? And the wedding? I suppose you think you're going to elope?"

"Maybe we are." I didn't want to elope. I wanted to see Thea in a white dress. I wanted to make it something she would look back on for centuries. But more than any of that, I wanted to be at her side, surrounded by the people who loved us. Currently, my mother didn't fall into that category. "Why would you care? Your true heir is back. You don't need to play pretend with me anymore."

"True heir, my ass," Sabine hissed. "We both know she has something up her sleeve. And I would never dream of missing my child's wedding."

"Even if it's to a siren?" I tested her. "You're sending me mixed signals, Mother."

"You won," she pointed out. "I acknowledged your engagement publicly. What else is there?"

Seriously. I wanted to ask how much time she had. Instead, I decided to focus on what mattered. "Respect."

"I have always—"

"Respect for Thea," I cut her off. "I know vampires are slow to change, but I'm not going to let you treat her like shit for the next century."

"Century?" she repeated, ice coating her words. "Do you know something that I don't?"

"No," I said quickly. Thea might change her mind when she learned more about being turned. I didn't want to jinx it. The thought of spending a human lifespan with Thea and losing her was too much to bear. "She's too young, but I assume."

"So, she will be my replacement." My mother took a seat next to the Christmas tree. Her blue gaze wandered to the window and the dark sky outside.

I didn't bother to remind her about Camila.

"Is that why you hate her?" I asked. "Because she has no intention of taking your place."

"Is that supposed to make me feel better?" She lifted her eyes to me. "There is a natural course to things. I won't live forever."

"Feeling ill?" I muttered.

"At least your mate seems to take this seriously." She crossed her slender arms over her dressing robe. "I must admit I'm impressed with her. She's clever."

"I could have told you that if you would have listened."

"You will excuse me if I found your obvious bloodlust too chaotic to be trusted," she said. "Perhaps it's time I get to know her."

"Now?"

"It is the holidays—unless you have other plans." I could tell what she thought of that possibility.

"Actually, we might be traveling soon."

"Before the new year?" Her response was icy.

"My sources found her mother, and it's complicated."

"The mother who rejected her for loving a vampire?" she asked.

I started to nod when it hit me. "How did you know about that?"

"There is very little I don't know about my children's lives," she said, continuing on quickly when she spotted my fury. "And, believe me, I wish that was not the case at times. However, I am aware of the situation with Kelly Melbourne."

"How aware?" I asked suspiciously.

"I know about the cancer and her disappearance," she admitted. "I assume she is also a siren?"

"It would seem so." I kept the rest of our theories about Thea's parentage to myself.

But my mother seemed to sense what was on my mind. "And her father?"

"Thea doesn't know him."

"And do we think that's a coincidence?"

I didn't, but I said nothing.

My mother sighed and got to her feet, smoothing the creases in her gown. "I am not your enemy."

Our gazes locked, and I knew she believed that, but I wasn't quite ready to forgive her. "You have done everything in your power to destroy my relationship. You even went to the Council to stop it in Paris."

I waited for her to deny the accusation, but she didn't. I'd suspected as much. Despite her fear the evening that the Council had visited and demanded I end my romantic relationship with Thea in favor of a magical union, I'd known she was too powerful to be overruled by her fellow Council members.

She hadn't been afraid of what they would do. She had been afraid of what I would do.

"You knew I loved her," I accused. "You knew that fate had picked her as my mate, but you tried to stop it."

"I am your mother." She took a step toward me, somehow looking smaller than she had my entire life. "I have dreamed of your future since I carried you in my womb."

"And a future that included a mortal wasn't in your plans?"

Her eyes closed and her nostrils flared as she took a deep breath. "There are things you don't understand about our world and your place in it."

"Not this shit again." I threw my hands in the air. I was so over the cryptic threats and mysterious warnings. "Camila says the same thing, but she says you're the one who can't be trusted. That the Council can't be trusted."

My mother didn't respond. She remained silent for a moment before she opened her eyes and looked over my shoulder.

"Is that true?"

I whipped around to find my sister standing behind me.

"I know about the Council," Camila said with a shrug. "The Mordicum knows about them."

"You know nothing," Sabine said softly. "You're too young to understand."

"Then tell us," I interjected. "Stop making excuses."

I glanced at Camila, who nodded once that she was with me on this. We wouldn't be best friends any time soon. Our relationship might never recover, but we both deserved to know the truth. Camila had lost so much. Even if her children were still alive, she would never be the same. My own mate had questions. I had no idea if the truth about the Council could offer any answers, but I needed to find out.

"Tomorrow," my mother said thickly. "Return with your mate, and I will tell you everything."

• • •

The house was too quiet. I pulled into the private drive, noting the lack of lights on inside. Night had swallowed the sky, moonlight spilling across the grounds. Jacqueline's car wasn't here, and I knew there was no way my best friend would have just dropped Thea off. But if they weren't here, where were they?

Cold dread sluiced through me, clenching my stomach. I parked the car and walked slowly to the entrance. Part of me already knew what I would find, but I refused to believe it until I opened the door and found the security system still armed. It was the utter lack of life—the lack of her—that confirmed my worst fear. Thea wasn't here.

Had they bothered to come back at all?

"Don't be a controlling asshole," I ordered myself, even as I felt my tether wrapping its viselike grip around me. There were a dozen other explanations for their absence. Maybe Jacqueline had decided to take her on a joyride. My best friend loved to drive with the reckless abandon of an immortal. I hoped she wouldn't put my mate in any danger as I imagined Jacqueline whipping that German death trap around the curvy cliffside roads of the island. With any luck, they'd simply gone out for a drink.

I walked to the kitchen, wishing I would find a note on the counter. Another futile hope. There was no sign they'd been here at all.

Taking out my phone, I wandered into the living room and dialed Thea. In the corner, our Christmas tree was dark. Neither of us had plugged in the lights this morning. It looked exactly like I felt—like Christmas hadn't come at all.

"Hi! You've reached Thea," her phone answered, and I hung up. I didn't trust myself to leave a message. I wasn't sure I'd be able to do more than growl anyway.

Rubbing my chest, I walked onto the terrace off the main living area and stared at the endless ocean stretched before me. The night sky sparkled on the gentle waves. There was a time when I would have felt instantly soothed. It was the reason why I'd chosen my private island in the Keys. The ocean spoke to me, calmed me. It always had.

Until now.

Nothing loosened the knot around my heart. I wanted to believe that Thea would walk through the door any moment, a little tipsy but none the worse. Something told me, though, that she wasn't out joyriding or drinking.

Giving into my tether's demands, I dialed Jacqueline's number. It rang four times, and I was about to hang up when she answered.

"Hey, Jules." She sounded cheerful, which I hoped was a good sign.

Then it hit me.

What if Thea wasn't with her at all? What if she'd dropped

Thea off and someone had been waiting here?

"Is Thea with you?" I asked through gritted teeth.

There was a pause so long that I died a million deaths.

"Hold on," she finally said.

"Hold on?" I growled into the phone. "Please tell me you have my mate."

"I have your mate," she said in a soothing voice that only grated on my fraying nerves.

"Put her on the phone," I ordered.

"Hold on, caveman."

Caveman? My fangs protracted as if my very genetic material took offense to the joke. Still, she wasn't far off. If she only knew. Every instinct in my body wanted to hunt Thea down and drag her back to my bed. Maybe I wasn't as far removed from ancient humans as I wanted to believe.

"Look, Jules," Jacqueline said softly, "she doesn't want to speak with you, but she said she'll call you later."

"Later?" I repeated like I'd never heard the word before.

"Yes, it's a time that comes after now," she said drily.

"I am about ten seconds from coming out to look for you." In fact, I was already striding toward the front door.

"That might be a problem." Jacqueline was tiptoeing around something. Whatever it was, it couldn't be good.

"Jacqueline," I said in a voice filled with nearly as much venom as what was welling in my mouth, "where is my mate?"

"Sitting across from me," she said far too innocently.

"And where are you sitting?" I asked suspiciously.

Jacqueline cleared her throat. "On my jet."

I swore under my breath, half glad that my best friend was nowhere near me—because I would have ripped her apart. The tightness in my chest increased until I felt like I might suffocate.

"You can't take her to Venice," I managed. "There's no telling what the Mordicum will do if they get ahold of her."

Jacqueline didn't say anything for so long that I checked the screen to make sure the call hadn't dropped. I still didn't know why these fucking mobile phones were an improvement, considering how fragile and finicky they were. But the seconds continued to tick on the screen. Finally, she spoke. "Talk to Thea."

It was what I wanted, but when my mate got on the phone, she offered a half-hearted, "Hello."

"Thea, tell Jacqueline to turn the plane around." Maybe part of her wished she hadn't left, and if so, the request would activate her tether.

"I need to find my mother," she said in a flat voice.

So much for that last hope. It felt like she'd punched me in the gut. No part of her questioned her decision to leave me and go to Venice. I knew she was upset with me—that she believed I'd damaged our trust—but I hadn't expected her to leave.

"You can't get her back," I told her. "Not without going to the Mordicum."

"Then I'll go to the Mordicum," she said, like she was adding an item to a grocery list.

"You don't simply walk up to the Mordicum!" I roared. She needed to listen. How could she be this reckless when she'd seen what they were capable of at the opera?

"I'm not afraid of those assholes," she hissed back, "and if I want to, I will simply walk up to the Mordicum, and you can't stop me."

I needed to switch tactics. I had to make her see reason. She wasn't just putting herself at risk; she was risking her mother, too. Maybe if she saw that, she'd wait until we could come up with a better plan.

"Thea—" But my half-baked attempt was cut off by the call ending.

I stared at the screen.

She'd hung up on me.

My mate had hung up on me.

My tether gripped me fully in that moment like a chain that had run out of slack. Even if it hadn't, I knew what I had to do. If Thea was going to Venice, so was I.

I only hoped that I wouldn't be too late.

CHAPTER TWENTY-FOUR

Thea

I didn't know what had gotten into me. Yes, I was pissed at Julian, but deep down, I knew why he hadn't told me about my mother. Because I would have demanded to go to her.

Like I was doing right now.

Unlike Julian's private jet, which oozed masculinity, Jacqueline's was clearly custom designed for her. I trailed my finger along the gold inlay of the polished white side table. Across from me, Jacqueline was busily texting, her legs thrown over the side of the plush leather seat. After a moment, she tossed her phone into her lap and sighed.

"Now we're both in trouble," she said with a resigned smile.

"If Julian is mad at you—"

"Not Julian," she said quickly. "My mother. I was supposed to go over for dinner this week."

"What?" I nearly jumped out of my chair, but my lap belt held me in place. "Why didn't you tell me? Can we turn around?"

"Nonsense. We aren't going back," she scoffed with a wave of her manicured hand. "I didn't tell you because you needed me."

"And The Rites?"

Her smile flattened. "I know. I'm terrible. I really will go through with it if it means saving my sister."

"But?" I prompted.

She shifted in her seat, folding her legs under her and ignoring the safety belt unfastened at her sides. "There was a reason I resisted marrying Julian. You know, other than the fact that it would be like marrying my brother." She gagged. "No offense."

"None taken." If she had married him, things might be very, very different right now. I couldn't even imagine what that world would be like. Just thinking about my mate sent guilt churning in my stomach. I pushed thoughts of him away and focused on my friend. "What was the real reason?"

"I was in love with someone else," she said softly. "Sometimes, I think she might have been my mate, but things were different back then."

"And you couldn't be with her because she was a woman?" I guessed.

"Vampires are far more relaxed about such things," she explained with a smile. "We've seen every version of sexuality there is, but The Rites are more conservative, if ruthlessly practical."

"They're all about making little vampire babies." Just saying it made my heart flutter. That's what The Rites wanted from me.

"Purebloods wanted to grow their family trees." She shrugged. "Who can blame them?"

"There's something I don't quite understand," I admitted. "If a baby is half familiar and half vampire, then why does it become a vampire? Do they ever become witches?"

"Not officially. There are rumors, of course. That some children are born and turned when they reach the age of the Frenzy."

"Frenzy?" I repeated. That sounded…bad.

"Full-blooded vampires like Julian and me are born vampires, obviously, but for those born to a familiar and a vampire, they age like humans until they hit the age of the Frenzy. Basically, sometime in their twenties—usually late twenties, but everyone matures differently—their vampire genetics begin to reveal themselves."

"And then they go into a Frenzy?"

"All vampires experience it," she explained. "Your appetite becomes voracious because your body is taking its immortal form."

"Your appetite? So you eat a lot?"

"It's not only our appetite for blood." She winked at me, and heat rushed to my cheeks. Of course it wasn't. "For pureblood vampires, it sometimes happens in the first couple hundred years. That's why no one attends The Rites until they're at least five hundred." Jacqueline fell silent, and I knew she was thinking about her sister. I saw her throat slide, and I wondered what unpleasant memory she'd swallowed. "I was a disappointment to my parents. Not lovely and docile like Camila. They threw us together all the time, hoping she would rub off on me. It didn't work. That's why they had my sister. Trying to force me to marry Julian was one last attempt to civilize me, I think."

"None of it makes sense." I let out a sigh. "It all feels so old-fashioned."

"It *is* old-fashioned." Jacqueline got to her feet and made her way to the wet bar. She didn't even sway as we hit a pocket of turbulence. "But vampires are the original elitist snobs. Trust me."

"I believe you. I've met Sabine." It was hard to believe anyone could be snobbier than her, but Jacqueline's parents sounded like they might be close. "So, this woman you loved. Was she human? A familiar?"

"A vampire." She took out a bottle of vodka and poured some into two glasses, not even bothering with mixers.

The fact that she had loved a vampire surprised me. Was that the real reason why she avoided attending the season and its parties? To avoid an ex-lover? "Is she...still alive?"

"She's gone." She downed her drink in one gulp. I just stared at mine. "She has been for a long time."

"I'm really sorry." I meant it. I couldn't imagine losing Julian. "What happened?"

Vampires were practically invincible. I knew there were ways they could be killed in addition to the violent methods I'd witnessed, although no one seemed keen on telling me how. I couldn't blame them for that. If I had a ticket to immortality, I wouldn't want to give away my secrets, either.

"She was forced to attend The Rites. We swore we would find a way to get through it. No one knew our secret—but she met someone at The First Rite, and everything changed."

My unease deepened, and I reached across and took her free hand.

"She was married by the end of the season." Jacqueline continued, blood-tinged tears sparkling in her eyes. "Whisked away by one of the most powerful vampire heirs in the world, and that was it. She never spoke to me again. She didn't even try."

"What?" I gasped, squeezing her hand. "I can't believe it."

A single red drop fell down her cheek as she lifted her face to mine. "I've never told anyone this."

"I swear I won't say a word."

"I know." She squeezed my hand back, offering me a sad smile. "I'm not sure I want to keep it a secret anymore."

"Don't," I said fiercely. "Never apologize for who you are."

"I never have. That's always been my problem." She drew away, tossing her blond hair over her shoulder. "There's something you need to know. Something Julian needs to know if I can get up the courage to tell him."

"Whatever it is, you can tell us." I might have only known her for a few months, but I loved Jacqueline like a sister.

"I'm not sure Julian will agree." She sucked in a deep breath. "I recently found out why she never spoke to me again. For all these years, I blamed her for what happened—for letting that male close to her. I blamed her for allowing herself to be tethered."

"No." It slipped quietly from my mouth as I started to understand.

"I've been so angry at her for leaving me and choosing him." She shook her head as if trying to banish the memory. "But she was a virgin, and he took advantage of that—and I can't help but feel that it's partially my fault. I'd lost my virginity centuries before, like most vampires. Most vampires are encouraged to go to bed with another virgin as soon as they hit adolescence. It ensures no tethering. But she was never allowed to socialize, and by the time I realized my feelings for her, we couldn't risk it. I'd told myself I was protecting her, but now I realized I left her vulnerable to a monster."

I couldn't believe what she was telling me. Her story's similarities had to be a coincidence. Ice filled the pit of my stomach, spreading until I felt numb all over.

A door to the private cabin opened, and the jet's lone flight attendant strode in with a pretty smile. She looked at our glasses before pausing for Jacqueline to acknowledge her.

"We'll be landing soon," the attendant told us. "Can I get you another drink before we start the descent?"

I nodded even though I hadn't touched mine. I already knew I was going to need more than a drink after Jacqueline finished her confession. My eyes locked with hers as we waited to be alone again. The flight attendant brought us our glasses and slipped away without another word.

I held mine so tightly I thought it might shatter as I waited for Jacqueline to speak. She downed hers first. "I don't need to tell you who it was," she whispered. "You already know, don't you?"

My mouth was dry, so I took a sip of vodka. It burned down my throat, letting me know I wasn't dreaming.

"Now do you understand why I can't tell Julian?" she asked. "I've tried to so many times. Maybe he wouldn't have cared back then, but after all this time... Time changes things."

"It doesn't change everything," I told her. "You should tell him." The friendship between her and Julian wouldn't change. I was sure of that. If anything, he might be able to support her better than I could.

Her shoulders sagged, but I saw the resignation on her face. She knew I was right. Why was she so scared to tell him? "I will. There's only one more problem."

One? I could think of a dozen. Before I could say that, she finally admitted the question weighing on her mind.

"What do I do now that Camila is back?"

CHAPTER TWENTY-FIVE

Thea

Water sprayed my face as the small wooden boat shot through the lagoon toward Venice. The sea was dark and choppy under the cloudy night sky, and I clutched a small handle near the cabin of the speedboat that had picked us up at a dock outside the airport. We'd landed on the Italian mainland half an hour ago. I'd been mesmerized since I stepped foot on the boat. Next to me, Jacqueline scrolled on her phone, seemingly oblivious to the weather or the city ahead. Meanwhile, my teeth chattered from the cold as I caught my first glimpse of Venice's lights on the horizon.

A gasp of delight slipped from me as I wrapped my arms more tightly around my torso, wishing my wool coat did more to stop the cutting wind.

Jacqueline glanced up and frowned. "You should go inside," she yelled over the sound of the boat's engine.

I shook my head, pressing my lips together to keep her from seeing them tremble. I'd always wanted to travel to Venice—the city responsible for some of the greatest music the world had ever heard. I couldn't believe I was here now, even if the circumstances were troubling. Even if my relationship with music had changed. Even if I wasn't sure how I fit into that world any more than I fit into the magical one. Or that I would be here to find my mother, to save her because she was like me—because that music was buried somewhere deep inside her. She kept it hidden. Just as she had hidden me. And for what reason? They had found her, and I had abandoned her.

Ignoring the pang of fear and pain that bolted through my veins at the thought, I focused on the outline of the buildings ahead. This might be my only chance to enjoy my visit. I hadn't come to sightsee.

A few minutes later, I pried my frozen fingers from the handle and crawled into the cabin to get a break from the icy weather. Jacqueline followed me inside, frowning.

"Your lips are blue," she fussed, unwrapping her Burberry scarf from her neck and draping it around the one I already wore. "If you catch pneumonia, Julian will kill me."

I refrained from telling her that Julian was probably going to kill us both for taking off without him. I reached up and wrapped the ends of the cashmere scarf around my fingers. "How do we find the Mordicum?"

"Can we unpack first?" Jacqueline asked with a flat smile, like she already knew she'd lost the coming debate.

"We can't wait. Who knows how long they've had my mom or what they've done to her." I swallowed the bile that rose in my throat at the thought. I'd been opening Christmas presents while my mother was being held prisoner. A fresh surge of anger rose inside me.

"It's going to take some time to find the Mordicum," Jacqueline reminded me.

"We don't have time," I exploded. What if she had been taken from the hospital? What if I'd been nursing a grudge over our argument while she was being tortured or worse? I couldn't bear to think about it.

Jacqueline's face smoothed into a reassuring calm as she took my cold hand in hers. "It won't take long. I have many friends in the City of Masks. We'll find them quickly, but Thea..."

"Yeah?" I fought to keep the annoyance out of my voice. She was trying to help me.

"We need to figure out what we're going to do when we do find them," she said carefully. "I don't think it's a good idea to just show up and knock on the door."

Yeah, there was that. She'd been listening when I'd told Julian I would walk into the heart of the Mordicum after my mother. I'd mostly said it because I was upset with him. The truth was that I didn't have a plan. I'd been trying to figure one out since we took off in the jet. I looked at her hopefully. "Suggestions? This is my first hostage negotiation."

"It isn't mine." Jacqueline's lips twisted, and I wondered how many times she'd dealt with something like this. Maybe I didn't want to know. "The trick is to have something to negotiate with."

"Like money?" I asked.

"Maybe." But she shook her head. "Most vampires have money. I doubt that will be enough to get them to release her. It has to be something that they want just as much. If we knew why they took her, we could come up with something."

Me. They took her because of me. It felt like a hand reached inside me and squeezed my stomach. I felt myself blanch even as I tried to shake the nauseating realization. "We know why," I said softly. "There's only one thing they want, isn't there?"

"We don't know that," Jacqueline said quickly, but she didn't meet my eyes. "Just because Camila said…"

It wasn't a coincidence that the Mordicum had captured my mother. Camila had come after me to figure out what magic slept in my veins. If I was a siren, like we believed, Mom must be as well. Had they figured that out yet? And why would they care?

"Why would they want me?" I asked the question preoccupying my thoughts.

"I don't know, but it can't be good," she admitted. The boat slowed, and Jacqueline tipped her head. "I think we're here."

I followed Jacqueline out of the cabin to find we'd stopped in front of a palazzo. I stared up its worn brick facade as the captain maneuvered the boat carefully to a set of ancient stone steps covered in moss. Water lapped at the lower one, and I was wondering how we were going to get in when the gates opened to reveal half a dozen household staff.

"Home sweet palazzo," Jacqueline told me as she lifted our bags and passed them to a uniformed man inside.

"This is yours?" I asked.

"I usually come for Carnival," she said before climbing onto the lower step, nonplussed as the water washed over her shoes. "I love a good party—always plenty of open-minded humans." She flashed me a smile as she held out a hand to help me to the dry upper step.

I'd been to a vampire orgy, so I suspected I knew just how open-minded vampires liked their humans. I paused and looked out over the lagoon, trying to get a better look in the moonlight. There was a bridge a ways down that connected a cobbled street to this side of the water. Tall buildings rose on either side. Each one had several windows flanked by wooden shutters. It was too dark to get a feel for the place, but even at night, Venice captivated me. In my chest, I felt warmth flare, as if my magic was responding to the city as well. I touched the spot over my heart, surprised. Usually, I only felt my magic in the presence of Julian.

"Is anyone here?" I asked Jacqueline in a whisper, wondering if my mate had somehow beaten us here.

Her lips pursed, but she turned to one of the staff. *"È un uomo qui? Signor Rousseaux?"*

My heart fell when he shook his head no. I wasn't sure why. It's not like I was ready to face Julian yet. But if he wasn't here, what was stirring my magic?

"Come on." Jacqueline nodded inside. The household staff rushed off with our bags, their footsteps fading to echoes in the distance.

I gratefully stepped inside the palazzo, ready to finally get warm, and my mouth fell open. The entry from the water opened into a massive open-aired courtyard. In the center, a large cistern had been converted into a fountain. The brick walls gave way to plaster walls painted with a half-finished fresco that looked suspiciously familiar.

"Um, who painted that?" I asked, pointing to it.

"Da Vinci," she said with a shrug as she kicked off her wet shoes. She continued toward a stone staircase that led to what I assumed was the first floor.

"Oh, *him*," I said, feeling dazed as I studied it. The subjects of this work weren't David or the Madonna but rather elegant creatures with dark eyes and women who held light in their palms. He'd painted the magical world here on these walls. Had anyone even seen it?

"The *piano nobile* is this way," she called down to me, her lovely voice bouncing around the cavernous space.

"Piano...?"

"It means the main floor," she said patiently.

After I shook off my shock, I followed my friend up the stairs. The entry was dimly lit but warm despite its stone floors and ancient walls. Jacqueline looped her arm through mine, guiding me past a pair of large doors draped on either side by heavy silk curtains.

"The garden is through there," she explained. "The tour can wait until morning. Your bedroom is through here."

"But—" A yawn cut off my protest.

"You need to sleep," she said firmly.

I didn't fight her. She was right, and until we had a plan, there wasn't much we could do. Jacqueline showed me to a guest room lit only by candles. The walls were covered with brocade paper in a deep red that shimmered a little in the candlelight. I paused for a moment to peek out the window to the dark lagoon below before she pushed me gently toward the four-poster bed. Heavy tapestries were pulled back to reveal black silk sheets and a small mountain of pillows.

"I'll be next door." She pointed to a silk rope hanging next to the bed. "If you need anything—food, water—pull that, and someone will come."

I nodded as I toed off my shoes and threw myself into the soft sheets. My eyelids felt heavy, like I'd never slept before. They were closing as Jacqueline crept toward the door. Before she could reach it, I felt another flare of magic. This time, it felt like a tug. I bolted upright, eyes wide and alert, and she stopped with her hand on the door.

"Thea," she called, "is everything okay?"

I rubbed at the spot again and sighed. "I think Julian is coming. My magic is acting up."

She snorted. "I don't need magic to tell me that. He'll probably be here when we wake up." She hesitated. "I can tell him to go to hell if you want me to. Just say the word."

"That's okay," I mumbled with a smile. It meant a lot that she was willing to side with me over him, but it wasn't like I could avoid my mate forever.

"Sweet dreams," she said, but I was already drifting toward them.

• • •

I woke in suffocating darkness, and it took me a minute to remember where I was. Sitting up, I discovered that the tug I'd felt before falling asleep had tightened like a vise around my chest. My hands clawed at my skin, as if I could free myself. After a moment, the chain loosened slightly, and I took a deep breath. The candles had burned out, so it took a moment for my eyes to adjust to my surroundings.

Moonlight poured through the window. I slipped from bed, drawn to it. As soon as my feet hit the floor, a tug redirected my attention, pulling me toward the door.

Jacqueline was right. Julian had come, and apparently he wasn't going to let me sleep. I grumbled under my breath about overprotective vampires as I searched for my abandoned shoes. After I felt two more tugs, I finally gave up.

The palazzo was quiet as I tiptoed into the corridor. The door next to mine was ajar. I peeked in to find the bed empty but rumpled. Jacqueline was up, probably seeing to Julian's arrival. Since I hadn't gotten the tour, I had no idea where to go. Turning, I started in the opposite direction only to find the tightness in my chest lessening.

Interesting.

Spinning back around, I took a step and felt it squeeze around me. I followed the sensation until it loosened again. As soon as I changed my path, it tightened again. It felt like the equivalent of a magical booty call. Not that I was going to let Julian into my pants that easily.

When I stepped into the entry, there was a strong pull toward the garden doors.

"Got it," I said, feeling silly for talking to myself. A single candle remained lit on a table a few feet from the doors, and I picked it up. Holding it in front of me, I went to the doors, expecting to see Jacqueline and Julian arguing in the moonlight. But the garden was empty. I'd started to turn away when a magnetic force yanked me back toward the door.

The ground was cold under my bare feet as I stepped into the garden. I held the candle up to look around, and instantly, a draft of wind snuffed it.

Crap on a cracker. I was not about to wander around a pitch-black garden looking for anyone, even my mate. He could come and find me inside, *under the covers*, if he wanted me.

My fingers turned the handle to go back into the house, but as soon as the door opened a crack, another gust slammed it shut. Awareness crept like a spider up the back of my neck, and I turned slowly to find I was no longer alone.

Although we'd met only once before, I recognized him even in the dark. Inside me, magic flamed to life, and I cried out as it burned so hot I thought I might spontaneously combust. I opened my mouth to beg him to stop doing whatever he was doing, but my eyes snagged on a limp body he held by the neck.

Jacqueline's blond hair streamed behind her still frame, her head twisted at an odd angle. She was dead. A scream rose in my throat.

"Silence," a deep voice commanded, snuffing out my cries like the candle. The scream shredded my throat as it tried to get free. But it was no use. I'd been compelled. I clawed at my neck, and the man groaned. "You may speak quietly."

There were only two words that came to mind as I stared, shell-shocked, at him. "Willem Drake."

"Thea," he greeted me.

My gaze darted to Jacqueline. Heart hammering in my chest, I looked away. "You killed her."

"She'll recover," he said, his eyes as dark as the night sky. "At least she will as long as you come with me."

I shook my head. "My mate will be here any minute, and—"

"I'm not afraid of Julian Rousseaux." He spoke his name with disgust. "Although I am disappointed in your choice."

Fury coursed through me, and I stepped toward him with a clenched fist. Was that what this was about? "I'm not, so if you think you're going to steal me away from him—"

"I don't have to steal you, Thea," he said with a wicked laugh. "You'll come with me whether you like it or not."

"I will, huh?" Even as defiance surged inside me, I felt the tug and yank of a chain dragging me toward our unwelcome visitor. There was nothing gentle or reassuring about it. This wasn't my tether inviting me toward Julian. This was a shackle, and Drake held the other end. I fought the urge. I wouldn't go with him willingly. "And why is that?"

He let go of Jacqueline, and her body crumpled to the ground with a soft thud. Willem reached out a gloved hand. "Because you don't have a choice. You will come with me because I am your sire."

CHAPTER TWENTY-SIX

Julian

I could swim faster than this.

Maybe it was his human eyes or the unearthly darkness of the murky lagoon, but it was well past midnight when the boatman maneuvered the water taxi up to the steps of Jacqueline's palazzo. I'd expected to find the house dark, but instead light shone through every window. Fear gripped me, and I reached out with my magic, searching for my mate. Concentrating on my tether, I hoped to feel her at the other end, but it felt nearly as taut as when I'd left Greece to come after her.

I didn't wait for the boat to dock completely before I bounded out of it and onto the wet steps. The boatman shouted something at me, but I was already pounding on the ancient gate that led into the private courtyard. There was a flurry of activity before a human servant rushed down the steps to let me in.

"Name?" he asked.

My patience was at an end. Thrusting a hand through the gate, I grabbed him by the shirt and slammed him against the door. "Rousseaux. Now, let me in."

He fumbled for his keys, the damp odor of terror leaching from him. "Y-y-yes, sir."

To his credit, the boatman stopped yelling after that. I dropped my hold on the servant, allowing him to open the doors.

I tossed my wallet at him. "Pay him."

"Right away," he said.

I started up the steps, taking them with mortal speed, not wanting to waste time compelling the captain. As soon as I was inside, I paused long enough to draw a deep breath. Jacqueline's sweet floral scent overpowered Thea's, but it was still there: the clove-spiked violet of my mate.

I had started in its direction when a few household staff rushed into the corridor and halted. Most backed away from me, but one— an older woman—held her ground.

"Where is she?" I demanded of the woman. She stared blankly at me, and I bit back a groan. *"Dov'è lei?"*

The woman pointed a trembling finger toward the back gardens. I didn't bother to hide my nature as I flashed toward them. Jacqueline's staff would be compelled. Most of them were likely members of the palazzo's *cortège*.

That made my fear flare brighter. They weren't afraid because a vampire had shown up in the night. Something else had happened here tonight. A memory of Camila's house the night of the fire came to mind. Her servants had been alert but terrified as they'd clustered helplessly outside the burning estate.

My empty stomach churned. I hadn't fed since last night. Not with the holiday bullshit preventing a moment alone with Thea. I'd gotten used to regular meals. I ignored the angry, clawing hunger inside me as I raced toward the garden.

There were no lights out here save for a few lanterns scattered near the door. My eyes fell on a single candle lying in the grass a few feet away, as if it had been knocked from someone's hand. I whipped around, looking for Thea, but only found more staff huddled around an outdoor chaise where Jacqueline rested. She pushed them away when she saw me, her face blanched white.

"Julian." Grief coated her voice, and I knew from hearing my name alone that whatever had gone wrong, Thea was involved.

I crumpled to my knees on the cold grass, only aware of one thing. I lifted my face toward the moon, breathing in the night air. A chill stung my lungs, but it was there. Faintly. Thea's scent. It hung like smoke from smoldering ashes in the air. It was a shadow—a remnant. Soon even it would be gone. As it faded, I felt the tether connecting us go slack, as if someone had let go of the other end.

"Nooo!" The cry disappeared into the night, and I collapsed onto my hands, my fingers searching the blades of grass as if I might find some lingering piece of her there.

A moment later, Jacqueline sank to the ground next to me. She reached a tentative hand toward me, but I jerked away. Falling back to my knees, I stared at my best friend.

Deep shadows, as dark as bruises, rimmed her eyes. The color hadn't returned to her face, making her skin so pale I could see every purple vein beneath the surface. Her hair was tousled like she'd just gotten out of bed, but bits of leaves and grass stuck out from it. A closer look revealed dirty smudges marring the white silk of her nightgown.

"What…" I couldn't form the question.

"Leave us," she called to the servants, her voice quivering. Once we were alone, she lowered her voice to a whisper as if she didn't trust them. "He came into my bedroom," she said, swallowing as she added, "Willem."

I couldn't speak, but I felt her words sap whatever lingering adrenaline I had in me.

"He broke my neck," she added quickly. "The servants found me in the garden and waited until I woke up. Julian, they searched the house. Thea…"

I didn't need her to finish the sentence. I already knew, just as I'd known my mate wasn't here as soon as I arrived.

Willem had Thea.

I thought of my sister laughing in the flames as he tried to burn her alive. I thought of how easily he'd kept her from us. Of what Camila had told me about how he'd raped her the night they met.

And now he had taken my mate as well. My brain replaced the images of Camila with Thea, and I gagged, choking on the scant liquid contents of my stomach.

"I'm so sorry," Jacqueline whispered.

I couldn't look at her. I didn't dare to look at her.

"We'll find her," she added passionately.

All I could do was laugh. In what condition? I kept that despairing thought to myself. "How?"

"The Mordicum. They must know where he is, right? It can't be a coincidence that they're here at the same time as him."

I managed a nod. She had a point, but it did nothing to soothe the ache inside me.

"Julian!" she called. "Don't fall apart on me."

Something snapped inside me. The world shifted and grew dark as I turned my fury onto her. "My mate is missing," I growled. Despair melted into white-hot rage. Wings beat in my chest as my magic bellowed to life, but there was only night and claws and fangs. With no golden kernel of Thea to hold my darkness at bay, it consumed me. "And I will tear this city and anyone who stands in my way apart until I find her again."

"That's better," she said with a sigh of relief. "But look at me. Please." I lifted my black eyes to hers, and she flinched from whatever she saw on my face. Jacqueline squared her shoulders and met my gaze. "We will find her. Whatever it takes."

I forced myself to nod. She knew contemporary Venice better than I did. I needed her help. I'd left here centuries ago under questionable circumstances. Then I was known as something else: the Scourge of Venice. I never thought I would be that creature again, but I'd been left with no choice. I knew that when the moment came, I would face Willem alone.

And then, I would rip his heart out and feed it to him.

CHAPTER TWENTY-SEVEN

Thea

I paced the length of the room for the hundredth time, searching the space for anything that might help me. I had no idea where I was. I had no idea how long it had been since Willem had carried me into the night. But I especially had no idea how the hell I was going to get out of here.

The room itself was nice—much nicer than I'd expected, considering I was a prisoner. Other than the fact it was locked from the outside, it might have been a guest room, albeit by vampire standards. If the room's walls were any indication, I wasn't in a palazzo. Rather than plaster walls or frescoes, I was surrounded by walls of cold, jagged stone that looked rather medieval. The king-size bed was outfitted with luxurious white linens and a half dozen feather pillows. It was the only seemingly modern object in the room. Lanterns were lit on either side of it. A desk that looked like it had been stolen from an ancient castle was wedged in the corner along with an even older-looking chair. The only other source of light was two small arched windows near the top of the twelve-foot-high ceiling.

I felt like I'd woken up in a gothic novel.

Except I hadn't woken up here. I'd walked right into it. Just like

I'd walked right to Willem Drake's side when he commanded it.

What the hell was going on?

Someone pounded on the door, as if some benevolent god heard my unspoken question. I took a few steps back as the metallic scrape of the bolt split the air. The door opened to reveal a girl about my age wearing a thin, nearly transparent gown.

"Hello?" I said uncertainly.

"Master Drake invites you to breakfast."

"I'm not hungry," I said slowly, but she simply stepped to the side like I hadn't spoken.

She was either compelled or a robot doing a damn good impression of being a vacant human. She didn't speak again as she stood there with the door open.

I had two choices: I could refuse and stay here, staring at her, or I could get out of this room and get some answers.

Although something told me that getting answers out of Willem Drake would only be possible if he allowed it. Taking a deep breath, I walked slowly out the door.

"This way," the girl said cheerfully.

She guided me down a corridor that only further cemented my feeling that I'd been taken to some type of old fortress.

"Do you work for Willem Drake?" I asked, wondering if she had any answers to give me.

She looked at me like I was speaking a different language. "I serve him."

Did I want to know what that meant?

I decided I didn't. Instead, I focused on memorizing our footsteps. I had no idea where she was taking me, but any information at all would be useful at this point.

There were no more windows. No glimpses out of the prison I'd found myself in. The corridor emptied into a large dining room, and I came to a stop when I spotted Willem sitting at the end of a mammoth oak table laid for a formal meal, although no food was present. Not that I would eat anything he offered.

My stomach grumbled in protest, but I ignored it.

"I'm so glad you could join me." Willem gestured to the seat across from him. "Please."

I took the chair without a word as Willem curled his index finger and beckoned my companion to his end of the table. She floated toward him, stopping when she reached his chair.

"My gratitude," he said. "You may serve me tonight as a sign of my appreciation."

He couldn't actually mean...

The girl stretched a reedy arm covered in scars, pride radiating from her. I averted my eyes but caught the glint of Willem's knife. I knew about the *cortège*. I'd seen them in passing at events, but this felt different. She was too thin, and there were far too many cuts on her arm. Still, the girl turned her palm without so much as a wince and let the fresh slash drip into a small silver bowl.

"I heard a rumor Julian Rousseaux took a mate," he said, his eyes flickering from the blood to me.

I didn't move. I didn't allow even a muscle in my jaw to twitch.

"I hardly cared when I first heard," he said, "though I was mildly surprised. Julian never seemed interested in a partner, but the rumors kept swirling."

"Even to you?" I couldn't stop myself. "It's hard to believe gossip reaches dead people."

"Yes, my death was another rumor." His sharp smile sent my stomach churning. "One easily swallowed. Gossip is gospel in the vampire world. Most immortal beings have lived to see it all, so they believe anything they hear."

"And when they find out you are alive?" I eyed my knife and fork, wondering if either might be a useful weapon.

"It will cause a stir, but nothing like the scandal when they realize what Julian has done to you."

I blinked. "Me?"

"Have you learned your true nature?" he asked. The *cortège* began to move away, but Willem caught her wrist. Lifting her arm to his mouth, he licked the faint trickle of blood that remained. Her eyes shuttered almost reverently, and my distaste morphed into revulsion. He smiled when he saw my disgust. "Humans serve a necessary purpose in the food chain."

"She's alive," I challenged him. "Not some piece of meat for you to nibble on."

"A hypocrite." He clicked his tongue at me, finally releasing the girl. She scuttled back to her place in the dark corner without another sound. "I should have expected that from a child raised by Kelly."

He let my mother's name dangle between us. I couldn't be sure if it was an olive branch or bait, so I let it hang there.

Willem swirled his goblet of blood like a snobby wine enthusiast. "You have no interest in how I know your mother or why you're here?"

"I assume you'll tell me." I crossed my arms with a slight shrug, hoping he couldn't pick up on how my heart had sped up. "You seem to love to hear yourself talk."

He was silent for a moment and so still that my skin began to itch. But even though he didn't move, his eyes shadowed.

"We should be clear on a few things, my dear. I am the head of my house. Not my mother, gods rest her soul. Or my wife, may she be damned. *Me*. And I find your sense of humor tiring. You will keep your little jokes to yourself."

"And if I don't?"

"This is a request. Next time, it will be an order."

"I don't take orders," I said coolly.

"You won't have a choice. I am your sire, remember? You will obey my commands, like it or not."

I swallowed as he circled back to what he'd said last night in the garden. Part of me wanted to know what he meant. Part of me suspected I already knew.

He smirked as he took a sip from his goblet. My eyes tracked the movement, my gums aching as I caught a glimpse of the blood. "Would you like a drink of your own? It can be arranged."

"No," I said quickly, but he snapped his fingers, and another of the *cortège* appeared from the shadowy corners of the room. The young man held out his wrist, but I shook my head. "I don't..."

"Liar," Willem murmured. "I sense your hunger. Why deny it?"

"I'm not... I don't..." I didn't know how to finish my own sentences.

"Tell me the truth," he demanded.

I felt tightness gripping me. I mashed my lips together, determined to tell him nothing.

"Have you drank blood before?"

"Yes." My answer slipped from me before I could stop it.

"Have your fangs appeared?" he asked next.

I nodded, the ache in my mouth growing stronger.

"Show me."

I opened my mouth immediately.

"Show me your fangs, Thea," he clarified with a sigh of impatience.

Before I could tell him that I didn't know how, a sharp sting replaced the ache as my fangs lengthened. My eyes widened as I realized just how much control Willem Drake had over me—over my body. He could force me to do anything he wanted. It was enough to make me want to vomit.

"There they are," he said. "Now, drink."

"I..." But I was already reaching for the young man's hand, already guiding his wrist to my mouth. I hesitated for a moment, realizing that I had no idea what I was doing.

"Give in to your true nature," Willem instructed.

I felt a tiny pop, as if his words had snapped my self-control, and I sank my teeth into the man's flesh. I hated it—hated how rich his blood tasted on my tongue. I hated how much I wanted it. I hated that I didn't want to stop. But I drank deeper, savoring how it heated in my throat. The world around me dimmed into shadows even as I became aware of the entire room. I heard Willem's slow heartbeat, the soft, even breathing of the other members of the *cortège*, and the gradual slowing of the man's heart.

"Finish him if you like," Willem said with a dark chuckle. "I have plenty more."

I jerked away and dropped the man's arm. Shoving my chair back, I wrapped my arms around my shoulders. The young man's skin was waxy, as if he was only a few moments from death. He swayed unsteadily on his feet, and I fought the urge to cry. I'd done that to him. I wouldn't do it again. I wouldn't allow Willem to turn me into a monster. "I don't drink blood!"

"All evidence to the contrary." He pushed the *cortège* away. "Go find your keeper."

I didn't ask what a keeper was. I could only guess. These humans were nothing more than cattle to him, compelled to do whatever he said.

"I'm not a vampire," I whispered.

"No," he said, a slow smile spreading across his face. "Not yet."

CHAPTER TWENTY-EIGHT

Julian

"Will they respond?" Jacqueline asked, watching my pen fly across a piece of heavy linen paper. Dawn crept into the room as the sun rose along the Venetian horizon. It had been hours, and we had no leads on Drake or the Mordicum. That left me only one choice: to ask for help from the source least likely to grant it to me.

"Let's hope," I muttered as I folded the letter into crisp thirds. I wasn't exactly following proper etiquette using her stationery, but I didn't have a choice. It hadn't occurred to me to send for the family insignia before I left Greece—not that my mother would have obliged. She would see my plan as reckless and refuse to be associated with the scheme. My best friend, on the other hand, felt responsible for my mate's disappearance. Even though I wouldn't admit I did as well, I shouldn't drag her into this mess. I slipped the letter into the cream envelope and paused. "Are you certain? You know what it might mean if I send this."

"Of course." She rolled her eyes. There was no hint of her usual smile. No sign that she hadn't recovered from her attack the night before. But her lack of humor was the only clue that she was upset. There had been no hesitation when I'd asked for a pen and paper to write a note to *Le Regine*, the vampire queens who ruled over the lagoons.

"Let's hope I can still find one of the *bocche di serpenti*." I stood and grabbed the jacket I'd flung across the chair back. The private mailboxes were hidden throughout Venice, disguised as sculptures and carvings of snakes—used by *Le Regine* to keep tabs on the immortal and mortal citizens of the city. The idea had been so successful that the Council of Ten had copied it for their own purposes. But while the lions' mouths the Venetian patricians had created had mostly been removed on Napoleon's command, the vampires' secret network remained active. I just had to get my bearings.

"One of my people can take it." She turned and spoke to the woman standing closest to her. A few moments later, the woman returned with two footmen.

Unease churned inside me as I watched the mortal disappear into the palazzo's corridor. I would stop at nothing to get Thea back, but I wasn't a monster. Not anymore. Sending someone else to deliver a request could catch the attention of one of the local *cavalieri*, the knights sworn to protect the queens. "Is that a good idea?"

"It's not the seventeenth century. The *cavalieri* are gone. No one is watching the old boxes." She passed the letter to one of the footmen. He disappeared out the door with my letter in hand.

Centuries ago, spying on the boxes might tell you as much as the letters placed inside them. But Jacqueline was right; that was lifetimes ago. Things had changed in Venice, and the message would reach the queens almost instantly, thanks to a spell cast long before magic slept.

Jacqueline yawned as she dropped into an armchair next to the fire. It was unusual for vampires to be tired, but not unheard of, especially after suffering a mortal wound. Considering that her neck had been snapped a few hours ago, she'd recovered quickly, even by vampire standards. But I saw the dark smudges under her eyes and the pallor of her skin.

"You should get some rest," I said, ignoring the rumble of my stomach.

"Isn't that the pot calling the kettle black?" Jacqueline pointed out, picking up on the noise. "You need to feed."

She'd been on me to feed since my arrival, as if she could calm me with a little fresh blood in my stomach. "I can't," I gritted out. "I promised Thea I wouldn't feed from anyone else." Just saying her name was like slicing open a fresh wound. I winced as my imagination began playing a reel of the horrors my mate was enduring at Willem's hands.

"That was stupid," Jacqueline said to my surprise. She swung her long legs up and tucked them underneath her. "What will you do when she…"

"Dies?" I finished for her, saying the word that neither of us wanted to say.

"Or becomes pregnant. It's not good for the baby if the mother's resources are being depleted by Daddy's appetite." She had a point, but I couldn't bring myself to do more than nod. The only thing worse than thinking about Thea was considering our future together—a future that hung by an ever-thinning thread the longer she was missing.

"I don't need blood," I said softly. My stomach growled again, as if outing my lie, but this time we both ignored it.

"If you won't feed properly, at least have some food." She picked up a bowl of fruit that one of the servants had brought to us earlier, and I frowned as I plucked a bunch of grapes from it.

I popped one in my mouth, chewed, and swallowed. "Happy now?"

"Ecstatic," she said flatly, putting the bowl back. "Julian, we'll find her."

I'd lost count of the number of times she'd told me this. At first it had been to soothe me. Then it was to soothe herself. Now it was just a habit. "There's no trace of her."

"He's probably got a glamour on her," she said gently. "The queens will know something, and I can send word to my—"

"No," I cut her off. "No one else knows about this. Not yet."

"Even the queens?" Her eyes fell to the door her servant had left through, letter in hand.

"I've only asked them for an audience."

She took a deep breath and nodded as she caught on to what I was saying. "You don't trust them. Why?"

"I don't know if I can trust them, but I do know that I'm unwelcome here."

"Did you really cause that much trouble?" She bit into a glossy red apple. After her attack, the food would help her more than it would help me.

"I was asked to never return," I said tightly.

"Asked is better than exiled."

"Their letter was strongly worded." And very clear. "I'm not welcome here."

Jacqueline shook her head. "I shouldn't have brought her here. I wasn't thinking."

"About my past?"

"About anything," she said. "I couldn't tell her no. I didn't want to tell her no. It was almost like…"

"Magic," I said gruffly. "We need to find out whatever we can about her siren lineage."

"We need to find her mom."

I knew she was right, but searching for Kelly Melbourne was moving further and further down my list. "We need to find Thea."

"Look." Jacqueline shifted in her chair, moving to bring her face in line with mine. "I know that, but what if Kelly can help us? She is Thea's mother."

"And I'm her mate," I roared.

Jacqueline fell silent as I rose and paced the room.

"I should be able to find her—to feel her! It's as if she just vanished. She was there and then…" I swallowed and turned toward the mantel, pretending to study an ancient clock still ticking above the fire. "I can't feel her anymore."

There was nothing on the other end of my tether. Her scent—

petals smoked in ash and spice—was entirely gone now. It was like she'd never existed.

"Why would Willem hurt her?" Jacqueline asked, drawing me back to my senses. "He could have done that before. He could have done it that day in Corfu, but he didn't. He wants her for something."

"I wish that made me feel better." It didn't. I thought of Camila and what she'd said to me. "There are some things worse than death."

"I know," Jacqueline said softly, and I heard a pain in her voice I didn't dare ask about.

"You should get some rest."

"Only if you do," she countered.

"Fine." I held out my hand to help her out of her chair.

She blinked as if my response surprised her. It wasn't that I wanted to sleep—or even that I would. My reasons were too personal to share even with her.

"I'll have Maria take you to Thea's room. I assume you'll be sharing her bed as soon as she returns to it." She shot me a limp smile. It was a pitiful excuse at a joke but a courageous attempt at optimism.

We made our way down the sun-soaked corridor that had been so dim and quiet when I'd arrived. But even in the presence of morning, I felt lost in the dark. I said goodnight to Jacqueline at her room and followed Maria to the next door.

"If anyone brings a message to me, notify me immediately," I commanded her.

"Of course. Is there anything else I can bring you?" the crone asked me as she placed a withered hand on the knob and opened the door.

Night-blooming jasmine roasted in a fire. Almonds crushed with rose petals and cloves to steep in sensuous tea.

Thea's scent hit me, and I resisted the urge to fall to the ground and trace it back to where she'd last been.

"I'd like to be alone." I slipped into the room and closed the door before I collapsed on it.

I had looked inside the space before and knew she wasn't hiding there somewhere—her scent was too faint—but I'd ordered the room to be left alone while we continued our search. Not only because it wouldn't do any fucking good to keep looking but also because I needed whatever scraps of her I had left to be kept safe. There were pieces of her scattered throughout the room. One of her shoes peeked from under the bed. A bag sat unopened in a chair near the fireplace. And on the nightstand...

I picked up her engagement ring, fresh fear pulsing through me. She had taken it off—likely to sleep—but what if...

I placed it on the table, refusing to let myself consider how badly I'd fucked things up between us. She wasn't missing because of Jacqueline; she was missing because of me. The thought was almost too much to bear. Instead, I sank into the black silk sheets and cradled her pillow in my arms. No one who saw me now would guess the horror I'd rained upon this city centuries ago. No one would think me a threat.

And they would be very wrong.

Because drinking in the faint remnants of her awakened the violence in my blood and the magic buried inside me. I wasn't breaking down; I was readying for what came next—for paying whatever bloody price I had to in order to hold her in my arms again.

Sometime later, a soft knock roused me. I shook sleep from me and went to the door to find Jacqueline there. Her hands twisted together as she stepped to the side.

"A message arrived."

"Where is it?"

"Waiting at the side door," she said.

I was already on my way. Two of Jacqueline's men waited by the door, which remained open to the street. On the other side, a woman in a red cloak stood silently, holding a large box. She wore the *moretta*, a black mask that covered everything but her eyes.

"She refuses to speak," one of the men told me, "but we assume she's here for you."

"She can't speak," I corrected him, nodding to her. The mask she wore was old-fashioned and meant to protect its wearer's identity—down to the sound of her voice. It was held in place by biting down on a bead sewn into the other side. Only one group still wore this type of covering—*Le Vergini*, the queens' personal handmaidens.

It seemed my letter had been received.

She took a step forward and held the box out to me.

This was their response? A present?

"What is it?" Jacqueline asked, coming up behind me as I lifted the lid. "Why would they send you that?"

I took one look at what was inside and knew it wasn't a present. It was an order.

I closed the lid and tipped my head to the handmaiden.

"They sent it to summon me," I told Jacqueline quietly as unpleasant memories rushed through me. "The queens will see me."

I only wondered what price they would demand.

My heart hammered as I nodded to the woman that I would return before closing the door and heading back to my bedroom. I was dimly aware of Jacqueline following, but my gaze seemed to narrow and constrict on the box in my hands. Was it a test or a punishment that my life had come full circle? That my future depended on the bloody secrets of my past?

I could barely stand the sight of the box and what it represented. I should have known the price they would demand. *Le Regine* wouldn't do a favor out of sentimentality. Shadows crept into my vision, as though they'd appealed to my basest nature. That's what they wanted, though. The queens had no use for a pureblood vampire gentleman. They wanted an animal. They wanted me to be a monster once again. And I would. I'd said I would do anything to get Thea back.

But would she want me after I became that beast again?

Warm blood coated my hands, and I dropped the box before I

realized it was my mind playing tricks on me. Its contents spilled across the mussed sheets: a tricorn hat, a black cloak, a leather *bauta* mask, and a folded piece of paper. Picking up the note, my unease deepened as I read the message scrawled in elegant script.

Return to us, il flagello, before asking favors.

Il flagello—the scourge. That was how I was remembered in the narrow alleys and canals of Venice. Several lifetimes had passed since I'd worn that mask or borne that name, but my sins weren't to be forgiven. Shame twisted my gut as I remembered the vow I'd made when I left. Not because I would break it, but because I wouldn't even hesitate before doing so.

"Maybe this is a bad idea," Jacqueline said, leaning against the doorframe.

"It's a fucking terrible idea," I grumbled as I picked up the hat, "but I don't have a choice."

"There are other people we can ask—your mother," she suggested. "*Le Regine* might be more willing to hear her out."

"Unlikely." Bitterness coated my words. There had been a time when the queens might have listened to my mother, but as their grip on the vampire world constricted, they'd clung to control of Venice more tightly. I'd left their service after they clashed with my mother over some secret or another—called home to see to family matters, and then forbidden to return to the city. My mother would have no sway over the paranoid queens, but she would be as pissed as they were over my return.

"I don't like this." Jacqueline wrapped her arms around her waist and held herself. "I should go with you."

"No." I turned to her, dropping the hat back in the box. "Someone has to be here if he makes contact."

"Jules…" Her teeth sank into her lower lip as she trailed away. She was holding back, and I knew why.

The chances that Willem Drake would send a message were slim. If he saw Thea as a hostage, there was a possibility, but he'd approached her in Corfu. It was much more likely he wanted her in particular. There would be no message, and we both knew it.

The truth was that I wouldn't drag Jacqueline into this. Not with the queens and not with Drake. My best friend could hold her own in a fight, but this was looking like war.

"I'm not going to just sit around and wait—"

"That is exactly what you'll do!" I exploded, the world turning black as I stalked toward her. "You won't go anywhere near the queens."

She held her ground with a mildly annoyed frown. "But I can't just wait around, either. I need to be helpful. This is my fault."

"You can't go after Drake. He's proven he can get to you," I said coldly. "I lost my sister to that psychopath. Now he has my mate. I won't lose anyone else."

"Camila is alive—"

"Camila is a monster," I roared, "because of him—because of what he did to her!"

Jacqueline clamped her mouth shut. She didn't dare contradict that. She couldn't.

"Fine!" She threw her hands in the air. "This has something to do with Thea's mother. I'll focus on getting to her."

"Call Camila." I could live with that. The Mordicum were dangerous, but my sister might be able to help.

"I thought Camila was a monster," she said coolly.

"She is," I murmured. "Maybe we need monsters on our side."

Maybe that was how I could justify what I was going to do now. "Okay."

"Don't do anything stupid." I slid the cloak around my shoulders. Its weight settled over me, heavier from the weight of the past it represented.

"I could say the same." But there was no amusement in her voice.

We both knew that I would do whatever it took to get Thea back, foolish or not.

"Here." She handed me the *bauta*.

I studied its familiar lines—the jutted angles of the chin, the rounded cheeks, and the exaggerated nose. Unlike most masks of its type, there were no gilded edges or painted flourishes. It was made entirely from smooth, worn leather that even now kept its shape. In the past, I'd worn it with black eyes. Humans thought dark glass rounds had been placed in the sight holes. Vampires knew not to cross my path.

I placed it over my face, and while the cloak had been a burden, some of the weight I carried lifted. As *il flagello*, I answered to no one but the queens. Whatever other factions were warring in this city, that still meant something. Their power might not extend beyond Venice, but here it was nearly absolute. Something I suspected the Council feared. Maybe that was why they'd severed ties with the queens not long after I'd left.

Of course that was before. Now, with the Mordicum and Drake here, it was possible they saw that power threatened—or worse, that they were losing control.

"People will think you're in costume," Jacqueline warned me as we walked toward the door. The handmaiden stood silently beside it.

I rolled my eyes. "I'll make sure they tag me on social media."

I was one step out the street-side door when Jacqueline caught my wrist. "Seriously, be careful."

Panic edged her voice, and I knew why. I was no longer the queens' favored butcher. I was a different man. I'd deserted them. I'd changed. At least I'd believed that before I'd slipped on the old mask. Now...

It felt like I'd slipped into darkness. The beast that paced inside me—the magic I held back even from Thea—stretched its claws and readied for the kill.

I nodded and slid quietly into the streets, the handmaiden at my side. Even in the light of day, the streets of Venice remained shrouded in darkness, its tall buildings blocking the sun. Jacqueline's home sat on the edge of the city's most residential district, so we encountered no one as we made our way past bakeries and businesses. Hardly anyone we did encounter noticed us. The handmaiden took the lead, although every step was familiar. How many times had I traveled the alleys in the dead of night, summoned by the queens? I could close my eyes and find my way, but still, I hung back, considering how to make my request.

The queens were slippery bitches at best. One poorly chosen word could seal my fate to them for centuries—if not longer. Deals made with them were sealed by magic; the eldest of them had never hidden the magic that burned in her veins, unlike so many of us. Instead, she'd used it to bind the desperate into servitude. If you were in her favor, she might grant your desires. My arrangement with them had been handled by my mother, and she had been careful to keep my autonomy. Most of those who served them weren't so lucky.

I hadn't been desperate before. I'd been bloodthirsty—eager to quash a growing rebellion. Then, Venice had been gripped by a terrible plague brought by vampires tired of *Le Regine's* influence. Is that why they'd summoned me now? Was the city on the verge of corruption again?

I followed my silent companion around a corner, nearly running into her when I found her stopped on the other side. In front of us, a group of twenty or so tourists clustered together, snapping photos of us and shouting over one another.

They wanted pictures.

"Fuck," I muttered, and my companion nodded—the only communication we'd had so far. At least we agreed on the damn tourists.

A teen grinned at us and started toward us, gesturing to his phone. Now they wanted us to pose? I was seriously considering if I could wipe them all out before any got away when the handmaiden lifted her hand and made a slight flicking movement with her wrist. The air around us shimmered, dazzling the tourists for a moment. Then, they turned and continued down another alley.

"You're a witch," I murmured, both surprised and impressed. That wasn't simple family magic or earth magic. It had the markings of true magic. No wonder the queens employed her.

She nodded again before inclining her head for us to continue.

It wasn't like she could give me other answers due to her mask. A long time ago, some claimed it added to a woman's mystery and allure. For those employed by *Le Regine*, it meant something else entirely. It was a symbol of allegiance but also power. Handmaidens only answered to the queens. No one else could question them, even approach them. The women were chosen for their skills and talents. Centuries ago, they might have served in the court, but if this woman was a witch, they wouldn't waste her on that.

Things had changed in Venice. Was this handmaiden special, or were there others? I stared at her red hood as we made our way to the court. She was not ordinary. Not with that power. There was only one purpose worthy of her—one I knew all too well.

It seemed the queens had a new assassin, and if so, what did they have planned for me?

CHAPTER TWENTY-NINE

Jacqueline

Had I lost my mind? Clearly, yes.

Near-death experiences had a way of making a girl question her priorities. Drake had snapped my neck, but he could have just as easily ripped my heart out or torn my head off. I wasn't sure why he spared me. Obviously, he didn't know about my relationship with his wife.

So, what was the obvious thing to do?

Call my ex, or whatever the hell Camila was to me.

Not because I needed her. No, Julian needed her. That was definitely why I was calling her. At least that's what I kept telling myself.

I paced across the marble floor of my bedroom, fanning myself. The servants had lit the fires, which made sense because it was winter. Winter in Venice was a chaotic affair. One moment, it might be a little overcast, and the next, it was raining. Sometimes it even snowed. Near the water in a drafty old palazzo, it could be bone-chilling. The fires were for the humans. Normally the heat didn't bother me. As a vampire, I didn't get cold. Not really. But I was healing. That meant I was overheated and itchy.

Oh, and irritated. Very, very irritated.

I paused in front of the window and pulled back the silk drapes to watch as the morning sun painted the canals with glowing light. It was less gray than normal. A gondola floated past, already showing the sights to camera-happy tourists. Normally I loved the city, but today, I wished I had never come.

I let the curtain fall back into place and hung up when I got Sebastian's voicemail. Part of me was relieved he hadn't answered. But the feeling was quickly replaced by shame. Julian had left an hour ago, and I'd been trying to reach Greece since then. I knew why he didn't want me to go with him to see *Le Regine*. I'd never been formally introduced to the vampire queens, although they sometimes came to balls or parties in the city.

I'd never been invited to meet them. A small blessing. Usually, they only met with people eager to sell their souls in exchange for their help.

Like Julian was doing right now.

Because of me.

Because I had fucked up.

Now Drake had Thea, and it was like history was repeating itself.

I couldn't lose someone else I loved to that psycho. I had to do something.

"Any luck?" Geoffrey, my butler, asked, bringing me another fresh glass of blood. He'd been force-feeding me since I was found in the gardens.

"No. Everyone must be asleep." I smiled at my old friend and took the goblet without complaint. Geoffrey was English, but he'd found himself stuck in Venice thirty years ago looking for work after falling out with the vampire he'd sworn himself to. Since I happened to think his old master was a prick, I'd happily employed him to look after my place while I wasn't here. There was no formal agreement. He wasn't compelled. We just trusted each other.

Looking at him now, I realized how the years had caught up with him. Lines creased his forehead, wrinkles crinkled around his watery blue eyes, and his suit wasn't as trim as years ago.

"Is there no one else to call?" he asked.

I hadn't filled him in on all the details. Mostly because I would probably have to draw a diagram or two to explain this mess. "The only other number I have is for Sabine."

"I see."

I'm sure he did.

"If I call Sabine, she will demand to know what's wrong." I sighed and dropped into a silk-upholstered chair. "The last thing we need is for her to come to Venice."

"Would she?" Somehow Geoffrey always knew how to get to the heart of the matter. It was one of the reasons I relied on him.

"Not for Thea," I said sourly. Sabine might have acknowledged her son's engagement, but she wasn't planning any bridal showers. "If Camila came, though, Sabine might tag along."

"And would Camila come?"

Now that was the real question. "I don't know."

Things had been tense in Corfu. Partially because she'd shown up without warning, but mostly because I'd been unprepared. Ever since Julian had told me she was still alive, I'd been trying to decide how I felt about her. I'd almost confronted her in Greece, but it had never been the right time. Maybe it never would be. Maybe love really could die, and ours had died along with the Camila I knew decades ago in that fire. All I knew was that I had no clue what she would do next or why she'd come back at all.

"She's hiding something, and if I could get it out of her, it might help."

"Then you should keep trying," he said gently. "Unless being near her is too difficult."

"Being near her is impossible," I whispered. One minute, I wanted to strangle her; the next, I wanted to scream. I told myself I wasn't in love with her anymore. Not after what she'd become.

But I kept thinking about kissing her. Just once. Just to see.

And there was no way in hell I was going to do that.

"Nothing is impossible."

I scoffed. "Who told you that?"

"You did." He took my empty glass from me.

"I wish I still believed that." I offered Geoffrey a half smile. If anything, the last few months had proven it true—to some extent. Julian had woken, which I'd begun to fear would never happen. Then he'd actually met his mate. And Camila...was alive. The most impossible thing of all. But these feelings twisting inside me? Those were impossible.

"Perhaps I could make some inquiries," he suggested.

It wasn't a bad idea. The household staff of vampires tended to stick together. Probably so they could gossip freely. Most compelled servants were forbidden to acknowledge the existence of the magical world to outsiders, but they could talk amongst themselves. "Be careful. I don't want to draw attention to the house," I said. "No mention of Mademoiselle Thea or Julian. Just see if anyone has heard about some rebel vampires."

"Venice always has its fair share of renegades," he reminded me.

He had a point. "This is a group. It's organized. They want to see change in vampire politics and customs. There have to be sympathetic households in Venice."

"And if they ask why I'm interested?"

That was trickier. I hesitated. There was really only one way to play this, but it meant walking a dangerous line. "Tell them your mistress wants to meet with them. That she's interested in their cause."

"I'm not certain anyone will believe that."

"Tell them I'm being forced to marry." It was almost true. It likely would be a done deal if I'd stayed in Corfu. "Tell them I'm looking for a way out."

His eyes pinched together, and I could tell he didn't like any of this. But he nodded. "I'll see what I can do."

Geoffrey excused himself, leaving me to the too-warm fire and my phone. Maybe he could get answers, but how long would that take? I took a deep breath to brace myself and dialed Sabine's number.

She answered on the second ring.

The damned didn't need to sleep, I guess.

"Jacqueline." Her greeting was a caustic mixture of mild surprise and deep annoyance. "To what do I owe this pleasure?"

"I was actually hoping to speak with your daughter."

"Camila?" I heard the annoyance shift to curiosity. "Why?"

"I thought we could go shopping," I lied.

"Do you know, Jacqueline, that when you showed up with that werewolf, I knew what you were up to?" She chewed on each word as if it was a delicacy. "But I never quite understood why."

"I like a little friction. Fur is good for that."

"You could have had my son," she reminded me, "and then none of this mess would have happened."

It 100 percent would have happened. Even if we'd gone through with the arrangement, there was no way that Jules and I would ever be romantically involved. We would have been at that party in San Francisco. He would have met Thea. I knew that because it was pretty easy to spot soulmates, and those two were soulmates. I kept all of that to myself. "Look, can I talk to Camila or not?"

"I'll ask her," she said pointedly.

I heard her muffled conversation through the line and realized she wasn't alone. A moment later, Camila spoke. "You want to go shopping?"

"Not really," I said quickly. "But I need to talk to you, and we should probably leave your mom out of it."

"Fine." She sighed. "Where should we meet?"

My heart did a little flip, and I hated it. "I'm in Venice."

"That might take me a minute," she said slowly, "but I'll see what I can do."

"Hurry. Julian needs us," I said and hung up. I didn't trust myself to stay on a second longer. Not when part of me wanted to add, *I need you.*

My heart could skip beats all it wanted, but I would never admit that to her.

Or myself.

CHAPTER THIRTY

Thea

My room might be nicer than a cell, but I was still in prison. No one had bothered me since my meal with Willem, so I'd gotten creative. The only two windows in this place were almost twelve feet off the ground. There was no way to see out of them without help. I'd dragged every piece of furniture I could move under them. None had been tall enough. The desk was the tallest and easily the sturdiest piece at my disposal. I was using it as a base.

Higher up, the stone walls became more jagged. Standing on top of the desk, I studied the stones. If I could get a foothold, I might be able to climb the wall. Olivia had forced me to go to a rock-climbing gym a few years ago. How much harder could it be? Spotting a small hole in the stonework, I licked my lips before wedging one foot into it, ignoring the sharp rasp of pain on my bare toes. My fingertips scraped over the rough stones until I found one above my head to grab onto. Clinging to it, I brought my other foot up, seeking purchase. Rough edges scraped my skin as I found a stone jutting out enough for me to plant my foot on it.

"Not so bad," I muttered, cautiously allowing my left hand to begin searching for something to help me pull up higher. My fingers closed over a rock, but as I gripped it, the stone juddered, and I lost my grip.

There was a moment of weightless surprise before my hip hit the edge of the desk. Pain shot through me as I tumbled onto the rug. My back hit the floor, knocking the wind from my lungs, and I gasped desperately for air as I lay in a ruined heap.

The door lock clicked open, but I couldn't even turn my head.

"What are you doing?" The thin *cortège* from earlier this morning darted into the room, the contents of a silver tray clattering along with her.

"Escaping," I mumbled. There was no point lying to her. My brilliant idea wasn't going to work. Not that I thought I could squeeze through the tiny windows, but I'd shoved a note in my pocket, hoping I might be able to throw it through the bars or something.

My college education had not prepared me for escaping vampire lairs.

"Why would you want to do that?" She put the tray down and came over to help me up. "Master Drake will not be pleased."

"Then let's make it our secret." I rubbed my hip. There was definitely going to be a bruise. I could only imagine what Julian would think of that.

Because he was going to find me.

"What did you think you would find out the window?" she asked, returning to her tray. She kept her back to me as she poured something from a teapot into a cup.

"I guess I was hoping for a view."

"Well, you're fifty feet up with only the sea below. Not much to see but water."

"Oh." The last hope I had in perfecting that plan fizzled. That meant I needed to change tactics, so I turned my attention to the *cortège*. "What's your name?"

I did my best to sound chatty, but she turned toward me, eyes narrowing suspiciously. "Natalie."

"That's a pretty name." I smiled at her. "I had a friend in

college named Natalie."

She shrugged, uninterested in this conversation. Before I could come up with a new topic to get her talking, she thrust the teacup in my direction.

"What's this?" I asked, but as soon as I glanced down, my stomach turned.

"It's fresh," she said primly. "I got it from one of the girls downstairs."

My throat constricted as my nose caught the iron-drenched scent of blood. "I don't drink blood."

"You do now." She smiled back at me, revealing rows of petite teeth. It was so innocent that a chill seized me. "Master says you need your strength."

Master. Sire. Willem Drake could call himself whatever he wanted, but if he thought he would have control over me, he was going to be unpleasantly surprised. He'd dodged every one of my questions this morning, including what he'd meant by claiming that he had made me a vampire.

I might not be human, but I wasn't a vampire.

I got carefully to my feet, trying not to spill the cup. The last thing I needed was a bloodstain on the rug. I held the cup out to Natalie. "Thank you, but I'm perfectly strong. You can tell him."

She moved toward the door, ignoring my outstretched hand.

"You will need to be stronger for what's to come."

Before I could ask her what she meant, she disappeared out the door. This time when the lock turned, I knew I would never escape.

CHAPTER THIRTY-ONE

Julian

She'd placed a glamour on us. It was the only way to explain the sudden lack of interest from tourists, especially as we made our way closer to St. Mark's Square. With each step, the alleys grew more congested with people perusing Italian leather handbags and vulgar tchotchkes aimed at travelers. We glided past all of them without earning so much as a curious glance.

When *Le Regine* had chosen their seat of power, they'd followed the church and the Doge by choosing the central part of Venice. It made sense at the time. These days? It was a fucking nightmare.

I was this close to throwing a few drifters into the canal to get through the crowd faster when we reached an unmarked alley. To the casual passerby, it was completely uninteresting compared to the bustling gelato shop and bistro on either side of the passage. The small shop at the end of the dank, dark alley attracted little attention. There was no sign. Its windows were filled with old, dusty books. The few souls that ventured never stayed long, in part because of the claustrophobic atmosphere but mostly due to the hissing feline that guarded the place against unwanted humans.

Few humans found themselves in the *Libreria Notte*. Even

fewer stayed more than a heartbeat.

Before we reached the door, it opened with a clatter, and two students scrambled out, throwing backward glances at the yowling ball of ginger rage chasing them.

I stepped inside, and the cat instantly calmed. She sauntered toward me, weaving in and out of my legs. The handmaiden stepped away from us, her dark eyes watching from behind her mask.

"Hello, Countess. It's been a while." I squatted to scratch her behind the ears. Her eyes squinted, her rage turning into a full-body purr. Behind me, I sensed a familiar presence. "And greetings to you, Conte."

Standing up, I turned to find the shop's proprietor. Like the city, he'd changed with the times, trading robes for a three-piece suit with a scarf knotted elegantly at his neck. The man's dark hair was swept back, glasses he didn't need tucked into his pocket. He looked every bit the part of a modern Venetian gentleman, for someone who'd driven the wooden piles into the swampy locks to build this city over eighteen hundred years ago.

"I thought you were exiled." Despite being Roman like my father, the Conte had developed a thick Italian accent in his years tending his post at the entrance to the *Rio Oscuro*. The position had earned him his title, gifted to him by both the Venetian aristocracy and the queens themselves.

"I was." I offered him my hand in friendship. The Conte didn't give a shit if I'd been exiled or not.

"And yet here you are." He took it and shook it firmly. "*Il flagello* has returned."

"Only for a visit," I lied. I'd always liked the Conte, but my business with the queens needed to be kept private until I understood the powers at play a little better.

"They might try to keep you," he warned me as the appropriately named Countess jumped onto the counter. She nosed his arm until he released my hand, her tail sticking straight up in annoyance at my lack of attention.

"I'm spoken for," I told him lightly. Now wasn't the time or place to mention Thea. Not while any member of the magical community might come in seeking entrance to Venice's hidden court.

"I see." He picked up the cat. "Regardless, let me be the first to welcome you back."

"Thank you." I tipped my head in acknowledgment. Turning, I gestured for my companion to continue past the stacks of teetering books to the back of the shop. Before I could follow, the Conte caught my shoulder.

"Be cautious in your dealings with *Le Regine*. They are not as they were."

Before I could ask what the hell that meant, he vanished behind another stack of books.

I walked swiftly to catch up with my companion. By the time I caught her, she'd already reached the cramped backroom. The musty scent of wet, molding paper filled my nostrils as I ducked in behind her. Most of the books and magazines in here were garbage, owing largely to a doorway opening directly to the canal behind the shop. Water seeped across the floor, catching the hem of my cloak.

"Shit." I suddenly remembered why cloaks were a pain in the ass.

The handmaiden didn't seem to care as she swept through the pooled water, moving toward the old gondola tied to a docking pole.

I had half a mind to take the damn cloak off as I trudged through the water. It soaked through my shoes, and I cursed again. Hauling myself into the gondola, I waited for her to join me, but she didn't move.

"Are you coming?"

She shook her head, the eerie mask as expressionless as her silence. Then she pointed north down the canal.

"I know the way," I said grimly. It was a bad sign that the queens wanted to see me. It was a worse sign that they wanted to see me alone.

Untying the gondola, I picked up an oar and dipped it into the murky water. The second the oar touched the surface, the world shimmered around me. The whirring of boat engines and shouts of tourists faded instantly, the city becoming as still and as silent as my recent companion. All around me, the age lifted from the buildings, revealing towering palazzi in their original splendor. Roses bloomed in flower boxes, unhampered by the winter chill. From an open window above me, the sharp notes of a pianoforte played. Magic hung so heavily in the air that I could taste it: the thick, earthy smell of wood and resin cut with the grassy scent of death and decay.

It only took a few strokes to reach the dock that connected the *Rio Oscuro* to the hidden magical quarter beyond. No one greeted me at the dock. I didn't bother to tie off the gondola. As soon as I stepped out of the boat, it began sailing slowly backward, returning to the *Libreria Notte*. It would come for me when I made my way back to the dock.

If I made my way back.

Unlike the magical quarters in Paris and Corfu, entrance here was by invitation only. Unfortunately, so was exiting the court.

More than ever, I wished I could reach inside me and feel that ember of Thea's magic. Coming here might have been a mistake. The queens could help me, but they could also decide to keep me—another way for me to lose Thea forever.

There was only one thing I could do: offer *Le Regine* something they wanted more than me. Whatever the hell that was.

The Conte's words stuck in my mind as I made my way through the stone square. The queens weren't as they were, he'd said. Now I understood what he meant. Centuries ago, I would have found myself elbow to elbow with flattering courtiers, each scheming to rise within a queen's estimation. Usually, they moved aside for me, whispering words like "assassin" as I passed. Today, there were none. No mindless flatterers. No two-faced friends to greet me. Other than the music playing somewhere in the distance, the place felt rather...dead.

When I reached the steps of the court, I found the gates closed. Roses lay scattered before them, some withered, some fresh. All the same sobering shade of black.

Mourning flowers.

If any city still had access to the magics that crafted these specimens, it would be Venice. Probably because the queens had locked away whatever familiar had the family magic to achieve it.

Pressing my palm to the gate, I opened it gently and stepped carefully around the flowers. Although the court had faded, it seemed someone had remained—someone brought these flowers— and given their loyalty, I wouldn't risk upsetting them.

The court itself was empty. Once, the gates had opened to magnificent gardens brimming with magical herbs and plants. Enchanted lights had floated overhead as the queens' favorites lounged, laughed, and entertained their keepers. Now, not a single blade of grass remained. Shriveled vines clung to the stone walls that separated the court's gathering place from the rest of the quarter. The magic that kept the *Rio Oscuro* alive and vibrant seemed to stop at the gates. It was like the whole place had slowly faded into nothing.

But the queens had answered. The handmaiden had come for me. None of it made sense.

I placed one hand on the dagger I'd slipped into my waistband, the weapon concealed by the cloak they'd sent, and walked through the massive oak doors into the throne room.

No one was in attendance. Cobweb-draped candelabras lined a path to the dais at the far end where the thrones sat. On the throne on the left—carved from the wooden piles that built Venice—sat the olive-skinned vampire Mariana. Her black hair rippled past her shoulders, glinting with the blue-green sheen of Venice's waters, and her blue velvet cloak covered her body, but I guessed that under it she wore clothing more suitable for the sixteenth century than the twenty-first. A large seashell topped the back of her throne, haloing Mariana like a crown.

Her sister-queen Zina sat quietly on the throne on the right.

Her face, so perfect after all these years, held no sign of recognition. No warmth. No greeting. That wasn't a surprise. Like the marble throne she sat on, Zina looked as if she'd been cut from perfect black stone. Her silver hair was wound tightly around her head. Carved into the armrests of her chair were two perfect masks: one happy and one sad. Both as perfect and unchanging as her.

And in the middle, the final throne. Centuries ago, the court had whispered it was made of moonstone and gold. Maybe the truth lay in the ancient, forgotten words carved into its body. Its arched back rose higher than the other thrones to reveal a serpent holding a crescent moon in his jaws. The throne was empty.

I'd hesitated too long, the empty throne catching me by surprise, so I rushed forward. Stopping short of the dais, I dropped into a low bow.

"Giuliano," Mariana greeted me. "You may rise."

Her courtly superiority grated on me. The queens were still playing court to an empty palace with an empty throne between them. How many outside these walls knew the truth? I'd come here for help getting to Thea. Now I knew I had wasted my time and jeopardized my freedom. I was glad the *bauta* was still in place to mask my reaction. I kept my eyes trained on the floor as I rose, worried that my annoyance might show there.

"You seek our assistance, *il flagello*," Zina said, no emotion showing on her smooth features. "But as you can see, we have been dealt a mighty blow. The gods have taken our sister."

"The gods?" I asked.

"Who else could kill one of us?" she snarled. For a moment, her mask slipped, revealing the vicious female that hid under her polished exterior.

"I apologize," I said quickly. "I find myself surprised to see Ginerva's throne empty."

"She was foolish," Zina answered cryptically.

I didn't dare try to get more out of her.

"So, we find we also require your assistance," Mariana added, sending a warning look in Zina's direction.

"I'm afraid my problem is a matter of life or death, Your Majesties. I am not sure I can—"

"Your mate," Mariana interrupted. "She has been taken by another vampire. It was against her will?"

Rage flared inside me, and I barely clamped down on it. "Yes," I gritted. "She is in danger."

"As are we all," Mariana said in a low voice. "A new queen must be crowned before the waters turn to blood."

Mariana had always been a weird one, so it appeared that hadn't changed. She saw portents in the tides and dreamed in prophecies. The trick was knowing which ones were fever dreams and which were warnings.

"What my sister is trying to say," Zina said irritably, "is that we need your mother's help before we will be able to assist you."

"My mother?" I felt my stomach hollow. The chances of getting Sabine to help *Le Regine* were unlikely—probably even more if she knew I needed their help to save Thea.

"Who else could sit on our throne?" Mariana asked. "We must reach her before it's too late, but she has ignored our messages."

I bet she had. The only thing less likely than Sabine helping them was her joining them.

"And my mate." I forced myself to return to Thea even as the small hope I'd felt when their letter arrived died. "I must find her."

"Then you must convince your mother to return." Zina lifted her head and stared me down. "You owe us that, *il flagello*. You left us without notice. See how our court has suffered?"

I doubted the lack of partying had anything to do with me, but I stayed silent, hoping they would mistake it for contrition. The queens could not help me. Not with their own power in shambles. It had been a waste of time to come here, but I couldn't risk that the lingering magic that protected the court from the outside world would keep me here. I would hear their request and leave.

"Three days," Zina said. "Tell your mother that she must come to us in three days' time. We will see to the other invitations."

I inclined my head. "Other invitations?"

"There are many vampires in Venice at the moment," she said, her sharp nails tapping the carved masks of the chair's arms. "All must attend, even those outside what you consider society. At least that is what Mariana sees."

Mariana nodded solemnly.

"The Mordicum? Willem Drake?"

Zina flinched as I spoke but nodded once. Suspicion crept up my back. Was one of them responsible for Ginerva's death? I decided I would risk asking the Conte. "*All* vampires."

"That could get bloody," I warned them.

This time, Mariana smiled, revealing small, sharp teeth. "That is why we have you back, *il flagello*."

· · ·

When I reached the docks, the gondola had returned for me, but the handmaiden was nowhere in sight. That was probably a good thing. I wasn't in the mood for company, even the company of someone who didn't speak. I waited until I'd stepped into the boat before I took off the mask. The Venetian air felt cool on my feverish skin. The *bauta* might be good for hiding my identity, but it was shit for airflow. Whipping the cloak off my shoulders, I wadded it into a ball around my mask and tucked it under my shoulder before picking up the oar.

The sun blazed high overhead as I dipped it into the water. It was already past midday, and I still had no idea where Thea was. The oar felt heavier in my hands. Maybe the canal's magic was resisting me. Or perhaps it was the defeat settling like lead in my stomach. Either way, it didn't matter. The queens' assistance depended on convincing my mother to drop her party plans and come to Venice.

I might have better luck putting up missing-person posters.

The passage back to *Libreria Notte* went slowly as I tried to decide what I was going to do. By the time I felt the magic fade from the air, I knew I had no other choice. The shop was as empty as I felt when I finally climbed out of the gondola onto its water-soaked steps. Once I was on dry ground, my one-cat welcoming committee greeted me. I offered her an absent-minded scratch that failed to satisfy her.

She followed me through the store, yowling for attention.

"Must you be so dramatic?" the Conte asked her from behind the shop's ancient register. Countess squinted her yellow eyes, lifted her tail, and trotted off to show she was offended. He sighed before looking at me. "No mask now, I see."

"It hardly seems necessary," I said, shifting the bundle under my arms. "Tell me the truth—does anyone come to court these days?"

His broad shoulders slumped as he shook his head. "Very few. You are the first in months."

Months? There had been a time when the court never emptied. *Le Regine*'s parties would continue without ceasing for decades. And now...

"When did Ginerva die?" I sensed her death had triggered the court's collapse.

"A few years ago, but the court has been quiet far longer."

A few years to a vampire could mean nine or ninety, but he'd answered the real question weighing on me. Zina and Mariana might remain on their thrones, but they ruled over a court of nothing and no one. "Then I wasted my time," I said furiously.

"Did you?" His question stopped me in my tracks.

"I came for help. It was a matter of life and death." I wasn't even sure why I was wasting time explaining myself.

"Your life?"

There was no point in hiding it from him. I'd been cautious before—afraid that someone might overhear us—but no one was coming to the *Libreria Notte*. No one was coming to visit the queens. Considering the Conte spent most of his days in the real world, he might be of more use than they were. "My mate's," I admitted.

"You really are spoken for," he said, blinking rapidly. "That will break the Countess's heart. But what danger is your mate in? Is she ill?"

"Taken." I hated the word. I hated what it implied. I'd let my guard down. It was my job to protect her. It was my entire purpose, and I'd failed utterly. "By an enemy."

"Venice has many enemies at present. I'm certain *Le Regine* made you aware of the threats within the city." He bent down, straightening a moment later with a bottle of Scotch. He didn't bother asking if I needed a drink. He just poured two and nodded to one.

I took it and downed it with one gulp. It scorched my throat and settled into my empty stomach like embers. The Conte studied me as I placed my glass on the counter.

"Perhaps you need something more nutritious," he suggested.

"I'm fine."

"All evidence to the contrary. I have some blood—"

"No. I do not need to feed. Not until she is found."

"That's foolish." He took a sip of his drink and winced slightly. "You need your strength if you have an enemy to face."

My throat knotted. I knew he was right, but I couldn't bring myself to consider feeding from another. It felt too much like giving up. "I made a vow to my mate not to drink another's blood."

"Your mate is...human?" he guessed.

"Mostly." I really didn't have time to explain that situation.

His black eyebrows lifted. "Your mother must be thrilled."

I forced a grim smile. But the mention of my mother reminded me I needed to return to Jacqueline and decide what to do. We needed to make a move. Quickly. Every moment we wasted put Thea's life at risk—and I'd already wasted time coming here.

"The queens asked you to speak with her, did they not?" he asked as I stepped toward the door.

I inclined my head. "A fool's errand."

"No, I fear it is not."

"Are you telling me that bringing my mother into this shit show is a good idea?"

"I'm telling you that you have no choice if you want to save your mate."

I stared at him. He couldn't be serious. Involving Sabine never made things easier. The Conte paused to pour us another drink.

"They want to crown a new queen," I told him. "There's no way Sabine will go for it. Not..." I stopped myself before I said something I might regret.

"Not with the court in ruins," he finished for me, but it wasn't the whole reason. I had no idea if he knew the truth about my time in Venice—or my mother's involvement in its abrupt end. "Without a new queen, the magic in Venice will die."

"It wouldn't be the first time that happened," I snarled. I'd witnessed it on the brink of devastation before. *Le Regine* would find a way to save it. No matter the cost. "I have more important things to do than worry about an abandoned court!"

But his next words cut my rage. "If the magic dies in *Venice*, it dies *everywhere*. Venice is the source."

"That's impossible." I looked at his bottle of Scotch. How much had he had?

"And if our magic dies," he continued, ignoring my interruption, "all magic dies."

"Did you read that in one of your books?" I rolled my eyes.

"You've walked the earth too long to be this arrogant. Without three queens on the throne, magic will continue to decline. Without a third sister-queen, they cannot feed the source." He paused as if waiting for his words to register.

"There are other sources," I said bitterly. "Right now, I need to find my mate." Each second without her was agony. The slack of my tether left me unmoored. I couldn't focus. I was being pulled in every direction by the dark beast it leashed. Maybe it had been a mistake to cage him.

"I suppose it won't affect your human mate." His words were full of disgust. "But will you leave her unprotected?"

The question slammed into me, and I lunged forward. My fists shattered the glass case before him, sending the register and whisky bottle flying into a stack of books. "I will never!"

Never *again*. I would never leave her unprotected again. I had failed her once. I knew it. He knew it.

Wherever she was, Thea knew it.

His lip curled as he picked a shard of glass off his scarf. "And what do you think will happen to you when all magic dies?"

"You can't mean…" I'd been too caught in my fear and shame to understand what he meant before.

"All magic will die, and with it, all who carry it," he repeated. *"Every last one of us."*

CHAPTER THIRTY-TWO

Thea

"You need to feed."

I'd lost track of the times I'd heard that in the last few days. This time was different, though. It wasn't the feeble voice of a *cortège* speaking. I looked up from where I lay on the bed, head swimming from the effort of lifting my head, and found Willem's stern face staring down at me. Natalie stood in his shadow, watching him with a reverence that might have made me throw up, if I had eaten anything.

"Give me some food," I grumbled, rubbing my empty stomach.

"Would you prefer it from the vein?" He beckoned Natalie to take a step forward. She moved to his side dutifully and began unwrapping a bandage from her wrist.

"I don't want blood." But even as I spoke, my gums ached and my pulse sped up. It pounded behind my eyes, making me feel even dizzier. "You have any pizza?"

My stomach growled, as if betrayed by the very mention of cheese and carbs.

Willem chuckled darkly. "You are only prolonging the inevitable."

"I'm not a vampire."

"Not yet," he replied, repeating what he'd said to me when I'd arrived.

I shook my head. I didn't believe him. I chose not to believe him. Because believing him meant believing things I wasn't prepared to accept—like my suspicions about what him being my sire meant. Or that if it meant what I thought, he was right about me being a vampire.

Or that Willem Drake was...

"Okay." I pushed myself into a sitting position on the bed. Maybe I was going about this the wrong way. "Let me rephrase. I don't want to be a vampire."

"I'll bite," he said, striding into the room. I cringed at his choice of words. "Let's pretend you have a choice. Why not? You've chosen a vampire as a mate. Surely, you want more than a mortal lifespan together, but you don't want to be a vampire?"

Had I found myself in couple's therapy with the psychopath holding me hostage? I clamped my mouth shut. Willem was trying to catch me with my guard down. I couldn't let him.

"You're as stubborn as she was," he said with a sigh.

Hairs rose along the back of my neck, but I maintained my silence. I didn't want to know who *she* was. I would not ask. If I didn't show interest, he would drop it. Eventually, they would give up and leave, and I would...starve?

"Your mother," he said, giving me the answer that I didn't want to hear.

A shiver raced through me as the truth began to take shape, and a moment later, my body was trembling like a leaf in the wind. I wrapped my arms around my waist, trying to get control of myself. I only shook harder.

"You take after her," he continued, standing completely still. It was unnerving. I'd been around plenty of vampires in the last few months, but Willem had none of the slight human characteristics that most of them had picked up. He didn't bother to blend in. He didn't even try, as far as I could tell. Hell, he could probably turn into a bat. "Tell me, has she kept her looks?"

Acid shot up my throat, and I swallowed it down. It burned more as it hit my empty stomach, and I winced.

"You need to feed," he repeated. "I would prefer not to force you."

I narrowed my eyes. Why would he care? I was his prisoner. Nothing he said would change that until he let me go or Stockholm syndrome kicked in—whichever came first. "Don't you mean compel me? You already kidnapped me. Why stop there?"

"A sire does not compel," he seethed quietly, his eyes darkening to near total black. "He commands, and his children *do as they are told*."

Children. The word clanged through me, echoing again and again in my tired brain until something inside me snapped. I was tired of the insinuations. Tired of waiting for answers. Because no matter what he said, one thing was true. "I am not your child."

"Obstinate little fool." He wrapped a hand around the post of my bed. "What will it take for you to believe me? I'm your sire."

"Who the hell cares? I'm not a vampire. Humans don't have sires."

"I forget how poorly educated humans are these days," he drawled. "Have you no idea what a sire is, little fool?"

I ignored him, training my eyes on a crack in the stone. I stared at it until I almost believed it was growing longer.

"I'm your father, Thea."

I refused to look at him—refused to acknowledge him. Refused the truth. But in the back of my mind, I heard Jacqueline's voice asking if my father could be a vampire.

It explained the fangs.

It explained why I enjoyed drinking Julian's blood.

It explained where the hell my deadbeat dad had been while I was growing up.

But as hungry as I had been for answers before, I wouldn't let myself listen to him. Ever.

"Fine." He threw his hands in the air. "Have it your way."

But he didn't leave. Instead, there was a flash of movement that made my head spin. When I managed to focus, Willem stood next to my bed, his bare hand curled around Natalie's slender neck.

"This is your last chance to do things the easy way," he warned me. "Feed from her." He flicked his thumb across her skin, and a thin trickle of blood dribbled down her throat.

I kept my mouth closed even as my fangs protracted and saliva pooled in my mouth at the sight. No, not saliva, I realized. Venom.

It was true. I was a vampire. Or, at least, part of me wanted to be, but that didn't make me his daughter. I knew how Willem lied and twisted things.

"My mother would never have touched you," I whispered.

"Because she hates vampires?" he guessed, pushing Natalie away. She stumbled toward the bed, and for a horrifying moment, I thought she would fall right into it with me. She caught herself at the last minute, pressing a finger to the blood welling at her throat. "Why do you think your mother hates vampires, Thea?"

I closed my eyes, recalling my mother's face that day in the hospital when she realized what Julian was. She had hated him. Not because he'd broken my heart but because of what he was. *Why did she hate vampires? How did she even know about them?* I'd wondered then. Not anymore. Not if it meant accepting...

"I am not a vampire, and I won't feed off a living creature," I said firmly. "Nothing you can do will change those facts."

Willem lifted an eyebrow. "Is that so? Kelly must be so proud of the headstrong woman she's raised," he said, disgust flitting over his sharp features. "So, let me be clear. You belong to me. You are my blood. You are my heir. And I can make things comfortable or miserable for you. I can also force you to do whatever I want."

Past the blood roaring in my ears and my pounding pulse, I forced myself to meet his eyes.

"You think so, huh?" I challenged him.

"There is no bond stronger than that of parent and child." His mouth curved into a wicked smile. "It's time for you to accept what you are if we are to move forward. I have plans for us, and time is running short."

"No!" I refused to go along with whatever he was planning. "Even if I believed you, I don't care if you donated some sperm.

You are not my father or my sire. You are nothing to me. There is no bond between us."

His eyes went black, and then something hot sprayed my face. The scent of iron bloomed in my nostrils as I blinked to find Natalie's surprised face staring back at me. The knife plunged into her stomach. She pitched forward a step, but this time she didn't catch herself. She landed next to me in a boneless heap, eyes wide, as a scream tore through the air.

My scream.

Pressing my palms to her wound, I tried to stop the bleeding. It was too much.

"It's too late for that, little fool. She'll die because of you. Don't waste her blood. It's quite delicious. And if you behave, I might consider healing her when you're finished." Willem's cold laugh tore through me. "Now, *feed.*"

And with one word, I no longer had a choice.

CHAPTER THIRTY-THREE

Jacqueline

"Brace yourself," I muttered. I stood in the courtyard next to Julian as the sound of an approaching motorboat grew louder. How like a Rousseaux to be exactly on time. A chill breeze brushed past me, and I shivered. Not from cold but from the ominous tension in the air. The moon hung in its full glory over Venice, casting the city in shadows that only reminded me of how deeply fucked we were.

Julian didn't say a word until the motor cut off. "This was your idea."

"Did we have a choice?" I asked softly so they wouldn't hear us.

His failure to respond proved answer enough. We didn't have a choice, but that didn't make this any easier. For either of us.

Geoffrey greeted our guests, but we held back.

"I hope this works," Julian muttered. He sounded hollow, as if he'd been twisted until all the life in him had been wrung from him like a rag. I suspected he still wasn't eating or feeding, but I was too polite to ask. For now.

He couldn't go on like this. Not feeding or sleeping or *living*. Gods, I hoped his mother and sister could help us. Or rather that they *would* help us. As if on cue, two cloaked figures entered the courtyard, hoods pulled low to cover their faces. It was all a tad dramatic, but vampires had basically invented the concept of overreacting.

"Mother," Julian said tightly, moving gracefully toward our guests. "Camila."

"Brother," his twin responded as she lowered her hood. Camila had always been beautiful, but in the moonlight, she stole my breath. The glow from the full moon seemed to fill her. It glinted off her silky black hair and turned her pale skin luminescent. My fingers twitched in my gloves, recalling how it felt to run my hands through her tresses and the velvet-soft feeling of her skin against mine.

Camila's dark eyes met mine and held my gaze. "Jacqueline."

I forced myself to swallow and turn away before I lost control of myself. "I hope your trip went smoothly."

Julian raised an eyebrow but didn't say anything. Instead, he directed Geoffrey to take their bags to the rooms we'd arranged for them. Sabine didn't even look my direction. Hood still raised, she swept past us and started up the stairs. Maybe she was practicing for her new role. As a queen, she could really let her bitch flag fly.

I restrained from cringing. This was already going off the rails. Turning, I gasped to find Camila standing next to me.

Close enough to touch.

Neither of us reached out.

"Are we reduced to small talk?" she whispered. "What a pity."

"Perhaps you've forgotten your manners," I said coldly, hoping she didn't catch the tremor in my voice. "I was being polite."

"Polite." She sank her teeth into her full lower lip as she chewed on my choice of phrase. "Interesting."

I resisted the urge to stare at her mouth—to think about how long it had been since I'd tasted it, since I'd felt it exploring my flesh. "We don't have time for games," I forced myself to say. "We need to talk."

"You're the one making chitchat," she reminded me. Her head

swiveled to her brother. "I think you'll find our mother less eager to discuss the matters at hand."

"She's here, though," I added quickly when I saw his jaw tighten. He had not been entirely convinced that summoning them was a good idea—queens or no queens. He might be right. Just convincing Sabine to return to Venice had been a feat, but it wasn't enough, and we all knew it.

"And she can be gone just as quickly," Camila told me.

"Keep your bitchiness on lockdown," I hissed at her. "He's been through enough."

Camila studied him for a second, and I wondered if she saw what I did: the circles ringing his eyes, the hollowness of his cheeks, the lifeless anger that pulsed from him. She sighed, softening some. "Fine, but you have no idea what you're asking me."

Maybe she still had a heart.

We stared at each other for a moment. "Then I guess it's time for you to tell me what I *am* asking. What is so hard about helping your family?"

"Let's not pretend." She laughed. "You've made it clear that we aren't *friends* anymore."

The brittle control I clung to snapped, and I turned on her. Keeping my voice low, I asked, "Why did you really come back, Cam? Because you clearly have no interest in helping your family."

"My family tends to get themselves in trouble. Why should I dig them out?" she snarled back.

"Because that's what family does. They put up with one another's shit. They show up for one another. They give a fuck." I swallowed against the raw disgust burning my throat. "Which, clearly, you do not."

Had I honestly believed she was capable of anything else? She'd let us believe she was dead for forty years. She'd let *me* believe it.

Her eyes flashed. "I came, didn't I?"

"Oh wow." I threw my hands in the air. "Someone get Camila a medal."

"I don't remember you being so judgmental." She huffed,

crossing her arms and maintaining her distance.

"Yeah, well, people change. You should know that better than anyone."

"I didn't have a choice."

"Neither did I." I met her glare without flinching.

There was a pause as we stared each other down. Tension hung around us as thick as the emotions swelling inside me, emotions I refused to show Camila. She didn't deserve the satisfaction of knowing how deeply her words cut.

How easily she could wound me.

Even after all this time, even knowing what I now knew, I couldn't believe she was standing here. As we took the last few stairs, Geoffrey met us at the top.

"I've shown Madame Sabine to her room."

"Take her to her room." I jabbed a thumb in Camila's direction.

She snorted. "Not having a slumber party, huh?"

My eyes narrowed as I pasted on a sweet smile. "I wouldn't go to sleep around me if I were you."

It was easier to hate her—to make her an enemy. Just like she'd done to all of us. So that's what I would do.

"Is that a threat?" she murmured.

I only shrugged as I walked away, leaving Geoffrey to show her to her room. But I smiled a few minutes later when he left and I heard the door lock behind him.

CHAPTER THIRTY-FOUR

Julian

Having Jacqueline, Camila, and Sabine in the house only meant one thing: bloodshed was imminent. I'd expected my mother to draw the first blood, but watching Jacqueline and Camila glare at each other, I wondered if they might come to blows first. Truthfully, I'd never understood what had ended their friendship. Jacqueline knew that Camila had been tethered to Willem, but it wasn't Camila's sudden disappearance from our lives that had wrecked things. They'd fallen out long before the wedding. Maybe it was purely an outlet for current frustrations, but I wasn't about to let their old feud distract them from our purpose. We needed to find Thea.

It had been three days, and every second was pure fucking torture.

"You look like shit," Camila told me as she joined us on the main floor. She'd changed out of her traveling clothes.

Our mother had yet to appear.

"Nice to see you, too," I said flatly.

"He won't eat," Jacqueline told her. "Or sleep. Or feed. He's basically a walking zombie."

Of course, I was the common ground that they finally found.

"Over her?" Camila sighed, her face slackening as if unimpressed.

Before I could throw her into a wall, Jacqueline spun round and pressed a bare finger into her sternum. "Thea is your brother's mate—a member of *your* family. Can't you see he loves her? Or don't you care about that? Don't you care he's in pain?"

"Love always leads to pain." Camila didn't budge an inch. She stayed pinned to the spot. "You should know that, or haven't you learned that lesson?"

"Oh, I learned it." Jacqueline's eyes narrowed, but she stepped back and allowed her hand to drop. "The hard way."

Camila brushed the wrinkle from her sweater. "So did I."

What in the actual hell was this about? "Can you two hate each other later?" I interrupted. "And worry about me less? All that matters is Thea."

"Of course," they both said, even though they sounded like they meant different things.

Camila started toward the garden, and Jacqueline tailed her like a prison guard.

I was half tempted to follow them before one killed the other, but the longer I waited to face my mother, the worse it was going to be. Plus, I suspected she was waiting for me to come to her.

I took the stairs swiftly, tuning out the bickering of my best friend and twin. My mother was in her room, overseeing the unpacking of her bags with a critical eye and a sharp tongue.

"Be careful with that," she ordered one of the maids who was carefully hanging a long evening gown. "It's Chanel."

"Yes, Madame." The maid did a sort of half curtsy before scurrying off with the dress.

"Does that mean you've made a decision about *Le Regine*'s request?" I asked.

"No, it does not." Sabine's words were clipped as she examined the floral arrangement on the hearth. "I am simply prepared for any occasion."

"You keep emergency gowns with you?" I didn't even have the

energy to roll my eyes.

"Perhaps my ways seem silly to you, but I'm here because you asked me to be."

"I asked you to arrange for the season to move to Venice," I reminded her. A request she had flatly refused.

"And you have yet to give me a good reason to do so." She plucked a lily from the vase and tossed it into the fire below.

"My mate has been taken. The queens demand it. Ginerva is dead. How many more reasons do you need?" I'd been foolish to think it was a good sign that she'd come. It wasn't.

"I would advise caution when speaking to me," she said coldly. "You are the one with your hand out, and you aren't telling me everything."

There was no way I was going to warn her about the queens and the empty throne. I couldn't risk her refusing to see them. Not until we could find Willem and where he was keeping Thea. If my mother knew what the queens were after, she would never agree to an audience.

"And you are the one keeping secrets," I said, switching tactics. "You were ready to tell us the truth in Corfu. About the Council. You said—"

"Don't ask for the truth while feeding me lies," she cut me off. "Why am I really here? Why does *Le Regine* want the season to move? They've never deigned to attend the season before. They have no power over the Vampire Council. They have their own simpering court."

"I don't think *Le Regine* sees it that way," I warned her. "They weren't asking to move the season; it was an order."

"Then they must have forgotten the treaty that establishes they have no control over the Vampire Council," she sneered.

"A treaty? I don't remember that."

"It was agreed upon when you were a child. After magic was cursed, we had to establish clear boundaries before we all killed one another."

"And the Council?" I challenged. "Do they have control over

the queens?"

"No, but the Council must respect them at court." She arched a brow. "Now do you see why it will be impossible to convince them to come?"

If my mother could not talk the Council into moving the season, no one could. Still, there had been a time when Sabine sent me to work for them—long after the curse and any treaty that followed. There had to be reason for it.

"Why did you fall out with them?" I asked.

"It isn't important." She dismissed the question with a wave of her hand.

"I think it is," I said softly. "What happened between you?"

"*Le Regine* clings to a world that no longer exists," Sabine said.

For the first time in days, I felt like laughing. "And we don't?"

"Not like this. They refuse to accept that magic will never awaken again. It's gone."

"Is it?" There was a time when I'd thought that. I'd never believed the stories about the curse. There were too many different versions of that story for any of them to be fact. But I'd lived long enough to know that magic had faded, that some of it had been lost or forgotten, and that some of it seemed to run like a current in the blood, making it as unreachable as if it, too, had been lost. But magic still existed. Thea had proven that to me.

"You sound like your sister. I never thought my children would become revolutionaries."

"We are hardly revolutionaries. You just said that the world had changed. Are you any better than *Le Regine* if you refuse to accept that?"

"Are you any less of a liar if you refuse to tell me what they actually want?" she countered.

I closed my eyes, knowing she wasn't going to let this go. Sabine could hold a grudge for centuries. I'd watched her do it. I didn't have that much time to waste. She wanted the truth? Fine. But she wasn't going to be happy about it. "They need to crown a replacement for Ginerva. She's dead. If they don't, the magic that flows in the *Rio Oscuro* will die. Allegedly."

I waited for her to gloat.

Sabine went utterly still, the color draining from her face. "That is not possible."

I hadn't expected that reaction.

It could only mean one thing.

"So, it's true?" I couldn't believe it. I trusted the Conte. He had no reason to lie to me, but I'd hoped he was being dramatic. I recalled what he had said to me. "All magic will die, and all of those with magic in our veins..."

"Yes," she said quietly. She shrank under the weight of this news. It was the first time my mother had ever looked vulnerable to me.

I cleared my throat, trying to process what all of this meant. It wasn't possible. "Even humans?"

It was why we fed off them—their unused magic kept us alive. It fed our own.

"Their magic is too diluted," she said in a thick voice. Crossing to an armchair, she took a seat next to the fire. "They don't require it to live. They won't even notice when it finally dies."

"But we..."

She nodded in response to my unspoken question. "Without it, we will eventually die." Sabine pinched the bridge of her nose with her long fingers. "I should have known this was coming."

"How could you have?" I asked slowly, joining her in the other chair.

"Don't be stupid." She grimaced as though she took personal offense to my apparent ignorance. "You've felt it. Magic fading. Fewer vampires. Why do you think the Council wants to see you married? The only way to protect our kind is to preserve the magic we have left."

"That's what this was about." I shook my head. "Then why fight my relationship with Thea? She has more power than any of us combined."

My mother leaned forward, lowering her voice like she'd done when I was a very young vampire and she wanted me to listen. "And why is that?" she asked. "Where do her powers come from? You are so blinded by lust that you have never stopped to ask these questions."

"Or maybe you're so blinded by prejudice that you never stopped to consider that Thea is exactly what we need," Camila cut in. I looked up to find her listening at the door. Jacqueline was nowhere in sight. "Why else would Willem take her?"

My mother's gaze was as sharp as twin daggers when she looked at my sister. "He was your husband. You tell us."

I opened my mouth to protest, her words triggering a dormant desire to protect my twin, but Camila spoke before I could.

"The only other reason he might take her should terrify you," she said to her before turning shadowed eyes on me. "And if that's why he has, we might already be too late."

I couldn't even consider it. It would drive me past any hope of return. Darkness rustled inside me as the beast stretched his wings, hoping I would give in and release him.

"Willem would never be so stupid to believe he could do that," Sabine seethed. "He knows what she is—it's perfectly obvious. He knows she isn't a witch. What good will she do him?"

"Obvious?" I countered. "Then why didn't you tell me she was a siren after we met?"

"I had no idea you were planning to fall in love with the poor creature. I assumed it was an infatuation."

Camila glared at her as she entered the room and joined us by the fire. For a moment, her face caught the flames' light, and I saw the female I'd known for centuries reflected there. Softness. Concern. But then her mouth twisted into a rueful smile—so full of spite, she looked like a monster. "And you have no patience for infatuations, do you?"

"Now isn't the time for personal vendettas. We need to decide what to do." Sabine sighed, pushing her raven locks over her shoulders like we were discussing a change to our dinner plans instead of the fate of my fiancée.

I'd had enough.

"We need to find out where Thea is being held," I interrupted.

"Your mate will keep," my mother replied. "I must speak to *Le Regine* at once."

"What?" I asked, but my blood was already roaring in my veins. Within me, beastly magic bellowed for release. "How can talking to two out-of-touch queens be what we need to worry about right now? You said yourself that they refuse to face the truth."

"The *Rio Oscuro* can be saved. Thank the gods for that," she muttered.

"Magic is asleep. Magic is dying." I hurled her words back at her, finally losing the last scrap of my control. "Which is it, Mother? You fear my mate. You think she's not good enough for me. She's human. She's not. Just tell me the fucking truth—or do you know what's real anymore?"

"Go on," Camila needled her. "Tell him the truth."

"You"—I spun around and pointed a finger at my twin—"are not helping."

"And you are an idiot." Before I could tell her what she was, she'd turned to our mother. "You've known this whole time, haven't you?"

"Known what?" I exploded.

"Never mind," my mother said.

I studied my sister for a moment, wondering if it would always be like this. She had changed. I knew that. But I'd been unprepared for her cruel games. I was unprepared for how much Willem had twisted her mind and warped her feelings. Maybe someday I would trust her again, but I couldn't imagine living to see that moment.

"What about you?" I asked Camila quietly before our mother could speak further. "Did you know that she was a siren?"

"I'll admit it took me longer to put together than I would like." Camila crossed her arms and stared defiantly down at me. "I heard the magic in her blood when we met, but I didn't know that she—"

"Enough," Sabine cut her off, a slight tremble in her voice. "No good will come from this. We must worry about the *Rio*'s source. Then we can deal with your mate's abduction."

"You were saying," I prompted Camila, ignoring Mom's interruption.

"The Mordicum has been seeking a siren for years," she explained to me, and the angry rush of my blood slowed in my veins, thickening into dread. "There have been rumors one was found in the States."

"Thea?" I'd known we were being hunted down, but I thought the threat came from the Council and Camila herself. Because of me. How could they have known about her before...

"I doubt it," Camila said with a dry laugh. "The rumors go back to the nineteenth century. Why do you think Willem wanted to go to America?"

Her words slammed into me, and I collapsed into my seat. She had hinted, and I had guessed, but nothing prepared me for the moment of reckoning I now faced. "Willem was looking for a siren," I whispered, dread churning inside me. I closed my eyes and sought the spark of Thea's magic inside me. It had grown fainter since she was taken. Now I couldn't feel it at all. I forced myself to look at my sister. "Why?"

"To breed." There was no malice in her words this time—no cruel joy. Instead, her eyes filled with sorrow as she delivered this final blow. "He's obsessed with magic—obsessed with finding a way to awaken true magic again. It's all he cared about. I was part of that obsession. The Drakes believed that with his blood and mine, we would create a truly powerful vampire."

I cast a sidelong look at my mother. Was this why she'd hidden Camila's children? Had she known? Sabine pressed her lips together and refused to meet my eyes. She could avoid me now, but I would force the issue. I needed to know the truth, and eventually, so did my twin.

Camila continued. "But Willem never believed that. He needed a wife to hide behind while he sought stronger magic, and there are no lines he wouldn't cross in his search."

"Did he find this siren?" I asked, though I suspected I already knew the answer. He had not. If he had, why would he need Thea now? Dark magic rose inside me, called to protect its master. Now wasn't the time to lose control. I needed answers. I needed to know what we were up against if I was going to find Thea, save her, protect her.

"Not to my knowledge," she said, choosing her words carefully. "At least, not until he found Thea."

It was my fault. I'd drawn her into this world. My magic stirred hers. It overrode her mother's glamour, undoing the sacrifices Kelly Melbourne had made to keep her daughter safe. I'd promised to protect her as my mate. I'd sworn that I would.

And I had led the devil straight to her doorstep.

"Why a siren?" I mumbled. Understanding this might be the only key to saving her.

"I don't know." Camila shrugged, offering me the smallest of smiles. It was nearly reassuring. "He's a bit of a collector. He was always seeking new magical creatures. Always locking me up and going off to follow rumors of fae sightings or werewolf packs, and sometimes..."

"What?" I demanded, but she shook her head. I rose to my feet and took a step toward her. "Just tell me. It can't be worse than what I imagine."

"Not even you could imagine such cruelty," she whispered. "I went into his study once. He left it unlocked, and the things I saw..." She trailed away, shuddering at the memory.

And now he had Thea. Now he was doing these unspeakable things to her. Now she was his to experiment on. My vision darkened as I felt talons clawing inside me, wings beating in my chest. My magic wouldn't be denied much longer. Even I didn't know what to expect when it finally broke free of the cage I'd kept it in all these lifetimes. I'd allowed it to come out to play with Thea, but I had never truly embraced it.

"I know why he wants a siren." My mother's voice broke into my nightmare. We turned to her. Half of me was filled with hope to have an answer—any answer—but horror tempered it, cooled it, and turned it to ice inside me.

I waited for her to continue. Each second she delayed felt like a stake to the heart.

"It is why I have fought your relationship with Thea," she explained slowly. "One of the reasons."

"Out with it!" Camila looked like she might throw her out a window if she didn't get to the point. I might help her.

"Being honest is new to Mother," I muttered, letting my disgust seep into every word. "She has to feel her way through it."

Sabine's lips flattened at the slight, but she continued. "I remember sirens," she began. "Such lovely creatures, said to be gifted by Demeter with the song of the living and the dead."

"Are you actually saying sirens were made by a Greek goddess?" Camila asked, stunned.

Even I had to admit I was surprised.

"You've always known there was truth to the old gods," Sabine sniffed. "But who knows? There is always some truth in myth. Look at us. Look at the magical world. Is it really impossible to believe?"

"Why did she create them?" I forced myself to ask. My mother wouldn't give me answers willingly, but I would get them out of her.

"To find Persephone. She gave them wings to fly over the fields and search for her, and when she learned Hades had stolen her daughter, she taught them to sing the song of the dead so that they could enter the underworld. But first, she taught them the song of the living so they could return. It's old magic—the magic of creation. Sirens could walk between life and death."

I found myself needing to take a seat. Sinking back into the armchair, I tried to process what she was telling me. "You should have said something."

"Would you have listened?" she challenged me, and we both knew that I would have ignored her. "I felt Thea's magic when we first met, but I didn't know what it was. I suspected siren blood ran in her veins, but it was so faint I assumed it was just the remnants of an old bloodline."

"The glamour," I whispered. "Her mother shielded her. It made her sick."

Sabine nodded. "It would. Magic as powerful as Thea's must have fought attempts to conceal it. Kelly must have struggled endlessly to contain it."

"But why hide it?" Camila asked.

"Willem cannot have been the first to hunt a siren," Sabine explained.

"Why?" I demanded, raking a hand through my hair. "What happened to sirens? Why would he want one now?"

"Because of what happens when our magic meets theirs." Her eyes shuttered for a moment, and when they opened again, ancient sorrow stared back at me. "I remember the sirens, and I remember what happened to them. Your mate is truly a rare creature."

Vampires guarded their own magic jealously. It wasn't spoken of, and it was rarely used. Most of us couldn't summon it even if we tried. My parents were old—ancient even by vampire standards— and I'd always wondered if they carried magic of their own. I wondered why we never talked about it.

"What happened to the sirens?" I asked. "Where did they go?"

Sabine lifted her chin, her grief turning to pointed resolution. "They were tracked down and eliminated."

"Eliminated?" Camila repeated. "You don't mean…"

"You killed them," I realized with horrible clarity.

"We had no choice," Sabine admitted. "The vampires had to kill the sirens. We couldn't risk what would happen if one of us bred with one of them."

I wouldn't allow her to spin this. Not knowing what was at stake.

I sprang out of the chair, shaking my head. "You murdered them!"

"We protected our species," she seethed, rising to meet me. "Sirens are a danger to us all. Why do you think the Mordicum wants your mate? Why Willem sought a siren? You have no idea what will happen if they manage to get Thea pregnant!"

"And me?" I asked in shock. "What if I got Thea pregnant? I thought that was what the Council wanted. Little vampire babies."

"Thea will never be allowed to carry your child." To my shock, she sounded almost sad about this. "I have tried to intervene, tried to break you two apart, tried to save you from that pain. But now you must know—you will never be allowed to marry her, you will never be allowed to have children, and you will be lucky if she's allowed to live."

No. The word wouldn't come out of me, but I found myself advancing on her. Somewhere in the back of my mind, I heard Camila yelling. A hand tried to grab hold of me and pull me away, but I shook free. And at that moment, as my tether tightened around me like the hands I wrapped around my mother's throat, I knew Thea was alive. I knew I had to protect her.

At any cost.

"We had no choice," Sabine managed to gasp as I choked her.

But I wasn't listening as I squeezed.

CHAPTER THIRTY-FIVE

Thea

Birdsong woke me, its cheerful melody piercing through my dream. It had been about the stranger again. His smile had been familiar, but I could never quite catch up with him. I rolled over, squeezing my eyes shut against the sunlight pouring into my room. It was no use. For some reason, my body refused to get on board with my regular schedule. Stretching my arms over my head, I felt the prickle of heat on my skin and snatched my limb out of the light. Yanking my covers up to my chin, I opened my eyes to find my bed curtains had been left open a fraction of an inch—just enough to let some of the cursed sunlight through.

If I could sleep through the damn day, it wouldn't be a problem.

Shimmying away from the slant of light, I caught the tasseled pull and rang for my maid. It had been another fitful sleep, full of those dreams, and I lounged against my headboard as I tried to wake up.

"Good morning, miss," Natalie called as she entered the room.

I rolled my eyes at her pleasant greeting. "Not really. When are they going to fix the windows?"

I felt like they had been broken forever. It was probably why I couldn't seem to sleep past dawn. How was I supposed to rest with all that stupid sunshine?

"Your father said they will be by tomorrow night to fit new shutters," Natalie said, pulling the curtains open on the other side of the bed. She extended her wrist, but I shook my head. I wasn't hungry. She frowned at the refusal but didn't say anything. "Couldn't sleep again? You only went to bed a few hours ago."

She was right. Half the house wouldn't be awake yet. But here I was—the first one in bed and the first one up. "When did the others go to bed?"

"Only about an hour ago." She held my silk robe up for me. "But your father is awake."

"He never sleeps," I said with a laugh. "He's too busy worrying."

A shadow passed across Natalie's face, but she smiled.

"What's wrong?" I asked.

"Nothing," she said too quickly.

"Liar." I stood, sighing with pleasure as the silk rippled down my bare skin. "What did you overhear?"

"He received a letter." It never took much to get Natalie to spill whatever gossip she'd overheard. "Anna said it looked like an invitation."

Now *that* was interesting. It felt like ages since I'd left the house. We'd been entertaining nonstop, but it wasn't the same. "Someone else in Venice is going to have a party? Thank God."

"You heard nothing from me," she reminded me as she guided me safely past the stray sunlight toward my dressing room.

But as soon as we were out of harm's way, I darted toward the door. "I'll get dressed later. I want to find out what this is about."

"He'll know I told you," she protested.

But I was already halfway down the hall. Thankfully, the rest of the estate's shutters were in working order and closed for the day. Not that anyone else had to worry about sunlight, but I understood why they preferred the dark.

I hated that I kept waking during the day and missing all the midnight fun.

I found my father in his study, a stack of old books piled in front of him and candles dripping wax onto the desk. The letter was there, too. Its envelope was sliced open and discarded. He looked like he'd stepped out of the pages of an old novel.

"It's the twenty-first century," I reminded him, pointing to the switch on the wall. "You could turn on the lights."

"It's not necessary." He closed the book he was looking at and moved it casually over the open letter. "Couldn't sleep again?"

I shook my head, pulling my silk robe more tightly. "Wide awake. I don't think I'll sleep through the day until those shutters are dealt with."

"I understand." His mouth turned down, his broad shoulders slumping. "I should have thought of it before you arrived."

"You didn't have time." I waved it off. Yes, he'd reached Venice before me, but it wasn't his fault. And as much as I wanted a good day's sleep, I was more interested in the letter. I sauntered to his desk and picked up a book from his stack. "What are you reading? And why is it in…"

I turned to study the book from a couple of angles, trying to figure out its language.

"It's an Anatolian dialect. Be careful. That book is older than I am." He reached for it, and I saw my opportunity. As soon as his hands were occupied, I swiped the letter from under the other book on his desk.

"A ball!" I shrieked and began to read it. "You are cordially invited to the Coronation Rites of—"

"You're not going," he cut me off and held out a hand.

A surge of annoyance shot through me, but I deposited the invitation. It wasn't like I had a choice, but it stung to give it up before finding out the particulars. "It's just a party."

"Nothing is just a party when it's hosted by a vampire." Opening the drawer of his desk, he tucked the letter inside before closing and locking it.

I crossed my arms and shook my head. Why was he always like this? I always obeyed him. Not that I had any choice. "You don't trust me."

"I don't trust *them*," he explained.

"But I'm bored." I flopped into the wingback that sat across from him. "We never go anywhere!"

"All our friends are here. Why do we need to go out?" He stood and looked down on me. "It's best you stay in. What if there was another accident?"

"I won't go hunting!" How many times did we have to go over this? It felt like we talked about nothing else. For days he'd fussed over me, and the worst part was that I couldn't even remember the stupid accident that had caused all the trouble. "I can't stay inside forever."

"Just a while longer," he said, dismissing my concern again. "When you're sleeping better. Have you fed?"

"Yes," I lied. I swear he thought every problem could be fixed with blood. But since we were always home, I was always feeding. It had been worse since the accident. I fed all the time. Probably because I was so bored.

"It will help your recovery," he reminded me, and I forced a smile. "I know I'm being overprotective."

"Yes, you are." I sighed. "I can take care of myself."

"Your mother thought the same," he said flatly, his words ending our disagreement. He had the trump card, and he was never afraid to use it. How many times had he told me the story of my mother's death?

"Nothing is going to happen to me," I promised.

"Not if you stay home," he agreed, moving around the desk. "After your accident, I thought I'd lost you, too."

I swallowed, feeling small in his shadow. Of course he was protective of me. After what had happened to my mother, how could he not be? But I couldn't help longing for the outside world. Not that I'd spent much time there. I hadn't been allowed. But sometimes, I swore it called to me.

"I need to see to something," he said. "I'll be home before nightfall."

"It's already nine! You should be in bed," I grumbled.

Father chuckled. "Worried about me?"

"Just annoyed that you get to run around at all hours while I have to stay home." I hated my stupid condition. I hated being stuck inside all day when I was awake.

"Why don't you try to go back to bed?" he suggested. "Have some warm blood and use one of the guest rooms."

I shrugged. "Fine."

There was a 0 percent chance I would take that advice. Even though I was tired, I would never fall asleep now. Not knowing that invitation was locked in his drawer. I only wanted to see whom it was from—there was no harm in that, right?

"You look sad." He helped me to my feet, and I winced at the sting of magic where we touched. I hated that feeling—it felt so wrong, but we never wore gloves in the house, and since I never left the house...

"I just wish I was normal." I wished my skin didn't burn in the sunlight. I wished I could come and go as I pleased. But it was no use. I was different, and everyone knew it.

"Never say that," he growled. "Do you know how many vampires would die to be in your shoes? You are pure, Thea. Vampires weren't meant for the day. We belong to the night."

"I know." Though I struggled to believe it. I didn't see my condition as a blessing like he did.

It was a curse.

I would never tell him that, though. I would never hurt him. Even if he drove me crazy, he loved me. He protected me.

Still, I couldn't stay cooped up here forever. I felt fine despite the poor sleep. Standing, I scrounged up a yawn. "Maybe you're right," I said, stretching my arms high. "I am tired."

He guided me toward the door. Once we were out of his office, he closed it and locked it, too. Just like the drawer with the mysterious letter in it.

He really didn't trust me. Whatever.

"Get some rest."

"I will," I said brightly as he leaned over and kissed my

forehead. "See you tonight."

I made a show of heading back to my room, but I hadn't given up. As soon as I was inside, I crept around the shaft of daylight to the bellpull and rang for Natalie.

She arrived, carrying a mug. "I knew you'd get hungry."

"Hmmm." I nodded, taking it from her and sipping the rich contents. "There's just one more thing I need."

She waited for my request, and I couldn't help grinning. My father didn't trust me? Fine. I was tired of trying to prove myself to him. If he was going to treat me like a prisoner, I would act like one. I might have to obey him when he was around, but when he wasn't, the servants had to obey *me*.

And I knew exactly what I needed. "Bring me the key to my father's study."

CHAPTER THIRTY-SIX

Julian

"I'll ask again. Where is Willem Drake?" The vampire's black gaze darted around, looking for escape instead of answering me. I had him pinned to a wall in the *Cannaregio sestiere*. Maybe he didn't know Drake, but I doubted it. I thrust his body higher, my fingers sinking deeper into his chest. The smell of his blood mingled with the damp air from the nearest canal—musty and wet. "This would be over a whole lot quicker if you answered me."

He scraped his shoes against the stones, trying to get leverage. "I don't know," he said with a thick Italian accent. He must be a local. "I have no idea who Willem Drake is."

"That's not what I hear." My captive had been at a local speakeasy—one of the few that managed to keep its doors open, due to *Le Regine*'s disapproval of the usual vampire vices—and he'd been talking about his new job for an English vampire lord— one who kept to himself. With the season in full swing, nearly every pureblood family was caught up with social events, and so were their servants. "You should be more careful who you brag to over absinthe. Someone overheard you."

"Fuck off," he snarled.

I barely noticed my rage surging. Being furious was becoming second nature after several of these spontaneous interrogations. I dug my fingers in a little farther, tearing through muscle. "Mind your manners before I rip your heart out."

"You're going to anyway."

"I see you're a pessimist," I said through gritted teeth. "Or you don't mind taking orders from wealthy masters. Wouldn't you rather try your luck and tell me than die? You'll live longer. Willem won't protect you."

"I'd only be tortured." He tried to pry free, but I was in too deep for him to get loose. "Either way, I die. I'd rather it be quick."

A low laugh peeled from my throat, but I wasn't amused. "At least we're getting somewhere. You do know Willem Drake."

"I know not to cross him."

"Where is he?" I demanded. "Tell me or—"

"He'll kill you." He panted. His eyes dropped to his chest and watched the bloodstain on his shirt grow. "If you let me go, I won't mention this to him. You don't want to go looking for him. You have no idea what he's capable of. He has a creature and—"

"Creature," I repeated. "What kind of creature?"

"I don't know. He keeps it locked away. Only household staff sees her."

Her.

It had to be Thea. My heart thundered in my chest as my magic stretched its wings and readied for battle. "Tell me where he is, and I can protect you."

"I'm a dead man already. Why should I help you?"

"Do you want me to say please?" I hissed.

"Even if I wanted to, I couldn't. The house has protections. I can't take you there. The glamour won't let you through."

"That is disappointing." I stepped back, allowing him to crumble against the wall. I pulled my hand away and surveyed my stained fingers.

The vampire tried to stand. If he was smart, he planned to run. But that was the funny thing about angry magic. It could be as fatal as poison.

And my magic was pissed the fuck off.

"What..." His question died on his lips, drowned by the black blood seeping from his mouth. He collapsed onto his knees, staring up at me in wide-eyed horror. His lips formed a single word: *"Flagello."*

Once again, my reputation preceded me. I was the scary story Venetian vampires told their children. I was the creature that stalked the shadows and dragged men from their beds. I was the Scourge, and Venice remembered me.

I stared down at the pitiful male. Bringing my fingers to my mouth, I licked his blood from my hands and considered my options. I could let him go. It's what I would have done a month ago. Maybe even a few decades ago. But he was a rat, and rats always scurried back to whatever holes they'd crawled from. "It's magic," I explained as he tried and failed to rise again. "It will wear off in a few minutes."

"Please." His thick tongue tripped over the word. "Have mercy."

"Mercy?" I repeated. I swiped my tongue over my thumb. "I can taste your last kill. Did you have mercy on her?"

This had been my job once—to punish the guilty and keep the queens' peace. Lists would arrive, and I would dispatch justice.

Until I found out I was being used. It had been an accident.

My target had tried to stop me. He'd lifted a bloody hand to my face to push me away—and I'd tasted it—his innocence. I'd never fed from my victims before. I'd had no idea until that moment. That innocent vampire had been on the list. How many other innocents had I killed?

I couldn't explain it. I didn't even understand it until my next assignment. I attacked first and fed, tasting the sins of the vampire I'd been sent to kill, tasting his victims. I'd known then that I was a pawn. When my mother had ordered me home, I'd left Venice willingly, but there was no place on earth I could go to escape what I'd done.

I'd chosen to be someone else. For a while, I'd been stupid

enough to believe I wasn't the monster they'd made me.

But now I was back, and between my absence and Ginerva's death, it seemed vampires were forgetting the rules.

"You aren't supposed to kill," I reminded him. Grabbing his shoulder, I lifted him like a heavy sack. He couldn't even fight me. "You're supposed to feed."

"I won't do it again," he promised, his tongue loosening. It seemed the poison was starting to wear off. "No one has been obeying the rules. *Le Regine* no longer enforces them. The Mordicum—"

My fangs ripped into his throat, not bothering to be discreet. He was right. No one was enforcing the rules—and nothing, other than Thea, tasted better than blood made rich by frequent kills. Its dark, heavy tang surged with magic and justice. Two mouthfuls would give me strength for a month—but since he wasn't walking away from this and I needed all the strength I could get, I finished him off and tossed him into the canal.

Familiar footsteps approached me from behind. "Jesus Christ. You're a fucking mess. If you're going to eat like that, wear a bib."

I turned as my sister strutted from the shadows. Swiping the back of my hand across my mouth, I discovered she was right. There was blood all over me. I shrugged. "I'm only doing what the queens ask."

"They asked you to run around murdering vampires?" She lifted an eyebrow.

"I am *il flagello*," I reminded her.

"Don't let it go to your head." She sighed as she looked me over. Unlike my bloody mess, Camila's cashmere coat was as pristine as freshly fallen snow. She wore it buttoned to her chin as if the cold bothered her. Her shoes—five-inch heels that looked like they could stake someone—were less practical.

"Going out?"

"Only to drag your ass back to the villa. Mother needs to speak with you."

I grimaced as I pulled my gloves from my pocket and drew

them over my bloodstained hands.

Camila spotted my disdain. "You'll have to talk to her eventually."

"Will I?" I doubted it. As far as I was concerned, Sabine Rousseaux was dead.

"Holidays will be even more awkward if you don't," Camila pointed out. "Look, she needs to go over the guest list with you."

"My mate is missing, magic is dying, and she's planning a fucking tea party?!"

"It's a dinner party," a lofty voice interrupted. Sabine rounded the corner. She hadn't bothered with a coat, but there was a scarf wrapped around her neck. I wondered if it was there to help her blend in or to hide the bruises on her neck from where my magic had marked her. To my delight, they hadn't healed as quickly as usual. "And I'm reconsidering your invite."

"Where should I send my regrets?" I scowled at her. Of course she'd followed Camila. I was getting sick of using my twin as a middleman, and Sabine was even less patient than me. But if she thought confronting me in person would change how I felt about her, she was wrong.

"You will be in attendance."

"I don't take orders from you." I started past her. I only made it a few steps down the cobbled street.

"I am still the head of this family!"

Despite everything, I smiled to myself as I turned around. "Perhaps you are, but I'm not a member of *your* family."

Her eyes bulged as she processed these words, and I wished Thea was here to see her face. It was almost as good as when my mate had challenged her to a cello duel. "If you think…"

"I'm a mated male. That's as good as married."

"As good as married and married are two very different things, son."

Her words reminded me of something that Thea would say. A pang shot through me. "I'm a member of Thea's family now."

"Thea might as well be dead," Mom hissed.

My brittle control snapped. "You better hope she isn't."

"Or what?"

"Or I'll finish what I started." My eyes dropped to the scarf knotted at her neck.

"Homicidal rage doesn't suit you." But she backed up a step.

"Can you both give it a rest?" Camila asked, sounding tired. If she was still fighting with Jacqueline, she'd probably already had her fill of arguments for the day. "Just tell him."

"Tell me what?" My heart jumped into my throat and lodged there. If something had happened to Thea, my mother might hear about it before I did, but I would have felt it—even with Thea's magic faint and growing dimmer by the day. I was sure of it.

"While you've been busy eating half of Venice's vampire population—"

"Trust me, they deserved it," I said.

"I've been to see the queens," she said, ignoring me. "And I've agreed to call the season to Venice."

"Fantastic," I said flatly, clinging to my anger. It was all I had left. If I lost it... "More dinner parties. That will solve all our problems."

Her mouth lifted into an arrogant smile. "It will solve your problem. I have a plan."

I waited, but I wasn't expecting what she said next.

"I've invited Willem Drake."

CHAPTER THIRTY-SEVEN

Julian

I missed Thea's eyes. The abandoned engagement ring sitting in my palm only reminded me of them. I missed how they lit up with laughter and crinkled around the edges when she smiled. I missed the tiny flecks of gold that danced in them. I missed the way they surveyed a room, drinking in every detail.

I missed the moment she opened them each morning.

It had been ten mornings since I'd woken up and found her glittering emerald eyes staring back at me. I wondered what she was looking at now.

Jacqueline knocked on my door and stuck her head inside. "Are you almost ready?"

"I'll be out in a minute," I said quietly, closing my hand around the ring.

I stood as she disappeared to make whatever last-minute preparations were necessary. Walking to the bureau, I found the chain Geoffrey had purchased for me earlier this morning. He hadn't asked me why I wanted it, which made me like him more.

Slipping Thea's ring onto it, I fastened it around my neck before I buttoned my shirt. I moved without thought. After all these centuries, my body didn't need my brain to tie my bow tie.

That was a problem because I couldn't get my mind off Thea.

Or, more precisely, the hope that tonight might finally deliver Willem Drake into our hands.

There was no way he'd be stupid enough to come, but that didn't stop me from obsessing over it as I dressed. I stepped into the hall in my tuxedo a few moments later and found my best friend waiting.

Jacqueline drew a deep breath before smiling brightly at me. I knew it was as false as my own calm facade, but I wished I could fake it as well as she could.

"Do you want this now or later?" She brandished my *bauta* and cloak, another cloak draped over her arm.

"Later," I said stiffly. "You look nice."

"'Nice'?" she repeated. "This is Gucci." She turned to give me a better view of her gown. Its black bodice plunged so deeply between her full breasts that two cream straps held things in place at the bust. The pleated gold lamé skirt fell into a short train behind the dress's low-cut back. She'd left her hair down, allowing it to fall in soft waves over her shoulder. But as lovely as she looked, I couldn't summon more enthusiasm. Not with what was at stake.

"You know you're beautiful. Why do you need me to tell you?" I asked.

Jacqueline snorted, shattering the ladylike illusion of her appearance. "Because girls deserve to hear it now and then."

"You look beautiful," I said with as much sincerity as I could muster. I crooked my arm and offered it to her. "Shall we?"

Her throat slid, but she nodded, taking a moment to carefully arrange our cloaks and masks in her other arm. She took my arm, and we headed toward the boat launch downstairs.

"Did your family arrive?" she asked.

"Yes. They're all here. Have you spoken to Camila?"

When Jacqueline had reached out to my twin for help, I thought they were turning a corner. But by the time my mother had arranged to take a residence for the family at court, not a single one of them was speaking to each other. Camila was pissed that

Willem had been invited. Sabine was being Sabine. And it seemed whatever fight had ended Camila and Jacqueline's friendship centuries ago had been rekindled. It had been a relief when the others left.

"No, I haven't," Jacqueline said in a clipped tone as we met our gondola.

I helped her inside it. The DuBois family crest was carved into the side of the boat. Jacqueline settled on the velvet seat and grimaced.

"It hasn't gotten more comfortable in the last two hundred years," she warned me.

I barely noticed as I took a seat next to her. Unlike the gondolas tourists could hail throughout Venice, ours was much older and much more private thanks to its *felze*, a small cabin for its passengers. It had shuttered windows on three sides and a pair of black lace curtains that could be drawn to avoid prying eyes. With hundreds of vampires making their way to the *Rio Oscuro*, we had to be careful or risk drawing too much human attention. The gondolier dipped his paddle into the water, and we began to make our way to tonight's celebration.

"Do you think he'll be there?" Jacqueline asked, peering through a crack in the shutters.

"I don't know," I admitted. "He's not stupid. He'll expect it to be a trap, but I'm not sure he can resist. As long as he hasn't figured out who sent the invite, he might show. He has to be curious."

"Everyone wants to know who will take Ginerva's place." She nodded. "Will they really crown Sabine?"

It seemed so, although nothing had been formalized. The Council would see it as a way to finally control the queens.

"I can't decide if it's the worst idea ever or the best way to keep her out of my business."

"She can't stop you from marrying Thea." Jacqueline placed her gloved hand on mine. "None of them can."

"They have their ways," I said softly. There was one very simple way to keep me from marrying her. We all knew it.

"No one will hurt her."

"I wish I believed that," I muttered.

"Your mother will intervene."

I laughed at the thought. "When did you get so optimistic?"

"She knows what you'll do if they try to hurt Thea," Jacqueline whispered. "She won't pay that price. She won't risk losing her only pureblood son over this."

I wasn't so sure. Most of the time, I couldn't be certain my mother liked me, let alone loved me. I kept the thought to myself. Jacqueline still had hope. I wouldn't take that from her, even though my own was nothing more than an ember in the ashes of my life. Any moment now, it would be snuffed out entirely.

The boat glided to a stop, and Jacqueline leaned forward, poking her head out of the curtains.

"People are starting to arrive," she told me.

I looked out to find she was right. "Sabine will hate that."

The only thing worse than being late to a party was being early to one. Gondolas and speedboats were stopped along the canal. Several had lanterns swinging from curved arms to guide their way along the dark water. Once they reached the enchanted part of the canal, it would be unnecessary. On the open water of Venice, darkness swallowed the city. The areas around the court had been instructed to close down for the night with all the vampires out. The fewer humans drawn to this part of the city, the better. Two security teams were circling around in motorboats to give instructions. I had no particular interest in being early, but before we could close the curtains, one of the teams approached us.

"Name," a bored vampire in tactical gear barked. The other shone a flashlight into the boat. Jacqueline coughed politely, and I groaned.

"She wants us there early," she muttered.

While most of us weren't speaking to each other, we'd all been notified of Sabine's plan. It sounded batshit crazy to me, but I was running out of options.

"Julian Rousseaux," I said to the guard.

His eyes widened, and he elbowed his partner, who was still shining his flashlight into our eyes. "My apologies, sir. Please proceed."

We drifted past the other gondolas filled with vampires in evening dress. The females dripped with jewels while the males displayed a curious variety of evening attire. A few of the suits looked to be from the eighteenth century. All of them wore masks.

Since we were the only ones allowed passage, we arrived quickly at the dock. When we stepped out of the gondola, I cursed. "Someone is making herself at home."

In the few days since *Le Regine* had called me to their thrones, Sabine had transformed the court from its grieving shadows to life itself. Lanterns flickering with fairy light lined the path that led from the dock to the magical *sestiere*. It was quiet now, but within the hour, it would be filled with courtiers, both vampire and familiar, as it had been in centuries past. We made our way to the gates, which were no longer closed.

The mourning flowers had been swept away and replaced with red roses in full bloom. Thorny vines snaked into the air to form an arch, holding the flowers in place with a spell.

"Are you ready for this?" Jacqueline asked as we crossed into the palace's courtyard. Before I could answer, a friendly cry split the air. A second later, I found myself enveloped in a hug.

"We tried to come and find you," Lysander told me, smacking my back in welcome. His dark hair was slicked back in an effort to make him look less like he'd just wandered out of some cave, but even in a tuxedo, he didn't quite fit.

"What kept you?" I asked, surprised to feel some relief to see my brothers.

Before he could answer, Sebastian caught me in another hug. He leaned in and whispered, "Don't worry. If Willem shows, we'll fuck him up no matter what Mom says."

"What?" I pulled back, but I didn't have time to press the issue before Thoren and Benedict welcomed me.

"The fucking canal wouldn't let us go," Lysander explained as they took turns hugging Jacqueline. "Mom ordered it not to."

"Of course she did." She would think that party prep was more important than my mate's life. "But what did you mean by no matter what Mom says?"

"He meant the order I gave them." Sabine appeared on the steps of the court, flanked by my father, who looked like he was about to implode, and a furious Camila. They all wore black—the traditional color of Ginerva's line.

"What order?" I asked slowly. Jacqueline grabbed my arm, as if to get a hold on me before Sabine answered. Camila's eyes narrowed in on the touch, and her face tightened into a frown.

"The same order I'm about to give you," Sabine told me. "No one is to lay a finger on Willem Drake tonight. Not even you."

CHAPTER THIRTY-EIGHT

Jacqueline

The trouble with vampire parties was always the lack of snacks. I tapped my foot, frowning as a waiter passed with another round of champagne. There was always plenty of that to be had, but I wanted something to chew on—something to distract me from Sabine's ridiculous plan. Because deeper down, something other than hunger turned my stomach: shame.

It was my fault that Thea had been taken, and so far, I'd done absolutely nothing useful to help bring her home. Standing around watching the guests arrive didn't feel like contributing to the cause. I glanced up and found a stone-faced Julian greeting people at the courtyard gates.

At least I hadn't gotten stuck with that job.

I swiped a glass of champagne from the next passing tray and downed it.

"You are supposed to sip champagne," a sharp voice informed me.

Suddenly, I wished I'd grabbed two glasses. I was clearly going to need more than one drink to get through this evening. Turning, I smiled at my mother. I'd suspected she would come, but I'd hoped she wouldn't. "Usually, I drink straight from the bottle."

"I'm sure you do." Her lips pressed into a thin line as she scanned me from head to toe. "At least you'll catch a few eyes in that dress. We should discuss what you will wear to future events, since you canceled our visit. You are still planning to join The Rites, I assume?"

Was I? I'd begged my mother to let me take Jessica's place. My sister was half a millennium younger than me—far too young to be married off. As much as I wanted to tell my mother no, I couldn't allow them to force a child into marriage. Before I could nod, the rest of my family joined us.

"Hey, big sister." Jessica grinned at me, her arm looped with our father's. "Fancy seeing you here."

For a minute, all I could do was stare. Relations with my parents had been strained for a couple of centuries. No one had been inviting me to family Christmas parties, but Jessica had managed to get letters to me. We'd even texted a few times in recent years. In my head, though, she was still a hundred years old—an awkward teenager by vampire standards.

But nothing about Jessica was awkward anymore. She was nearly my height, helped a little by strappy gold heels that lifted her a few more inches off the ground. Like me, she shared our mother's looks, but it was strange to see her with curves in a dress that our mother had chosen to showcase her assets. The rose-colored gown had a full skirt that split in the front to reveal a shorter skirt that showed off her legs. Its strapless neckline hugged her breasts and nipped at her slender waist.

"You look gorgeous," I told her as she adjusted her opera gloves, which were made from the same fabric as her gown. "You've grown up."

"That's why I'm here." Her grin faltered as our father cleared his throat.

I took a deep breath and faced him. "Hello, Daddy."

"Jacqueline." He said my name smoothly, without betraying a hint of emotion or sentiment. "It's been a long time since we last saw each other."

"That will happen when you're disowned," I said before I could stop myself.

My mother's gasp punctuated the air, but she caught herself quickly.

"Or did you banish me?" I asked, unwilling to let her off the hook. "I can never remember."

"Let's not talk about it," Jessica burst in before I could stop her. "Let's just see what eye candy we can find."

"Eye candy?" I repeated. She might not look like an awkward teenager, but clearly, she was still in the throes of adolescence if she was worried about looks. I only hoped she was well past the Frenzy. Maybe I needed to pull her aside and remind her that vampires married for life—and vampires lived long lives.

"We've discussed this," my father said with a sigh. "You need to worry about position, not attraction."

"Is that what you did?" I smiled at him. He ignored me, but we all knew it was the truth. My parents' marriage was more like a treaty than a relationship. "And she doesn't need to worry about it at all."

My mother rolled her eyes and turned to Jessica. "We've discussed the right families, remember?"

"Wait," I said slowly as what they were saying processed— or rather, who they were saying it to. "Jessica doesn't have to get married. Why coach her?"

"If she can make a match this season, she might as well."

"Absolutely not." I'd been holding back my temper, but now my fuse was lit. "I said I would take her place."

"And you will, *officially*," my mother added. "But she's out now. We already introduced her at the Solstice Ball."

Of course they had. I'd been too distracted by Camila's arrival that evening to keep tabs on them. "If you're going to force her to get married—"

"What is one season?" my mother hissed. "The Council doesn't care about her age."

Another reason for me to tell the Council to go fuck themselves.

"Is everyone losing their minds? She's only three hundred."

"Jessica is far more mature than you were at this age."

My sister bit her lip, looking nervously between us. "Please don't fight. I don't mind."

"You never do," I mumbled. That was the problem. She was the good kid. The one who did as she was told, didn't ask questions, and followed the rules.

To my surprise, the cheerfulness faded from her face. Jessica narrowed her eyes and leaned closer. "I can make my own decisions."

Before I could respond, my father stepped between us with an upraised hand. "There is Antony Devlin." He waved to the older familiar to catch his attention. "Their line has produced an heir every generation."

"Good breeding stock, huh?" I said as my gut twisted. Not only was I stuck here while my family tried to pawn me off on some old familiar like a trading card, but I was also shirking my duties to Julian. "If you'll excuse me, I see Julian."

A hand latched around my wrist before I made it a single step. "Stay and say hello to Mr. Devlin."

I glared at my mother but didn't try to pull away. Instead, I cast a pleading look at my sister. "Maybe you should find someone to dance with."

"There's no music." Jessica blinked a few times, looking genuinely confused by my suggestion.

"There will be," I said, shoving her toward the center of the courtyard as a quartet took their places nearby.

"Your sister will stay and meet him, too," my mother said firmly. I couldn't help but feel she was lining up her merchandise and preparing to haggle. She moved closer to me and lowered her voice. "If you have any brains in that head, you'll choose a husband and get it over with."

"I'm not ready to be tied down," I muttered.

"Silly child, a marriage for a female vampire isn't a shackle. It's a key."

I didn't have a chance to ask her what that meant before

Devlin approached. Music filled the air around us, but there was nothing romantic about it. Devlin had to be at least forty-five. It shouldn't matter, since I was clearly older than him. But humans didn't just age more quickly; they matured faster, too. Judging from his receding hairline and permanent scowl, he might as well be a couple of thousand years old.

"Daphné." He bowed his head to my mother before forcing a smile for my father. It looked painful. "Stewart."

"It's lovely to see you here." My mother sashayed closer to him. "We wondered how many others would make it on such late notice."

"A rather unexpected change of plans," he agreed. "But I was happy to follow." He didn't look happy, though it was hard to tell if he was displeased or if his face was just stuck like that.

I had a couple of questions for Devlin, but one stood out. Why was he unmarried at his age? Humans didn't usually wait around. Not with their lifespans.

"Are you alone?" I asked, earning a furious glance from my parents. "Traveling alone, I mean?"

"I have a few of my people with me," he said, studying me for a moment, "if that's what you meant."

I nodded, pinning a fake smile on my face. It wasn't exactly an answer to my question. But, for whatever reason, it seemed he was single.

"Jacqueline is our oldest daughter," my father told him.

"Much older than her sister?" Devlin asked like we weren't even here.

"Only by about six hundred years," I said flatly.

"A woman, then"—he sounded a little too pleased—"if you'll pardon the phrase."

I was about to tell him that I would not pardon him when he held out his hand. "Care to dance?"

Dancing with him was about the last thing I wanted to do, but my hesitation gave him a chance to eye Jessica. A burst of protective instinct shot through me, and I grabbed his hand. "Let's dance."

I dragged him to the center of the courtyard, where a few other couples had drifted. Devlin took my waist and led me into a waltz. At least I could get a better look around while I was dancing.

"I was surprised to hear the DuBois family had two daughters on the market this season," Devlin said as he spun me.

I caught a glimpse of Julian watching by the gates. He almost looked like he might smile. I guessed if my misery made him laugh, I could suffer for a minute.

"The market? You make it sound like we're cattle."

"Of course not." He sounded annoyed. If I wanted to get rid of this guy, that was a good start. "I simply meant that you are both eligible."

"Jessica is only three hundred—or did my parents fail to tell you that?"

"Three hundred?" he repeated, sounding shocked. "But you're…"

"Old enough." It was better to keep the non-damaging information to a minimum. He seemed to like the idea that I was older. The last thing I needed was to wind up with a middle-aged familiar suitor.

"Perhaps you would like to go to—" A tap on the shoulder cut him off.

"I'm sorry." Camila smiled sweetly at him. I knew better than to trust that smile. Arsenic was sweet *and* deadly, after all. "Can I borrow her? My mother needs to speak with her."

"Of course," Devlin answered, dutifully releasing me. His scowl returned. "We can finish our dance later—and you can answer my question."

I forced a smile. No way in hell were we finishing anything later. I followed Camila away from the dancers toward a corridor that led to the back kitchens. I wasn't sure if I should be grateful to her for intervening or worried that Sabine had asked for me.

My gaze drifted down Camila's back. Her off-the-shoulder gown swept low in the back to reveal her creamy skin. A lump formed in my throat as I tried to tear my eyes from her, but then she passed under a hanging lantern. The light caught her skin, revealing faint scars marring her flesh. Without thinking, I reached out and ran my finger down one.

Camila stopped abruptly, and I nearly ran into her. Snatching my finger back, I tried to paste a disdainful look on my face as she whipped around.

"What are you doing?"

"The s-scars," I stammered, wondering why after all these years, I still got tongue-tied when she looked at me. "Did Willem—"

"I meant dancing," she cut me off, flinging her index finger back to the party. "I thought you were looking for Willem." Camila's glare cut through me, but I refused to back down.

"I can do both," I said through gritted teeth.

Her mouth parted, and she blinked before composing herself. "I apologize. I thought we were here to help Julian. Not find husbands."

"I'm not finding a husband!"

"Please. Your parents were practically drooling over him. I hear he comes with a large dowry—his first wife left him her fortune."

The lump in my throat felt like it might choke me. I swallowed, but it did no good. "How could you think I care about any of that?"

"Don't you?" Camila challenged, bringing her gaze to meet mine.

There was a time when I'd thought I might drown in those eyes. Looking into them now, I realized I still could. Maybe that was always the trouble between us. Our love was deadly.

"I have my own money," I said thickly.

"You mean you have your parents'—"

"*My* money," I cut her off. "They weren't too thrilled with the werewolf stunt. I had to take care of myself. Turns out I'm excellent at investments."

"Is that so?" Camila finally looked away, and I nearly gasped for air.

"You would know if you'd stayed in touch," I said coldly. I was no longer the broken-hearted girl she'd left behind. But I wasn't the girl she'd fallen in love with, either. I could never be either again. I'd made myself into someone new from the pieces she'd left behind.

"I didn't have a choice." For a second, her hard edges softened, revealing the truth. "You don't know what it's like to have your life stolen from you."

"So you became this?" I asked. "You joined the Mordicum. You attacked innocent people."

She swallowed, looking past me to the night sky. "Why did I think you would understand?"

"Why would I?" I shot back. "You could have come home. You could have reached out to your family. You could have reached out to…" I nearly choked on the final word, unable to say it.

Me.

"Because I deserve to be angry!" she screamed. "I deserve to hurt. I earned it. I bled for it."

She was right. The realization hit me so hard I could have fallen over. "I understand."

"No, you don't," she said forcefully. Camila took a step toward me and another, slowly backing me toward the wall. "Because if you did, you wouldn't look at me like that."

She was so close that I could smell the orange blossom of her perfume. A wave of memories washed over me: stolen kisses in the library, afternoon walks through lavender fields in southern France, the way she looked the evening of her presentation—the night she'd met Willem.

"Like what?" I asked breathlessly. "How do I look at you?"

Her throat slid, her own breathing picking up as she closed the last bit of space between us. "Like you hate me."

"I don't hate you," I whispered, staring into her eyes. "That would be easier."

"Easier than what?" Her tongue swiped over her crimson lip.

I reached to stroke a fingertip along that lip, suddenly wishing I hadn't worn gloves. "Loving you."

Neither of us turned away. We stayed locked there, our bodies barely brushing together. Neither of us made the first move, either. The world was different now. Maybe it could be different now for us, too.

But had we changed too much?

"Jacqueline." My name was a kiss on her tongue. I shuddered a little as I remembered that voice—the one that murmured my name in the dark.

I slipped my hand around her neck, catching it at the base, and urged her closer. She didn't resist, and when our lips met, the centuries apart didn't matter. Our differences didn't matter. There was only me and her. It felt like no time had passed at all.

Tightening my grip on her, I pulled her closer. She sighed against my mouth before slamming me into the wall and deepening the kiss, which was starting to get pretty serious when a gentle cough interrupted us.

We scrambled apart, but it was too late. We'd been caught.

"Well, this explains a few things."

CHAPTER THIRTY-NINE

Julian

It seemed I had finally found something to take my mind off Thea—if only for a moment. The moon hanging overhead provided just enough light to make out the couple pressed against the ancient stone wall...making out. I should be shocked, but for some reason, I wasn't. Now everything made sense.

Camila yanked out of Jacqueline's embrace, and both turned wide eyes on me. My sister raised a hand to her swollen lips before flattening her mouth into a thin line.

"It's rude to sneak up on someone," she said, planting a hand on her hip.

"I'm sorry." I couldn't help but laugh. "I didn't expect to find you both skulking about a dark alley."

"We weren't skulking!" Jacqueline straightened and brushed her dress back into place.

"I suppose you weren't." I couldn't keep myself from grinning. It hurt a little after all this time. I couldn't remember the last time I'd seen Jacqueline so flustered. I wasn't sure I ever had. My best friend was usually composed, as though she knew she was the center of attention. Right now, she looked out of sorts.

"What are you smiling at?" Camila asked. "Nothing was going on."

I caught Jacqueline flinch out of the corner of my eye. The kiss explained a lot, but so did each of their reactions.

"Cam," Jacqueline murmured. "Maybe—"

"What do you want?" My twin crossed her arms over her chest and glared at me.

I glanced between them. Jacqueline looked torn between crying and screaming, but Camila was as haughty as ever. This was going to go sideways really fast. We didn't have time for their drama. Not right now.

"Willem is on his way," I informed them. "We received word from the security team."

The mood in the air shifted. Camila drew herself up, squaring her shoulders and looking positively murderous. I knew better than to trust that look. How would she handle coming face-to-face with him?

"Should I greet him? He's technically still my husband." Her lips puckered on the final word as if it tasted sour on her tongue. Jacqueline's mouth fell open. I couldn't decide if she was shocked by Camila's behavior or her suggestion.

"I don't think that's a good idea. We should stick to the plan."

Camila rolled her eyes. "We both know Sabine's plan is shit. Do you really think we can distract him for that long?"

She glanced at Jacqueline, expecting support, but received only silence.

"It's the best plan we have." I actually agreed with Camila. I wasn't certain why our mother thought we could keep Willem occupied long enough to trace his movements through the city— with or without the locating spell a local familiar had crafted from her family grimoire.

"I bet a sword would work better," she said with a shrug.

I did, too. I kept that to myself. "I'm sure Mother doesn't want anyone to spoil her party."

"You mean she doesn't want anyone to spoil her chance at the crown," Camila said bitterly.

I wouldn't put it past my mother to make tonight about herself, rather than Thea. Now that Sabine was being tapped to take Ginerva's empty throne, she couldn't afford to alienate any vampires. Not until she wore the crown officially.

"We should get going," Jacqueline interjected. She started back to the party without looking at Camila. "I should be at the docks when his boat arrives."

"I guess I'll just keep to the shadows," Camila said glumly, "and wait to be summoned."

"We all get to do our part." I might not like our mother's plan, but I suspected she was wise to keep Camila away from Willem. We needed answers from him, and my sister was far more likely to drive a sword through his heart.

I fell into step beside Jacqueline, waiting until we were a safe distance away to speak. "If you get into trouble, get out and come get help."

"This is not my first rodeo." She snorted. "I can handle myself."

"I know that, but…I don't want to lose anyone else to Willem." Pain laced my words. I'd considered every scenario. Sometimes, when my tether felt slack and lifeless, I panicked. There was a possibility that Willem had already finished with Thea, and if he had…

I didn't want to consider it.

I couldn't.

I had not waited nine hundred years for a reason to live to lose her like this. No matter what it took, I would get her back.

"So, back there…" Jacqueline interrupted my thoughts. "I should have told you about us."

"Us, huh?" My sister and my best friend—that complicated things. Part of me was over the fucking moon for the distraction, though.

"Not really." Her mouth dipped into a frown. "Not anymore."

"It started before Willem?" I guessed.

She nodded. Yet another reason for me to hate the bastard.

"Why didn't you tell me?"

"I think we might have, eventually. We had a plan."

"What happened?" I asked as we reached the courtyard.

She swallowed. "Things didn't go accordingly. Let's hope tonight's plan goes better."

I couldn't disagree with her there. "We'll talk about this more later," I said, swiftly adding, "if you want to."

"I do," she said softly. "I could use some advice."

A dark laugh slipped from me. "I think you'd be better off finding Thea then."

That earned me another frown. "You were my best friend first."

"So, Thea doesn't know about you two?" I asked with a raised eyebrow.

Jacqueline looked away, heat flooding to her cheeks. I couldn't blame her for going to my mate with this. It wasn't like Jacqueline was with a total stranger. Camila was my sister. That changed things, whether I liked it or not.

"After she came back, I had to tell someone."

"I get it." I actually did. "It sounds like we both need to find Thea."

"I will," she swore. "Tonight."

I forced a smile, not wanting to undermine her resolve. I wished I felt as sure as she sounded. We'd scoured Venice, looking for Thea. And Willem was no idiot. He wouldn't leave her unprotected.

"I wish I could come with you." I looked up at the moon, wondering if Thea was looking at it, too. I'd much rather leave this bloody party to search for my mate than be stuck here. But that was my part to play. Willem needed to see all of us here— our entire family. He couldn't suspect we had anyone tracing him. Since he'd never known Jacqueline, she was our best bet to go after Thea. If I tried to leave, he might follow. So I was stuck here, being a pawn on an unused chess board.

I wasn't even allowed to rip the bastard's head off.

"I'll bring her back," Jacqueline promised.

I wanted to believe her.

God, I needed to believe her.

But hope might be the death of me.

"Good luck," I told Jacqueline. She nodded and slipped into the crowd. He couldn't see us together without risking suspicion. It was better if Willem didn't know she was here.

Though I couldn't stop myself from walking toward the gates. The crowd parted for me as I passed through them, ignoring anyone who tried to speak to me, until Mariana stepped into my path. All around us, vampires and familiars gasped and dropped their heads. She looked the part of a queen tonight. A tiara of pearls sat on top of her long, seaweed-black hair, and she wore a sequined gown in a dozen shades of blue and green that shimmered like the ocean as she approached me.

A few days ago, the court had been nearly deserted. Now everyone was treating them like royalty again. It was insane what a fancy party could do for a situation.

I inclined my head in greeting but didn't bow.

"*Flagello*," she murmured, twisting her spindly fingers together. "I must speak with you."

"Now isn't a great time," I said carefully. The last thing I needed was my sister's homicidal ex around a pissed-off vampire queen. I glanced toward the gates, wondering if Willem had made it to the dock yet.

"This cannot wait." She grabbed hold of my arm at the wrist, her bare fingers sending a shockwave of magic surging through me. It had been a long time since I'd felt that much power in a single touch.

I tried to pull away gently, but she tightened her grip and sent something else surging through me: a vision.

A vision of Thea.

It was a flash so brief that it almost destroyed me.

"What do you know?" I demanded. A few nearby guests shrank at my tone, but Mariana shook her head slightly and pulled me away from the crowd.

"We cannot speak of it here," she whispered, looking furiously around us. My eyes followed hers and landed on a sight that made my heart nearly stop. Willem had arrived—and he wasn't alone.

Before I could break my promise to my mother and attack Willem, Mariana continued. "You know who she is? In the vision, you are connected to her—linked."

I couldn't tear my eyes from Willem or the petite cloaked figure next to him. Half of me felt like I was being dragged toward them and the other half felt like I was being pushed away. Was it my tether? Was it reacting to Thea? I took one step forward before Mariana's next words stopped me.

"Please tell me she isn't your mate."

CHAPTER FORTY

Thea

Sneaking out had been the easy part. With my father gone, there was no one to hover over me. Getting into this party was proving more difficult. I tugged my velvet cloak around me as I bypassed a group of tourists. They watched me, whispering to each other. The problem with wearing a floor-length gown and cloak in Venice was that I both fit in and stuck out. I turned a withering glance on them, and they scattered like cockroaches toward the nearby lights of St. Mark's Square.

I had no idea what I was looking for. I was unfamiliar with the city, so I didn't know where vampires might congregate around here. They probably weren't sipping espressos at Caffè Florian.

Continuing down the cobbled street, I paused at the mouth of a dark alley. The dank odor of seawater floated toward me, and I started to walk away. As I took one step, something tickled the back of my neck. Reaching up, I touched the spot, but the tingling grew stronger. Dread worked its way into my bloodstream as I stared toward the end of the passage. What was down there?

"This is how stupid girls get killed," I muttered to myself as I walked into the shadows. But I wasn't a girl, and I wasn't stupid—so why did I feel so anxious? The feeling grew with each step. By the time I arrived at the passageway's end, my stomach was churning, but all I found was a musty old bookstore that looked closed.

I searched for a sign, but there was none. The exterior was so dirty I could barely see through the windows to the haphazard stacks of books there. It was nothing. No one was here. I turned to head back, chalking it up to my imagination, and discovered a ginger tabby cat sitting in a puddle of moonlight.

"Well, hello. Where do you belong?" I asked.

The cat turned its head and studied me. With a soft mewl, she rose and sauntered to my feet.

"Are you lost?" I bent to scratch behind her ears and discovered she was purring loudly.

"You must have the magic touch."

I spun around, nearly jumping out of my skin, to find a well-dressed male watching me from the shop's doorway. "What... I mean, who..."

I had no idea what I meant.

"I didn't mean to alarm you." His voice was melodic, almost hypnotizing. He stepped from the shadows into the small shaft of light outside the bookstore. "The Countess doesn't take to most people this way."

"The Countess?" I repeated.

He gestured to the cat with a slender, gloved hand.

"The cat," he explained.

"Oh." Duh. Of course that's what he'd meant. My gaze lingered on his gloves. He was a vampire, but he was doing a remarkable job of passing for a human.

"Are you lost?" he asked in a pointed way.

Maybe it was a mistake to trust a random vampire I met at the end of a dark alley, but then again, how bad could he be if he had a cat? A cat named Countess?

"I have an invitation." I slipped the card out of my pocket, glad I'd left the envelope with my father's name on it at home.

His dark eyebrow lifted as he read it.

"I'm new to the city. I'm a bit lost." It was easy to sell because it was mostly true. I was just leaving out the part about not being invited.

He looked up and studied me for a moment, his eyes narrowing with curiosity. I was about to back down the alley when his nostrils flared. "Interesting," he murmured.

"What?" I asked, stopping before I really started.

"Nothing." He dismissed his remark with a wave of his hand. "You will need to book passage on the *Rio Oscuro*."

I sighed and nodded. That much I knew from the invitation. I extended my hand to take it back, but he held it out of reach.

"I was just leaving. If you care to join me, I know a shortcut."

I swallowed, feeling a lump form in my throat. This had bad idea written all over it. If I were smart, I would head right back down the alley, find the canal he'd mentioned, and charm some nearby male into taking me. Instead, I found myself nodding.

Maybe it was the cat, but I trusted him. If my father found out, he would lose his mind. But my father wasn't going to find out. He wasn't even going to know that I'd gone out. It had pissed me off when he'd asked Natalie to accompany him, but taking one of the *cortège* had its uses. She'd promised me—not that she'd had any choice—to keep him distracted so I could slip into the party. Not that she understood why I'd come. How was I supposed to explain this wasn't about mere curiosity? I needed to get a glimpse. I felt like my whole body was being dragged toward some hidden place in Venice.

"I suppose we should introduce ourselves." He opened the bookshop door and flipped on a light. The cat followed us, rubbing against the silk skirt of my gown. "I'm the Conte."

I guessed that explained the cat's title. I stuck my hand out. "Thea Dr—" I cut myself off before I said my last name. This guy might be nice and have cats, but my father was always clear. Our enemies were everywhere.

"Please come in, Thea." He stepped to the side to allow me into the shop.

The shop wasn't much better inside than outside, so I lied, "This is nice."

He tipped his head and loosed a throaty laugh. "You are very polite. I assume you were recently turned."

I frowned and shook my head, but he was already walking into the labyrinth of books. For a minute, I stared, wondering if I should run for it. I might be able to take out a few tourists, but did I stand a chance against a male—and from the looks of it, *ancient*—vampire?

"I won't bite," he called over his shoulder, adding, "I've already fed."

At my feet, the Countess meowed impatiently before following him. The cat trusted him. I would, too.

The books continued into a back room where, like many of the buildings in Venice, it was open to allow a boat to dock. Water seeped into the shop, spoiling books, but the Conte ignored it and went straight to where his store met the canal.

"My gondola will be along in a moment," he told me.

"You have a gondola?" I don't know why that impressed me so much. My father had one. I suspected most vampires did, even ones with rundown bookstores.

"It is one of the perks of my position."

"Position?"

"I watch over the entrance to the *Rio Oscuro*," he explained, eyeing me. "You must be *very* new...to town."

I refrained from rolling my eyes at the insinuation. Instead, I smiled. "I am." Before he could pepper me with more questions, a dark shape floated out of the shadows. I gasped as a gondola appeared from the haze.

"We should hurry," he explained, offering me his hand. "Others will be along any minute."

I accepted his outstretched hand and climbed into the boat. Once I was seated, the Conte picked up a paddle and dipped it into the water. The boat lurched forward, and I scrambled to grab hold of my seat. As soon as we were moving, he took the seat across from me.

"Have we met before? There is—if you'll pardon the expression—something familiar about you."

I shook my head. "I've never been to Venice. I must have one of those faces."

He tapped a finger against his cheek. "No," he said slowly. "It's something else. A scent."

For a moment, I almost smelled it, too. Jasmine and woodsmoke. Rose petals studded with cloves. But just as quickly as I caught the scent, it vanished.

"Was that you?" I asked him in awe.

He held a finger to his lips and winked at me. "It will be our secret."

I nodded. I hadn't met many vampires with actual magic. Some of the household staff whispered that my father had magic, but I'd never seen it. Then again, there had been some odd moments of late. Things I couldn't explain.

Things that felt a lot like magic.

"This will be your first time visiting the court, I assume." It was more of a statement than a question, but I nodded anyway. "At the gates, they will ask your name and present you."

"What?" I yelped, starting to stand in the gondola. It swayed dangerously, and I sat back quickly before we capsized. "I don't want to be announced."

If someone yelled my name at the party, I would definitely get caught. I turned around to see how far we were from the bookstore and spotted another black gondola drifting behind. Even if I wanted to, it was too late to turn around. My eyes strained in the dark to make out two masked figures in the boat behind us.

"Is there a particular reason?" His wide mouth twisted as though he found me funny.

I could lie again, but something told me he would know.

"I'm not exactly supposed to be here. It's my father's invitation," I confessed.

"And why didn't he ask you to accompany him? You must be old enough to take The Rites."

The Rites? Where have I heard that before?

There was another tickle at the back of my neck. I swatted it with my hand. "He doesn't think so." Another easy lie to tell because it must be true. Why else would he keep me at home and away from the rest of society?

"You can be my guest, but you must do me the honor of a dance." He reached inside his coat pocket and withdrew a curious black mask. Handing it to me, he said, "This may help, but I am afraid you won't be able to speak."

"Thanks." I took the mask and looked it over. Two holes were cut for my eyes, but that was it. There was no strap. No opening for my mouth. The Conte leaned over and tapped a button that blended so well with the fabric I had missed it.

"You hold it in your teeth," he explained. "*Le Regine*'s handmaidens wear them. Or they did."

"Did?" I swallowed at that ominous insight.

"Only one remains. Much of the court has left in recent years, but soon they will rise again, when the three queens assume their thrones."

"I see." I really didn't, but since I was just here to crash a party, did it really matter?

Music wafted toward us, growing louder until a dock came into view. The notes swelled inside me—calling me, beckoning me like the greeting of an old friend. It was mesmerizing, and I was so lost to it that the Conte coughed to get my attention. Security guards stood on either side of the dock, waiting for us, and I quickly put the mask to my face and bit down. It wasn't terrible, but I found myself glad that I wasn't one of these handmaidens.

"Conte Notte," my companion announced himself, "and guest."

I stilled, waiting for them to ask my name and ruin our plan.

They tipped their heads and offered their hands. I took one and climbed out of the boat.

"Welcome to court."

The Conte joined me, crooking his arm, and I slipped mine through it. "Shall we?"

He guided me toward the gates as the strangest feeling came over me.

I'd never been here before, so why did it feel like I was coming home?

CHAPTER FORTY-ONE

Julian

"Sir Willem...Drake." The male announcing his arrival stumbled over his name. Every head in the courtyard turned as whispers slithered through the crowd.

Willem showed no signs of caring as he strode forward, dragging his petite guest along. My heart stuttered, half from hope, half from fear. Willem hadn't bothered with a mask or cloak. Apparently, he didn't plan to hide. That was his second mistake.

The first was showing up here—invitation or not.

"Is that female your mate?" Mariana repeated. I spared a single glance at her.

"Her?" I asked Mariana, looking at the companion at Drake's side.

"No." She stepped before me and whispered, "The woman in my vision. The one I just showed you."

I couldn't tear my eyes from Drake and his guest, but I managed to nod.

"When you find her, you must bring her to me immediately, Giuliano."

"Why do—"

She was already gone. That saved me the trouble of telling her

I wouldn't be bringing Thea to see anyone. Not until I'd examined every bit of her for injuries and then kissed every bare inch of her skin in case I'd missed something. My mouth went dry as a dangerous hope bloomed inside me.

But now was no time for optimism. Optimism was reserved for innocents and fools.

I looked around for my family and instantly spotted Sebastian, then Thoren and my father. Turning, I discovered they were all here. Each seemed to have taken a position in the courtyard that would prevent Willem's escape. Sabine might have ordered us not to attack, but we didn't have to let him get away.

I didn't care about Willem. Instead, I darted through the crowd, trying to get a glimpse of the woman accompanying him. Her cloak's heavy hood obscured her face, but she was short and well-dressed.

"Did the bastard actually bring her?" Lysander murmured as he joined me.

It was exactly what I was thinking. There was no way. Willem wasn't that stupid. My heartbeat picked up, rattling my rib cage as I tried to remember how to breathe.

And then, I felt *her*.

Or, rather, I felt our tether. It fell like a heavy chain around my neck. The bond between us was looser than before, but the connection was still there. Lightness and darkness linked together—a complex combination of her and me. I was a slave to this love, but I would choose no other master.

"She's here," I snarled. Grabbing my brother's forearm, I yanked him along.

Lysander slipped a hand inside his tuxedo jacket and drew out a small knife with a curved blade. "I guess we're giving up on the plan."

"The plan was shit." I echoed our sister's earlier words. Drake's companion turned just as a stout male with beady eyes stepped into our path. I cursed under my breath and started to shift in another direction. My escape was cut off by a loudly gossiping and completely oblivious group of Italian vampires, and he approached me with a sinister smirk.

"Boucher," I greeted him coolly, peering past him.

"How strange that we haven't met since Paris, but I hear you have been otherwise engaged." He nodded his hello to both of us and followed my gaze. "Another vampire back from the dead. First, your lovely twin, and now her husband. People are calling it a miracle."

"More like an omen," Lysander said drily.

Boucher lifted his thick black brows. "Given their connections to your family, I expected to find you all quite *happy*."

"Happiness isn't a Rousseaux family trait." I watched as guests surrounded Drake, completely enveloping them both in a crowd. I shot Lysander a look. "If you'll excuse me..."

"Eager to greet your brother-in-law?" Boucher guessed. An undercurrent of malice ran through his words.

I paused and studied him for a second before tipping my head. "Yes, if you'll excuse us."

I was taking a step away when Boucher said, "And you must be eager to return to your mate."

My patience snapped like a twig, and I whirled around to grab him. Hoisting him into the air by his lapels, I snarled, "What do you know about Thea?"

Boucher glanced down at my hands with more interest than fear. "Nothing everyone here doesn't already know." He cleared his throat, and I let him go. "You can't make inquiries all over Venice without news spreading. You know how it works in this city. The serpent mouths are everywhere."

Of course, people had been tattling. The *bocche di serpenti* were probably crammed full of complaints. Was that why Mariana had demanded to see my mate? Had word spread all the way to their grief-stricken court that I had taken matters into my own hands?

"Don't believe everything you hear," I warned him.

"Then should I not believe what they say about your mate

being a siren?" His dark eyes gleamed with barely restrained greed. "As a patron of music, I find myself desperate to speak with her. If I had known in Paris..."

Word had traveled. I might as well have written a tell-all book. The smirk played at Boucher's lips again, and I knew he was baiting me. Over the centuries, we'd had an uneasy relationship based mostly on our mutual interest in the arts. More than once, I'd thought of him as a friend, but always one to be kept close. I never had quite trusted him. Now I never would.

I leaned closer, lowering my voice so no one around us could hear. "If you so much as look at her without my permission, I will sew your ears shut and make sure you never hear another fucking note of music in your life."

"You *are* properly mated now. Only a mated vampire would threaten such violence against an old friend," he said in a clipped tone.

"How many vampires do you know?" Lysander asked with a soft laugh.

"I don't have time for this," I muttered, turning my attention back to Drake.

He was gone.

The crowd had dispersed, Willem and his guest along with it.

"Fuck," Lysander said, reading my mind.

I poked my finger into Boucher's chest. "If I find out you had something to do with this—*any* of this—I'll make my first threat feel like a blessing."

Boucher's smirk widened into a toothy grin. "I have no loyalty to Drake." He bowed his head, eyes flashing. "And now I have no loyalty to you. Best of luck, Julian."

He turned and made his way through the crowd, pausing to start a conversation with a group of Japanese vampires nearby.

"Why don't I think he meant that last bit?" Lysander asked with a sigh. "Was it wise to make him an enemy?"

"Boucher is cuckoo. He doesn't belong, and he never has," I told my brother as we made our way through the party, searching for Drake. "The question isn't whether I should treat him as an enemy. It's who does he really serve?"

"I always thought of him as self-serving."

"So did I." And that had been a mistake. In the past, Boucher had slaughtered the cast of more than one stage production, compelled theater owners, and worse. But his violent outbursts had masked the truth. I'd thought his love of music had driven him to madness on those occasions, but he had always found a champion—a vampire willing to stick up for him and get him out of trouble. That meant he was in the debt of other vampires—*many* other vampires. "Can we put someone on him?"

"With Mother practically planning her coronation speech, I'm not sure she'll want to spare any security." Lysander sounded grim. He stared across the courtyard, and I followed his gaze to find my mother speaking with Zina.

"And to think, I believed she would reject *Le Regine*'s offer."

"Me too. I wonder what changed."

Magic, I thought. She was doing this to keep magic from dying entirely and to keep all of us from dying with it. It was the only reason my mother would abandon her modern lifestyle to sit on the throne—even if she would only be required to visit Venice once a year to hold court. Despite her proclaimed indifference to her soon-to-be sister queens, she had grabbed hold of the opportunity with both hands. Maybe she simply wanted to be a queen.

But nothing with Sabine Rousseaux was ever simple.

"If she won't spare someone, we'll have to do it ourselves," I decided.

Lysander nodded. "I'll speak to Thoren."

Our stoic brother was the obvious choice. Despite his massive size, he tended to blend in well. If any of us could keep an eye on Boucher without being noticed, it was Thoren.

"Tell him to be careful." I didn't know who currently held Boucher's purse strings, but my gut told me if he was up to something, he wasn't acting alone.

"I will," Lysander promised. He held out his hand, extending the knife he'd taken out earlier. "Is it a mistake to give you this?"

Willem's smug face flashed to mind, and I shook my head. "Keep it."

I didn't need a weapon against Willem. I would end him with my bare hands and drain every drop of magic from his blood. Nothing less would satisfy me.

My brother didn't say anything, but we shared a look of understanding. It didn't matter what our mother had ordered. Willem Drake wasn't walking out of this courtyard tonight.

"I'll find Thoren." Lysander left me on the outskirts of the party to speak with our brother.

As I surveyed the large stone courtyard, my frustration mounted. Drake was nowhere to be seen. Had he left? I closed my eyes and concentrated on the tether that bound me to Thea. It was there, as heavy and reassuring as it had been when I felt it fall into place after its long absence. I gave in to my magic, letting the darkness swirl inside me. It felt the magic in our tether and grabbed for it, hungry and ready to devour. I'd always thought of my magic as a curse. I'd always fought it. But now, as it gripped my tether to Thea and drew it taut, I was thankful. Opening my eyes, I followed the invisible chain, knowing where it would lead me.

I was so close. We were so close.

I smelled burnt sugar and candied violets. The scent that had drawn me to her the night we'd met was guiding me home.

CHAPTER FORTY-TWO

Thea

I'd never been around this many vampires. Even before the accident that had forced my father to return here to seek magical assistance, we'd kept to ourselves. I'd always thought that meant other vampires were solitary creatures like my father. Any contact with other vampires—like the ones staying with us now—was at our private homes.

But as I walked amongst the crowd, I realized I was completely wrong. Most of the guests staying at our house looked like my father, acted like him. But here, vampires of every race mingled under the roses blooming over the courtyard. Fairy lights guided us toward a female in a black lace gown that curved around her pale shoulders. It clung to her curves in a way that nearly made me blush. No wonder she was surrounded by others who hung off her every word. As we passed, she paused and looked directly at me.

Her eyes, which were bright blue even in the moonlight, pinched at the corners, and an unnamed fear throttled my throat. Did she recognize me? Would she drag me right to my father? I was about to bolt when I remembered my mask.

"Sabine," the Conte whispered to me. "She will likely be announced as the future queen at midnight."

I nodded, unable to participate in conversation due to my strange mask. I didn't know what sadist had come up with the idea to hold a mask by your teeth, but he was an asshole. Still, it was doing its job.

He guided me around Sabine and her fans, but we didn't make it far.

"Conte?"

My companion paused with a sharp inhale before pivoting toward Sabine's crisp voice. "*Buona sera*, Sabine," he greeted her stiffly. "I did not wish to intrude on your conversation."

"I appreciate your conscientiousness." She sounded like she was lying, but the Conte didn't call her out. He probably didn't want to piss off a future queen. I couldn't blame him. "I was wondering if this was the handmaiden we spoke of earlier. I wish to discuss some important matters with her."

Those brilliant eyes tracked along my body, as if trying to see past my mask and cloak.

"No, this is my guest," he said.

I could have kissed him—if it weren't for this mask—for not telling her my name. If she was going to be queen, she definitely knew my father.

"What an odd choice to wear the *moretta*." She looked over me again, and I swore I felt the venom in her words. "I do want to speak with the handmaiden as soon as possible. I assume you can arrange that."

"Of course. I will see to it." The Conte bowed his head, but his whole body was rigid when he straightened back up.

Sabine turned back to the people waiting for her attention without so much as a thank-you. She might be the next queen, but she struck me as entitled instead of regal. Something told me that if I knew her better, I still wouldn't like her.

"Would you care to dance?" the Conte asked me.

I shook my head and gestured to a dark alcove. He escorted me to it. I tucked my body in the shadows and took off the mask. I flexed my jaw, stretching out the tension that lingered from holding the mask in place for so long. "I don't want my father to see," I admitted, holding the mask back out to him. Getting out of here had to be a lot easier than getting in. I knew where the dock was now. I could get back there and wait for a boat. "Thank you for bringing me."

"Keep it. You might need it." He took my other hand and brought it to his lips, pressing a kiss to the back of my glove. "If I can be of assistance again, please find me."

"I think you might have your hands full with her majesty," I said, glancing to where the haughty woman held court.

His mouth lifted. "You may be right. Are you certain you will be okay without an escort?"

"I'll be fine," I promised him. "I know how to keep out of sight."

"Don't be a stranger, Thea. You must visit both of us. The Countess will want to see you again."

"I'll visit." And I would. The bookstore might be a health hazard to humans, but I would never forget the Conte's kindness. "And thank you again."

He moved into the party with an easy smoothness I envied. Would I ever feel that comfortable amongst my peers? Maybe when my transition was complete, it wouldn't be so daunting. That's what my father said, but deep down, in a place I never showed anyone, I doubted him.

I stepped from the shadows just long enough to stop a passing server.

"Blood or champagne?" he asked, lowering his tray. It held a dozen or so flutes, half filled with bubbles and the others with a thick crimson liquid.

I snagged a glass of champagne with a smile. Even in polite society, I didn't trust unknown blood. I sipped it slowly, grimacing a little as the bubbles hit my tongue. I'd liked champagne once, but now, it tasted off. Everything had since I'd begun my final transition. I hoped it wouldn't always be like that, or else I would really miss champagne—and chocolate.

Pressing into the alcove, I scanned the party. I still wasn't sure why I'd come. I didn't know anyone. The vampires and familiars my father knew didn't move in these circles. It was a little weird, actually. When I'd asked my father why he was going, he'd said he didn't have a choice but that it wasn't a safe place for me. Despite that, I felt like I belonged. I couldn't explain it.

There was absolutely no way I was going to walk out there and start small talk with strangers. Though, at the same time, I didn't want to leave. The force I'd felt pulling me to this place was stronger than ever. It was like chains had bound me.

A few couples took to the dance floor, moving with the elegance of centuries. Others mingled under the rose arches, the stars twinkling overhead like the lanterns that surrounded the courtyard. As I watched, something tightened around my chest and tugged at me. Staring into the crowd, I looked for the source of this magnetic force, but all I found were masks and strangers.

And then I saw him.

My father stood on the other side of the party. Natalie was at his side, her hood drawn over her head. I wished I could sink farther into the shadows, but a cool stone wall was at my back.

"Maybe next time," I said to my glass of champagne before placing my mask over my face. My father was already distracted—several male vampires had approached him—and if I stayed hidden, I wouldn't be caught.

And I didn't want to be caught.

I never remembered my punishments, but I never forgot them, either. They teased and scraped below my memories, etching fear into my brain. I suspected my father's magic was to thank for that. I'd seen what he'd done to those who displeased him. Just a few days ago, he'd chained a vampire in our dining room. The male had been drained nearly to death and then forced to watch us dine. He'd snarled and wept and begged—and then one morning, he was gone. I wasn't brave enough to ask what had happened to him. I wasn't sure if it was better if he was dead or alive.

I doubted my father had ever been that cruel to me, but my

scars told another story. Natalie wouldn't tell me how I'd received them, and I couldn't remember. He had forbidden me from even speaking of them, but it wasn't like we could pretend they didn't exist. Some of them were even...

My face heated as I thought of the places I'd found the pearly crescent-shaped scars. Maybe that's why he refused to talk about them. He couldn't be responsible for those scars—not directly.

He had to know who'd given them to me, and since I was pretty much never allowed out of his sight, he must have been present. It had to be the remnants of a punishment.

From the shadows, I spotted another figure approaching my father, and my mouth fell open.

Sabine.

They knew each other. The Drakes were an ancient line, and she was going to be queen. As she neared him, my father turned so I could see his face. It contorted with fury, turning into the beast that even I feared. Next to him, Natalie dropped her hood, and several of the males he'd been speaking to fell back. Only one remained close to him. His body was turned from mine, but even from the back, he showed no signs of fearing my father. I was a little impressed. Maybe he was stupid. Maybe he was brave. Not that there was much of a difference between the two.

Sabine placed a hand on the male's arm, but he threw her off and stalked away. She stayed, speaking to my father, as the other male headed away from the courtyard into the dark.

"Ouch!" I yelped, placing my palm on my chest as the tightness I felt before became suffocating. I couldn't breathe. I was being torn in two by invisible forces. I took a step toward the party, hoping to loosen its pull on me. As soon as I did, another invisible rope yanked me away—away from the party and the blooming roses and my father.

Away from where I should belong and toward the dark unknown.

I couldn't stop myself from following. I kept my eyes on my father as I wove through the crowd. He looked angrier than ever as he spoke to Sabine, but at least she was distracting him. No one noticed me as I darted around their conversations. With the mask on, I felt nearly invisible.

When I stepped out of the courtyard, the night swallowed me. There were no magical lanterns to guide my way. Time had cleaved the moon to half its fullness and already started to carve it slowly to a crescent, so there was little light ahead of me. But I didn't stop—I couldn't stop.

I was being dragged, and then I heard it—a whisper in the night carried on the wind.

Thea.

Someone was in my head.

CHAPTER FORTY-THREE

Julian

Her scent unfurled as our eyes met, wrapping its smoky jasmine and sweet spice around me. But the tether binding my heart told me she was real. It stretched between us like a live wire. Thea placed a hand over her heart, and I felt the touch as though it were my own.

I took a step forward, afraid I imagined her. Thea shrank away with wide eyes.

"Thea?" I whispered again.

Every fiber of my being wanted to grab her, throw her over my shoulder, and run as far and fast as I could from all of this, but something locked me in place. It wasn't my tether, even though I felt its desperation to please and protect her—to win her back.

No, it was something I'd never expected. Ice sluiced through me as her fear hit me.

She was afraid. But instead of drawing me closer, her fear repelled me. It held me in place. It protected her—from me.

She was afraid of *me*.

I couldn't let her slip through my fingers. Darkness gripped my tether, and I tried to seize control. Whatever was happening—whatever she'd been through—it was my responsibility to protect her. I reached for her, and she jumped back. My body reacted, forcing me to my knees, even though all I wanted was to touch her.

My knees hit the stone, and I fell forward to my palms, my tether keeping me from her. "Thea." I groaned her name and tried to lift my hand as she stared at me. "For fuck's sake, *please*."

"How do you know my name?" The "please" had snapped her out of her daze, and she took a small step toward me. She stopped just out of reach. Her throat slid as she studied me, hands twisting together. "Who...who are you?"

Until that moment, I hadn't lost hope. Not entirely. I'd clung to it like a man lost at sea with only it as a life raft. Now her words ripped it from me. My wounded heart shattered as my mate looked down at me with a stranger's eyes.

"You know me," she said softly. Gathering her skirt in her hands, she dropped to the ground before me.

She was so close but still out of reach. Even if my tether would allow me to move, I wouldn't. Not while she was looking at me like this. Not while her sweet scent grew damp with fear.

"You called my name. I heard you in the courtyard." Her voice took on an edge of desperation.

I shook my head. I hadn't called out for her. How could I with Willem so nearby? I couldn't risk it, even if he finally knew the real reason his presence had been requested by *Le Regine*. But she had heard the part of me that hadn't stopped thinking her name since the moment I'd found her gone from our house in Greece.

"You heard my thoughts," I said gently, afraid that the truth might scare her more. Whatever was wrong with her, she didn't know me. She didn't recognize me. But if she'd heard me, maybe I was wrong. Maybe everything wasn't lost.

I just needed to reach her.

"You're crazy." She started to straighten up, her body shaking.

My nostrils flared as her adrenaline spiked. *Don't go.*

Two words. They were all my tether would grant me before it constricted with enough force that I crumbled to the ground. It was going to snap me in two if I kept trying to reach her physically or mentally. But I didn't care. I couldn't. If she walked away now, I was dead.

I couldn't survive if she left. How could I, without my soul?

Please.

I blasted it at her, and my body arced, my spine nearly splintering as my tether tried to silence me. There was nothing but pain. Hell clawed at me, ready to drag me to oblivion. My mouth parted over a dry tongue and formed her name. If I was going to die, I would die with her on my lips.

A scream split the night air, and my tether gave way. I slammed into the stone and felt something inside me crack. I'd broken a bone. Maybe a vertebra. It hurt like hell, but it was nothing compared to the pain I'd felt as love tried to destroy me.

Thea's face swam over my bleary eyes. Maybe it was some remnant of her humanity, but I watched as she slipped off her gloves. She hesitated for only a moment before her fingers brushed my forehead.

"My love." I didn't know if any sound escaped me, but I knew she heard me. Confusion twisted in her eyes as she touched my chest gingerly.

"What is happening?" she sobbed. "Why... What did that?"

Her whole body shook, and I realized with horror that she had felt it, too. Somewhere in the haze that enveloped her mind, she'd felt the tether torturing me. I had put her through that pain.

"I'm sorry." I tried to look into her eyes, but the world was growing dark.

She cried harder, and I knew I'd broken more than a bone. Not that I could feel it. I couldn't feel much, actually—only a cold emptiness that seeped from my blood to my flesh. Thea's face grew panicked, her breaths coming in fast, hard gasps. "I saw you in my dreams." Her voice cracked as she spoke. "I think I've been waiting for you."

I tried to lift my hand, wanting to brush away her tears, but I couldn't feel it anymore. "I waited for you, too. It was worth it. *You* were worth it."

I had waited for her for so long, and I would do it again. I would fight through eternity to find her.

Even if this was how it ended.

"Don't leave me," she pleaded. She bent forward, brushing her mouth to mine one last time.

I smiled as her lips left mine, my cheeks wet with her tears and her taste on my tongue. "I'll see you in your dreams."

And then, I died.

CHAPTER FORTY-FOUR

Lysander

I heard the scream first, but I wasn't the only one. A half dozen others had followed that sound of alarm, including half my family, the queens' handmaiden, and a few strangers. That meant there were a lot of witnesses to this mess, and I... I just stared.

Some of the guests began to whisper, and some cried. But I just stood there as Thea's body slumped like a rag doll over my brother—both of them entirely still, save for their blood seeping across the pavement. My brother was dead. His mate, too. And all I could do was stare until a dark figure stepped in front of me.

Sabine swayed on her feet, a low keening vibrating from her body, and I caught her just in time.

"Release me," she hissed, still shaking.

Before I could, the world rocked under my feet. A few people around us shouted before the earth shook a second time. A few feet away, the pavement cracked, creating a deep chasm that had to run all the way to the water below us. There was a clap of thunder overhead that shook the ground again, and a few vampires fell to their knees. A male lost his balance and swayed over the open fissure before the handmaiden grabbed his shirt and hauled him onto solid ground.

"What the fuck?" I muttered as my mother overcame her shock and squirmed out of my hold. I let her go and braced myself for another earthquake or whatever the hell had just happened.

"Is it a volcano?" someone yelled.

Considering we were in Italy, it wasn't the stupidest question. But the timing was a bit suspicious, especially with the scene before us. It reminded me of a passage I'd read once in an old grimoire I'd found in Prague.

"'When light falls and shadows burn, the dreamers will awaken the storm as above and as below,'" I whispered, wishing I could remember the rest of the prophecy—as though some five-hundred-year-old book might explain this shit show.

A strong hand clapped me on the shoulder, and I looked over to see my father's grim face. "We should get their bodies before…"

He didn't need to finish that thought. *Before all hell breaks loose.* I nodded and followed him, grateful that he could think clearly. It was like something from a nightmare. As if in response to my thought, there was another loud crack and the earth split a few feet away. The ground continued to rock gently as if the lagoon below it was boiling. A few people fled toward the courtyard. Others remained frozen in place, waiting for another quake.

I followed my father to where Julian and Thea lay, my calves straining to keep me upright as the ground shifted and shook. Half a lifetime of digging in the desert had prepared my legs for something like this. When we reached them, Sabine stood silently by, as if the world wasn't collapsing around her. I followed her eyes to where my brother and his mate lay dead.

A hundred battles should have prepared me for seeing their broken bodies, but they hadn't. Nothing could have prepared me for this. It hit me like air on an open wound—stinging and deep. Pain filled me, punctuated by sharp throbs that threatened to send me to my knees.

My brother was dead.

A few minutes ago, Julian had been alive and threatening

Willem Drake within an inch of his own life. Now? I could barely face it. It felt surreal.

"She'll be light," my father said quietly. "Get her feet."

Light. It was a coincidental choice of words. Still, it pricked at my memory. I cleared my throat, hoping to hide the rawness I felt creeping up it. "The others?"

"Sebastian is getting the boat. Thoren and Benedict are dealing with other matters."

My father meant they were dealing with crowd control. Naturally. Benedict would smooth things over, and Thoren would scare people away. They were a perfect combination. That was how it had always been. We all had our parts to play. I had answers or knew where to find them. Sebastian was as slick as an oiled fish. And Julian was the one we followed.

We'd only just gotten him back...

"Son," my father said, drawing me back to the task at hand.

I swallowed the emotions welling inside me and bent to wrap my hands around Thea's delicate ankles. She might have been a feather. She was so easy to lift. I couldn't bring myself to look at her—at those vacant eyes—so I looked to my father.

"Put her next to him."

I followed his instructions, helping him place Thea on her back. He stepped over her, lifting her hands and placing them over her wounded heart. I turned away when he leaned over and closed her eyelids. When I looked back, he'd done the same to Julian.

"We should take them to Jacqueline's," Dominic said, approaching my mother and me.

"Jacqueline's?" Her voice was hollow. I'd never heard her sound so lost. Even after Camila had died, she'd been angry in her grief. She had raged like the east wind. Now? It was like she wasn't here at all.

"Wherever," I murmured, understanding his suggestion. "Just away from here." I didn't give a shit about gossip or scandal. Every vampire in town, if not the entire world, would know they were dead by morning. There was no hiding this. But what we needed was a moment to regroup and figure out what the hell had happened.

"You aren't taking her anywhere!" a deep voice bellowed, and I turned to find Willem stalking toward us. Thoren was a few steps behind him, his own expression murderous.

Anger flickered in Sabine's eyes as she rounded on him. Her rage crackled in the air around her, and I took an instinctive step away without leaving her side. "Kidnapping my daughter-in-law does not give you claim to her," she thundered, and for a second, I swore I saw lightning strike in the distance. "Leave this place."

Willem's lip curled into a beastly snarl. "She's my child. I think that's claim enough."

I might have cared about what he was saying, but I was past that now. It hardly mattered. Thea was dead. Julian was dead.

From the corner of my eye, I saw the handmaiden moving in the shadows. She crept closer as they argued before sliding past them.

"Liar." Sabine hurled the accusation at Willem. My father and Thoren flanked her, guarding their matriarch without a word. "She's no vampire."

"I never claimed she was," he spat back. "She's far more extraordinary."

There was a split second of hesitation on my mother's face before she shook her head and clung to her accusations. "You wouldn't dare. Not even you!"

What was he suggesting? Sabine seemed to know, but she seemed as unlikely to share as he was, and there was the other matter: I didn't know whether to believe Willem's claim that he was Thea's father or not—and I didn't really care. What did it matter if they were both dead? I stepped quietly back so no one would mark my movement. If anyone noticed, they didn't say anything. They were too absorbed in threats to notice me moving toward the bodies.

The handmaiden was bent beside them, her fingers drifting over Thea's bare hand. A thick hood obscured her face. She didn't look up from her silent vigil until I stepped beside her. When she did, her mask kept all but her eyes hidden from view.

"What are you doing?" I asked her.

Her eyes fluttered behind her mask, but she continued to stare at me. After a moment, she glanced at the bodies before reaching up and removing her mask.

The hood kept half her face in shadows, but there was enough light to make out the rest. My heart slammed like a fist into my chest when I saw the scar that carved across her cheek, down her chin, and onto her throat, as if she'd been slashed by a very sharp blade wielded by someone who wished her dead. Her lips pursed thoughtfully, drawing my attention away from the scar to her mouth, full and untouched. I knew she wore the mask as part of her livery, but maybe she wore it to cover those lips, that striking, scarred face that I could barely tear my eyes from.

"They can be saved," she whispered, and I blinked, my attention returning to the hellscape before us.

"They're dead," I said flatly. The last thing anyone here needed was false hope, myself included.

"The queens have the power." She rose to her feet and moved closer to me. "We must take them to the others at once. There is a prophecy."

I knew a lot of prophecies. I'd spent a considerable amount of time chasing prophecies, fortune, and glory around the globe. I'd read thousands of books. I'd even seen my fair share of miracles. But vampires didn't come back from true death. Neither did mortals. Not anymore.

"Not with an empty throne," I shot back. "Sabine hasn't ascended, and even if she does, the magic you would need doesn't exist anymore."

As soon as the words left my mouth, a rumble of power nearly sent me flying. I stumbled forward a step, my eyes darting around me as I cursed under my breath.

"I know you felt that," the handmaiden said.

"What?" I asked. "The earthquake?" Or maybe there really

was a volcano under us—that would be bad.

She rolled her eyes. "Earthquake? I heard you were smarter than that, Lysander."

She had? I was about to ask her where she'd heard it and how she knew my name when the sky turned into a glittering shower of sparks. The few remaining gawkers shouted and ran as tiny flickers rained down on us. My eyes fell on one of the nearby fissures and discovered dark smoke billowing forth from it.

"Come on." She grabbed my hand. "Help me get them to the queens. They'll know what to do."

"But—" I glanced toward my mother, and the handmaiden yanked my arm.

"Sabine can't help us," she hissed. "She isn't the queen we seek."

"There won't be enough power to bring them back from the dead." For some reason, even as I argued, I found myself picking my brother up and hoisting him carefully over my shoulder. Whatever hesitation I'd felt earlier was too clouded by the sheer insanity going on around me.

"Thea isn't dead." She lifted Thea into her arms, cradling her limp body.

But Thea was. Not even a magical creature could survive that wound. Thea's wide, unseeing eyes stared back at me from over the handmaiden's shoulder. There was no life in them. She was gone.

"She can be called back to this world," the handmaiden said.

She made bringing someone back from the dead sound a little too simple, but what did I have to lose? I was about to point that out when she started to carry Thea off. I glanced over my shoulder and found Sabine and Willem screaming at each other. The strange woman's plan sounded futile, but I didn't have a better one. It was probably better than letting Sabine or Willem get ahold of the bodies.

"What now?" I demanded as I caught up to her.

"Thea walks between death and life," she explained in a hurried whisper. "We have to show her the way back to us."

"And how the fuck are we supposed to do that?" I asked as we slipped into a hidden passage.

"You ask a lot of questions." She shot me a shy smile before she answered my question. "With magic."

"Oh, *that*," I said flatly, adjusting my brother's weight on my shoulder as the passageway narrowed. I didn't want to think about why he felt so heavy, and if there was a way—any way—to save him, I couldn't ignore it. No matter how crazy it sounded. "Okay, one more question: how are we going to do that?"

"By placing her on her throne."

CHAPTER FORTY-FIVE

Thea

*D*eath. It wasn't what I expected.

Mostly, I hadn't expected anything. I'd never really gone in on the pearly-gates-and-harp-music version of the afterlife. Or the fiery-pit-of-doom version, for that matter. And whatever this place was, there were no angels or devils waiting around to greet me. Because instead of oblivion—instead of a sudden and abrupt end—I found myself walking in a thick fog. On either side of me light and shadow danced, each seizing a moment only to retreat for the other.

Hello?

The word formed in my thoughts and somehow seemed to float in the liminal space around me as though I'd spoken it aloud. I was here, but I wasn't. I spoke without saying a word. I was in my body and liberated from it. And despite the strange purgatory I found myself in, my mind was clear for the first time in… I remembered everything that had happened.

Willem had kidnapped me. He had stolen me away and forced me to drink blood until I was dizzy with need for it—until I couldn't think—and then someone else had come. A woman I didn't know. I'd been half out of my mind when he laid me on an altar. She had opened an ancient grimoire and begun to speak in a strange, forgotten language.

My stomach turned over as I saw what had happened next. I reached to rub it, but there was no movement—no hand to place on my absent abdomen. I was here and not here. I was lost, even as more memories surfaced, and I found myself back on that altar.

Where was I? Who was I? I stared at the room's stone walls. There wasn't a single window. The only light came from a dozen flickering candelabras stationed around me. A damp chill hung in the air, and I trembled as I wrapped my arms around my naked body for warmth. It was not unlike being born, I supposed.

A male moved into view over my head. He looked familiar, I thought, as he placed a blanket over my shivering body. "You are my daughter. Thea Drake."

Thea. I was Thea. Yes, I knew that.

"H-h-how did I get here?" My voice quivered as I tried it out for what felt like the first time.

"There was an accident." His dark eyes were soft as he helped me to sit up. "You were taken from me. Do you remember?"

I tugged the blanket around my shoulders as I tried to recall anything. There was only darkness. Biting my lip, I shook my head.

"You will," he promised. "I will help you."

And he did. He fed me blood to strengthen me and told me stories about my life. About the mother who had stolen me when he'd discovered her secret. About how she had died.

"She was a siren," he told me as we sat by the fire a few hours later. "She cast a spell on you to make you forget who you are—who I was."

"Why would she do that?" I asked, peering at him over the rim of my goblet.

Firelight danced in his eyes as he stared at the hearth. "She wanted you to be like her, but I could never let you become that."

"A siren? Why?"

"Because sirens destroy men," he explained. "They lure them and seduce them to their demise."

The blood I was drinking turned to ash in my mouth. I forced myself to swallow it, still clutching the goblet. "Is that what she did to you?"

"She tried," he admitted in a gentle tone, "but vampires are not as easy to destroy as humans."

"I don't understand. If she wanted to hurt you, why have a child? Why have me?" My throat bobbed as I spoke.

"It was no accident that your mother chose me—chose a vampire. If she had taken a mortal man to bed and conceived a child, you would simply be a siren," he explained. "But she knew a secret that my kind has fought to protect."

I placed my cup on the table next to me, suddenly feeling like I might vomit. "What is it?"

I half expected him to refuse to answer. As it was, he took his time and studied me before he finally spoke. "The daughter of a siren and a vampire can harness the powers of both her parents. She can become something that both our species fear—something more powerful than both of us put together."

I almost didn't want him to continue. Did I want to know what secret power ran in my veins? Did I want to know what harnessing it would cost me?

"Sirens once flew between life and death," he said. "Your mother's kind was created by the gods to seek out those lost to the underworld."

His words sparked something in my mind, a flash of memory too fleeting to grab ahold of. I shifted in the leather chair, drawing my knees to my chest before I nodded for him to continue.

"Vampires are forbidden from entering the underworld," my father explained.

"Why?" I blurted out.

"Our long lives offended the god of the underworld. It is difficult to kill a vampire. We do not die as easily as mortals, and often we can heal from a wound that would kill a human. We can even experience physical death temporarily and be resurrected."

I wanted to ask him what killed vampires—if the faded memories I had of vampire stories weren't stories at all, and he really could die by a stake to the heart; if there were other ways. But something kept my questions locked inside me.

"We are not welcome in the afterlife," he told me. "We

become shadows."

"But sirens are welcome?"

He nodded once but offered no further information.

"And me? Am I more siren or vampire?" Would I die and find myself in this shadow world he spoke of, or would I rise again as he would?

"That is for you to choose," he said gently. "Your mother tried to choose for you."

"To force me to be a siren?" I said with disgust. "Why?"

"Because you would not only be able to move between death and life—you could control them. You would be more powerful than either a siren or a vampire. You would be a creature of both worlds, able to take life and grant it." He paused, meeting my eyes. "Thea, you would be a succubus."

A succubus? I'd heard of those nightmare creatures. They were the stuff of ancient folklore. Stories told to terrify children into staying in their beds after dark. I'd never thought they were real. But why would my father lie to me after all he had done to protect me? "Aren't they demons?"

"We make demons out of what we misunderstand," he said with a dry laugh, "and we make villains out of what we fear. All creatures seek power, and if they believe another species has more power, it is easier to destroy it than bow to it."

"But I don't want power," I whispered. Not like this. I had no desire to control life or death.

"I'm afraid that there is no choice," he said softly. He moved in his seat, placing his forearms on his knees. "The sirens will come for you. They will never allow us peace. They will try to blind you with lies and trickery."

"Why?"

"Because war is coming." He sounded sad as his head bowed. "Vampires have hidden amongst humans for too long. We are divided. We no longer see the same future we once did."

"And sirens? What about my mother's people?"

A muscle in his jaw twitched. "Your mother was the last of her kind, as far as I know, until you."

And I was only half siren. "What happened to them?"

"Sirens were hunted down and killed. Most creatures believe they went extinct centuries ago."

"Who hunted them?" I demanded, anger surging through my veins as if I already knew the answer.

My father didn't speak for a long time, and his face softened with apology when he did. "Vampires. Vampires destroyed them all."

It had all been a lie, but there was truth in it. Like this strange space I found myself in now. It was both, and it was neither. My mother had sacrificed herself to protect me from my father—and his people, who'd exterminated hers. I had no idea what dark magic she'd called upon or how she had found it, but she'd spent her life trying to keep him from finding me. It might have worked. I might have had a quiet, normal life.

If I hadn't met a vampire first.

How many of the vampire elite I'd danced and dined with over the last few months remembered sirens? Had they forgotten the threat over the years? Or would they come for me like Willem had? Not to use me, like I'm sure he planned to do. I sensed that bit of truth in the memory. It was my father who wanted power. It was he who had hunted down my mother and seduced her. Had she even known what she was then?

No, they wouldn't come to use me. They would come to kill me. I was sure of it.

But now they didn't have to. I was dead.

Wasn't I?

I thought of what my father had said. Sirens walked between life and death. I wasn't a succubus. Not yet. I wasn't sure how I knew, but I felt the truth in my gut. He hadn't succeeded in turning me into one, but he had tried. Was that why my skin burned in daylight? Had I begun to change? Could it be stopped? Reversed?

Did it matter if I was stuck in the space between worlds? Between light and darkness?

Because I wouldn't be used by him—or anyone. I was safe here. I felt that, too. But for how long? Was I doomed to walk through this haze alone for eternity?

Or was Julian here with me, lost as well?

If I could walk between life and death, I would find him. I didn't care what it took or how long I wandered.

Before me, the fog parted slightly but only to reveal that dance of light and shadow. Life and death moved seamlessly to some silent music, and then, like magic, I could hear its notes.

Darkness crashed and swelled, colliding with the high, bright notes of life. Each played its own melody that somehow entwined to create a bittersweet song that filled me with despair and hope, longing and fear.

And somewhere, Julian was there in that music. I'd followed him into death, and I knew what I had to do now. I walked toward the storm before me, turning my thoughts inward as I searched for him—for the tether that bound us. Not the leash that chained him to me but the bond that linked us as one. A bond that could never be broken. Not by life. Not by death. It was timeless and unending.

True magic, I realized. What else but true magic could fuse our souls as one?

And I was still here, and so was he.

So, I strode forward, and as I walked into the storm, I heard his voice gliding along that beautiful, dreadful music. I reached out for him, feeling for that thread that bound us together. But before I could seize it, the storm changed. It surrounded me, its music roaring in my blood as shadows and light wrapped themselves in tendrils around me and yanked me out of the fog.

"Julian!" I screamed his name over and over until I was hoarse. Until I felt two hands grip my shoulder and shake me.

I opened my eyes to find myself sitting in the middle of a room, my hands clutching the intricately carved arms of a chair. Looking to my left and right, I found two more chairs. No, not chairs. *Thrones*. Looking down, I discovered mine was as well. My chest was bloodied, but I felt no pain.

Until my gaze shifted to the floor before the thrones, where my mate's body lay broken before me.

CHAPTER FORTY-SIX

Thea

"Nooo!" The moan slipped from me. I reached out as I threw myself forward, struggling against the two strong hands hauling me back onto the throne. My eyes darted wildly over to find it was Lysander! Betrayal barreled down my spine, and I bucked off his grasp. "What are you doing? Let go."

"Not yet," he said. His mouth flattened to a grim line, and he nodded in the other direction, where a hooded woman knelt by my side, watching.

I turned my attention to her. "Please. You have to let me go." A sob cracked my words. "My mate."

I needed to reach him, if only to touch him. If only to quiet the pounding in my chest that demanded to be near him. It was the only way to soothe my ravaged soul. But it also might help me find his voice again—the one I'd heard calling through that strange silent world of light and shadow. I needed to know if he was still there. I needed to know if I could still hear him.

Tears threatened to blind me, and I turned my agony toward the stranger, allowing it to show and praying she had a shred of sympathy inside her.

"Giuliano will survive," she said with a thick Italian accent.

Giuliano. It took me a second to realize she meant Julian. I'd never heard him called that, but it was clear she knew him. The name must be a remnant from a past life. I didn't really care. Not now. Not with my mate bloodied on the floor at my feet.

"I need to go to him," I pleaded.

"You need your power," she said softly. "The throne will help. It's a conduit to the *Rio Oscuro*'s magic. Give it a few more minutes to heal you."

"What the hell are you talking about?" I demanded. They made it sound like they'd plugged me into a magical charging station. But I wasn't who mattered now. Each moment, I felt the memory of his voice slipping further and further away. "I need to get to Julian. I heard him!"

"You heard him?" Lysander asked slowly. I turned to see his eyes skip from the strange woman to his brother's body.

"Yes," I said, losing patience. "I was somewhere"—how the hell was I supposed to explain the limbo I'd been in?—"somewhere else. There was music and light and shadows. I could hear him. I could feel him. He's still alive."

He had to be. I'd been wrong before—out of my mind, thanks to Willem's magical interference. I didn't know what was going on, but Julian was here. He was close. I felt it in my bones, felt it in my blood.

"Light and shadows?" Lysander muttered, and I tensed, expecting ridicule. Instead, he murmured something under his breath: "When light falls and shadows burn, the dreamers will awaken the storm—"

"As above and as below, magic to magic, darkness to darkness, true love to true magic," the woman whispered.

"I can't remember the rest," Lysander said, his eyes wide and watchful and entirely focused on her. "Do you know the grimoire it came from? What it means?"

"I've studied it extensively." She looked down, a faint flush coloring her cheeks.

They were…flirting. A strange urge to break both their necks flashed through me, but I resisted. I didn't have time for that mess or for them to continue their cryptic conversation. "You said he would survive. How?"

The woman paused before answering me. "You. You can heal him."

"How? He can't drink my blood. He..." I fought the rawness rising in my throat like the ache growing inside me. That couldn't be it. I hadn't already failed him.

"Not your blood. Your magic," she told me. "You will need strength to summon the song of the living and call him back from limbo."

"Limbo?" I repeated. It couldn't be. I heaved a breath. "That's where I was?"

She nodded. "Did you hear the music of life and death there?"

"You were in *limbo*?" Lysander asked in an incredulous voice.

I ignored him and twisted my hands around the carved arms of the throne. I'd heard music there, but I'd had no idea what it was. I definitely had no idea how to channel it.

"Yes, you do," she said, as though reading my thoughts. "It will be easier, though, if you call your sisters here first. Their magic will boost your own."

"My sisters? I don't..." I shook my head.

"*Le Regine* are your sisters," she explained. "They have been—"

"Waiting for you," a female voice interrupted.

I lifted my head to find two vampires approaching. The speaker's black hair cascaded down her back, catching the light from the lanterns overhead and glinting like seawater. Next to her, the other female was silent, like a statue carved from black stone, except for the silver hair that waved past her shoulders. They both wore high-necked gowns of ivory chiffon, but each had a different crown resting atop her head.

"I understand now why the visions told me to invite Giuliano back to our court," she continued. "I assumed it was to make peace with his mother—to offer her our empty throne. It wasn't until tonight that the veil lifted and I saw the truth. It's you we've waited for, sister."

Sister? I lifted an eyebrow, glancing to Julian's brother to see what he made of all this. He only stared at the queens.

And I didn't care. "I don't give a shit about your visions," I snapped. "All I care about is saving my mate."

"And what price will you pay?" the silver-haired queen asked. Her lips barely moved as she spoke.

I knew my answer as surely as I knew the heart beating inside my chest. "Anything."

There was no price I wouldn't pay to save him. I would give up my soul, my very life, if it meant saving him.

"Your mate experienced true death," the other queen told me as she climbed the few steps to the dais where the thrones sat. "To save him, you must offer him your own life."

"I will," I said quickly—too quickly, because Lysander clamped a hand around my wrist.

"Think of what you're doing," he said quietly. "Julian would not wish to live without you."

"And he will not," she interrupted us. "She must offer her life to call him here. Vampires do not enter the underworld. He walks in limbo. He must be bound to something here to call his soul back to his body."

I swallowed. It couldn't be that easy. "We're mates," I said, adding, "and we are tethered."

"Yes, you are mates." She inclined her head as she came to stand before me. "But you are no longer tethered. A tether cannot survive death."

Her words hit me with a fresh wave of grief. It swelled inside me, and I fought to keep breathing. Even though we had never wanted our tether, it had linked us together. And Julian had never abused that power over me. But that power... That power had killed him.

"How?" I finally asked. "How do I do it?"

"To bring him back, you will call upon the song of the living and offer it to him. If he accepts, his life will be bound to yours."

"What do you mean by bound?" Lysander asked suspiciously.

"As she lives, he will live."

"And if she dies?" he demanded.

"Julian will die as well," the silver-haired queen continued. "But there are other things to consider. You will grant him access to *our* magic." There was the bitter edge of distaste in her tone, and I wondered if it was because she didn't want to share her power or because Julian had pissed her off in the past. Probably both.

"I will pay any price," I said fiercely, tears swimming in my eyes. "Any."

"You are too weak," she replied, her lips finally moving into a slight sneer. "You will require our assistance, and I am not convinced he is worthy of using our magic."

"Zina," the other said, her voice full of warning. "This is not the time."

"I believe it is a perfect time, Mariana. We do not know this siren. She is not like us. Will she sit on the throne? Will she reign?" I opened my mouth to protest, but her next question was like a blow to my stomach. "Will she give up her life to this court?"

"I already told you I would," I said hotly. How many times would she make me say it, wasting precious time?

"Do you even know what it means?" she snarled, her stonelike features contorting into that of a beast.

"Anything. I will give you anything," I swore again, and as I spoke, I felt something heavy circle my head. I reached up and felt a crown—one that came from nowhere—now resting on my head.

Lysander's eyes widened at the sight, and I knew what it meant before Mariana spoke again.

She smiled at me, and the crown felt heavier, like a weight confining me to this throne—to this life. "Magic has chosen you. Welcome, sister. Now let's bring your mate back to life."

CHAPTER FORTY-SEVEN

Julian

Death was not peaceful. Not that I deserved peace. I'd done terrible things in my life. I deserved worse than the shadow world I found myself in now. Vampires never worried much about heaven or hell or the underworld. Not when we lived for millennia. But I'd always secretly thought it might be peaceful, unlike living.

That was before her...before I had a reason to live. Before I knew what I would lose when death claimed me. Now? Eternity stretched before me—a realm of darkness and shadows deprived of any light, even *her* light.

I might as well be in hell. I'd prefer physical pain or torture to this nothingness. Because the lack of her—the lack of her light, her smile, her existence—*that* was hell.

I continued into the shadows, searching for signs of anything or anyone, but I was alone.

And then I heard a soft melody in that vacuum of nothingness and saw, for just a moment, a sparkle of light flash in the distance before billowing black clouds swallowed it again.

I opened my mouth to call her name, or I tried to. I tried to look down. I tried to lift my hand. I wasn't really here. At least my body wasn't. I'd become something else. I'd become a memory, but

I didn't care. Something like hope wrapped itself around me. The light. The music.

She was alive.

And nothing mattered if I could cling to that. I could find my peace in this neverendingness, and maybe sometimes I would see that light glinting or hear her music to remind me that not all of me was lost. Not if she lived.

Even...even if she had forgotten me. Even if that tether that had tied us together had been sundered.

And so, as I became darkness and shadow, I faded into memories of her.

CHAPTER FORTY-EIGHT

Thea

"It's not working." I resisted the urge to cry as I knelt over Julian's body. Cold stones bit into my knees, but I barely noticed. There was so much blood, even now after it had stopped seeping from him, his heart no longer pumping it through his veins. It covered my hands and my dress, mixing with my own.

"Listen," Mariana coaxed. She stood beside me, her shadow falling over his body. Her sister—or, according to them, *our* sister—Zina, had not left her throne nor spoken since the crown had chosen me.

"I'm trying," I said through gritted teeth, straining to hear the song she spoke of.

The one I'd sensed while in limbo.

Lysander moved into view, and I lifted my head to meet his eyes. What I saw there twisted like a knife in my stomach. Pity. He didn't think it would work, and with each minute that passed, I was beginning to agree with him.

"Thea," he said my name softly, "if you don't—"

"Out!" Mariana commanded, no hint of softness to her now. "She needs to concentrate."

"Why?" Zina called from her throne. "He's not the first

vampire to die. He won't be the last."

White-hot anger boiled inside me, threatening to unleash itself on her—needing to find an outlet before the rage and guilt ate me alive.

"Perhaps if you helped," Mariana replied carefully.

I felt my control slip, but before I exploded, there was a commotion in the distance.

"Aurelia." My companion turned to the cloaked woman. "Make sure no one gets in here. And take him with you."

My eyes met Lysander's as Aurelia approached him. He nodded slightly, shadows catching the sharp planes of his face as if to promise he would be nearby and ready to help.

But he couldn't help me. No one could, it seemed.

When they were gone, Mariana relaxed. "It will be easier now."

"I doubt it," I grumbled, because I was running out of what I needed to keep trying. Not magic. Hope. Each second stole more of it from me, and soon there would be nothing left at all.

When that happened, I didn't know what I would do. I'd tried to follow him into death, only to be hauled back here—the real hell.

"Listen for the music," Mariana said for the hundredth time.

I closed my eyes and tried, but the melody I'd heard in limbo was unlike any I'd ever heard before. I didn't know that song. Taking a deep breath, I tried to fade back to limbo, but there was nothing but silence now. Disappointment swelled inside me as I looked back at her. "What does it sound like?"

She paused, her eyes pinching at their edges. "I don't know. Only sirens know that music."

And I wasn't a siren. Not really. I bit back a scream of frustration. Only half my blood contained the magic that I needed to call upon. The other half…

"I can't do it." My voice sounded hollow even to my own ears. I dropped back and pulled my bloody hands from Julian as the last glimmer of hope began to fade. In its place, grief threatened to overwhelm me. It dragged at me like a hidden current, and at any moment, I would be pulled under.

I wasn't sure I even wanted to fight it anymore.

"She's not strong enough," Zina proclaimed from her throne. "I told you."

"The crown chose her," Mariana said softly.

"The crown chose poorly."

I didn't bother to disagree. Zina was right. Whatever power had called the crown to me was gone. Extinguished. There was nothing left except two broken creatures, both dead in their own ways.

"I'd like a minute alone," I whispered, swallowing back the words that wanted to follow: *to say goodbye.* There would be no farewells between us.

"I'm not sure." Mariana hesitated, and I saw the doubt in her stormy eyes.

But Zina had already risen from her seat. Delight danced in her eyes as she approached me, the only emotion on her stoic face. "Come," she said to Mariana. "Let her have these final moments."

Final moments.

I didn't process their departure as I considered what she meant. If she was right, this was the end. Eventually, they would come for Julian, and I would be forced to part with him. But I wasn't ready. Not when I'd felt him so clearly only an hour before. Not while I could touch him.

His blood had cooled. It no longer warmed my hands. Now it felt slick and oily, and I was torn between wanting to wipe it away and wanting to let it cling to my skin. This was all that was left of him, and it wasn't fair.

I didn't realize I was crying until a tear fell onto the back of my hand and met with his blood. There would be no wedding. No children. More tears fell until I could barely breathe. I thought of all the places we had planned to go. I would see none of them. Why would I want to, without him there by my side? I gasped as each second brought more loss. I would never catch him watching from the shadows as I played my cello again. We would never build a new home in Paris to replace the one his sister had destroyed. There would be no reverent touches. We wouldn't make love in the moonlight.

I'd spent so much time, recently, wondering about what the future would bring, feeling uncertain about what to do next, that I'd lost sight of the truth. The future was always right there. It was his smile. It was grumpy exchanges with his brothers. It was his hands finding my body in the dark of night. The future—the only future worth having—was us.

It was him.

Without it, I wanted none of this. Especially not a stupid throne or a stupid crown. I tried to grab the crown to hurl it away from me, but it resisted, as though it wasn't simply an object but a living thing that refused to be rejected.

"I don't want you!" My scream echoed around the empty room and came back to fall on me. Collapsing against his middle, I dissolved into the weak creature I knew I was. If I was what they said, I could save him. I could call upon this stupid song. I could heal what I had broken, but I was nothing. I wasn't a siren. Or a vampire. I was just some half-breed that had no place in this world, and if I couldn't save him, I didn't want this world anyway.

So, I let myself cry and scream until my throat was shredded and there were no tears left, only the ghost of them throbbing behind my dry eyes. I thought of the night we'd met—when he'd looked at me like he might rip me apart—and softly began to hum the *andante con moto*. The last song I'd played before he charged in to save me and changed my life forever.

It wasn't the song of life that my kind was supposed to wield. It was the exact opposite—a song about a maiden meeting death— and I finally understood it. I'd thought it was the story of an innocent fleeing from the clutches of an ill fate, but it wasn't. It was about loss. The frantic desperation that accompanied that grief. It was fear and wild hope and panic…and, finally, acceptance. I couldn't remember more than the part we'd played. I couldn't recall anything past that final bit of the quartet, except Schubert's sense of resignation. Not relief, because it held too bitter an edge.

And I couldn't hum any more as I came to the end of the *andante*. I wouldn't. Instead, I found a new melody, one as sweet as the taste of *his* kiss at midnight. It changed into the longing I felt when he touched me and the quiet contentment I found in the safety of his arms. I wrote his eulogy—my final farewell—in music, because there weren't words for what I felt for him. There was no way to capture everything he meant to me and everything he would continue to, except through the notes that swelled and flowed from me.

When I reached the last lingering note, I knew that this song had no ending. We had no ending. We were the true magic, and maybe that's why the crown had mistakenly been called to my head by that symphony our bond had written. But for now, I'd finished my work, and silence fell.

A hand coasted up my shoulder, and it took me a moment to feel it—to feel *him*.

"My love." The words were anguished and brittle, but they were his.

I sat up, and his hand fell away, landing on the stones. Julian groaned, a sound of true pain that twisted inside me. I grabbed hold of it and dared to finally look at him. Blue eyes stared back at me, flashing with lightning as the magic did its work. I stared as the bone protruding from his chest retracted. Color returned to his pale skin.

"Thea." Agony twisted his voice.

I hushed him. "Don't talk. Just heal."

I pushed onto my knees so I could brush back a bloody strand of hair from his eyes—his eyes that were full of life and love and a future.

Our future.

We stared at each other until I had no idea how much time had passed. I couldn't tear my eyes from him—from my mate.

Until a smile danced across his lips. "Can I speak yet?"

I laughed, nodding, as tears filled my eyes again.

"Good," he said. "Why are you wearing a crown?"

CHAPTER FORTY-NINE

Julian

My mate reached up to touch the crown that graced her bowed head. Diamond shards rose from its band like rays to mimic the sun. In the center of the sunburst, a delicate serpent, *Le Regine*'s oldest symbol, held aloft a crescent carved from moonstone in its jaw. Her nose wrinkled, drawing attention to her freckles, and she sighed.

"Oh, that," she said flatly. "It doesn't matter."

But it did matter. Because I recognized that crown, knew whose head it once rested upon and what it meant that Thea wore it now. I raised my head and looked around the room, unsurprised to find us near the queens' dais. The throne room was empty, but it had been cleaned since my last visit. No doubt in preparation for the sisters to welcome their newest member. It was supposed to have been my mother. But if Thea wore the crown, then...

"What happened?" I asked softly, knowing this was her story to tell.

She paused before finally speaking in a brittle voice. "You died."

I nodded because I wouldn't deny that fact. But there was more to all of this than that, and we both knew it. "I'm here now."

There was one more moment of hesitation before her mouth

opened and the story spilled from her. I listened quietly as she told me about Willem—about who he was to her—and then continued to tonight's events. When she finished, tears shone in her emerald eyes.

"I didn't have a choice." She wrung her hands together. "I would have done anything to save you."

"You don't have to justify yourself to me." If she knew what I'd done to find her, the vampires I'd tortured as I'd hunted her, would she even look at me the same way?

"You don't mind?" Her teeth sank into her lower lip, drawing attention to her mouth. Suddenly, my pants felt tighter. At least I appeared to be recovering quickly.

"Mind?" Carefully, I pushed up until I was sitting next to her. There wasn't the slightest twinge of pain. It was almost like none of it had happened. If it weren't for her crown, I might have thought I'd imagined the whole thing.

"That I..." She gestured to the crown, as though she couldn't bring herself to admit what she'd agreed to by wearing it.

"I'm just picturing you wearing that crown and nothing else." I didn't bother to paint the rest of the picture—her straddling me, her face contorted with anguished bliss—but judging from the heat that stained her cheeks, she'd imagined the same thing.

"I don't know what they expect from me," she admitted. "I think it was a mistake."

"Thea." I savored the way her name tasted on my tongue before dropping my voice to a lower octave, knowing others would be nearby. Taking her hand, I brushed my thumb along the back of it. I knew there was no way to soothe her ragged nerves, but maybe I could help her accept what she'd done. "You brought me back to life. It wasn't a mistake. The crown chose you."

She opened her mouth to protest as the doors to the throne room burst open. My mother, followed by a dozen others, flowed into the room, all of them stopping short when they saw us sitting there.

"Julian." Sabine's lips formed my name even though no further sound issued from her. She pressed her hand to her chest. My father stood next to her, confusion warring with relief on his face.

"It worked." Lysander's voice finally cut the silence. "It fucking worked."

The woman next to him hushed him with a harsh glare.

"As I said it would," Mariana announced as she swept past them and headed toward us. Her sister, walking beside her, sniffed slightly—the only sign on her stone face that she was disappointed at the outcome.

Mariana smiled at us as the two queens ascended the dais and took their respective thrones. As soon as they were seated, she called in a lofty voice, "Join us, sister."

Thea's eyes met mine, her teeth still chewing on her lower lip, and I knew it was the last thing she wanted to do. Not only because I was here but because she hadn't processed what had happened— who she now was.

"Go on," I urged her in a low voice only she could hear. "Take your throne."

"But..." Her fingers locked tightly around mine. "What about you?"

"I want to be the first to bow to you as my queen." I leaned closer, brushing my mouth against her ear. She shivered a little, and I smiled. "And later, I will kneel before you and show you my allegiance properly."

With one smooth movement, I stood, to the shocked stares of my audience. In fairness, even I was surprised by my rapid recovery. Perhaps the *Rio Oscuro* had granted Thea the strength to heal me, but I was surprised not even an ache lingered.

Bending, I offered her my bare hand, and she took it, earning a shocked gasp from one of our onlookers. When she was on her feet, she didn't move. It took effort not to pick her up, throw her over my shoulder, and cart her away. There were too many people here for a proper reunion, and with the newfound energy of my resurrection, I was itching to get her alone. I was about to cave in when Sabine snapped out of her daze.

"What is going on?" she demanded. Her eyes darted from the crown on Thea's head to me and back to my mate. They narrowed into slits as she started piecing things together. "What did you do?"

I gripped Thea's hand tightly, squeezing it once in warning. *She's baiting you.*

Thea laughed quietly, as if to say she knew, but she didn't back down from my mother's question. Instead, she dropped my hand and sauntered toward Sabine, her hips swishing in her bloodstained gown. When she reached her, Thea lifted her chin as though she still wasn't nearly half a foot shorter than my mother. Her height hardly mattered, given the power radiating from her like a halo of sunbursts. "What did I do?" she repeated. "I saved your son's life."

Sabine blinked. For a moment, she almost looked taken aback by Thea's answer, but then her haughty mask slipped into place. "And stole the crown."

"The crown was given to me," Thea said in a quiet voice that demanded to be heard, "and if you're more worried about that than you are about your son's life, then you need to get your priorities in fucking order."

Neither of them backed down, even as a murmur of approval rippled through the crowd. Out of the corner of my eye, I spotted my brother twist to smother a smile. Others arrived and flooded into the court before the next round could begin.

"Is it true?" Sebastian's voice carried through the room. He pushed past the onlookers until he spotted me and his shoulders slumped with relief. But he didn't stop like the others—didn't seem awed by the sight of the queen at my side. Instead, he rushed forward and embraced me. "I'm glad you aren't dead."

"Me too," I said, smiling despite the developing situation.

"And don't worry—I'm armed," he added with a whisper.

I guessed I wasn't the only one expecting things to go south quickly.

"Will no one answer my question?" Sabine commanded the attention back to her. "Why is she wearing that crown?"

The answer came from behind the crowd as a deep voice

bellowed, "Because she is more powerful than you—*all* of you."

I stepped slightly in front of my mate as the throng parted to reveal Willem. He'd taken off his mask to show his arrogant, if grim, smile.

"You aren't welcome here," I said. "Leave."

"I was invited," he snarled back at me. A few of the other guests flinched and backed away, but not a single member of my family so much as blinked.

"An oversight," Sabine said, turning to him. "Now, please excuse us while we sort out this mess."

I knew exactly what "mess" she referred to, but before I could remind her about what Thea had said about priorities, my mate stepped around me.

"Leave," Thea commanded him, her voice clear and strong. Even with dried blood staining her gown, coating her hands and face, she looked regal. But maybe because of all the blood, she also looked like someone who shouldn't be fucked with.

I reached for the tether that connected us, ready to protect her if needed, but it was gone. In its place, there was something else: threads of light and shadow that seemed to be woven into our very beings. I made a mental note to ask her what else she might have done to bring me back to life, but before I could worry about it, Willem laughed.

"I see you are no longer in thrall," he said. "That doesn't mean I have no claim to you. I am your father. You are my daughter, and—"

"I belong to no man," Thea said in a deadly whisper. "I know what you did to me, so consider this the only gift of filial duty you'll ever get from me. Leave now, and I will let you live."

"Thea, there are matters—"

Thea raised her palm, and a blast of wind cut off his response. Willem flew backward, his back cracking as it collided with the stone wall behind him. For a second, he remained pinned there before Thea flicked her wrist and he collapsed to the ground. She'd done it—attacked him with true magic, I realized, a little horrified but mostly impressed.

All around us, our audience began to back away, whispering with wide, fearful eyes, until Mariana called out, "Tonight, you have witnessed a new era's birth. Magic has awakened. Can you feel it?"

The whispers grew louder. Some of the vampires drew off their gloves as if to inspect their palms for signs.

A few steps away, my father shook his head, his face pale. "It can't be."

But I already knew it was true. I knew it was responsible for bringing me back to life. Still, there was so much I didn't know. None of that stopped me from taking one look at my mate—my mate, who had not only brought me back from the dead but awakened magic as well. It thrummed in my veins, and I wondered if she felt it, too. Later, I would ask her, but first, I knew what I had to do.

Pivoting my body to face her, I winked. Thea's eyebrows lifted, her mouth forming a question. Before she could broach it, I dropped to my knees, bowing my head. "Queen," I said, smiling around the word. "I offer my life, my body in your service. I will protect and serve you until death and beyond."

Sorrow filled her eyes at my words, and I knew she was thinking about earlier—that the until-death part held new meaning to both of us.

Everyone watched us carefully, their masks removed. Somehow I knew enemies lurked behind many of the friendly faces. No one could be trusted. Not with a new queen on the throne. Not with magic surging through our veins.

Her eyes met mine and held for a moment, her sorrow transforming into fierce determination. Let them come for us, and they would find out why she wore that crown.

I reached out, my dark magic wrapping around her light, and took her hand, lifting it to my lips. "Long live the queen."

ACKNOWLEDGMENTS

I want to start by thanking the readers for being part of the FRV family. I am grateful every day to write new words and new worlds for you. Thank you.

Huge thanks to Louise Fury, my badass agent and biggest cheerleader. To the team at The Fury Agency, thank you for looking out for me and bringing my books to new readers all over the world.

Thank you to Liz Pelletier and the entire Entangled team for being behind Filthy Rich Vampires! Thanks to Yezanira Venecia, Jessica Turner, Heather Riccio, Lydia Sharp, Curtis Svehlak, Brittany Zimmerman, Angela Melamud, and so many more for all of your hard work.

Thank you to the team at Tantor for bringing FRV to audio! Thank you to Dialogue Books for bringing FRV to the UK, to the teams at Blanvalet for bringing them to Germany right from the start, and Wydawnictwo Kobiece for taking a chance on my vampire lovers! Thank you all!

My life is a literal commune, and I am so blessed to have my husband and sister working beside me. Thanks to Josh for helping me develop these books into their best versions. Thank you to Elise for keeping me on track, positive, and for all the cake.

A huge thanks to Shelby for proofreading and keeping everything going when I can't. To Elsi, Christina, Jami, and Karen for keeping the Facebook group running smoothly and posting the best memes.

Thank you to Graceley, Kai, and Paper Myths Media for their fabulous work spreading the love all over social media. You're the best.

Thanks to my kids for laughter and love every day. A huge

thanks to my daughter for being my brainstorming buddy, to my son for being my grilled cheese master, and to my little one for being an endless source of joy.

And to my husband—there is no one else I would want by my side through all of this, for better or worse. Thank you for twenty-five years of true love.

Filthy Rich Vampires: Three Queens is a steamy romance full of extravagance and an ending that will leave you on the edge of your seat. However, the story includes elements that might not be suitable for all readers. Violence, familial estrangement, blood rituals, beheadings, mind-altering substance use, and death are shown on the page, with sexual assault and discussions of cancer in the backstory. Readers who may be sensitive to these elements, please take note.

*Don't miss the exciting new books
Entangled has to offer.*

Follow us!

 @EntangledPublishing

 @Entangled_Publishing

 @EntangledPub

AMARA
an imprint of Entangled Publishing LLC